TOO DARK CITY

TOO
DARK
CITY

Murder in **Black** or White?

Kalamazoo: 1948

JOHN GERTS

John Streg Publishing

Acknowledgments

Cover art: John Gerts
Contributing Editors: Steve Gerts, Paul Gerts, Marda Gerts,
Margretta Dumas

Research: John Gerts

Thanks to Terry Gerts, my life mentor.

Dedicated to Margretta,
my inspiration,
my love,
my life.

Printed in the United States of America
First Printing, 2023

ISBN 978-1-7326034-8-6

John Streg Publishing

1 | Misty, Morning

Wet streets and a heavy cloud cover persisted after the evening storm. Fog caused by cooler air rose from the damp pavement, swirling around the streetlights, engulfing the few unsteady bar patrons heading home to their hotel rooms and boarding houses.

A police car using only its running lights emerged from the fog, slowly moving west on Kalamazoo Avenue. The patrolman in the car swung a searchlight mounted above the left driver's mirror, illuminating a couple in a passionate embrace. The man and woman broke apart and began to hurry south at the corner of Kalamazoo and Edwards streets.

Near Burdick, the spotlight picked up another man walking near the curb. The man stopped, took one last drag on his cigarette, and tossed the half-smoked Camel aside. He turned toward the light and extracted his left hand from his jacket pocket, demonstrating that he carried no weapons.

He knew the drill.

"You there," said the policeman, training the spotlight on the man's face. "Where are you headed at this time of night." The patrolman in the passenger seat leaned across his partner to look at the man squinting from the bright light.

"Come on, Rookie," said the patrolman to his partner. "That's Moses Webb. He's not a problem."

The energetic driver of the patrol car wouldn't let it go. His instinct made him wary of coloreds.

"I asked you your business," the driver said, irritated.

"And I told you to keep rolling, Alex," said the rider. "He's coming off his shift at the garage."

"Well, if you're sure, Ross," said Alex.

"I'm sure. Moses used to be on the force. Now roll."

The police cruiser turned north on Rose Street. Soon, there was silence in the early morning except for a trickling rivulet from the rain and the click of the walking man's heels.

Moses proceeded to the corner at Burdick Street. The police stop had raised his blood pressure. For a moment, he recalled the first demeaning disruption he experienced at nineteen. At the time, the policeman had drawn his revolver, keeping a steady aim on the third button of Moses' shirt. The gun had terrified him. Tonight was the sixth stop he had endured. Moses was thirty-eight now and had a routine down pat. Slow movements, no smiling, no backtalk. There was no guarantee, of course, and perhaps he was just lucky, but to date, he had escaped the brutality retold to him by men he knew.

Police take one look at Moses and assume trouble. Over six feet tall with a seventy-five-inch reach, Moses trained for six years to be a professional boxer after quitting high school. He had slimmed considerably in the years after his last fight, and his arms didn't quite match since the shooting. Moses was still considered a threat in some circles due to his skin color.

He looked left down Burdick toward Southworth's Paints and Oils.[1] His apartment above the store was two buildings down, just five blocks from the Cities Service Station[2] where he worked. Instead of turning, Moses walked on, then turned north on Rose Street. If Reggy Camden was still losing money in Sofie's game, three blocks to the north, Moses could herd him out of there. Reggy's woman would give Moses a five-spot for bringing Reggy home before he lost all of his poker money. He might not be in the game at this hour, but it was worth a shot.

Three men were smoking up ahead. Indistinguishable in the fog, one man leaning against the picket fence in front of a well-kept bungalow. The other two men seemed to be paying close attention to the leaner.

Moses thought of crossing the road to avoid them. Instead, he hunched his shoulders, edged into the street, and passed by peacefully. The conversation dropped to a murmur behind him. Then he heard quiet footsteps, which he ignored. Ignore, run, or fight. Moses sensed his choices were down to two.

As a youth in Baton Rouge, Moses wrestled with these choices several times. He was fast back then; running was the best option. As he grew beyond his teenage years and his size and weight increased in the ring, he would turn and face two or even three bullies. All of that was ancient history now. Now, he could no longer jab with his left. He could only raise the useless arm enough to block blows. Besides, he was up north now. Less of a worry.

An excruciating pain on the back of his thigh from either a steel bar or blackjack sent him down on one knee, ending all thoughts of options. Moses raised his left arm as far as he could while kneeling to deflect a frontal attack from the two men now facing him. A steel-toed shitkicker boot to his ribs added to the pain in his leg and sent Moses sprawling on the cold, wet pavement. Another kick rolled Moses onto his back. He curled into a ball and covered his head with his arms as the attackers pummeled and kicked him with the blackjack and shitkickers, keeping Moses grounded.

"You're one of them scabs come here from Indiana, ain't you," said the big man. Moses tried to catch a glimpse of the man, but with the fog, all he could see was the outline of the brute, equal in size to himself, and the boot he used to kick him.

Too dark.

He would not forget those combat boots.

"You bunch from Detroit won't break our strike. I'm telling you, leave," said Boots.

"I live here," said Moses. "I don't work at the Shakespeare company.[3]"

"Shut up," said one of the other men, kicking Moses in the head. Moses' world began to spin, and just like in the ring, he shook his head to clear it as he grabbed the leg of Shitkicker-man, holding on for no reason but to bury his head in the man's pant leg for protection.

Through the fog on the street and the fog rattling his brain, Moses heard a screen door slam, then the pump action of a shotgun being racked and loaded with shells. Moses perceived a woman's voice loud enough to wake the entire block.

"You men get along and leave that other one alone," she said. "I don't care if I hit all of you. I'll shoot if you're not gone in ten seconds. Make up your mind."

The men moved off quickly, vanishing in the fog. The woman stared at Moses lying in the street for a while, then turned and returned to the house.

Minutes later, the ringing in Moses' right ear stopped. He rose, dizzy as if the count had reached eight. Somehow, he would have to make it to his apartment despite the burning aches in his leg, side, and head.

Only five blocks.

Moses stumbled into the alley heading east and limped to Burdick Street. He stopped and hugged the first lamp post he came to. Leaning his head against the cold, wet pole, breathing hard, the beaten man relaxed for a spell, trying to ignore the pain in his side.

Need to get home without the police, friends, or enemies seeing me broken.

His reputation as the Northside neighborhood enforcer depended on his formidable, never-back-down demeanor. His clientele would be reluctant to hire him if they knew he couldn't stand up to an indignant husband, gang bosses, or the "man."

I'm getting too old for this shit.

Moses slowly hobbled to the Paints and Oils store without further contact. Climbing the stairs was excruciating. He unlocked his apartment door, gingerly peeled off his clothes, took three Bayer tablets, glanced at the alarm clock on his bedstand, and crawled under the covers. The time was 1:53 a.m., and the calendar on the wall indicated the day, Thursday, September 16, 1948. Sleep was heaven-sent.

2 | Dr. Alexander

The wind picked up in the morning, whistling through the small gap in the window beside Moses' bed. Moses turned over to read the time on his alarm clock. The movement caused all the previous night's pain to return. It was ten minutes past noon. He hadn't missed a day of work in more than two and one-half years of employment as a mechanic at the service station. If he stayed in bed, rumors would be inevitable that he had finally met his match, his maker, or both.

The apartments above the Paints and Oils store included a small Dixie stove and oven, a sink, and a new Westinghouse refrigerator. Moses shuffled down the hall carrying his paper roll and found the toilet unoccupied.

Returning to his room, Moses poured hot water heated from the stove into the sink to shave and sponge bathe. He usually showered at the service station after work. When Moses looked at the back of his thigh and right ribs, his dark skin did not camouflage the purpling bruises. He would continue to bathe in his apartment until his bruises healed.

Moses swallowed three aspirin before slowly dressing. He ate two bowls of Cheerios and milk, although his jaw hurt like hell when he chewed. The red scuff mark above his ear from the kick in the head was (thankfully) not too noticeable, but the headache hadn't gone away. He decided to spend money on a visit to the doctor's office. He practiced casually walking the hall outside his room, thinking he could fake a somewhat normal step.

The walk to Dr. C. Allen Alexander's[4] office, five blocks up Burdick, took Moses fifteen minutes, double the time it would take at his usual gait. The office was next to Van Avery Drug Store[5] on the corner at North St. Moses hoped Doctor Alexander would prescribe a strong pain medicine so he could work through the pain.

Sitting at her desk, the doctor's outer office receptionist wore a name tag: Nadine Cross.

"Name?" she asked.

"Moses Webb," he answered.

Nadine referred to her appointment calendar and glanced at the chairs along the wall to her left. A woman sat near the receptionist's desk, clutching a handkerchief and occasionally sniffling. A man in a herringbone suit, possibly in his forties, sat in a chair seven feet from the woman, thumbing an edition of Life magazine.

"Do you wish to make an appointment, Mr. Webb," said Nadine, "we are quite busy this afternoon, as you can see."

"I can wait," said Moses.

"What's the nature of your visit, Mr. Webb," said Nadine, "for my notes."

"I had an accident last night and hurt my ribs on this side," Moses said as he pulled his shirt up to show Nadine one of his bruises. The waiting woman winced when she saw the purple bulge. Nadine took note without emotion.

"It will take quite a while, Mr. Webb, but you may take a seat."

Moses sat between the two patients and picked up a copy of Ebony magazine.

The gentleman tipped his hat. His left hand stayed in his lap, wrapped in a towel spotted with blood that seemed to be acting like a crude bandage.

"Did you get that bruise at the strike," asked the gentleman."

Moses shook his head. "No."

"My name is Larry Phelps. I sell vacuums to maintenance departments and homeowners."

The man pulled a business card from his pocket, handing it to Moses. "The Shakespeare Company is one of my accounts."

"How did you hurt your hand?" asked Moses.

"I was delivering our Model 27^6 Hoover and tried to get past the pickets out front. I may have gotten a busted hand for my trouble." Phelps held up his wrapped fist. "I was a bit persistent because I didn't get my commission until I delivered and got a receipt. Plus, Jim Miller had promised me a Wonderod if I gave him a deal.

"Guess I won't be fishing for a while."

Moses shrugged sympathetically. Notwithstanding the previous night's altercation, he knew about the strike at the Shakespeare Company. Everyone in Kalamazoo did. The pickets and the police involvement were causing rising tempers on both sides of the issue. More than a week had passed since early September when the strike began, and neither side was ready to compromise. The employee contract expired back in July. Everyone in downtown Kalamazoo seemed nervous and on edge. The Shakespeare manufacturing plant is just three blocks from where Moses and the salesman sat in Dr. Alexander's waiting room.

"The policeman driving me over here told me I was lucky," said Phelps to the whole room. "He said the police force is ready for anything. The rumor is that union people from Detroit may come here and join the employees. Communists and anarchists. The cop sounded confident that the police force could handle them. Easy to brag with that Thompson sub-machine gun and bulletproof vest I saw when he put my vacuum cleaner in the patrol car's trunk."

"I don't see how he can be that confident," said Moses. "The fact is that headquarters is still short of at least six patrolmen. There's a big crowd at the plant, and it's getting bigger each week. The company still won't negotiate."

The woman sitting near the receptionist leaned toward Phelps, "My brother is picketing," she said, "and he is the farthest thing from a Communist you could imagine, with medals from Normandy to prove it."

"I'm sorry, ma'am," said the salesman, "But I don't consider a broken hand a peaceful demonstration."

The door to the examination room opened. A nurse leaned out, calling the woman in for her appointment.

"Guess I ruffled her feathers," Larry said.

Moses shrugged.

Fifteen minutes later, the examination room door opened, and the lady emerged, walking stiffly by Nadine without looking at Phelps, and walked out of the office. Mr. Phelps was called into the inner office.

Moses read his magazine for five more minutes while Nadine shuffled papers. Then, Nadine beckoned Moses to her desk, lowering her voice.

"I'm looking at your medical record, Mr. Webb," said Nadine, "A note has been attached next to your wife's name under next of kin. Would you like to update that with another name?"

"My wife is no longer in the picture," said Moses.

"Oh, I'm so sorry, Moses."

"Divorced, eighteen months."

Nadine lowered her head and looked up at Moses, batting her eyes, "Under your insurance, if your injury requires care, the doctor provides in-home assistance. A nurse could call on you. I'm sure that could be arranged."

Moses looked Nadine over with new interest. She was cute, and his eyes wandered down the buttons on the front of her starched nurse's uniform. He considered the prospect, but the pain of his injuries cleared his head.

"I should get your number, in case."

Nadine wrote her telephone number on the back of the doctor's business card and handed it to Moses.

The examination room door opened. Phelps stopped at Nadine's desk to set up a follow-up appointment. His hand was now bound in a splint. Moses was called into the examination room. He sat down and waited a few minutes for Dr. Alexander. When the doctor entered the room, he shook Moses' hand and looked at his clipboard.

"Bruising, a rather brutal bruise, the nurse notes," said the doctor, "Remove your shirt and sit on the examination table."

The doctor was the picture of professionalism. He wore a crisp white shirt and dark tie, tacked at the second button. His white coat sounded like sandpaper as the stiffly starched fabric shifted with his movements. His stethoscope hung from his neck, and he wore an expensive-looking watch. His balding head and overall appearance presented an air of intelligence, notwithstanding his objectionable (to many) skin color, which was not as dark as Moses'.

Moses did as requested. The bruises had grown to cover most of his left side, from hip to chest. Some areas were darker than when he woke up at noon. Some of the edges of the bruises had dark yellow streaks.

"I notice that removing your shirt caused quite a bit of pain. Can you point to areas that seem most affected?" asked Doctor Alexander.

His whole side was painful, but Moses pointed to five areas that hurt the most. As he indicated each location, the doctor probed gently and occasionally not so gently.

"I'm trying to determine the extent of the damage to your internal organs," said the doctor. "So far, I think you escaped long-term or permanent damage. Without an X-ray exam, I can't be 100 percent certain, but I don't think that is warranted yet. If any areas exhibit sharp pain, like a knife in the side, we'll get you into Borgess Hospital for X-rays."

Moses dropped his drawers to show Doctor Alexander the bruise on the back of his thigh. That bruise wrapped around the circumference of his leg, but the doctor came to the same conclusion. "Nothing broken. How did you get these injuries, Moses? Don't tell me you fell down the stairs. We know each other better than to waste time telling stories."

"Does it matter, Doctor Alexander? It happened," said Moses.

The doctor shrugged. Moses was a familiar patient. After the shooting at the Eastside drug store, Dr. Alexander had worked on Moses in the Borgess Hospital emergency room. He had extracted one slug from Moses' upper arm and another embedded in his clavicle, positioning the broken pieces together and immobilizing the left side from shoulder to wrist in plaster. He was one of three surgeons who worked on placing the shattered arm and shoulder in the traction contraption that a bedridden Moses dealt with for twelve weeks.

"Are you still exercising that left arm, Moses?" the doctor asked.

To answer, Moses raised his arm, hand extended nearly as high as his shoulder, hiding the pain and effort to do so.

Dr. Alexander nodded, "I would remind you as I did three months ago after you dislocated that shoulder. The next time that happens, you may never use that arm again."

Moses showed the doctor the head wound. Doctor Alexander proceeded with several cognitive tests, afterward stating, "No sign of concussion this morning, but if you feint or become dizzy, have someone help get you back here immediately."

"Sure, Doc," said Moses, "I'll be careful."

"Right," said the doctor, rolling his eyes, "I'll prescribe four days of Morphine tablets for the pain. Take them only when the pain is unbearable. Go easy.

I know you help a lot of our folk around here, Moses. I don't want to know how. Maybe it's time to step back."

Moses thought for a moment. "I might say the same of you, Doctor Alexander; you're not much younger than me."

"At least come out to the cottage on Sherman Lake for bass fishing. I guarantee you'll catch a good dinner," said the doctor.

"Sure, Doc, I'll be out one of these days." Moses privately thought of shooting himself before being coaxed into a boat holding a fishing pole, waiting hours for fish to bite a worm on his hook.

Give me the damn pills so I can get to work.

3 | Karson's Dilemma

The Kadian tablets prescribed by Dr. Alexander barely lasted four days. Moses would not have been able to work without them. Garage work is physical, muscular work. Keeping the rest of the crew from discovering how injured he was meant taking an additional pill ahead of his self-imposed schedule. The following Monday, Moses returned to the doctor's office for another four days of medicine.

When Moses wasn't working, he sat very still in the one overstuffed chair in his apartment, letting the healing continue. When the buzzer rang for the apartment building entrance, Moses reached an arm to the wall and pressed the button to release the building lock. He could hear through the door somewhat heavy steps climbing the stairs. There was a knock on the door. Moses didn't get up. He just said, "Come in."

The door opened, and Thomas Karson shuffled in. Moses knew the big man; he played pool with him on occasion. Today, he looked mournful, apologetic. Thomas had an expansive butt, and blubber hung over his belt. Naked, he must look like a big black goose.

"I need help, Moses," said Karson.

Moses quickly answered, "I can't help you, Thomas."

"You've got to, Moses," moaned the man. "You remember what I did for you."

"Not really," said Moses.

"Sure you do," Karson continued, "Five years ago now, I think. You arrested that dealer at the fairgrounds. You had just gotten the cuffs on him. You didn't see another guy coming up from behind carrying a brick.

'Behind you, Moses!' I yelled, in time for you to turn around and knock that scrounger into the dust.

"You owe me, Moses."

"What is it, Thomas," said Moses. "Your wife tied up with someone again? Why don't you leave her? I told you when I chased the idiot out of the county that it was a one-time deal. Not my kind of work; leave her."

"You got paid a hundred even for that job, Moses. No, the wife and me are great. But I got an outstanding IOU that Mirsh bought up. He's charging me thirty-five percent interest per week. I need Mirsh to be reasonable. I can pay fifteen dollars a week and pay the debt off in eleven weeks. But I can't ever clear the debt at thirty-five percent interest."

"I don't see how hiring me helps you at all, Karson," said Moses. "My services would cost you at least fifty bucks. I don't see how that benefits you."

Karson looked like he was about to cry. "It saves me a broken finger at week two, week four, and so on. I ain't never been in a fight in my life. I can't stand up to a guy like you can, Moses."

"Alright, Thomas," said Moses, speaking through his morphine fog. "I'll quietly check out the situation this week. If I can see a possible outcome that keeps us both from getting our fingers broken, I'll let you know next week. This will square us if I pull it off. Got it?"

"Thanks, Moses."

Karson rose and left the apartment. Moses stayed in his chair, kidding himself that he would be well enough in a week to confront this Mirsh character.

Moses visited Dr. Alexander's office the next day, flirting with Nadine and pleading for another week of pain medicine. The doctor was away performing an appendectomy at the hospital. Nadine took Moses' hand in hers, rubbing the back of his hand and arm in sympathy. She retrieved a Dr. Alexander signed prescription from her desk drawer for patient emergencies, which she filled in with another week of Kadian[7] tablets. Outside, on the corner of the street, Moses swallowed the first tablet without water.

The pain of his bruises gradually decreased when turning a wrench at work. Either he was healed enough or taking enough morphine pills to blunt the pain. Regardless, he spent time in the pool rooms playing pinball before going to work, waiting for Mirsh to show up.

On Thursday, he heard someone call out the man's name, offering a game at one of the pool tables, and Moses looked him over. The Pool Room and Cigars store on W. Michigan Ave. only had room for three tables. Natural light filtered through two four-foot square windows consisting of eight-inch square glass blocks caulked together. One of the tables was under repair because of a four-inch tear in the cloth. Mirsh was a small man with quick movements. His hands were delicate. He held the cue gracefully and with confidence. He looked like he could handle himself in a fight, perhaps turning the cue stick around and using it as a weapon. Mirsh's eyes seemed too close to his pug nose. Moses watched the man's quick, jerky movements, his eyes darting around the room. The man reminded Moses of a weasel or a ferret.

Moses followed Mirsh into The Crescent Moon Saloon two days later, offering him a cigar at the bar.

"I have a loan I'm hoping you can help me with," said Moses.

Mirsh's eyes widened. "Let's discuss it in my office, the booth in the corner, all right?" said Mirsh.

Sitting down, Mirsh offered Moses one of his Chesterfields. Moses declined but tapped out one of his Camels and lit up. A waiter approached with two glasses half filled with Coca-Cola. He grabbed a flask from the inside breast pocket of his vest, poured a shot into each glass, and returned to the counter.

"How can I help you. I got money to lend, but I gotta tell you, I don't lend it out for my health. My fee is steep," said Mirsh.

"Nothing like that," said Moses, "My name is Moses Webb."

Mirsh's eyes widened again and then narrowed to slits. Ferret-Face had obviously heard of Moses.

"Keep smoking, Mirsh, and leave your other hand on the table.

"Now to business. You're holding an IOU of Thomas Karson's for one hundred fifty dollars. I will buy that IOU from you for that amount plus an additional fifty dollars for your trouble. We're both about making money, and I wish to be fair."

Mirsh couldn't resist a smirk. "That's not going to happen, Webb," said Mirsh. "I'll just hang on to my current arrangement with Thomas."

"You mean the one that includes broken fingers and exorbitant interest?"

"If that is what it takes to repay the debt, so be it."

Moses took a slug of coffee and doused his cigarette in Mirsh's mug.

"Let's relook at the situation. You may not have heard that I was previously a detective with the Kalamazoo Police Department. I still have friends at headquarters. In fact, patrolman Ross Kirkpatrick is a whistle away out the front door as we speak."

"You've got nothing on me."

"I'm not suggesting I do. But I can put you down and walk away without Officer Kirkpatrick taking a second look. Be smart. You can ply your trade just as profitably in Benton Harbor as Kalamazoo, and no one's fingers or toes need to be broken."

Mirsh's chocolate complexion had grown paler as Moses spoke. He began to edge his left hand off the table. Moses banged his hand hard over Mirsh's and squeezed his wrist. Mirsh, still holding his cigarette in his other hand, thought about burning the back of Moses' hand.

Anticipating the move, Moses let go of Mirsh's wrist, slapped the Chesterfield away from Mirsh's right hand, and again slammed Mirsh's left hand against the table, squeezing hard as Mirsh grimaced in pain. Many in the pool room noticed the commotion but, knowing Moses, stayed out of the disagreement.

"OK, the IOU amount plus seventy-five dollars," said Mirsh.

Moses smiled. "I can go up to sixty. We'll do the exchange in the alley. I show you the cash, and you show me the IOU."

Outside the pool room, Ross Kirkpatrick was nowhere in sight. Mirsh began to suspect he was never there. Ferret-Face turned toward Moses once they were out of sight in the alley. Moses extracted a roll of bills from his pocket and began counting out two hundred and ten dollars.

Mirsh seemed excited at the sight of the money roll and reached for his back pocket and billfold, presumably to retrieve the IOU. Instead, he bent quickly and extracted his switchblade from his boot.

When he straightened, Mirsh judged how close he needed to be to Moses to slash his throat. He took a step forward, forgetting about the long arms of the boxer.

Moses jabbed with his right three times, dazing Ferret-face. He head-faked to his right. With a useless left arm, everything had to be done with his right. Moses started low and followed through with his whole arm and shoulder, offering a staggering blow to Mirsh's temple. Mirsh dropped to one knee, shaking his head to focus but still holding the knife. Moses grabbed the wrist that held the blade and squeezed until the switchblade dropped to the alley. He picked up the weapon and threw it down the alleyway as far as he could.

Moses twisted Mirsh's arm behind his back, forcing him to stand, extracting a wallet from the man's hip pocket. Then he threw the little man to the ground. He found the IOU, put the two-hundred-ten dollars under the clip, and tossed the wallet to Ferret-Face.

"Time to head out on US-12. Benton Harbor is calling, right?" said Moses.

Mirsh, rubbing his hand and wrist, said, "Yes."

Moses figured it would take Thomas Karson about sixteen weeks to pay Moses back at fifteen dollars a week.

4 | Conduct Leading To Divorce

The 1945 two-door Desoto Deluxe up on the Globe hoist in the Cities Service garage needed the rear brakes rebuilt. Moses had just replaced the oil and air filter on a '40s Chevy Special Deluxe blackout 2-door. He disconnected one of the brake lines on the Desoto and started working on a second line when he heard his name.

Turning, Moses pulled his rag from his hip pocket and cleaned the oil off his hands.

"Hello, Harry," said Moses, pointing to the small box tucked under the arm of Harry Martensen, the area Nusbaum auto parts salesman and friend. "I see you brought the solenoids I ordered."

The two men shook hands. Harry seemed not the least bit worried about the grime on Moses' hand. One dirty colored hand and one clean white one in a firm grip. Obvious friends.

"Hand delivered, as promised," said Harry. "I charged the parts to the garage's account back at the warehouse." Harry pulled a folded two-copy receipt out of the inside breast pocket of his suit coat, placing it on a nearby car fender for Moses to sign. Moses did so, ripping off the top sheet of the receipt and walking it over to the manager's desk. He gave the second copy back to Harry. Moses thought for a few seconds, then snapped his fingers.

"Another problem came up that's right up your alley," said Moses. "A customer is bringing in a Cadillac late this afternoon for me to work on. Along with the clutch, he says the radio is on the fritz. Do you have time to look at it? Maybe tomorrow?"

"Ah, something interesting for a change," said Harry. "If you pull the radio, I'll bring my meter, and we can check it out. I'll go home, milk the cow, eat dinner with Sarah and the kids, and return. Say around seven o'clock tomorrow evening."

"Great, Harry," said Moses. "Say 'hi' to the wife and kids."

"So long, Moses."

Moses smiled as Harry left the garage. It was strange how comfortable Moses felt when Harry was around. The boxer grew up cautious in Baton Rouge. He wasn't distrustful, just wary. Harry was different. After the war, the salesman moved from Chicago to St. Louis to Gobles, Michigan. Harry was a radioman, eventually stationed on Iwo Jima after the big bombs dropped.

He was as tall as Moses but a skinnier man Moses hadn't met. They both enjoyed playing basketball, something they had in common that broke the ice. They met by chance one day on the Douglass Community Center[8] gym court. Harry wasn't a great player, but he unselfishly passed to Moses, an excellent shooter, who usually scored. Harry was an outstanding defensive player, and his long arms and timing allowed him to block many shots. They made a good team.

Over the last year, Harry had helped Moses on four occasions. Besides his radio expertise, Harry was an amateur photographer. The coal bin at his farm became his dark room after he converted it to oil heat. He had a decent camera and telephoto lenses. Twice, Harry accompanied Moses on stakeouts. That was the other thing about Harry.

His car. Moses couldn't help from loosening up with the man during a four-hour wait in the car.

The next night, Harry showed up with his meter and found two issues with the radio within fifteen minutes.

"This tube is kaput," said Harry, holding it close to the lamp on the workbench. "Plus, this burnt spot on the chassis indicates a blown resistor."

"So, you can fix it?" said Moses.

"Of course. Replace the tube and resistor. Fifteen minutes of solder. Recheck the circuit. Good as new. I'll have to check on the price of the parts. I'll do the labor for the fun of it. I miss the challenge."

Moses knew oil, grease, nuts and bolts, and MIG welding. Electrical circuits and electronics were science fiction to Moses but not to Harry. A captain in the new Army Air Forces and a reserve officer, Harry could still send Morse code at thirty-five words a minute.

Harry took the radio to the shop, tracked down the needed parts, and waited five days for them to arrive. A half-hour after they came, the components were installed, the soldering was complete, and the unit passed a dry run. After his last sales appointment, he drove to the Cities Service Station and set the radio on Moses' workbench.

Moses hooked the radio up to a spare car battery and listened to WKZO[9] Kalamazoo for a few minutes as he spoke quietly to Harry.

"Might you be interested in a one-night stakeout?" asked Moses. "I've been approached by a friend of mine. The client is the wife of a Northside slum landlord. She hired me because she thinks I blend in better around here.

"She has suspected that his Thursday bowling night is, in reality, a time for horizontal relaxation with one of the secretaries at the paper mill. She is sick of the guy's excuses and wants a divorce. I know of the man. I served him building code violation notices when I was in the force. He's a Vice President at the Shakespeare Company with real estate holdings in the Northside neighborhood. His buildings are run-down shitty death traps, yet the rents keep going up. The renters are screwed as much as the VP's secretary. I know two families living in one of his dumps trying to buy a house in the Westwood neighborhood. Bankers turned them down, even though they had good, steady jobs and a down payment.

"He's a confident bastard. I followed him in a yellow cab to the Burdick Hotel[10] and found out he rents the same newlywed suite every Thursday.

"From the roof of the building across Michigan Ave., we have an unobstructed view of that suite.

"I need you, your camera, and your telephoto lens to record what they do in that room. We're talking one thousand dollars split sixty/forty when the divorce is final."

"Thursday, you say," said Harry. "That's Sarah's choir rehearsal night, but I'll hire the babysitter myself for that money. Four hundred dollars. Count me in."

Moses spoke to his boss the next afternoon, requesting permission to quit work early on Thursday for personal reasons. An hour before the end of his shift, he was in the pit, unclamping the oil filter on one of the black and white KPD police cruisers. He heard a voice echo through the shop. A woman's voice.

"Mr. Webb."

Moses wasn't sure he had heard his name. Everyone in the shop called him Moses. Mr. Webb didn't register.

"Mr. Webb," repeated the voice. "Can I speak to you?"

Moses finished with the clamp and let the filter dangle on the oil supply line attached to the side of the filter.

"I'm in the middle of an oil change at the moment," said Moses. "I can be with you in about fifteen minutes."

"I have to go to work shortly myself, Mr. Webb."

Moses glanced toward the voice and gawked at a pair of the best-looking legs in nylons he had ever admired. Starting at garters visible beyond the hem of the knee-length pencil skirt and ending in brown heels, Moses' view from the pit made him blush. When his wife left him, the ordeal soured him. It had been a long time between women, and Moses was not about to turn away.

"I'll come up," said Moses.

He wiped his hands on his shop cloth and climbed the ladder out of the pit. Coming around the car's passenger side, he met the woman from the driver's side at the hood ornament. The legs matched the rest of her. She wasn't short. In fact, she came up to Moses' chin in her two-and-a-half-inch heels.

Her dark skin matched the man standing before her, unusual in Moses' experience. Shapely, the suit jacket couldn't hide that. Moses decided to focus on her wide brown eyes. When she saw him looking at her, she removed the red-rimmed glasses and quickly stuffed them in her purse.

"My name is Eileen Simmons, Mr. Webb," said the woman. "My friend Mildred Compton said you could help me."

"How," said Moses.

"What?" said Mrs. Simmons.

"How can I help?"

The woman seemed to lose courage. "It's about my son," she stammered.

Moses thought to give Mrs. Simmons time to collect her thoughts. "How is Millie? I've never seen anyone work so hard at gardening with such terrible results."

Mrs. Simmons looked quizzically at Moses, so he backtracked again.

"Oh, don't get me wrong. Millie is a good friend and a great gal, but she can't grow a weed."

Eileen Simmons chuckled. "I'm afraid you're right," she said. Tugging on her jacket, she took a breath and began again.

"I'm worried that Marvin may be getting into trouble. He's sixteen, and I don't want him taking after his father."

"I notice you're not wearing a ring, Mrs. Simmons," said Moses.

"No," said Eileen, "I mean, yes, I'm married to Leroy Simmons, but we have been separated for nearly two years."

"I still don't know how to help you, Mrs. Simmons, much as I want to. I'm probably not great with kids. Never had one of my own. Definitely not my area of expertise. I used to be a detective, but I never worked in the juvenile department."

"Mildred thinks you can handle anything," said Mrs. Simmons. "Listen, I won't take any more of your time away from your job, and I do have to get to work. I'm a third-shift nurse at Bronson. Could we meet and discuss my problem further? I'm willing to pay whatever is reasonable."

There was no way that Moses would let this gorgeous woman go without seeing her again.

"I could meet you Friday in Woolworth's at two o'clock. After I hear the details, I'll decide if I can help."

"Thank you," said Mrs. Simmons as she hurried off. Moses watched every second of her departure.

She looks just as good from behind.

***

On Thursday, Moses showered before leaving work to meet Harry. Before walking to his apartment, he took one of his two remaining Kadian tablets. His shoulder had bothered him all morning. It didn't hurt exactly, but Moses needed to concentrate on the stakeout without being distracted by aches and pains.

Harry pulled up to the curb where Moses waited in front of the Paints and Oils store. Together, they drove to the parking lot of the ten-story Hanselman Building[11], the tallest skyscraper in Kalamazoo. Each of them carried a large leather attache case into the building and asked Willie, the elevator operator, to take them to the offices of Campbell, Haskell, & Kurtis Attorneys at Law. Their office suite on the seventh floor was conveniently located across from the seven-story Burdick Hotel bridal suite. Moses had successfully accomplished three "favors" for John Haskell, and the after-hours use of the lawyer's office would repay those favors.

Under an arrangement with Haskell, Willie opened the suite's front door. All other offices were behind closed and locked doors. The board room was unlocked, and Moses and Harry closed the blinds and set up the camera gear. Harry had brought two cameras. He set up two tripods and attached a camera to each. Each camera's telephoto lens focused on different objects in the two adjoining rooms across the thirty-foot-foot gap between the Burdick and the

Hanselman buildings. At 9:15 p.m., a light illuminated the first room, and Harry, looking through the camera, observed a blond cross to the table throwing her coat on the chair. She didn't stop with her jacket. The woman seemed to be preparing for the arrival of the Shakespeare Executive. She took a fifth of bourbon from her purse and set it on the table. The light in the second room went on, and Moses observed the secretary as she crossed to another door, entered a third room, and returned to the first room with two rock glasses, setting them on the table near the bourbon. She opened the bottle, poured herself two fingers, and gulped it down.

Next, she unbuttoned and slipped out of her blouse. Reaching behind her back, the blond unsnapped her bra and threw it over her blouse and coat. In the privacy of the room, she hefted her breasts with both hands and admired herself in a mirror Harry couldn't see. Finally, she dug makeup out of her purse, glossed her lips, and fluffed her hair.

"Sorry, Moses," said Harry. "I'll bet they won't reach your room and camera when your mark appears. She's ready now. The woman has a nice figure, I would say, and she enjoys the tease. The skirt, stockings, and heels stayed on. That's it."

"Enjoy the show, Harry," said Moses. "Just make sure to take the pictures."

The woman didn't have to wait long. There appeared to be a knock on the entry door, and the topless secretary let the VP in. He was already tugging at his tie. The blond handed him a drink, and he downed it while feasting on the breasts of the woman before him. She did a slow turnaround and bent over, wiggling her ass at him, which invited a slap on her butt by the man.

The blond turned back around and waved her tits at the man. She picked up the bourbon and entered the bedroom while Moses watched with the second camera. The man picked up the glasses and followed her.

"Did you get anything?" Moses asked.

"I believe I did, Partner," Harry said. "I'd say we can pack up and leave right now unless you're hoping to capture the humpity dumpty."

"That would be ideal," said Moses.

Harry, the photo guru of the team, took over Moses' camera, capturing the two rolling in the sheets, snapping pictures that included the faces of the bouncing couple in the light of the bedside lamp.

In twenty minutes, the woman sat up on the side of the bed, lit a cigarette, and slugged more bourbon down.

The man took hold of her wrist to pull her back to the bed while chugging more bourbon from the near-empty bottle. The woman shook him off.

Moses and Harry, incredulous, observed what looked like a heated exchange between the naked couple, and then the man yanked the woman by the wrist back to the bed.

The woman, now visually upset, jumped out of bed and began to dress.

Unbelievably, the man slapped her so hard that she sat back down on the edge of the bed, rubbing her cheek, apparently crying. The man hit her again, and she fell prone on the bed face down, dazed. He used his tie to bind one of her wrists to an iron bedpost and his belt to tie her right wrist to the other side of the headboard.

"Moses, we need to call the police," said Harry, hurrying to the boardroom phone. "I didn't sign up for rape."

"Hold on, Harry," said Moses. "Let me think."

"You better think fast, Moses; this is serious."

"I know it's serious, Harry, but suppose you make that call. If the police are involved, it'll mean a police report, and that will mean a splash in the Gazette, and you can kiss our thousand dollars goodbye. The wife won't need us.

"No, there's got to be a better way."

Harry frantically began dialing for the operator.

Moses crossed to Harry and pushed down the hook switch.

"I've got an idea," said Moses. "Give me the phone and look up the number for the Burdick Hotel."

Harry thumbed through the directory lying on a side table and eventually called out the number as Moses dialed.

"Hello, my wife and I are in rooms 712 or 716. I can't recall right now, but we just heard a woman screaming in the room across the hall. I think it's the bridal suite. They're having a huge fight, and I'm afraid the woman might be getting beaten to death. You need to get your security team up here and get that woman some help. I'm telling you, this is a matter of life and death. Hurry."

Moses hung up the phone.

"We'll give them three minutes," said Moses. "If they don't show, we'll call the police. What's he doing now?"

Beaded sweat dripped off Harry's forehead, yet his complexion had drained of color. He was clearly anxious for the helpless woman across the way. He could see that the man had stuffed his t-shirt in her mouth, effectively gagging her.

She could still kick with her feet. The idiot straddled her behind her thighs to force entry.

Moses took over the first camera, focussing on the bridal suite's lounge area. Keeping still while looking through the camera was no problem; he felt no pain. Yet his headache seemed to be getting worse. As the seconds ticked by, he began to sweat like Harry.

"Moses, the guy has jumped off the bed," said Harry. "He's looking around, trying to decide what to do. He must have heard someone in the hall.

"OK, now he's untying the woman. He tossed her clothes at her. He's hopping around, trying to get into his pants.

"He's coming into my view, Harry," said Moses. "Two men just entered the room. One of them is crossing into the second room."

"Yup, that man is getting an eyeful. The woman is really disheveled and nearly falling down drunk. She's showing the hotel dick her wrists."

"That's it. Let's get out of here," said Moses. Both men packed up their equipment. Moses scanned the room to ensure there was no evidence of their presence and left the law offices. Moses made a beeline to the alley in the back of the Burdick in time to see a hotel security man escort the Shakespeare V.P. to his car. The woman was escorted separately to the hotel limousine. Moses turned around, meeting Harry at his car in the parking lot.

"That is that," Moses said. "The hotel doesn't want publicity any more than the VP does. I'll report to the wife as soon as you develop the film. She or the secretary can decide if and when to press charges against that asshole. Either way, the divorce settlement should be to the wife's satisfaction."

"The whole ordeal has left a bad feeling in my stomach, Moses," Harry said.

Moses rubbed Harry's back, trying to ease the apparent tension in the man's shoulders. "We may have saved that woman from more hurt, Harry; I hope it wasn't too much for you. You were a huge help."

Harry shrugged and chuckled. "Hey, a peep show and Dragnet episode on the same night. Sarah is not going to believe it."

5 | Eileen

Eileen Simmons sucked on the straw buried in her chocolate malt at Woolworth's[12] on South Burdick. She sat on a corner stool at the end of the soda fountain. Moses entered the store and strolled over. He took the seat around the corner of the bar, facing Eileen. Dressed in grey slacks, work boots, and a white shirt, Moses left his brown leather jacket on but doffed his tan fedora and set it on the stool beside him.

"Good afternoon, Mr. Webb," Eileen began, "Thank you for meeting with me."

"My pleasure, Eileen," said Moses, and he meant it. "May I call you Eileen? I checked at the hospital; you've worked there for over eleven years, five in Emergency and five in Pediatrics. Impressive. Your colleagues have nothing but good things to say about you."

"I'm not sure I'm comfortable with you running around inquiring about me," said Mrs. Simmons.

Moses' lip curled. "I'm sorry, but didn't you approach me, Mrs. Simmons?

"Just to keep things straight, you've seen where I work. I like my job. I do favors for friends and friends of friends that I feel are worth helping. I expect to be paid for my efforts, so I do background checks, just like I did when I worked at the police department.

"Do we continue?" he asked.

"I apologize, Mr. Webb," said Mrs. Simmons. "I do want your help."

"Good enough, then call me Moses." Moses waved at the soda jerk. "Hey, Benny," he shouted down the bar, "I'd like a pineapple shake." Then he turned back to Eileen.

"Alright, Eileen, do you really think I can help with your sixteen-year-old?"

"I need to know that he is OK, Mr. Webb… Moses."

Moses could read Eileen's concern in the furrows of her brow. "The other day at the garage, you mentioned your husband," he said.

"Yes," said Eileen, "Leroy Simmons, people these days call him Pot if that tells you anything."

"I know him," said Moses, "Or rather, I know of him. he hangs around the train station and Bus depot. He sells knockoff watches, rings, and other contraband from a suitcase. I've heard he sells marijuana and heroin in the alley behind the restaurant. I sympathize with your concern. He has a mean streak and leans toward violence. He sometimes carries a snub-nosed revolver in a hip holster under his coat, although the cops that stop and frisk him have never found it on him."

Eileen was amazed. "You seem to know much more about Pot than I do these days," she said.

"I couldn't take on the favors I do without knowing the people and places on Kalamazoo's north and east sides, good and bad."

"I see," said Eileen.

"Three years as a street cop and two as a detective has supplied me with plenty of scrapes and scraps of history," said Moses, "My naturally curious nature keeps me current.

"If you are separated from Leroy, how much influence can he have on your boy."

"That is what I want you to determine, Moses," said Eileen. "I just don't know. A good friend of Marvin's died three months ago. Heroin, according to the Gazette. Marvin was with him when he died. Maybe that scared Marvin enough, but I've got to know."

Moses watched tears form in the corners of Eileen's saucer eyes. "Let's take a walk," he said, "over to Bronson Park; get some air and have a more private conversation."

By the time they reached the park, Eileen had dried her eyes. The couple sat near the Fountain of the Pioneers.[13] The flowing water covered their conversation. The walk gave Moses time to think out a possible strategy and cost of helping the woman he hoped to get to know much better. Something about her sparked heat in Moses. He wanted her; he knew that much. At the same time, he wanted her respect; maybe there was more to this than heat. Helping her might gain him a foothold. A favor… that no doubt would cost him more than what Mrs. Simmons would be able to pay.

"Here's what I can offer," said Moses. "A three-week contract, depending on your resources. In the first week, I would learn his routine: school, work, and after-school activities. My work schedule precludes nighttime observation except for the weekend. You'd be in charge of his after dinner time."

"Marvin doesn't work during the school year," said Eileen. "After supper is homework time. He actually excels in his studies without my prodding."

Moses nodded, "He sounds like a good kid. If his grades aren't suffering, I doubt if you have anything to worry about," he said. "In the second and third weeks, I would get close enough to record or overhear anything untoward."

"I believe that plan would ease my mind," said Eileen.

"Mind you," said Moses, "from what you have told me about Marvin, I'm already pretty sure nothing will come of this. If you decide to proceed, how much have you set aside to hire me, Eileen?"

"I have saved three hundred dollars," she said. "I can give you one hundred dollars now as a retainer. I'll get more if you need more than three hundred dollars."

Moses smiled, covering her hand resting on her lap with his. "I calculated my time and expenses as we walked," he said. "Two hundred fifty is what I came up with. Of course, if the investigation continues after three weeks, I would charge you more, but we'll worry about that when the time comes."

"It's settled then," said Eileen, handing him five twenty-dollar bills from her purse. "When can you start?"

"On Monday," said Moses. "Help me out. What does he like to do after school, hang out at the soda fountain, sports, pool?"

Eileen had a quick answer. "Basketball. My father played baseball in the negro league for the Cleveland-Buckeyes club. Marvin is taller but just as athletic. He hopes to make the Junior Varsity team at Central High School. Practice starts in November, I believe."

Moses could have kissed her. Basketball was his own favorite sport. He and Harry played in pickup games down at the YMCA, the Douglass Community Center, and the outdoor courts at Lincoln School.

Wow! An easy $250.00 and the chance to part the best legs on the Northside.

6 | Marvin

Moses shifted into daylight mode at the break of dawn on Monday. Typically, he would start his day at noon, at some point, work out at the Y, and be at work by 3:00 p.m. He shifted his second shift starting time from 3:00 p.m. to 4:30 p.m. to accomplish Eileen's favor. If Marvin dallied on his way home until 5:00 p.m., Moses could still get eight hours in by skipping lunch at the shop and working until 1:00 a.m.

As he prepared for the day, the jar of Kadian tablets beside the sink called to him. He hadn't taken one the night before, and still, nothing was hurting. If he took another pill now, the whole day would be easy.

Then he thought of Eileen. He was hooked on her. She already had one hophead to deal with. Before changing his mind, he dumped the remaining pills in the sink and flushed them down.

At 7:00 a.m., Moses waited a half block from the corner of Parsons and Walbridge streets, out of sight of Eileen's home at 416 Parsons. From there, Moses followed Marvin to Central High School, a thirty-minute walk. Marvin entered the school from Dutton Street, and Moses followed the throng of kids inside, looking like a parent heading to the office. Marvin turned left from the entrance and stopped at his locker on the first floor, traded a couple of his books, and proceeded to a third-floor classroom. Moses got close enough to Marvin in the crowd to note his lock combination and height, already over six feet. Eileen's father's athleticism had been passed along to Marvin. He was thin at the hips and probably still growing. Marvin's complexion was a light caramel, understandable since Pot was Caucasian.

Kalamazoo Central High School[14] is a massive four-story red-rust brick and grey stone skirted building built in the early '20s. The school takes up half a city block. Upwards of 1200 students attend. The auditorium has a seventy-foot fly on the stage with main floor seating and two balconies. The entire student body fits in the audience for assemblies.

At 2:30 p.m., Moses was back at the school, shaking from the absence of morphine. He walked back and forth along the Westnedge St. block until he spotted Eileen's son emerge from the Dutton St. entrance. Moses followed the boy back to the north side of town. Marvin didn't go directly home. Instead, he stopped at the Van Avery Drug Store on N. Burdick. He came out of the store unwrapping a Three Musketeers candy bar, then continued up Burdick to the Lincoln School[15] basketball court. Moses held back.

Within twenty minutes, there were fifteen kids shooting baskets and picking teams. Marvin seemed in demand, but Moses observed no drugs or other misbehavior, nothing other than Marvin's skill on the court. He was fast, one of the fastest. The teen also seemed like someone Moses would have picked for his team. He wasn't physically aggressive, depending on his speed and dribbling skill to work his way into position for a shot. Moses watched him make four baskets and three layups off of steals. Others on the court participated in good-natured and sometimes not-so-good-natured verbal jabs after an inevitable hard foul. Not Marvin. He was quiet, shrugged off fouls, and won every game he was in.

Moses enjoyed watching from behind a car parked just fifty feet from the court, becoming lost in the rhythm of the games. Around 4:30 p.m., Marvin and four friends walked off the court, heading for their homes, dropping off a friend now and then. At the corner of Parsons and Edwards streets, Moses spotted two young boys up ahead talking to an older boy and exchanging money for a ceramic jar of weed. The older boy finished his dealings with the two younger boys and quickly approached Marvin and his friends. Marvin didn't acknowledge the older boy's presence. Three of the dealer's friends appeared at the next corner. Two of the gang wore short leather biker jackets. The third teen wore a short Sharkskin jacket with a turned-up collar. The gang blocked the way, enticing Marvin's friends to try their product. Marvin pushed through and kept walking, never looking back. When he reached the intersection at Porter St., Marvin signaled the two remaining boys and entered his house. Again, Moses was pleased with Marvin's conduct, a teenager handling what life threw at him with aplomb.

After work, when Moses entered his apartment, he looked for a moment for his bottle of Kadian. He was exhausted and shaking. That night, he didn't get much sleep, soaking the sheet wet with sweat. Thoughts of Eileen helped him through. He had survived worse conditions before.

Tuesday at 7:10 a.m., as Marvin left the house, Eileen's car rounded the corner from Walbridge Street, and Marvin waited while she parked in the driveway and climbed out of her Ford Deluxe. After a brief exchange with his mother, Marvin continued his brisk walk to school. Moses lingered, watching Eileen climb the porch stairs and sashay into the house, deciding the night of sweat had been worth it.

What was it about a woman in a starched white uniform?

Even wearing her fall jacket, Moses fantasized about helping her off with it and everything else she wore. Moses picked up Marvin's trail a couple of minutes later.

That afternoon, Marvin walked out of school carrying a load of books and notebooks, some apparently belonging to the girl walking close by his side. The couple headed north on Westnedge. Moses watched the boy and girl interact all the way to Northside. He couldn't ascertain how far the relationship had progressed, but at the very least, Marvin had a girlfriend that Eileen was unaware of.

Moses was presented with a quandary. Should he report this development to Eileen? Marvin may just be waiting for an opportune time to introduce his girlfriend to his mother. Marvin may be dating someone else in a week. He was certainly good-looking enough to warrant multiple girls' attention.

On the other hand, this girl had to be one of the prettiest girls of color in the school. Perhaps rivaling the beauty of Marvin's mother. She had bright, perfect teeth and an easy smile. She wore her hair long and straightened. Her body shape made her appear to be two years older than Marvin. Moses decided Marvin was as hungry for this girl as he was for Marvin's mother.

Marvin walked the girl to her house on Bosker Avenue while Moses kept some distance away. The girl's mother hung laundry in the backyard, and Marvin and his girlfriend entered the home. Moses made a note of the address. An hour and fifteen minutes later, Marvin emerged from the house, danced down the front porch stairs, red-faced in Moses' opinion, and walked the rest of the way to his home, carrying just three textbooks and a blue denim three-ring binder.

Wednesday, Marvin repeated his Monday routine, and Thursday saw a repeat of Tuesday, with Marvin again spending time at his girl's house.

Friday, Marvin sat next to his girlfriend at the home football game held at Kalamazoo College's Angell football field. Kalamazoo Central played Battle Creek Central on the two-year-old football field.[16] Marvin ignored the game. Moses thought he seemed more interested in keeping his girlfriend warm. However, the crowd was enthusiastic, cheering the home team to victory in the college's fancy stands and football field Central School called home.

On Saturday, Marvin didn't leave the house until 1:00 p.m. A typical teenager, sleeping in. Moses followed Marvin for twenty minutes as he walked downtown to the YMCA[17] at the corner of West Michigan and Park Street, near Bronson Park. Marvin went to the weight room and worked on curls and squats with the deadweights. Moses waited a few minutes, entered the room, and began lifting weights in the opposite corner.

Fifteen minutes later, Marvin left the weight room and went to the gym to join the next basketball game. Marvin would be playing alongside men in their 20s, 30s, and 40s and one man who looked to be in his sixties. Marvin seemed to enjoy running circles around the older men. He was known here and appreciated. Moses watched from the running track surrounding the gym's perimeter above the basketball court. Moses smiled. He loved the sweat smell, the action, and the snap of the net as a basketball swished through the rim.

Sunday, Eileen and Marvin popped out of the house at 9:40 a.m. and walked the four blocks to Mt. Zion Baptist Church[18]. Moses always thought the crenellations on the bell tower made the church look like a castle. He could hear the enthusiastic gospel songs, shouts of hallelujah, and amens, where he watched from the corner of the street.

Eileen was easy to spot and easier on the eyes when she left the church with Marvin in a shimmering dark navy dress and fur-collared black overcoat.

It was after 2:00 p.m. when Marvin slipped out the backdoor of his house and sauntered south three blocks to the Douglass Community Center. The gymnasium was practically new, having been completed in 1941. Several of Marvin's friends were waiting for him in front of the building. So was Marvin's girlfriend.

Marvin sent his friends into the building and stayed outside with the girl, looking around for watching eyes and bending over her for a kiss. After a short discussion, Marvin entered the structure, and the girl followed ten steps behind him.

Again, Moses could find nothing untoward in Marvin's actions and adventures. No drugs, no shoplifting, no fighting, no gangs. At most, Moses thought the boy was old enough to discuss condoms and the responsibility surrounding pregnancy. It's not his job. But absent his birth father, Moses wondered who might provide the lesson.

In the second week of his contract, Moses observed a repetition of Marvin's first-week routine. On Friday night, however, Marvin walked first to his girlfriend's house, and then the two walked to the State Theater[19] downtown. Several of Marvin's buddies and their respective girlfriends met Marvin at the theater. The group took in the movie together. Moses enjoyed the show as much as the kids did: John Wayne and Montgomery Clift in *Red River*.

On Sunday at the Community Center, Moses joined the pickup games. Marvin played on the same team as Moses during the third match and unselfishly passed the ball to Moses several times when he was open for a shot.

Basketball is a communal sport. Players know each other by their frequency in the gym or sometimes by their nicknames, Magic, Curly, or Springs (referring to how high a player could jump.) Given names were less consequential. No one, young or old like Moses, or in between, showing a particular skill, whether it be shooting, passing, or defending, was denied time with the ball. Exhausted from his third game, Moses left the court for the showers. Marvin seemed to be just hitting his stride and stayed on the court.

Moses sat on a bench near the building, smoking. Marvin's girlfriend leaned against the wall to the right of the entry, waiting for Marvin. Marvin emerged with two friends. At the same time, a man waved at Marvin from the direction of Ransom Street. Marvin recognized the man and waited for him to approach. The bench Moses sat on was close enough for him to overhear the conversation.

"Hi, Son, I came over to watch you play," said the man. "Guess I missed out."

"Yeah, Dad," said Marvin. "I'm done for today."

The father-son exchange clued Moses that this was Leroy Simmons. There were no hugs or handshakes, but no animosity was evident to Moses.

Leroy wasn't short; he probably was just shy of six feet tall. If he had ever had a summer tan, it was long since gone. His pale complexion contrasted with Moses'. As far as Moses was concerned, Leroy's pencil-thin mustache and long bulky jacket made him look comical, like a clown from a carnival. He smiled broadly on approach, and all his teeth were evident. Moses couldn't understand the fit between the man and Eileen.

"Hi, Malcolm, Terry," Leroy said while nodding at Marvin, "Are you three staying out of trouble?"

"Sure, Mr. Simmons," said one of Marvin's friends.

Leroy turned his attention to the girl.

"And who is this, Marvin?" Leroy said.

"Oh, sorry, Dad," said Marvin. "This is Sheila Rohan, a friend of ours from school." Since Sheila was just one of the group, Leroy had, as yet, not figured out which boy she might be attached to, if any. Moses made a note of Sheila's name in his notebook. Now, he could do a background check.

"Sheila, eh?" said Leroy. "Say, you are mighty cute, girl. Hell, if someone as cute as you had been around when I went to school, we would have been in trouble. I would have seen to that."

The crude remark made Moses squint. Drawing again on his second Camel cigarette hid the slight shake of his head in dismay.

Marvin stepped in front of Sheila, looking with a menacing smolder at his father, and said, "That's enough, Leroy." Marvin took Sheila firmly by the arm and led her away. Malcom and Terry followed.

"Hold up a minute, Marvin; I need to talk to you," said Leroy. "It will only take a minute."

Marvin reluctantly stopped. "You guys go ahead. I'll catch up with you at Van Avery's. I want to get a Dad's Root Beer."

Sheila looked up at Marvin, sweeping her hair behind her right ear. "That's fine. Your dad's a piece of work. I guess you warned me, but I want nothing to do with him."

Marvin shrugged and turned back to Leroy. Moses had watched the exchange between Marvin and Sheila but hadn't heard the conversation. When Marvin got close to Leroy, Moses could listen to every word.

"What," Marvin said.

"I need fifty bucks," said Leroy, a look of astonishment swept over Marvin's countenance. "Now, wait!" Leroy backtracked. "There's a deal I heard about that will take a little more cash than I have," said Leroy.

"I don't have fifteen bucks to my name, Dad," said Marvin.

"Well, your mom has a lot more than that. She still keeps her cash in her breadbox?"

"I don't know where she keeps it, and I don't care. I'm not going to steal fifty bucks for you."

"It ain't stealing, Kiddo," said Leroy. "Loan, short-term loan. I'll put it back two weeks from today.

Moses, listening, sat on his hands, head tilted on his shoulder, trying to appear napping on the bench.

Throttling this asshole would be a pleasure. Then Moses remembered the gun, supposedly hidden by Pot's long jacket. Care would be taken, but he would still crush the scum. Moses knew he shouldn't be thinking of Eileen now, but he couldn't help himself. She needed to get this bastard out of hers and Marvin's life. The creep wasn't helping her son at all.

"Dad, I'll loan you my fifteen bucks; you'll just have to find another way to get the rest," said Marvin.

"Alright, I'll talk to your mother myself," said Leroy.

Marvin made his excuses and set off for the drugstore. Moses was torn. In the two weeks following Marvin, he had observed nothing but a good kid who loved basketball and possibly a beautiful and levelheaded girl until today. His immediate reaction was to switch his assignment from Marvin to Leroy. He was curious about this fifty-dollar supposed loan. The money wasn't enough for Leroy to invest in anything. Was it the beginning of an extortion pattern with increasing amounts week after week? Moses decided he would cut off his shadow work on Marvin and, with approval from Eileen, start keeping track of Leroy.

7 | Report

Moses knew Eileen worked the third shift, and Marvin went to school during the day. He predicted she would sleep between eight and three and then make dinner for Marvin and herself. That would give her time to watch over his studies before heading to work at Bronson.

On Monday morning, before starting out for Eileen's house, Moses held out his right hand, fingers spread, at eye level, a foot in front of his nose. The shakes were gone.

Moses observed Eileen arriving home from work and Marvin walking to school. Instead of following Marvin, Moses knocked on Eileen's front door.

Eileen was surprised at his presence but invited Moses in, attempting to smooth the wrinkles of a night's work out of her uniform. Moses noticed blood spatters on the left side of her skirt.

"I was just having some toast for breakfast," said Eileen, leading the way to the kitchen. "Would you like coffee?"

"Toast and honey and coffee, thank you," said Moses. "If you can stay awake, I'd like to give my report."

Eileen shuffled between the toaster and the coffee pot. When the plate of toast was buttered and coffee poured, Eileen put both hands on the table but didn't sit down.

"I want to hear your report, Moses, but if you don't mind, a shower and a change out of these clothes will allow me to concentrate. Do you have time?"

Moses did have time. He spent it eating his toast and honey, downing the coffee, and daydreaming about Eileen in the shower.

Twenty minutes later, her hair pulled back in a knot, Eileen, refreshed, made-up, and somewhat awkwardly smiling, entered the kitchen. She wore a navy blue house dress with a pattern of tiny yellow and red flowers. The dress showed off Eileen's incredible cleavage. She sat down opposite Moses at the kitchen table.

"Alright, Moses," she said. "I think I can handle whatever you have found out."

"Eileen, you are fortunate to have Marvin for a son. I didn't research his grades but assume, from what I learned, that he does well in school."

Eileen smiled and nodded in agreement.

"He certainly is skilled on the basketball court," said Moses. "For his age, he is probably the best player in Northside, if not the city. He can hold his own playing with college kids and adults."

Moses referred to his notes, highlighting Eileen's son's daily routine and activities. He told her Marvin was respected by his friends and other players on the basketball court. Marvin avoided trouble and steered clear of drugs, dealers, and gang members. Because of the reputation he had on the basketball court, outside influencers, for the most part, left him alone.

"So, you're telling me all is good," said Eileen, letting her breath out in relief. "I shouldn't worry."

"Well," said Moses, "I left some items out of my initial report. Now, don't get me wrong. I wanted to stress the many positive points in Marvin's favor.

"Before I speak of my concerns you might want to consider, can I ask some personal questions?"

"You can ask," said Eileen. "I may not have answers, but go ahead."

"OK, first of all, Marvin has a girlfriend. Her name is Sheila Rohan, and she lives on Bosker Avenue. Were you aware he was going steady?"

"No," said Eileen, "I wasn't. I may be prejudiced, but I think Marvin is extremely handsome. I guess it isn't too surprising that girls find him attractive."

"True, Eileen, and I think you would like her. She is stunning but seems to have her feet on the ground. Marvin is very protective of her. Maybe Marvin could ask her over so you could meet Sheila."

"Is pregnancy your concern, Moses," asked Eileen. "Teenage boys are hard for me to fathom. Marvin's father should help with those issues."

"Yes, but he won't help, will he, Eileen," said Moses. He didn't know how far he should overstep his agreement concerning the boy. "No, I think you will have to take on the topic.

"Listen, just remind Marvin to respect his girlfriend's feelings and future. Marvin is smart enough to determine a path based on that basic premise."

"All right, thank you, Moses. I'll talk to Marvin," said Eileen. "So that's it. Nothing else?"

"Another personal question," said Moses. He was ready to take the plunge. "What about Leroy? Are you considering divorce?"

Eileen stood up and cleared the dishes off the table. Her back was to Moses, and as she rinsed plates, stacking them near the sink, she said, "He is my son's father. Marvin still loves his dad despite their very apparent differences. I have lived with the current situation for my son's sake."

"What about you, Eileen. Doesn't Leroy sometimes stay over?" said Moses.

"Yes, he sleeps on the couch, sometimes. Sometimes, he's drunk. Usually, he is broke and needs money. Perhaps the time has come to divorce the man."

Now, it was Moses who sighed with relief. He told Eileen about Leroy pleading with Marvin to take money from Eileen's hidden kitchen stash.

By the way," said Moses, "If you keep money there, move it or put it in the bank. One thing I have already learned about Leroy is his lack of conscience when dealing with his son or you."

"Oh, Moses, that sounds a bit scary," said Eileen.

"You should be frightened, Eileen."

"OK, I'll put the money in the bank tomorrow morning after work." Eileen sat back down at the table opposite Moses, "Is there something else?" she said in reluctant anticipation.

"Another incident involving Leroy as well. There was an altercation between Marvin's girlfriend, Sheila, and Leroy, who made a lewd remark to Sheila in front of Marvin.

"Marvin defended Sheila, and nothing violent occurred, but Sheila definitely appeared upset, and Marvin was mad as hell, mad enough to start something with his dad."

"The man is an idiot at times," said Eileen. "Most of the time, I guess. He really crossed the line. Didn't he?"

"Yes, no question," said Moses.

"I'm reluctant to put Marvin through the finality of a divorce. I'm hoping Marvin will attend college. Maybe then," said Eileen. "Then we'd both be ready."

"After a two-year separation, I bet Marvin is mature enough to withstand that final step," said Moses. "Perhaps he would welcome it. He is ready to make his own path, what with basketball, a steady girl, and good friends."

"I'm just not sure," she said.

Moses saw an opening and said, "Then let me help you make sure."

"What do you propose, Moses."

"First of all," said Moses, "You don't need to spend any more money for me to tail Marvin. In fact, I want to come clean with the kid for my own benefit. It's time we trusted him again, and he'll never trust either of us without learning the truth about your concerns and my involvement. The sooner, the better.

"I actually like connecting with Marvin through basketball and would enjoy pursuing more playing time with him. Regarding our contract, another seventy-five dollars will finish the matter."

"Are you sure, Moses," said Eileen. "I'm so grateful for what you've done and how you have gone about it. I can afford to pay more; believe me, you're worth it."

"I'm not done yet," said Moses.

Eileen looked confused, "What more could you do, Moses," she said.

Moses stood, walked to the sink, found a glass in the cupboard to the left, filled it with water, and drank. He placed the glass to the right of the sink and returned to face Eileen over the table, putting both hands on the chair back.

"I propose switching my focus from Marvin to Leroy," said Moses. "Something is up with that man. He's too cocky. He's a penny-ante schemer. Yet, he appears ready to take someone down or be taken for a sucker himself. I want to prevent you and Marvin from going down with his ship."

"How long would you need, Moses?" said Eileen. "How much might this cost?"

"There may be minimal expenses for supplies. I sometimes have a partner I work with, and he would need compensation.

"Up to now, I have contracted with you because you are a friend of a friend of mine. I expected to be paid accordingly. Moving forward, if you let me, I would do this as a favor to you because you are my friend. No charge. Understand?"

"I think so," said Eileen. "How would you work it?

"When I know something and have details to report, I'll include you. Otherwise, I'll work independently. No one will know I'm on a case."

"Do you expect to find something shady?"

"Based on what I have seen so far, I'm sure I'll find something way beyond shady. As sure as I was that I wouldn't find anything shady concerning Marvin."

"How will you proceed, Moses," asked Eileen.

"Sooner than later. Before I work at the station this afternoon, meet me at Lincoln School. Let me explain what I did, basically giving him the same report I gave you until the part about Sheila and Leroy. He may have a problem with me after I tell him. In that case, I think it best to get out of your life."

"That would be a real shame, Moses," said Eileen. "I think you are having a positive influence on Marvin. On me as well."

"Well, we'll see," said Moses. "If Marvin's OK with things, I'd like to take you both to The Pacific Club[20] for dinner on Saturday. Maybe cut the rug a bit. A celebration of a clean slate. Marvin could bring Sheila along."

"Sounds like a gas, Moses; I… we haven't been out to dinner in ages."

Eileen's smile, the look in her eyes (yearning), and the lingering handshake at the front door as Moses left sent electricity up his arm.

Moses returned to his apartment for a nap. Before lying down, he pulled out the typewriter he had bought at the army surplus store after the war and transferred his report notes to paper. His hunt-and-peck typing method took an hour and contained five mistakes, but he hoped Marvin would appreciate the effort.

Marvin, Eileen, and Moses converged on the parking lot at Lincoln School at 3:45 p.m., and Eileen introduced Moses to her son.

"I've seen you around. We played on the same team once last week, right?" said Marvin.

"Yes, you ran me into the ground," said Moses. He motioned the three to the picnic table next to the parking lot. Moses, seated, unfolded his typewritten report and handed it to Marvin.

"To give you a little background, Marvin, I'm a mechanic at the Cities Service Station on Kalamazoo Ave., but I was a detective for the Kalamazoo Police Department. Your mother has been concerned with your safety since your friend Richard Sternaman died from a heroin overdose two months ago.

"This report is kind of a diary of your activities for the last two weeks. As I reported to your mother, she has nothing to worry about. That report is exemplary, and I didn't even embellish it with the times you hit the winning shot of a game."

Marvin looked stunned. He stared at his mother, who reached out and placed her hands on his.

"I just didn't know how to talk about Richard," said Eileen. "He was such a good friend of yours. I was scared, Marvin, terrified something might happen. If I lost you, I would be lost as well. Moses has brought me to my senses. I am sorry I doubted you even for a second. I promise I never will again. Moses had nothing but good things to say about you."

Marvin stood up, circled the table, bending over his mother, hugging her neck and shoulders. Then he straightened. "I'll read it later, Mom; I want to get in the next game." He started to walk away, stopped, and turned back to his mother, "Sometimes, Mom, you can be as dumb as Dad."

***

Eileen picked up Sheila at her house. She also picked up Moses, waiting at the curb on Burdick, and then she drove to The Pacific Club on Riverview Drive. The restaurant was crowded and decorated for Halloween. Marvin waved at the local jazz band on the small stage fronted by Marcia Gibbens, a singer Marvin and Sheila knew from school. Marcia smiled back while singing Nat King Cole's song, *Nature Boy*.

The waiter delivered the group's beverages, setting each soft drink above the dinner plate. Next to each place setting was a cutout Halloween face glued to a wand. The server took the group's dinner order and left. Shortly, a nattily dressed negro gentleman approached the table and addressed Moses, "Good to see you, Moses."

Moses rose from his chair and shook the man's hand. "Hello, Jr.," said Moses, "Eileen, this is Council Hawes,[21] the owner of the Pacific Club.

"Council, this is Eileen Simmons, her son Marvin, and his friend Sheila Rohan."

Mr. Hawes took Eileen's hand, "Welcome, Mrs. Simmons," he said, acknowledging the two teenagers.

"Moses, this beautiful lady is way beyond your station. You must have accomplished quite the favor."

Eileen patted Moses' hand. "Your club is amazing, Mr. Hawes."

"It would be spectacular if Moses talked the police chief into using his pull to move our liquor license along."

"I talk," said Moses, "But bigwigs don't listen to me any more than they do you, Council."

Eileen was curious, "In a dry town like Kalamazoo, I could understand it would take some time. How long has it been?

"Well, after the war, I came home from the South Pacific, kicked around a bit, and then got the idea for this place. So more than two years so far."

"You see, Eileen," said Moses. "Only city-recognized clubs can serve alcohol in the city. I'm a member in good standing here. I paid my ten dollars, but it doesn't mean much until Hawes Jr. gets his permit."

"The thing is, Mrs. Simmons," continued Council, "I know of three country clubs that applied after me, and all three of them are up and running and serving martinis."

"That's not right," said Sheila.

"Look around, Sheila," said Mr. Hawes. "I lived and fought with whites, blacks, Irish, and Cherokee. I'm bringing that kind of fusion here to the Paradise, with the sounds of jazz holding everyone together."

"Is Kalamazoo ready for a club like this?" asked Marvin.

"We beat the Nazis, Marvin; there is hope in that. Enjoy your dinner, folks. Moses, don't be a stranger."

After dinner, Marvin grabbed Sheila and went off to jitterbug.

Eileen leaned into Moses. The music increased in volume as the band became more lively. "How well do you know the chief of police, Moses."

"He's been decent to me since the shooting, set me up in my apartment over The Paints and Oils store.

"It took six months of exercise before my arm worked at all. I was ready to return to work when Ethyl put her foot down.

"She couldn't live with the danger she said followed me on the job. I quit my dream job as a detective. The chief helped get me the job at the Cities Service Station. Six months later, Ethyl left me for an Encyclopedia Britannica door-to-door salesman. I had no clue.

"I had a tough time finding a place that would rent to me after the house was sold. A divorce like that sets you back, so there wasn't much I could afford.

"Chief got tough with my landlord on some building violations. The landlord relented and rented the apartment to me. It's perfect. Close to downtown and work and my old neighborhood. Enough of that."

"How about a dance, Moses," said Eileen. "It's been years, so you may have to excuse my feet."

"Sweet, Let's show off that killer diller dress. It looks like Marvin's a great dancer. Rhythm. A big part of basketball as well."

"This has been a wonderful evening, Moses."

"I expect a kiss at the night's end to return the favor."

Eileen didn't hesitate. She rose on her high-heeled toes and kissed Moses. Moses latched on, gently squeezing Eileen, feeling her breasts against his chest, a tightness in his groin nearly betraying his excitement.

8 | Tournament

The next day, Moses sat in the back of the Mt. Zion Baptist church nave. When the service ended, Moses approached Marvin. Eileen had moved into the Sunday school classroom setup for congregation coffee.

"Hey, Marvin, do you have a minute?" asked Moses.

"Sure."

"I noticed at the 'Y' last week that they are holding a church league basketball tournament next Saturday and Sunday. Might you and some of your friends be interested in playing? I'd be willing to sponsor your team." said Moses.

"Uh-huh," said Marvin. "Still trying to get in my Mom's good graces, right."

"I don't think it would hurt, that's true," said Moses, "but you know how much I like basketball. It would be a good tune-up for JV tryouts at Central next week. I could act as a coach along with a friend of mine."

"I can round up five of my friends," said Marvin. "That gives us one sub. But a team? We've never actually played on the same team together."

"If you can gather them up this afternoon for a practice at the Armory, that would have to be enough. Say at 3:00 p.m."

"OK, I'll call around. See you at three."

***

When Harry Martensen finally found the unlocked door to the massive Kalamazoo Armory Building[22] on Water St., he still had a minute's walk to the other end of the cavernous hall. Moses and Marvin had wheeled out the basketball hoops onto the ends of the laid-out court stretching crosswise at that end of the building. Marvin's friends were warming up with layups. Harry met up with Moses on the sideline.

"Glad you could make it, Harry," Moses said. "I thought we should keep to a few fundamentals, maybe a give-and-go play through a screen, and then just let them scrimmage.

"Marvin found six kids who wanted to play, allowing us two on the bench. If we run with them in the practice scrimmage, we can play five-on-four; what do you say?"

Harry nodded. Moses blew his whistle and called the boys to center court. He introduced Harry as the defensive coach. He reiterated his plan to practice running, dribbling, and passing for a half hour before dividing into two teams for a practice scrimmage: five on four. A couple of the boys grimaced.

"What's the matter," said Marvin. "Never played with a white guy before?"

"Listen," said Moses. "Next Saturday, you'll be playing basketball against teams from all over the city. Yours will be the only one from Northside. If you make the JV team at Central, which is a big, big if, you may never see another brother the whole season. Get used to it."

Moses spent the most time passing. He pointed out how fast the ball could move down the court on a fast break instead of the guards dribbling down. "Push the ball down the court. Team work. Keep your head up. Pass the ball forward."

Dribbling elicited the same series of comments from Moses. "If you are looking down at the ball or your feet, you'll miss opportunities for a shot or a pass to an open cutter," he said.

Harry took over the practice, explaining the necessity of defensive and offensive rebounding. He showed them how to block out an opponent to gain access to the rebound. Each player took a turn trying to get to the ball by maneuvering around Harry while Harry guarded their approach to the basket. Each player practiced blocking Harry from getting to the ball on a rebound.

After observing the skills of all of Marvin's friends, Moses put the best four players on one team with Marvin, while Harry, Moses, and the two remaining boys made up the other team.

Moses began the play by hustling the ball down the court to his shortest teammate, who passed it to his friend. After three dribbles, Moses yelled to the ball handler to look up. Harry was racing down the court on the right side. The dribbler threw the ball baseball-style in Harry's direction, out of Harry's reach and out of bounds.

"That's OK, Mike," said Moses. "That's the idea. Lead the runner next time, and work on your chest pass. Two hands give you more control."

Marvin's team brought the ball down, dribbling and methodical. When they came near the basket, Harry was all over the ball. They finally passed the ball back to Marvin, who took the shot, a perfect bank from the right side for two points.

While Marvin's friends gloated, Harry took the ball out of bounds and passed it inbounds to Mike, who immediately passed it to Moses. Moses dribbled five steps and passed to Harry, speeding down the court. Harry took two steps and fired the ball back to Moses, cutting toward the basket for an easy layup.

Marvin gathered his team. "These old geezers can run. They obviously have played together a lot. I've watched Mr. Webb. He can shoot. We need to double-team him every time down the court."

Even with the double team, Moses could shoot over the shorter high schoolers and kept the game even. Harry blocked three or four shots. Eventually, Moses and Harry were leaning over, holding onto their shorts, exhausted. Marvin and company could have gone another hour, but Moses called the practice over.

"I hope the practice helps you out for next week. I put down your team name as the Northside Zion Zealots. If you think of a better name, I can change it. The first game is at 8:30 a.m. Saturday. Be at the 'Y' by 8:00 a.m."

***

The Zion Zealots gathered around Moses after the warm-up. Moses tried to calm the boys' excitement. "Here are your jerseys provided by the 'Y' for the weekend. The other team has uniforms, so you'll start with the dark side. Harry, any words?"

"It looks like No. 25 is their main offense," said Harry, "but No. 6 looks pretty good as well. Block out under both baskets and get the rebound."

Moses looked at each of the faces before him as he said, "Boys, this is a single elimination event. If you lose, you are out. I guess you are playing a favored team of seniors in high school. The organizers matched you with them to eliminate you quickly. You are all sophomores except for Mike, who is a junior. My bet is that you can outrun them."

Moses looked over at the other team huddled with their coach. "How about trying a little strategy. The game will consist of two ten-minute halves with a running clock. In a boxing match, you've got to pace yourself, and that's what I suggest for you guys. They don't know you, and they especially don't know Marvin.

"Marvin, let your other four teammates run the daylights out of them and feed Mike or Keith the ball for the first eight minutes. If the score gets too lopsided, we'll change tactics in the second half.

"Otherwise, Marvin, hold back, stay in rhythm, and see what happens."

As predicted, the older team slowly built up a lead. Mike and Keith made the majority of points for the Zealots, and Marvin took two shots, sinking them both. Marvin's team used the fast break lesson from their one practice to eventually wear out the other team. At the eight-minute mark, the team representing the episcopal church from the south side of town was up by ten points.

Marvin had been feeding Keith until then, but at a signal from Moses, Zealots started feeding Marvin. Marvin was fresh, relaxed, and anxious to contribute. He made six points in the last two minutes before the scoreboard clock timed out for the first half. His team sat down for the three-minute half, only four points behind.

When the referee called for the second half to begin, Marin was still rested and in control. Moses didn't say a thing except, "Have fun." The Northside Zion Zealots went ahead after two minutes in the second half and eventually won the game by twelve points.

The second game started at 10:30 a.m. This time, the Zealots faced a team of apparent sophomores. The Christian Reformed Church players seemed embarrassed to play on the same court as Marvin's team. Both sides relaxed and played the game for fun. The Zealots won by eighteen points.

The third game in the afternoon was more intense. There seemed to be underlying hostility toward Moses' team of a different color. Fouls were hard, and the faces of the players were set in scowls the entire game. Marvin scored twenty points despite the bruising affair, and the Northside team win was never in doubt.

Moses gathered the team after everyone had showered. "That was a good day. You represented the Northside neighborhood with real style. Look it up. Tomorrow, the last two games will be against players who have beaten as many teams as you have. Or you may be out after the first game. Try to get a lot of rest. Harry scouted the last three teams. They are all talented, with a lot of depth."

That evening, Moses knocked on Eileen's door. She asked him to sit in the living room. Marvin and Sheila were already there, studying. "I won't stay, Eileen," said Moses. "I just wanted to encourage you to attend the game tomorrow at 2:00p.m. That may be their last game."

"I'll be there. I can't wait," said Eileen.

"Me too," said Sheila, "Unless that will make you nervous, Marvin."

"Maybe," said Marvin, "But I still want you there. If I don't make the Central JV team, it may be the only time you see me play."

***

The first game on Sunday was scheduled for 2:00 p.m. Moses looked over at the other sideline. The other team surrounded their coach. One player stood out because he was nearly a head taller than the others. Moses nodded to Harry as the Zion Zealots crowded around them.

Harry nodded at Keith. "Don't look now, fellows, but you'll have to win this game with defense. I can't believe that kid can be in high school. He must go 6'5" or 6' 6". Keith, what do you think?"

"I watched him during warm-ups," said Keith. "He ain't so tough. Look at his legs. A fan would blow him over."

"Everyone, hustle back on defense after you make a basket. Keith, try to keep that big stick out from the basket. Let's see if he can shoot outside of the paint. The rest of you help Keith; try to double up on that tall guy." Harry drew a picture on his clipboard to illustrate his point.

Moses clapped Marvin on the back. "You can bet they scouted our team as well," he said. "Marvin will probably be double-teamed. Mike, come up from your forward position and set a pick on Marvin's defender. Marvin, alternate between heading for the basket or stepping back for a catch-and-shoot. Be quick. If that big kid comes at you, try a head fake and go for the basket. Remember, everyone, crash the board."

Marvin was rubbing his shorts. Moses threw him a towel to dry his hands; he looked nervous.

"Marvin, have fun out there," said Moses.

Marvin did have fun. Time and time again, he shook off the other team's defenders and made points. Keith fouled out two minutes after the start of the second half, but by then, the Zion lead was comfortably in double digits. With a running clock, the Eastside team couldn't catch up. Near the end of the second half, Moses glanced up at the running track. Eileen was leaning over the rail next to Sheila. They were smiling and enjoying their favorite player. Eileen noticed Moses looking up. She waved and gave him a thumbs-up.

The Zealots had to wait for the other semi-final game to be played. Moses and Eileen took the team to Woolworths for a hamburger and Coke at the soda bar. Harry stayed behind to scout the strengths and weaknesses of the two remaining squads.

After lunch, the group returned to the 'Y.' The kids relaxed while playing bumper pool on the two brand-new tables in the youth lounge. They still had an hour to wait.

Thirty minutes before game time, Moses called for the pool cues to be racked and gathered the team for Harry's scouting report. "What can I say. Both teams were outstanding. The winner consisted of another bunch of sizable seniors. Box out your man and grab the rebound. Run the fast break. That is your strength. Moses. Anything else?"

"No," said Moses. "Let's go and play the game. You fellas have come a long way. Win or lose, hold on to that."

The First Methodist Church, the oldest established church in Kalamazoo, had a large congregation. The church basketball team was active in the area and traveled to neighboring Battle Creek and Lansing to participate in tournaments. The starting five were all seniors, and the bench held ten more players waiting to play. They played disciplined basketball. They were well-coached. The Zealots were terribly overmatched in size and experience.

Despite the hurdles, Marvin, Keith, and the rest of the team played with heart and speed. Marvin scored eighteen in the first half, Keith added ten, and Mike scored two. Still, the Methodist Marauders were ten points in the lead at the end of the half.

In the second half, the Marauders brought in a steady stream of fresh players to defend Marvin. Marvin shed his shirt, wearing only the borrowed 'Y' jersey. His shorts were soaked with sweat. The rest of his team fared no better. They were all exhausted, and the Marauders continued to score.

With two minutes to go in the game, the Marauder's coach ensured all his players participated. Marvin poured buckets when the second string came in, scoring eight points before the final buzzer.

The Methodists lined up opposite the Baptists, and everyone shook hands. The players on Marvin's team were too tired to be upset or mad at their loss. Seniors congratulated sophomores. Despite the color differences, an atmosphere of respect filtered through the gym.

The man approaching Moses after the game was a bit taller than Moses. He had dark hair, broad shoulders, and an easy gait. Moses guessed he had played basketball at some level, high school, college, or pro. His three-piece suit fit him well for not being professionally tailored.

"Hello," he said. "Have you got a minute?"

"Sure," said Moses.

"My name is Bob Quiring."[23]

"I'm Moses Webb. What's on your mind?"

Mr. Quiring reached out and shook Moses' hand. "I apologize for keeping you away from the kids and the locker room," he said. "I'm the varsity coach at Central. I caught most of your games this weekend. You've done great things with your team."

"I didn't do much, just sponsored the team, mainly," said Moses. "Marvin Simmons is the son of Eileen Simmons standing over there. You might say she is a person of interest to me."

Bob Quiring shook his head, "You're selling yourself short. These kids worked together as a team, and that kid, Marvin Simmons, you say that's his name. He is a person of interest to me. Does he attend Central High?"

"He does, and he's excited about trying out for the JV team next week. Would you like to meet him? He's as level-headed as they come."

"Yes, I'd appreciate it."

The two sauntered over to Eileen, who was listening to Marvin, Keith, and Mike recount their favorite moments of the game.

"Eileen, this is Mr. Quiring," said Moses. "He's the varsity coach at the high school."

"Pleased to meet you," said Eileen, shaking Bob's hand. "This is my son, Marvin, and his friends, Keith Gerlach and Michael Pelton."

"Hi boys, sorry for your loss; a little more rest between games, and I believe it would have been a nail-biter," said Mr.Quiring.

All three boys shook the coach's hand. "We're all planning to try out for the JV team, Mr. Quiring," Marvin said.

Mr. Quiring tilted his head ever so slightly at the comment. Moses saw it, and so did Eileen. The boys were oblivious.

"It's a tough workout," Bob said. "There will be great competition for those twelve slots on the team. We'll have to see."

"Hit the showers, boys," said Moses. "Next stop is The Pacific Club. Council Hawes is sponsoring a celebration dinner for your second-place trophy.

"I'll meet you after I shower, Eileen."

Eileen sat back on the bleacher while Moses headed for the men's locker room with Mr. Quiring.

"Mr. Webb," said Bob, "I hope I didn't get those kids' hopes up too high. I hope you can understand what pressure I'd be under if I put them on the team."

"If they are the best players," said Moses, "They deserve to be on the team."

"I don't disagree with you at all, Moses. I'm doing my best to move forward, but I must be cautious or out of a job."

"How cautious," asked Moses.

"Well, Marvin, for instance," said Quiring. "He will be a top player, no doubt. The JV team, for sure, may be The Varsity. From the stands, he'll look like the rest of my players.

"Your team…

"Too dark."

Moses felt his stomach tighten. He had no ring to step into to take out his frustration. With great effort, he swallowed, saying, "I hope you will keep an open mind and give the others a chance, too. Marvin will play better for you with friends around him."

"If they show up," said Bob, "they'll get a chance. Nice meeting you, Moses."

By the time the team sat down to dinner at The Pacific Club, the final loss in the tournament was ancient history. Harry had driven home and brought back his wife, Sarah, who hobnobbed with Eileen. Everyone had a good time except for Moses. His stomach wouldn't unknot. Bob Quiring may be trying, but Moses suspected the boys in Marvin's group would not see it as adequate.

The alcove at the east entry of the Kalamazoo Armory Building offered some relief from the biting November wind and snow swirling around Moses' boots. When he finished his second cigarette, Moses thought, *to hell with it*, and walked home. Without possessing a Union Card, he had failed to gain entry to the strike meeting. Yet, Leroy had strolled right in.

Moses had followed Simmons on and off on his own time and convenience for the last three days. The 1:00 p.m. Union meeting was Leroy's first activity that Moses registered as unusual. Most of the time, Leroy moved from one corner of the Michigan Central Railroad Station[24] to another, hawking watches or leather belts. Sometimes, if the mark looked gullible enough, Leroy would take them behind a neighborhood dumpster and sell them a hand-rolled cigarette rubbed in incense to imitate marijuana.

At times, Leroy would greet a familiar customer enthusiastically. The two would walk around the block, knock on the door of the dilapidated bungalow where Leroy slept most nights, and enter. Five minutes later, the two would emerge, smiling. None of Leroy's customers looked interesting, important, or noteworthy to Moses.

But the attendance at the Union meeting baffled Moses. Leroy's behavior seemed out of character. He didn't seem the type to think about work conditions, politics, family life, or anything not involving easy profit.

As Moses unlocked the door to his apartment, he heard someone climbing the stairs. The clicking sound of high heels meant a woman might be coming to see him. Moses went in and looked around. His gym clothes were piled on the overstuffed chair. He gathered them and threw them in the basket in his closet. There was a knock on his door. *Maybe it would be Eileen.*

Moses opened the door as a heavy whiff of Lavender perfume filled the doorway. Nadine, the receptionist from Dr. Alexander's office, mainly stood on one foot, one hand placed high up on the door frame and her other on a cocked hip.

"Your place is so close to the office I thought I'd stop by and check on your progress," said Nadine.

"I've got to start getting ready for work in a few minutes," said Moses.

Nadine walked past him, checking out the apartment. "This is quite nice, Moses. Is that a new refrigerator?"

"It is. Quite convenient. Would you like something to drink? I can heat water for tea. That's easy. A soft drink, maybe. I received a fifth of whiskey as appreciation for a favor."

"Ooh, I could use a little of that whiskey. It was a cold walk over here."

Moses poured two fingers of whiskey into rock glasses, punched out four cubes from the ice tray, and invited Nadine to sit in his big chair.

Nadine instead pulled out one of the two kitchen chairs from the small table, turned it around, and sat down, crossing her legs, which Moses had to admit looked long and shapely, great.

"It would be best if you sat in your chair, Moses. I'm fine right here.

"How are your injuries, Moses? You haven't been by for any more pills."

"Don't need them. They were getting too easy."

"So you're healed?"

"Pretty close. My ribs still hurt when I work out, but I take it easy with lifts on that side."

"That's good; I'll make a note in your file."

"Say, Nadine, I'd like to get in touch with the husband of that patient the Doc treated while I was in your office and showed you my bruised ribs."

"I'm not sure I can do that, Moses. Patient confidentiality, you know."

"I'm not looking for medical information, but she said her husband worked at Shakespeare and was on strike. I'd really like to talk to him about the strike. What do you say?"

"I can't see the harm in that," said Nadine, fiddling with the top button of her blouse, which accidentally popped free of the buttonhole. "I'll call you when I get in the office tomorrow and give you her phone number."

"Sweet, I have to get ready for work, Nadine."

Nadine stood up, tossed back the rest of her whiskey, set the glass on the kitchen table, and walked toward Moses, saying, "Don't you have a little more time for me, Moses?"

Boldly, Nadine encircled Moses with her arms and kissed him, hugging him tightly.

Moses was caught off guard but not surprised and not about to turn down advances from the pretty receptionist. He broke the kiss and looked down at Nadine. Her eyes were still closed, and her lips were still parted. It had been a very long time for him. He gave a thought to Eileen. Then, the heat of Nadine's body drew him in again, and he kissed her, returning her ardor.

There was nothing for it.

Moses drew back and attacked the rest of the buttons on her blouse.

***

The phone in Moses' apartment rang shortly after 9:00 a.m. Nadine was at the office and offered Susan Deering's phone number. She was the patient Moses sat beside at Dr. Alexander's office on his first visit. Moses hung up after a few pleasantries and innuendos passed between Moses and Nadine about the romp the day before. He next called Mrs. Deering, who answered on the second ring. When Moses explained the reason for his call, Susan passed the phone to her husband, Walter Deering.

Walter worked on a reel fabricating machine at the plant when he wasn't on strike. "Mr. Webb, my wife told me about meeting you in the doctor's office. I'm not allowed to talk with non-union members about the strike."

"Mr. Deering," said Moses. "I'm trying to gather information about a man named Leroy Simmons. I know he attended the rally yesterday. Do you know Leroy, Walter?"

"I know he worked in fishing tackle. The only time I saw him was in the lunch room. He was at the table next to my friends and me. He was trying to sell this fancy-looking man's ring to anybody who would listen. Two days later, he was gone. We thought he was an idiot hawking stuff in the lunch room. Apparently, so did management."

"OK, thanks, Mr. Deering. Would you mind if I kept in touch? I'm curious to know if he attends another rally. He is not the type, and I think he might spell trouble."

At 3:00 p.m., Moses called Eileen. "Sorry if I woke you up, Eilleen. I have a couple of questions."

"That's OK, Moses," said Eileen, yawning into the telephone. "I need to get up and think about dinner. How can I help?"

Moses pictured Eileen with disheveled hair and wearing lounge pajamas. Smiling, he said into the phone. "I found out Leroy worked for Shakespeare. Do you know how long he worked there?'

"Less than six weeks," said the voice on the phone. "Actually, only thirty-eight days. Leroy said he quit. His sister told me he was fired."

"Apparently, he was there long enough to join the union," said Moses.

"I don't know about that, Moses. It doesn't sound like him."

"Work it out," said Moses. "Leroy worked at Shakespeare for a few days after the CIO contract expired. He quits or is fired, and within days, the Union goes on strike."

"But why, Moses. What could he be up to?"

"I still don't know, Eileen. But you can bet someone is pulling his strings. He's attending the Union rallies. From what I've learned, that is completely out of character for a hustler like Leroy."

"What are you going to do, Moses?"

Moses hesitated, deciding how long he wanted to stay on this course. Nadine certainly complicated things.

Have I got a thing for nurses?

"Keep working the case," said Moses after hitting his head with the receiver, clearing his hesitancy.

Moses closed his eyes during the ensuing long pause. Finally, he said, "I hope I discover Leroy's scheme soon. It's getting cold out."

"How about coming over for Thanksgiving Dinner," said Eileen. "It's less than a week away. That would warm you up,"

Moses hesitated again, a little too long.

"I… apologize, Moses," she said. "You probably have another obligation."

"No, no. Well, The Cities Service Station may need me to work. I'll have to let you know."

"I hope you can make it," Eileen said, trying not to sound disappointed over the phone. "I'd like to see you."

"I'll certainly try to make it," said Moses.

"By the way, Marvin made the JV team."

"I expected he would. How's he doing? Does he like the practices? High school basketball is pretty grueling."

"He always comes home exhausted and sore."

"What about Keith or Mike? Did they make the team?"

"No, just Marvin."

"On Thanksgiving, I'll talk to him. He's playing in a white man's world now. I know from boxing how tough that can be. Joe Louis opened a lot of doors for me when I was competing. Marvin will have to open a door for Keith, Mike, and the rest."

"He shouldn't have to deal with any of that, Moses. That would be a worry," said Eileen.

"Like it or not, he'll be the poster boy in Kalamazoo."

***

On Saturday, Moses worked out at the 'Y' at noon. The rest of the day, he watched a grubby white man wander from one corner of the train station to another, looking for suckers.

Leroy was having a pretty good day, as far as Moses could tell. Moses stayed in the shadows of neighboring buildings to avoid being identified.

At five-fifteen, a 1948 maize yellow Ford Coup stopped next to Leroy, and two men jumped out. Each man hooked one of Leroy's arms and hustled him into the automobile. Moses didn't have time to register the men's features. The car turned and sped away, heading perpendicular to Moses' position. He missed the license plate number and couldn't identify the features of the third man waiting in the car or the driver.

Sometimes, not owning a car limits an investigator's options.

Who owned that beautiful Ford, and who were the players in the car?

***

The next couple of days tried Moses' patience further. Nothing unusual occurred in Leroy's routine until Tuesday when he never left the stash house where he stayed. Moses figured it was Leroy's day off. Plywood covered most of the windows of the stash house, preventing Moses from verifying Leroy's presence.

Moses had never observed Leroy shooting up. He never even saw him smoking marijuana. Leroy sucked once or twice on one of his fake incense-laden hand-rolled jobs to convince some kid it was real.

According to Eileen, Leroy did indulge in a drinking spree on occasion. Since Leroy showed up on his favorite street corner the next day, Moses decided that he had slept off a night's bender the previous day.

In mid-afternoon, Leroy walked over to the Armory. The strike rally had been moved from Thursday to Wednesday due to Thanksgiving. Again, Moses was turned away, but he waited an hour and fifteen minutes out in the cold until the rally finished and members began to stream out of the building. Instead of following Leroy, Moses approached Susan Deering, waiting for her husband in their car, parked in the Armory parking lot.

He exchanged 'Hellos' and 'How are yous' with Susan, and when her husband approached the car, Moses shook Walter Deering's hand and asked if he had noticed Leroy in the meeting.

"Yeah, he was in there," said Walter. "I stayed in the back next to an exit, so I saw him. I've heard of police raids at rallies in other cities, so I stay aware of my surroundings."

"Anything unusual on Leroy's part?" asked Moses.

"It seemed unusual that he would even own a pen and notebook. He wrote down the dates the Leader told the crowd of our impending Detroit CIO collaboration."

"Dates?" said Moses.

"The week of December 6th to the 13th. Out of 700 workers at our plant, over 500 are here, and they are members of Local 3619. We want all 700 employees in the union. Strength in numbers. The Detroit Union members coming here will demonstrate that strength to the holdouts."

"Interesting."

"Well, we'll see. Both sides of this stalemate need to start talking, but management hasn't budged much."

"I'll keep an eye on Leroy. It was nice meeting you, Walter. Good seeing you, Susan."

"I don't see how Leroy could mess up the works, Moses, but if you get wind of anything, can I expect a call?"

"Certainly."

Moses walked back to the train station. Leroy had taken up his position and was hawking a watch to a well-dressed man waiting for the next train. As dusk became dark, Leroy left his post and walked to the flophouse where he stayed. Moses took off for The Cities Service Station in the other direction.

Moses spent his shift replacing a snapped piston in one of the police patrol cars. At the end of his shift, he was dog-tired. He showered and walked home.

At the top of the stairs, Nadine was knocking on his door. She turned to Moses and smiled slyly. "I can't stay tonight, darling, but I decided we should celebrate Thanksgiving our way."

Once they were in his apartment, Moses took her coat and threw it on his chair. He tugged her dress up over Nadine's garters to her waist and pushed her back toward the bed. Nadine stepped away and stripped off her shift.

"Let the celebration begin," said Moses.

10 | Thanksgiving

Moses woke up before ten o'clock on Thanksgiving day, not knowing why. Nadine left shortly after one o'clock that morning, so Moses felt rested and relaxed. He couldn't explain why his mind wandered to Eileen Simmons. Moses decided to take her up on her dinner invitation. Maybe he was just hungry. He dialed her number. "Good morning," said Moses when Eileen answered the phone. "Am I still invited for Thanksgiving Dinner? They didn't need me to work today at the shop.".

"Yes, more than welcome, Moses," said Eileen.

Moses was introduced to Carlene and Scott Thomas, two of Eileen's cousins. Sheila had also been invited. Marvin entertained her in the living room, listening to Hopalong Cassidy on the radio.

Scott and Moses talked football and cars while Eileen and Carlene finished preparing the gravy and the cranberry roll. The table in the dining room was already set. Eileen asked her guests what they wished to drink with dinner. The wine was offered, but Scott requested a beer, so Moses also suggested a beer for him.

Apparently, Scott had agreed to be the designated turkey carver. He took his position at the head of the table and, after cutting away the turkey legs and wings, began slicing the closest breast and doling pieces onto plates. Moses and Marvin requested some of the dark meat and healthy slices of the breast meat.

Dinner rolls, an apple and strawberry jello salad, mashed potatoes, and green bean dishes were passed around the table. The gravy boat made the rounds.

With forks on the table, Scott lit a cigarette from his pack of Chesterfields from his jacket pocket. Eileen started clearing food and dishes from the table. "Apple pie is coming; I'll make the whipped crème."

Moses wished to savor the turkey dinner longer, so he helped Eileen clear the table rather than smoke. Eileen did not hide her shock. "You don't have to help, Moses; I can get these,"

"It's no bother, Eileen," said Moses. "These months living as a bachelor have made me into a housekeeper. I like a neat kitchen."

"Have you spoken to Marvin yet?" said Eileen.

"I'm about to right now."

Moses wandered into the living room. Marvin and Sheila were quietly sitting next to each other, holding hands.

"How does it go with you two?" asked Moses.

"I'm OK," said Sheila. "Marvin's grown another inch since we ate at The Pacific Club."

"I've been eating my Cheerios," Marvin kidded. "Seriously, Sheila, I'm no taller; you must be shrinking."

"How are your legs holding up, Marvin?" asked Moses.

"My shins get sore," said Marvin. "The varsity team doctor makes me ice them for twenty minutes after practice. That seems to calm them for the walk home."

"We play our first game tomorrow night at six thirty before the varsity game."

"Too bad I have to work. Do you think you might get some playing time?" said Moses.

"He should," said Sheila, her voice clear and commanding. "He's the best guard on the team, by far, Moses."

"Sheila, I've told you I'll be lucky to play five minutes," said Marvin.

"That's cockeyed, Marvin," said Sheila.

"Not really, if you think about it," said Marvin. "The mayor's oldest boy is on the team, and the son of Mr. Esker, the physics teacher, is the starting guard. I'm telling you, I'll be lucky to get on the court."

"That's the right attitude, Marvin," said Moses. "Play as if those guys are your best friends. Do the same in practice as well."

"It's tough, Moses; I don't get many touches of the ball. My Northside charm doesn't affect my teammates or the JV coach much."

"Well, I know the varsity coach has his eye on moving you up. Just keep playing hard, and maybe you'll get a chance to make your mark," said Moses, heading back into the kitchen. But Marvin had more to say. "The bigger problem is that my friends aren't saying much to me either since I made the team, and they didn't."

Moses turned back, gripped Marvin by the shoulder, and said, "That's something I was afraid might happen, Marvin.

"The thing to do is to try to talk with Keith one-on-one. Explain to him what it might mean to him and Mike if you stay on the team, get more and more playing time, and next year on the varsity team, you might have some pull in his direction."

"That's a tough conversation, but you should try. What do you think, Sheila?"

"I'm not on the team," said Sheila, "but Keith might come around. If he does, the rest of our friends will be easy or not worth keeping."

The Eileen-baked apple pie was cut into generous pieces, plated, and set down before each chair around the table. The whipped crème was passed around so each diner could spoon their preferred amount onto their pie. Marvin, Scott, and Moses ate a small second piece. That was it; dinner was over.

In another hour, Moses and Eileen were alone in the house. Marvin was walking Sheila home. Scott and Carlene had left for their home in Grand Rapids. Moses sprawled on the couch, leaning back against the cushion. He felt full, lazy, and uneasy.

What to do, what to think. Nadine: Pretty, full of sex, sexy, accessible, and straightforward. Eileen: Stunning in comparison, capable, responsible, a companion, and, what's more, an excellent cook.

In the middle of these thoughts, Eileen entered the room, sat at Moses' hip, and ran a hand over his chest. She leaned over and kissed him. Straightening, she said, "Thank you for joining us for dinner."

"That dinner was fantastic, Eileen; you're terrific," said Moses. "And Marvin... I like that kid. You have raised him right. I'm damned if I wouldn't want a boy like him."

"That's nice of you to say," said Eileen. "I worry about him too much, I suppose."

"Just enough, in my opinion. Marvin is coping with light skin in a too-dark city neighborhood, a new team and coach, a pretty incredible girlfriend, and his studies. How many mothers can glow about their kid like that."

"As you say, I am very proud of him. Still, I get the impression that you see a black woman with a kid, like a chain around your neck; you're a guy used to being free and easy."

"Perhaps, actually, not at all. Before the drugstore shooting, I was 100% committed to my marriage. Afterward, as well, until my wife left."

"Why did she leave, or am I getting too personal again."

"What did your friend Mildred tell you about me?"

"Just that you had experience with law enforcement and were trustworthy."

Moses thought about that proclamation for a bit. If Eileen had known he was enjoying Nadine's company while at the same time having a pretty serious conversation with the gorgeous woman sitting next to him, she might have reconsidered her trust. Moses looked down at Eileen's perfectly shaped legs.

There's nothing for it.

Moses wanted to see how his fascination with Eileen would play out. He would call it quits with Nadine.

"The nickel tour of my life: I didn't finish high school. I started boxing when I was sixteen. I trained for five years and won seventeen decisions and two knockouts. I lost twelve bouts. I had the technique, skill, and stamina. I lost the will and the anger it takes to get to the next level. Plus, my family needed money when the depression hit. I worked as a mechanic at The Baton Rouge Refinery,[25] a skill I inherited from working on cars with my dad on Sunday afternoons.

"I married Edith in '34, and we moved to Detroit. We lived there until 1937. I passed my GED exams and received a Master Mechanic certification at a Ford plant."

Curious for Moses to continue, Eileen fetched a cold beer from the refrigerator, poured half into a glass for herself, and handed the bottle to Moses. She sat beside Moses and asked, "Was yours a happy marriage then?"

"I sure thought so," said Moses. "In '38, Edith and I moved to Kalamazoo because I was hired as an auto mechanic at the Checker Motors Company.[26] I loved that job. It was challenging, and I felt proud of every cab that drove by, no matter what city we visited.

"Then Pearl Harbor. I went in to enlist and was turned down due to my flat feet. I tried three times at different recruiting stations with the same result."

"Maybe it was meant to be," said Eileen.

"Because so many men from Kalamazoo were enlisting, the Kalamazoo Police Department was short-handed and hired me as a patrolman. I felt connected to the war effort by keeping people safe here in Kalamazoo while others faced danger overseas. I was assigned to the Edison neighborhood but moved to Northside the following year.

"When the war ended in '45, my rank was raised to detective, and I was assigned to most Northside cases.

"In 1946, September 14th, I remember walking to the precinct headquarters to get my assigned patrol car. Brian Statton, my partner, met me in the car. It must have been over seventy degrees, a beautiful, sunny day.

"Later, it was turning into dusk outside, and we were cruising by the Eastside Drug Store when Brian pointed to a guy leaning against the building near the drugstore entry. Suspicious behavior back then was a sixth sense, so I pulled over, and my partner and I approached the man. He took off running, and Brian followed him.

"I entered the drugstore, and when I came around a display case and could see the pharmacy checkout counter, the druggist was handing over a stash of pills to a man pointing a gun at him.

"I reached for my gun, but the robber turned toward me and fired immediately, twice."

Moses pointed to the two entry points where the bullets hit him, knocking him back. "The robber fled while I bled all over the display case."

"That sounds awful, Moses," said Eileen. "I suppose it wasn't like the movies, was it?" she said.

"No, it wasn't," said Moses. The bullets hit bone and fragmented my clavicle, sending shock waves of pain through my entire body along my skeleton."

Eileen impulsively leaned down and gave Moses a soft, lingering kiss while brushing at his hair. When Eileen straightened, Moses gulped more beer and said, "I better finish the sad story… Or not if you'd rather I kissed you again."

Eileen laughed, "Later, I'm so tense now; I've got to hear what else has happened to you."

"That's about it, Eileen," said Moses. "The rest is just melodrama. Recuperation took twelve weeks. Edith forbade me to go back on the force. I was unemployed for half of 1947, then the police chief got me a job at the Cities Service Station, and he arranged the rental room above The Paints and Oils store when Edith left."

Eileen knelt before the sofa and slowly massaged Moses' left arm as he lay. "So it took a long time to heal," she said. "Is your arm OK now? And what about these favors you do. They're not as dangerous as being a policeman, are they? I've never seen you with a gun."

"I have a gun. I keep it in my dresser at the apartment but never use it or carry it," said Moses.

"I guess I can understand your wife's concern. It's a consideration."

"Be that as it may, Eileen. My arm and shoulder will never fully recover. I do what I do for people with minimal risk, but I must admit, I like solving people's problems as much as I like making an engine purr."

"I see," said Eileen. Moses could tell Eileen was calculating her own risk in their association.

"With all these true confessions, it's time I learned your story," said Moses. "How in the hell did a beautiful girl like you get hooked up with Leroy Simmons, and what are you doing about it."

"Moses, I hired a lawyer on Tuesday to draw up divorce papers. I'll sign those when they're finished, tomorrow or the next day."

"Good, that answers one of my questions."

"What can I say about Leroy. He hasn't always been a street peddler. I met him while working at the Oaklawn Hospital[27] in Marshall, Michigan. Leroy was an ambulance driver in Battle Creek, where I'm from, but he was unemployed because of the Depression. I guess I've supported us ever since.

"What can I say? He's a salesman. Initially, he was a charmer, a dancer nearly as good as you. There were so many people out of work I didn't think I could blame him for not having a job. Nurses are always in demand.

"Marvin wasn't an accident. I always wanted children, which made me more assertive when he was born. Then, the war hit, and the Army opened and renovated the Percy Jones Hospital[28] in Battle Creek. I rented an apartment nearby so

I could walk to work. When we entered the war, the hospital was ready with 1500 beds. I had all the work I could handle and could afford daycare for Marvin. Leroy worked in and around the hospital on and off as an ambulance driver, security guard, and handyman. Nothing lasted, and none of the jobs held his interest.

"At some point, while I worked and studied for my nursing credentials, I lost track of Leroy's problems. I was too focused on Marvin and nursing. Leroy drifted away for days at first and then sometimes weeks. I finally heard from a friend that he was dealing, and people called him Pot."

Moses rubbed her shoulders as Eileen talked, attempting to ease her tension. "You have had your hands full," said Moses. "Raising two children, Marvin and Leroy.

"How did you end up in Kalamazoo."

"Near the war's end, Borgess Hospital[29] in Kazoo advertised for nurses. The pay was better, so I spent weekends dragging Marvin around to houses for sale in the city. I went to the bank and qualified for a low-interest FHA,[30] 30-year mortgage, as long as the house was in Northside. For one reason or another that I never understood, the homes for sale in Westwood, Westnedge Hill, or the south side became unavailable after I toured the property.

"I'm still fixing this place, but I'm doing OK. Leroy has always been a transient here.

"As I told you, I finally told Leroy I was through with him, except for his relationship with Marvin, which has deteriorated."

Moses reached down and pulled Eileen up to him on the sofa. Their kiss was long and gentle, the history of tension they both lived with draining away.

Shortly, the back door banged shut. Moses sat up on the sofa, and Eileen stood up, straightening her dress as Marvin walked in, casually wandered to the stairs, and went to his room.

11 | Con Artist

On Friday, Moses had to leave for work at three o'clock. He checked twice, but Leroy never showed up on his preferred corner at the train station.

Saturday was different; many people traveled in and out of the city. Leroy kept busy. It looked to Moses that black market alligator belts were selling well for Leroy. At 1:45 p.m., Leroy unexpectedly started walking east and south toward downtown Kalamazoo. Across from the Pool and Cigar Shop, Leroy stopped and smoked a cigarette.

A car drove up, and Leroy directed the driver to park next to the pool hall. Moses gambled and hurriedly entered the building before the vehicle finished parking. Scanning the booths, he noticed two empty in the farthest corner. He sat down and studied the Gazette left on the bench. Two men and Leroy entered and took the only booth available, right next to the booth occupied by Moses. His back was to the group, but he could hear every word.

One of the men put an arm around Leroy's shoulders. "What did you find out at the meeting, Leroy," said the man in a voice familiar to Moses, although he couldn't pinpoint a connection.

"All I know so far," said Leroy, thumbing through a little notebook, "is that the Detroit contingent will be coming between December 6th and the 13th. They're hoping fifty cars will come over. That could mean as many as three hundred demonstrators from Detroit added to the five hundred workers from here."

"That's communism in action," the man questioning Leroy said. "Just like the boss suspected. What do you think, Cyril."

"I don't care, as long as I keep getting paid," Cyril said.

"How about me," said Leroy. "When do I get my money."

The voice Moses almost recognized said, "Get the exact day and time those Detroit Union boys will show, and you'll get your money. You better be ready when they get here if you want more."

"I'm taking all the risk so far. I need an incentive if your boss wants that date, Owen," said Leroy.

The two men stood and started to leave. Owen threw some bills on the table in front of Leroy. "There's one fifty," he said, "but you better deliver, or I'll take back that money and half of your hide with it."

Moses followed the three men outside. They stopped at the corner of the building for a smoke. Moses got a good look at the two strangers. One of the men was the same height as Moses, perhaps fifteen pounds heavier, with blond hair styled in a flat-top crew cut. Something clicked, and he looked at Owen's shoes. Owen, Shitkicker-man. The painful kicks had not been forgotten. Moses now had a first name. It is somewhat unusual. Surely, someone around town could provide him with a last name. Then, he would find and isolate the man, threaten and scare him, and repay the pain.

***

Sunday, a day of rest. Moses checked out Leroy's usual haunts and couldn't locate him. Returning to his apartment, he brainstormed ways to find the shitkicker, Owen. If lucky, he would discover Owen's name and location on Monday. Moses planned to check in at police headquarters and find out from Ross Kirkpatrick Owen's priors, if any. He was about to lie down to read and nap when he heard a knock on his door. A knock he identified as Nadine's.

Might as well get this over with. Moses opened the door, and Nadine strode into the room wrapped in her ankle-length winter coat and fur collar.

"Nadine," said Moses. "This isn't a good time."

"That's OK, Moses. I can't stay," said Nadine.

"What is it, then."

"Don't I get a hello kiss?" she said.

Moses leaned in, gave Nadine a peck on the cheek, turned, and walked to the stove, picking up the coffee pot.

"I'm having coffee," he said, pouring a cup.

"None for me, thanks; perhaps something stronger."

"Listen, Nadine, you're a great gal, but showing up here unannounced is not right."

"Why not? It's a short walk from my place. I like to be spontaneous."

"It's too much."

Nadine circled behind Moses and wrapped her arms around him.

"You've never minded before."

"Things have changed; I can't do this anymore."

Nadine circled in front of Moses again and began toying with his shirt buttons. Moses turned his back to her and set his coffee cup on the table, saying, "Nadine, I've met someone."

"We've been good together," said Nadine, ignoring the statement. "We have fun. Next time, I'll call ahead. It's not complicated. I want you, and you need me."

Moses heard rustling behind him as if Nadine had shed her coat. He saw it land on his armchair.

Moses turned around. Before him stood a woman, easily a match to Lena Horne in beauty, wearing only a pale yellow negligée and red high heels. Nadine had pulled the nightgown off her shoulders to reveal a provocative view of the curves of her breasts. The hint through the fabric of rock-hard nipples reminded Moses of why Nadine was so hard to resist. Nadine had walked over in the freezing weather wearing nothing underneath her coat but the slinky nightdress. Moses imagined there was nothing underneath it but Nadine's milk chocolate skin.

Fuck it.

Moses alternated between pulling on his shirttails and unbuttoning his shirt. Suddenly, he was in a hurry.

***

Leroy was at his post by 10:00 a.m. Monday, Moses watched him from a bench outside the train station while seemingly reading the newspaper. Two men approached Leroy, and the trio walked around the corner to the group of garbage cans in the alley. Moses hustled around the other end of the station, practically on the run to a position he had often used behind a pair of giant maple trees. From there, he could observe and listen to Leroy conduct his transactions unseen.

One of the men, wearing a leather flight jacket and fur-lined trapper hat, grabbed Leroy's coat lapels.

"Tell us who you have been talking to, snitch," said the man. "You have no interest in our cause. Why are you hanging around the meetings?"

"I'm interested," insisted Leroy. "I worked there. Listen, Jim, when the strike ends, maybe I'll return to work with you guys."

"That's bullshit," said the hatless man. "You were worthless during your time on the job. Hell, I would have fired you."

"We're on to you," said Jim. "A security committee member saw you talking to outsiders at the pool hall."

"They're friends of mine, that's all," said Leroy.

"Oh, yeah? What are their names," said Hatless-man.

"I don't know their names yet," said Leroy, "I just met them."

Jim leaned in and punched Leroy in the gut. "Names," he said. Leroy doubled over, choking. Moses watched, expecting Leroy to reach under his coat and pull his gun, but the con man was in too much pain.

"I tell you, I don't know names… Just met them," said Leroy.

"You're lying," said Hatless-man.

"No, I'm not," said Leroy. "Give me a minute."

Leroy tried to straighten up, struggling to breathe, biding time.

"Listen, I just met those guys, but I bet I can get their names for you by tomorrow. I have to make something for my trouble; these guys are dangerous. Say a hundred dollars now and two hundred more when I give you their names."

"We don't have that kind of money to hand out," said Jim.

"Then get it," said Leroy. "Take it from the strike fund. I'll wait here. One of you be back here in fifteen minutes with the hundred dollar deposit, or I'm taking off. We'll meet tomorrow at the same time, and I'll have found out their names."

Jim sent Hatless-man after the money and to report to the strike security committee.

In twenty minutes, Hatless-man returned. Leroy still hadn't pulled his gun. Moses decided Leroy wasn't currently wearing it or that Leroy was confident that the strike committee would come through with the money.

The latter did come to pass. Jim returned with an envelope and handed it to Leroy, who stuffed it inside his shirt.

"Count it," said Jim.

"Nah, I trust you guys," said Leroy.

"Count it," yelled Hatless-man.

Leroy withdrew the envelope, peered in, and counted the ten dollar bills. One hundred dollars total, as agreed.

"Now," said Jim. "If you don't have those full names by tomorrow, or if you don't show, we'll find you and take back more than one hundred dollars. If you value your face, you'll be here."

***

Back at his apartment, Moses tried to figure out Leroy's piece in the Shakespeare strike puzzle. Moses had overheard two important meetings involving Leroy. In the second meeting with Jim and the hatless man, Moses understood that Union officials were aware of Leroy's duplicity to a certain extent.

The other meeting, which included Owen and another nameless accomplice, was an attempt to acquire information on the involvement and impending action of the Detroit Unions in Shakespeare's Union affairs.

But why? It was clear that Leroy was conning both sides. He had collected $250.00, with a promise of triple that amount, by providing essential information about each group to the other. As long as Leroy's involvement with both parties went undiscovered, Leroy stood to make lots of money from both sides.

Of course, the downside for Leroy was getting caught by one or the other faction at conning the other group. If that happened, Leroy was as good as dead.

What could Moses do? Since he now knew what Leroy was up to, bringing in Harry to help gather evidence seemed warranted.

Another thought occurred to Moses. With what he knew, he could persuade (strongarm) Leroy to leave the State and never return. Moses rejected that idea immediately. Eileen and Leroy's divorce was essential to his own future.

Moses still had to identify Owen and as many of his cronies as possible. The divorce would be assured if he could prove Leroy's participation in a crime. That's another reason to bring Harry and his camera in on the case.

What crime, extortion? Moses doubted if any of the players Leroy was involved with would prosecute. No, there had to be something else going on. And who was directing these factions. Union leadership, on the one hand, but was it an overzealous union member, an officer, or the whole committee.

Who was Owen's boss? Moses was sure he held the key, whoever it was. Again, Harry and his car might be necessary to access Owen and his boss.

***

As Moses dressed for his shift that afternoon, the apartment phone rang. Walter Deering sounded excited.

"Moses, have you found out any more about Simmons that would help my committee," he said.

"I doubt it," said Moses. "You should know as much as I do. Your security committee just paid Leroy Simmons one hundred dollars this morning."

"Yes, but the timing has just become crucial to our cause. Can we talk for a minute? Is anyone with you?"

"No, how can I help?"

"OK, we've never really talked about the actual strike. Which side are you on, the management or our Union?"

"I'm sorry, Walter. My involvement in your Union's doings is strictly personal. I want Leroy out of the way as a favor to a friend. I'm staying out of taking sides."

"I doubt if you will succeed in staying neutral, Moses. For now, I will trust that you are at least against Leroy Simmons. What I'm about to tell you might allow you to benefit your friend and help us as an added benefit. Are you willing to listen?"

"Certainly, Walter. If I can legally get rid of Leroy Simmons, I'm in. Leroy is the biggest bum I've dealt with since I left the police force."

"Alright, I'll tell you what is happening. Even the police won't be able to stop us if you tell your buddies on the force."

"I stop short of breaking the law for friends, Walter, Union members, or Management. Remember that."

"Understood, Moses."

"So, what's up?"

"Moses, I'm sure you know we have been joined in our fight for fair negotiations by the national CIO organization.[31] Specifically the Detroit branch. Today, action is being taken to publicize our joint effort. Peacefully, mind you, but forcibly.

"The Detroit CIO branch has organized a fleet of forty cars filled with workers driving in a flying squadron from Detroit. Our two unions will meet in Galesburg tonight, probably in less than two hours. The vehicles are moving bumper to bumper along US12."

"I thought that was all set up for the week of the 6th to the 13th," said Moses.

"In our public meetings, we gave out those dates. No one knew the real date until yesterday," said Walter.

"That was smart. It will cost Leroy money and a beating, probably."

"Tomorrow morning, at dawn," said Walter, "more than 150 CIO members from the Great Lakes Steel Plant in River Rouge will join our 400 Local 3619 members for a demonstration at the Shakespeare plant."

Moses still couldn't figure out the purpose of Walter's call. "What exactly are you thinking I can or should do," he said.

"Keep an eye on Leroy Simmons, Moses," said Walter. "My committee will mingle with the demonstrators to ensure a peaceful rally. Leroy is a wild card. I don't have time to babysit him."

Moses didn't mention it, but Owen, Shitkicker-man, might also be cause for concern. He would watch them both, "I'll do what I can," he said. "I can't say blending into the crowd with my skin will be easy."

"You'll be fine, Moses; I'll let my committee members know you'll be there. You'll be able to stay lost in the crowd."

"Walter, do you know a member with the first name Owen?" said Moses.

"No, but I'll ask my committee if it's important," Walter said.

"Yes, It's important."

12 | The Shakespeare Factory

The muscles in the mechanic's back were tight. He decided to take as hot a shower as he could stand in the gang bathroom down the hall to wake up. The alarm this morning at five-thirty guaranteed no one else would join him in the bathroom.

Moses had left work at 11:00 p.m. last night, having finished using the hoist to pull the engine out of the 1942 Pontiac Chieftain Streamliner coupe. He would examine the block for cracks at work tonight. The effort had guaranteed a good night's sleep.

Moses glanced out the window to check the weather. Technically, it was still fall, which in Michigan meant winter. It was pitch black outside his window; no stars winked back at him. Cloud cover and cold, typical Michigan. The radio said it was 42 degrees, with a high today of 45. He was dressed in Levi 501 jeans he had bought at the army surplus store at the war's end. (Only defense workers were able to get them during the war.) He put on his heavy alpaca-lined mouton-collar work coat. He wore his workday fedora in case it snowed later, although there were only vestiges of the last snow on some street corners. The sidewalks and streets were clear.

The Shakespeare factory and administration building were three blocks northeast. Dawn was still an hour away. At the corner of Kalamazoo Avenue and Edwards Street, cars blocked the intersection in four directions. Cars were lined up bumper to bumper, heading north and south on Edward Street and east and west on Kalamazoo Avenue.

Moses tested the doors on a Chevy coupe; all locked. All the cars were abandoned.

Curious, Moses walked the entire block that housed the Shakespeare plant. Cars blocked Ransom Street and Pitcher Street back down to Kalamazoo Avenue. Two cars side by side prevented traffic flow in either direction.

As Moses completed the circuit of streets surrounding the Shakespeare compound, he noted the arrival of a half dozen police cars, apparently surprised at the completeness of the automobile blockade. The police could not breach the wall of vehicles, and any cars or people inside the effective perimeter would not be getting out without running into Union members.

Hundreds of men and women congregated in the parking lots near the plant. Moses kept to the shadow of the building across Kalamazoo Avenue. Three more police cars arrived, parking near the others. Moses knew that neighboring police forces must have been notified and joined their fellow officers. Still, the policemen were outnumbered ten to twenty to one by strikers. It would have been suicide for the police to try to intervene. Tear gas may have been effective, but at present, officers seemed content to observe the peaceful demonstration.

The strikers became active as dawn broke over the Kalamazoo River, waving their signs, lettered with demands for higher wages and Union representation. Committee members set up two dozen G.I. Pocket Stoves to warm the hands of the demonstrators. The Union members formed several large marching circles in front of the Shakespeare Administration office building and on all sides of the plant. A handful of police officers mingled with the strikers, guns holstered, strapped, and buttoned down.

As the activity of the demonstrators settled into a pattern, Moses decided he should try to find either Leroy or Owen. He was sure finding one would lead to the other.

Squatting near one of the pocket stoves, Walter Deering beckoned Moses to the fire. "I haven't seen Leroy this morning," said Walter. "Maybe he won't show."

"It's finally light enough to look for him," said Moses, "Hard to spot in this crowd."

Fifteen minutes later, Moses noticed Leroy at another G.I. Pocket Stove. Luckily, Leroy had not spotted Moses. Moses stayed twenty feet behind Leroy.

It didn't look like Leroy would be carrying a sign and marching. He was at the furthest rest station from the marching circles as possible. Moses watched four men and Owen approach Leroy. They all crowded around the stove, hands extended to gather the heat.

Moses couldn't make out the conversation and didn't dare get any closer. The discussion turned angry when Owen jerked Leroy to his feet with a tight grip around his arm. Owen pointed first at the Administration building and then toward the east side of the plant. Two men and Leroy took off in the direction of the administration offices. Owen and the other two men started out in the opposite direction.

Deciding to stick close to Leroy, Moses followed Leroy's trio past the office building to the management parking lot. A few cars were in the parking lot, stranded within the perimeter of the barricade. Leroy and one other man smoked. The demonstrators circling in front of the management offices were in calling distance of Leroy, but nothing seemed to be happening. Moses thought he might be missing what Owen might be up to and took off running to intercept Owen.

Moses found Owen and two buddies fighting with three Union men over favored positions around one of the G.I. Pocket Stoves. Owen had already bloodied the nose of a picketer and was now shoving another man so hard the man fell into the crowd. Some in the crowd pushed back. A scuffle ensued over nothing. The elderly policeman at Owen's elbow panicked and withdrew his gun from his holster, pointing it into the sky at arm's length. Owen stopped working the small man over, moved behind the patrolman, signaled his two accomplices, and shoved the unaware policeman hard from behind. The gun went off, the shot echoing across the barricaded area, sending demonstrators, especially the women, into a screaming frenzy.

Owen and friends immediately began spreading the news that the police had attacked the peaceful proceedings at the demonstration. A large contingent followed Owen the eighty feet to the entrance to the plant, where Owen found a five-pound rock, which he picked up and hurtled through a front window of the plant.

The policeman, whose gun went off, desperately explained the situation to two other policemen who joined him. The crowd menacing the factory had grown instantly to fifty men, and they poured into the factory, pushing past the one patrolman and scabs protecting the front entry.

The speed at which Owen had instigated the conversion of the peaceful demonstration into a violent riot amazed Moses. He now realized that Owen wasn't just a street thug but a trained mercenary paid to disrupt. That was the goal all along. Leroy was the dumb pawn in a larger scheme.

Moses felt helpless watching men release their frustrations and inhibitions for the strike, unleashing mob rule against an inanimate equipment building. He turned back toward the management parking lot to see what Leroy was up to.

Leroy and his partners had gathered thirty frenzied rioters and had rocked one of the cars onto its side. They were working on turning over a second car when Moses caught up to them. Moses had no desire to get mixed up with that crowd, either. The cars proceeded to get turned on their side, one by one, until all seven cars rested on their side. The parking lot looked like a scrap metal yard.

Leroy looked like a wild man leading the crowd from the parking lot back to the factory, rushing through the entrance. Moses followed. No one noticed or paid attention to him. Moses lost sight of Leroy but found Walter in the front hallway, his lower lip swollen and blood covering his chin and neck. His left ear looked red and puffy.

"Moses, I can't believe this is happening," said Walter.

"Nothing you could do," said Moses. "Nothing, anyone, could have done to prevent this riot. Me, the police, or your committee."

As they tried to be heard over the chaos in the building, Moses saw men turning over cases of parts that skittered across the floor. He heard glass breaking as tools were being thrown through windows.

The temporary insanity of good men and women is difficult to sustain. Within a half hour, people were walking around listlessly, filing out of the building and staring vacantly around, waiting for instructions from their Union leaders. Many looked embarrassed. Some still maintained a scowl.

At 1:00 p.m., the cars in the barricade started moving as the Detroit CLI members began the long drive back to

Detroit. Moses didn't find Leroy or Owen among the wandering Union members reforming the picket line at the factory. The police seemed to be questioning people still hanging around, but they learned nothing about how things got out of hand. Some said the gunshot caused the trouble. Some said the strikers were to blame.

Moses couldn't be sure either, except that Owen was in the center, causing chaos. Had the policeman fired his gun just before being knocked to the ground? Had Owen bumped the policeman's elbow? Had there been a second gun?

Moses regretted not having time to call Harry for help on the case. His camera may have collected the evidence everyone would be looking for now. The flying squadron, the massive demonstration, and Leroy's participation had occurred too rapidly for Harry's assistance. Moses decided to call Harry in the morning. There was still work to be done, and Owen hadn't been paid back yet.

***

For the next four days, Moses concentrated on his job at the garage. The shop received some of the business of repairing the cars overturned in the riot. While he replaced dented or vandalized body panels on sedans and coupes damaged in the riot, Moses contemplated how much more he wanted to be involved with the strike and its aftermath.

The Kalamazoo Gazette[32] put the riot front and center on page one. The reporter spoke of Governor Siegler flying in to survey the damage. State police troopers eventually joined the Kalamazoo police to protect against further plant vandalism. Company officials estimated the damage to the factory to be $100,000.00.

Strikers stood in solidarity with the Union during interviews by reporters, offering "No comment" when questioned. The owners and upper management of the Shakespeare company were nearly as reticent as the Union members in explaining the events of December 1st. The descriptions of the events were sketchy at best, contradictory in many cases, and sources remained unnamed. Owen or Leroys' name never appeared in the newspaper, and no one had been arrested.

Moses needed evidence that the chaos was instigated by less than ten men under the direction of Owen, Shitkicker. For personal reasons, Moses wanted proof. He wanted Owen to pay as much as he wished to see Leroy gone. The mechanic concluded that the beating from Shitkicker was a deliberate ploy to delegitimize the strike and intimidate scabs in defiance of court orders. The more agitation Owen spread through intimidation of strikers and scabs, the greater the chance that the strike would fall apart entirely. It wasn't a red scare. The "goons," called out in the Gazette, were turning the community against workers and favoring Shakespeare's management and police.

On Saturday, Moses found Leroy working by the train station. Leroy didn't stand on the corner and wait for travelers. Instead, when someone approached the intersection, either coming out of the station or walking toward it, Leroy emerged from the shadow of the station's overhang and quickly walked up to the mark.

Leroy worked intermittently and randomly, generally keeping out of sight in the shadows, like the rat he was.

At midmorning, as Moses watched, a green Studebaker Commander coupe pulled up and parked in a ten-minute parking spot in front of the station. A woman wearing a long brown wool coat and scarf holding down her brown hair emerged from the Studebaker and stood on the corner.

Leroy strolled up to the lady, but she was no mark. Moses couldn't hear the ensuing conversation, but it quickly escalated into an argument. Leroy kept shaking his hands at her. Whatever the problem was, Leroy was not owning up to it. The woman's body language told Moses that she was threatening Leroy. Leroy became more and more agitated. He took his billfold from his hip pocket and showed the woman that he only had a few dollars. Moses knew from days of spying on the rat that he kept his cash concealed in a money belt, which he only accessed when alone, near the garbage cans behind the building.

Finally, the woman flipped off Leroy, shrugged, got in her car, and drove off. Leroy stayed on the corner, hugging himself to keep warm, shaking his head, and pacing. Moses decided it was the perfect time to catch him off balance and question him.

Moses walked over to the corner. "Leroy, hang on a minute," he said firmly. "I need to get in touch with Owen. He owes me money, and I intend to get it."

"What about my money?" said Leroy, "and who in hell are you, anyway."

"Not your concern; name's Moses; I work over at the Cities Service Station. I know cars; that's why my job was to throw that Molotov cocktail at the milk truck by the loading dock while you were trashing the place."

Moses had read in the Gazette about the milk delivery van set on fire the morning of the raid. No suspects were in custody for that bit of arson, and Leroy and Owen had been busy with their own tasks. Moses took a chance by taking credit for the fire that destroyed the truck. Leroy seemed to buy the story.

"I haven't seen Kressbach since that morning," said Leroy. "He's like a ghost, but when he shows up, watch out."

"Owen Kressbach had better watch out for this," said Moses, holding up his fist. If I don't get my money by tomorrow, there will be hell to pay."

Leroy looked up at the big man standing in front of him. He noticed how the mechanic's coat bulged at the chest. There was no slope in Moses' shoulders. Long arms led down to the oversized fist he brandished.

"Well, I don't know where he is, but I'm telling you, he don't like your kind. Watch out."

"How much does he owe you?" said Moses. "When I find him, I'll get what he owes both of us."

"Five hundred," said Leroy without a blink. "Tell him when I get that money, I'll blow town and won't make trouble."

Owen Kressbach. Moses now had the mercenary's full name. On Monday, Moses would be at police headquarters at the start of Ross Kirkpatrick's shift to continue the background check of shitkicker-man.

13 | Gather the Pieces

Church on Sunday at Mt. Zion Baptist was loud with the praises of Christ and the myriad "Amens" from the congregation. The morning's joy for Moses was walking behind Eileen and Marvin down the center aisle to their favorite pew. Moses had hung Eileen's coat on the rack in the back of the narthex. She elicited stares from breathless men in the congregation, Moses being no exception. He focused on her exquisite legs when she walked. Eileen wore a bright cerulean skirt and a white long-sleeve blouse with lace fringe at the wrists. Marvin had on a two-piece suit and paisley tie. Moses wore slacks, a white shirt and tie, and his leather jacket. He carried his fedora. Eileen grasped Moses' hand when he sat and didn't let go until the first hymn.

Moses didn't hear much of the sermon and was not one to offer an "Amen," but he had a solid baritone voice and enjoyed singing. Eileen followed the alto line in the hymns, and Moses thought her voice sounded husky and sexy.

Eileen invited Moses for Sunday dinner, which he accepted. He helped with the preparation (cutting up vegetables) and the clean-up.

Marvin wanted to hear about the raid of the Shakespeare plant. Moses didn't say much except that he was there and observed many people making fools of themselves. Eileen asked about Leroy's participation, and Moses again didn't say much. He didn't wish to poison the man in his son's eyes. Let Leroy do that in person.

At two o'clock, Moses walked home. He had just sat down with the Sunday edition of the Kalamazoo Gazette when Nadine knocked on his door with her distinctive knuckle wrap.

Moses opened the door just a few inches. "Nadine, I told you last week that I am done with these Sunday afternoon surprise visits. You've got to call first."

Nadine put a shoulder to the door, caught Moses off guard, and forced her way past him, throwing her coat on the easy chair. At least she was still dressed.

"I mean it, Nadine. This must stop," said Moses.

"I know, Moses," whined Nadine, "but I feel so… so good today. I want to party. Come to me, and I'll show you a good time."

Nadine's behavior was erratic and unlike anything Moses had seen before.

"Sorry, I'm not in the mood," said Moses.

"Ah, Mosey Wosey, I'm so hot and wet for you. You gotta cool my engine, and I mean right now."

Nadine picked up her coat and threw it on the table. Sitting down, Nadine hiked her skirt and spread her legs provocatively. "Come here, baby," she said."

Moses finally figured things out. "You're higher than the Hanselman building, Nadine. What are you on?"

"I brought along some for both of us, Moses. I've been crushing those Kadian pills. I take a snort every once in a while. Come on, try a line or two with me. Let's screw our brains out. I want to feel you inside me."

"Nadine, that is going to get you fired."

"I am careful. No one knows. I feel so good."

"We're done, Nadine." Moses picked up Nadine's coat and pulled Nadine out of the chair." Nadine swayed while Moses helped her get her coat on. When Moses let go of her to open the door, Nadine nearly fainted, falling back onto the chair, almost unconscious. Moses figured she was moving from a morphine high to a dangerous low. He forced her to drink a glass of water and then made a pot of coffee.

After two cups, Nadine seemed to wake up again. Then she was all over Moses, pressing against him. Moses helped Nadine down the stairs, walking her home while holding her up. Once in Nadine's apartment, Moses made tea. When he thought she could be alone, he helped dress Nadine in her PJs and put her to bed.

***

On his way to work the next day, Moses stopped at the Water Street Police Station[33] around the corner from his apartment. The duty sergeant sent Moses back to the locker room. Ross Kirkpatrick, who worked the second shift like Moses, was adjusting the tie of his uniform.

"What's up, Moses," said Ross, "You can't get this place out of your system or what?"

"Something like that," said Moses. "I think I know one of the men who instigated the riot at the Shakespeare plant. I thought you might want to get on the teletype to Detroit and Washington and see if they have a record of this man: Owen Kressbach. He's my height, has brown hair, hazel eyes, goes about 175 pounds, and wears steel-toed shitkicker boots."

"Moses, don't tell me you were mixed up in that nightmare," said Ross.

"I observed from a distance, Ross," said Moses. "I have nothing but eyewitness accounts, no physical evidence."

"I'll get someone to run his name and leave a message at the front desk. Are you still at the same phone number?"

"Thanks, Ross. I'd love to locate the creep for personal reasons."

"Ah, a favor," said Kirkpatrick. "A favor for a pretty woman you don't deserve, right?"

"You're right, my friend, but I keep trying."

***

Moses tried reaching Harry at Nusbaums on his first break, but the receptionist said he was on a sales call. Moses left a message to have Harry call him at home or the Cities Service Station.

Harry stopped in at the garage around 6:00 p.m. the following evening.

"Sorry, Moses," said Harry. "I was out of town yesterday and most of today. What do you need? I hope I didn't hold you up too much."

"We don't need anything for the shop," said Moses. "I need help documenting the activities of a rat.

"It's too complicated to explain here at work. Could you give me a half hour to explain tomorrow morning? I'll buy you a big breakfast at Woolworths. How about it? You'll be paid for your time and materials."

"I'm intrigued, as usual, Moses," Harry said. "Sarah is saving for a new electric wringer washing machine. See you tomorrow at seven o'clock."

***

Moses outlined his proposal while eating scrambled eggs with toast and coffee the following day.

"I'm gathering physical evidence on a grifter that works the street corners near the train station," said Moses.

Moses reviewed his initial task involving Marvin, Eileen's son.

"That kid can play basketball, sure," said Harry. "He reads the court well, and he's fast. Shoots well from the perimeter. You say he made the JV team. Makes sense."

Moses proceeded to explain his relationship with Eileen, Marvin's mother.

"Eileen is married to Leroy Simmons. He is the one we need to keep an eye on," said Moses. "She's filing for divorce, and I want to see she gets every break in the decree.

"Our man, Leroy Simmons, participated in the riot at Shakespeare. He even instigated a lot of the vandalizing. The violence that occurred that day was the direct result of goading by this guy and his accomplice, Owen Kressbach.

"If we watch Leroy close enough, Kressbach will show himself. I want photographs, hopefully of the two of them. Also, there is a woman with whom Leroy has argued. I want to find out how she fits into this thing. Neither Leroy Simmons nor Owen Kressbach is the brains behind the riot. Their boss is who we're trying to nail, and we may need your car to follow Leroy or Owen to a meeting with him.

"I figure we can work in shifts for ten days. If we have no success by then, I'll drop the case. I'll work Leroy from 9:00 a.m. until 2:30 p.m. If you could take over from 3:00 p.m. until 7:00 p.m., that should cover him.

"If we can document the scheme's members, I'm betting we can get substantial compensation for our trouble from the Union or the management at Shakespeare, depending on who is pulling the strings."

"If these assholes meet at the same place," said Harry. "I suggest recording them. I've been experimenting with the remote radio control of a miniature tape recorder. I'm unsure about a criminal case, but a recording would undoubtedly influence a civil suit."

"You're the radioman, Harry," said Moses. "I bow to your expertise. Bring both your cameras, and I'll use one on my shift."

It was midweek when Moses returned to his stakeout of Leroy. The long-range telephoto lens attached to Harry's camera made it possible for Moses to take position seventy-five feet from the corner Leroy worked. He stayed in the shadow of an alcove next to the alley rear entrance of the Kemp's Clothing Store. There was even an exhaust fan blowing slightly warmed air out of the building next to a ledge where Moses could rest the heavy camera. Moses clicks pictures of Leroy's clients, primarily out-of-towners, trying to buy Harry's watches.

The stakeout provides no revelations by Moses or Harry for the next two days. Friday's high school basketball game was moved to Saturday afternoon to allow for a conflict in scheduling the Oakland Gymnasium[34] at Western's East Campus, where the high school home games were played.

14 | Game Night

Moses rode with Eileen. She also picked up Sheila and drove to the parking lot for the gymnasium. Marvin had walked to the school an hour earlier.

The parking lot was filling up quickly. The varsity team had won all but one game this season, and talk of going all the way in the state tournament was already circulating. The JV game, which Marvin would be playing, came first. The three of them rode the funicular[35] up the hill to the gym. The view overlooking the city on the clear, crisp winter afternoon added to the anticipation of excitement for Marvin's game.

The KCH band filled one of the bleacher sections on the home side of the court. Every few minutes, as the stands filled, the band played the Central High fight song. The cheerleaders took the court and showed off their acrobatic skills and gymnasium-filling voices. Eventually, someone requested over the loudspeaker that attendees slide together to allow more fans to sit in the bleachers.

The players from both teams ran onto the court and began their layup routine. When the scoreboard counted down to two minutes until the start time, the KCH coach called his team together for a last conference. Then, the starting five players shed their warm-up outfits and wandered to center court for the tipoff. Marvin sat on the bench in the center of the reserve players.

The teams seemed evenly matched through most of the first two quarters. The rival Battle Creek team pulled ahead by six points. Number thirty-five on the Bearcats team led all players in scoring. He stood two inches taller than the players on both teams. Stretching his long arms high, he received the basketball while standing close to the basket. Without dribbling, thirty-five could turn and shoot a quick, short shot.

Sheila and Moses sat calmly, waiting for Marvin to come off the bench and join the game. Eileen was more enthusiastic. She had attended Battle Creek High School and occasionally, during the match, would rise from her seat excitedly when they scored.

With ninety seconds left in the second quarter, the Giants coach called to Marvin, who stripped off his warm-up jacket and entered the game. As the point guard, Marvin dribbled down toward the KCH basket and passed to Kevin, the other guard. Twelve seconds ticked off the clock. The ball was passed four times before being returned to Marvin.

The defensive player guarding Marvin blocked a possible run to the basket. He allowed Marvin space to shoot, figuring Marvin, as a last-minute substitute, wouldn't fire off a shot. Wrong. Marvin took his set shot and scored two points. Sheila jumped up, shouting his name.

Up by four points, the Bearcats worked the clock down to the last few seconds and then passed the ball to their tall center, who made another basket, putting his team back up by six points.

During half-time, Sheila went off to find her friends, and Moses bought popcorn to share with Eileen.

"It's been weeks since I've seen Leroy. My lawyer says the paperwork for the divorce will be ready on Monday. Is he still in town?" asked Eileen.

"Oh, he's still working the train station," said Moses. "Tell your lawyer to try serving the papers around ten o'clock on the northwest corner of the building, at Rose and Ransom St. He'll most likely be there. He may be in the shadow under the eave, but if your lawyer stands on the corner for a minute, Leroy will probably approach him."

"Good," Eileen said, "He better sign them. I hope he signs the papers." She sat quietly for a minute. "Do you think he will sign, Moses?"

"I'm certain he will sign on the dotted line," said Moses. Leroy would soon be under immense pressure to get out of town, given the failed extortions he had attempted with the Union and Owen's group of thugs. The photographic evidence Moses accumulated of Leroy's schemes would further convince the grifter.

The third quarter of the basketball game did not go well for Marvin's teammates. The Battle Creek High School team had adjusted their defense and completely shut down the Kalamazoo Giant offense. Marvin sat on the bench but yelled encouragement to his teammates. Halfway through the quarter, the varsity coach, Bob Quiring, came out of the locker room and sat beside the JV coach.

With one minute left in the third quarter, the coach called time-out. Battle Creek was up by fourteen points. Moses clenched his fists to keep from vocalizing his frustration.

Put Marvin in and give him the ball.

Marvin left the huddle and went to the scorer's table to check in. Play resumed with Marvin inbounding the basketball to Kevin, who took over as point guard. Marvin came down the right side of the court in front of the KCH bench, and Coach Quiring nodded. Kevin passed the ball to Marvin, who passed to Loren on the baseline. Loren passed it back to Marvin, who immediately faced the basket and let the ball fly. Two points.

Battle Creek missed their next attempt, and the rebound came out to Kevin. Kevin hustled the basketball upcourt and passed to Marvin, streaking ahead on the right side. Marvin dribbled in for a layup.

When the BCHS guard crossed center court on the next possession, Marvin rushed up and frantically smothered him on defense; the guard tried a bounce pass to his teammate, but Marvin anticipated the pass and intercepted it. As the Giants set up their offense, Marvin again took a pass from Loren. Marvin did a stutter step and faked left. The defensive man nearly tripped, trying to cover Marvin. Marvin dribbled on a tear to the basket and snaked his way past the center. He did a neat reverse layup from under the left side of the basket for two more points. The Giants were now down by eight points, and the buzzer sounded to end the third quarter.

When the fourth quarter started, the Battle Creek team began to stall, passing back and forth among their players while the clock ran down. But there was a problem: they weren't adept at that style of play. The nervous BCH forward on the right side received enough pressure from Loren to throw the ball out of bounds.

The defense is now keying in on Marvin on every play. The defensive guards pressured him and Kevin as they crossed the center line. Marvin received Kevin's pass and dribbled to his left.

Someone from one of the highest bleacher seats on the Battle Creek side yelled, "Go, Bearcats. Run that nigger off the court, you Bearcats. Go, Bearcats."

Moses heard, as did Eileen, who squinted through violent eyes, craning her neck to locate the source in the Bearcat stands. Most of the spectators in the gymnasium grew quiet momentarily, wondering who the Bearcat fan was talking about. No one in the stands could visually identify Marvin's racial background, but some from Battle Creek had grown up with Eileen and knew of her interracial marriage to Leroy Simmons.

On the court, the slur was lost in background noise and the concentration of the players.

Marvin now saw Loren open in the corner. Marvin looked once at Phil at the left corner, turned his head slightly, and fired a baseball pass to Loren running at the basket. Loren made a short bank shot.

Marvin committed a foul on the tall senior, who missed his attempt to score from the foul line. Phil was fouled on the succeeding KCH possession as he put his shot up. The ball circled the rim and dropped in. Phil did not miss his extra point.

The Bearcat coach called off the stall in favor of a screen for their center, whose hook shot, this time, hit the front of the rim. Loren got the rebound. He threw a long pass to Marvin, but three Bearcats rushed back, disorganized, on defense. Instead of trying to get to the basket, Marvin pulled up, set his stance, and took a long set shot. The ball banked off the backboard and through the basket.

The Battle Creek Bearcats led the game by only one point with two minutes left in regulation. Both teams nervously stepped up the pace of the contest with misses by both sides. Then Marvin took a long shot that hit the iron hard, bouncing high. It looked to Moses that Marvin realized he had missed but also calculated where the ball would come off the rim. He swept up the rebound about five feet from the basket, and without putting the ball on the floor, he jumped up and hooked the ball into the basket. Kalamazoo Giants were ahead for the first time in the game.

But the Bearcats got the ball to the tall center, who made his hook shot for two points to go back up by one point. Time was called by the KCH team with fifteen seconds left on the clock.

The five Giants huddled up with both coaches. The players were bent over, pulling on their shorts, exhausted. As Moses watched the huddle, he saw the varsity coach key in on Marvin, who let go of his shorts and stood tall, nodding in agreement. It didn't look like the coach had a specific play in mind, but he looked hard at the four other players to indicate the importance of getting the basketball in Marvin's hands.

The Bearcat Center stood next to Marvin as the players assumed their positions on the court. The opposing coach had assigned the long-armed center to guard Marvin, the player who had nearly single-handedly led the Giants back into the game.

The referee blew his whistle. Kevin put the ball in play by passing it to Marvin, who immediately made a bounce pass back to Kevin as the opposing center stuck close to Marvin. Kevin passed back to Marvin just before crossing the center line. The tall center ran toward Marvin, arms waving. Marvin signaled Loren to come up from the post to set a screen. Marvin passed to Loren on his right and swept behind him. The Bearcat Center decided to tie up Loren until the clock ran out. Loren faked a pass across to Kevin and instead passed right to Marvin, cutting around the three players.

Marvin caught the pass, squared up, and took his shot twenty-one feet from the basket. Sheila and the Kalamazoo crowd, already on their feet, went crazy with excitement when the basketball passed cleanly through the net. The Giants went back up by one point.

The BCHS coach immediately called timeout to set up his final play. After the timeout, the Bearcat point guard inbounded the ball to one of his forwards, who winged the ball seventy feet at the center, standing to the left of the basket. The line drive pass gained height and went beyond the outstretched arms of the Bearcat center. The game was over. Marvin's team and the crowd celebrated the Kalamazoo Central Giant victory, the derogatory comment from the stands buried or forgotten.

***

Marvin and Sheila wished to stay for the varsity game. Thay planned on heading to Louie's Trophy House for a soda and Hamburger with Curtis and his girlfriend. Eileen told Marvin to be home by midnight.

Eileen parked near the Paints and Oils Store, and the two climbed the stairs to Moses' apartment.

When the door was closed, Moses turned Eileen to him and kissed her. He was not frantic, and she was a bit shy, but the thrill of the basketball game lingered in them both, and when Moses led Eileen toward the bed, she came willingly.

Moses began to unbutton Eileen's dress in the back as he kissed her again. Eileen stepped back and shrugged the shift to the floor. Then she tugged at Moses' shirt, pulling it out of his pants and undoing the buttons. Moses shrugged the shirt to the floor on top of Eileen's dress, pulled his undershirt off, and tossed that on the pile.

Still in garter, stockings, and bra, Eileen lay on the bed and stretched her arms wide to invite Moses to join him.

He lay next to her, and they kissed. Moses moved to Eileen's neck with his kisses, reaching around to unclasp her bra. He didn't wait for her to slip out of the lacy cups. His hand covered her right breast and brushed her nipple. Eileen opened her eyes and smiled at Moses.

A knock on the apartment door startled them both.

No. Not tonight. Please, God, not tonight.

Eileen was already sitting on the side of the bed and refastening her bra. She bent over and gathered her clothes as another insistent knock reverberated in the apartment, even louder than the first time.

"You better get that, Moses," said Eileen. "Your neighbors will be hearing the commotion."

Moses threw on his undershirt, glanced at Eileen, and, seeing she was more or less dressed, went to the door.

Nadine, preceded by her lavender perfume, entered the room. She halted when she saw Eileen. Nadine quickly recovered from the shock of seeing another woman with Moses and said, "Did you forget about our weekly get-together?"

"We don't have a weekly get-together, Nadine," said Moses. "You should leave."

"I see," said Nadine, "Providing a little favor for someone else tonight?"

Meanwhile, Eileen had put on her coat and hat. "Goodnight, Moses," she said. "I'm sorry I interrupted,"

Eileen slipped out the door. Moses didn't recover soon enough to come up with anything to say. Even though he shooed Nadine away within five minutes, the night had turned into a disaster.

15 | Marvin's Threat

Monday after Saturday's game, Moses clicked only a few photos of Leroy selling pot by the garbage cans in the back of the train station.

On Tuesday, Leroy changed his routine. Moses followed him downtown, keeping Harry's camera slung over his neck by its strap and concealed in the fold of his coat. Leroy entered Schensul's Cafeteria and came out in half an hour, wiping his mouth on the sleeve of his dirty coat. As customers emerged from the restaurant, Moses could smell Schensul's fantastic fried chicken.

Leroy walked west on South St. and then south on Westnedge. At the corner of each cross street, Moses watched Leroy take a swig from a flask he kept in his right-hand coat pocket. Moses thought the odds were good that Leroy would hunt up Marvin at school. Moses decided he would have to be late to work and raced ahead to take up a strategic position on the side of a giant oak tree at the corner of Dutton and Pearl Street with a clear view of the Dutton Street entrance to Central High eighty feet away.

Moses focused the camera on the entrance and saw Sheila leaning against the building to the left of the entry. The bell had not wrung; Sheila must have been released early. Leroy appeared and went right up to Sheila, too close. Moses decided Leroy must be drunk to accost the girl outside the school. The grifter spent less than a minute talking to Sheila before he encircled her with one arm, grabbing Sheila's left wrist in a restraining grip.

The bell rang, dismissing school. Leroy pressed his body against Sheila so tightly her right arm was pinned between them. She couldn't fend him off as he pawed at her breast and skirt with his right hand.

Moses clicked a series of ten photos and then began to run to Sheila's aid. The third person exiting the school was Marvin, followed by his friends Phil and Loren, the forwards on Marvin's basketball team.

Marvin grasped Sheila's distress instantly and grabbed Leroy by the back of his collar, yanking him around and down to the ground. He kicked him twice. Moses was close enough to hear but stayed back, surrounded by the high school onlookers.

"Get up, you fucking pervert," said Marvin. "You're drunk; I can smell you."

Phil and Loren hauled Leroy to his feet and stayed close enough to assist Marvin in handling his father.

"I'm sorry, son," said Leroy. "I came here to see you. I had a few nips on the way here. You know how I get."

"Yeah, I know. If you ever get within fifty feet of Sheila again, I'll destroy you, father or no father."

"I've got to get some money to leave town," said Leroy. "If you and your mother can front me this last time, I swear I'll leave here, and you'll never have to deal with me again. I'm desperate; people are coming after me."

Moses watched Marvin seem to soften. "Come over to the house tonight," said Marvin. "I'll talk to Mother. We'll scrape together what we can, but I'm done with you. Stay out of my life, never look at my girl again, or I'll come after you myself."

Phil said, "I don't know your dad, Marvin, but I'm not sure he's learned the lesson yet." He punched Leroy in the stomach. Leroy gagged after the forceful blow and doubled over in pain. Loren straightened Leroy up again and lifted a fist to strike him across his jaw. Leroy had recovered enough to sweep his coat back and grab his revolver from his hip holster.

"You two get back," Leroy said. "This is between Marvin and me and his mother. Get Back." Loren and Phil immediately jumped back five feet. Moses lifted his camera up and into focus, snapping four pics.

"See, Marvin," said Leroy. "This is how desperate I am. I don't usually carry my gun, but they're after me. I gotta protect myself."

Marvin approached Leroy and caught him with a fist to his left cheek and eye. "Don't ever pull a gun on me or my friends again." Leroy staggered and dropped to one knee. Marvin put his arm around Sheila and walked off.

Moses returned to the train station and found Harry sitting in his car, waiting for Leroy to show. He summarized the altercation at the high school for Harry.

"I'm afraid I've got to ask you to watch Eileen's house tonight: 416 Parsons Street. If Leroy shows up and isn't out of the house in fifteen minutes, find a phone and call the police. Then, go home to Sarah and the kids. We'll see if Leroy shows up tomorrow. He may or may not be leaving town."

Moses set off for the Cities Service Station. He promised the 2nd shift supervisor he would work late the next three nights to make up his time. The manager agreed.

Harry kept a diligent, wakeful eye on Eileen's house that night. Leroy never showed.

***

Moses made himself as comfortable as possible in the shadow of the rear entrance to Kemp's Clothing Store in the ten-degree weather. He was thankful for the warm air pouring out the vent near the ledge where he balanced Harry's camera and telephoto lens.

Moses figured the cold snap would curtail Leroy's sales activity, but at ten o'clock, Leroy showed up. He was hawking men's ties today. Nothing occurred while Moses watched that warranted a snapshot. At 2:45 p.m., Moses hung the camera strap over his head and walked to work.

At 4:30 p.m., Moses was called to the shop telephone. Harry was on the other end of the call. "What's up, Harry," said Moses.

"I thought you would want to know," said Harry, "that Leroy was a no-show at Marvin's house last night. I waited until ten, and I'm confident my cover wasn't compromised."

"Nothing happened on my watch today, Harry. Let's see what happens this evening. I'll be working late to make up some of my time."

"OK, Moses," said Harry. "I'll call tomorrow at this same time. Hopefully, it won't get any colder tonight. I bought another pair of winter gloves and wrote them on your expense sheet. That Leroy creep is sure dedicated to making money the hard way."

"I find most crooks are that way. Keep me posted. Thanks, Harry."

***

The weather turned a little warmer, with a high temperature of thirty degrees on Wednesday. Still, nothing interesting happened on Moses' watch of Leroy. At work, he received some news from Harry.

"Moses, a woman joined our man on his corner last night. They argued, and she began smacking Leroy around as if she could kill him.

"I don't know if it is the same woman you saw with Leroy, but I wondered why Leroy didn't let her have it. He just took the abuse. At one point, he brought out one of his gold watch knock-offs and handed it to her. She threw it down on a patch of dry pavement and took her heel to it."

"Can you describe her, Harry?"

"The meeting occurred just before the streetlights came on. I can't tell you the woman's hair color, but she wore a heavy fur-collared coat. I took several photographs of her and the two of them arguing. I may be able to change the exposure on one or two of the photos when I develop them. Hopefully, you could identify her then."

"If Leroy didn't fight back," said Moses, "She must be important. Maybe she's the boss, or she represents him. I bet she's trying to get back the advance money they gave Leroy. I think he is scared to death. He'll break soon."

"Alright, Moses," said Harry. "I'll see what happens tonight."

"Great, Harry. I'll try to identify the woman if you could develop some photos soon. I'll ask Ross Kirkpatrick if I can look at the police mug books to find her. We've agreed that we'd wrap this thing up by tomorrow, whether or not we have anything substantial. Our photographs should help the divorce proceedings in any event."

***

Moses put on his coat and took a last swig of his coffee before trucking to the train station. He was ready for this to be the last day of the stakeout of Leroy Simmons. Then the telephone rang. Harry Martensen was calling from his desk at Nusbaums.

"From your description of this man, Owen Kressbach, I'd say he met with Leroy yesterday," said Harry, describing the man to Moses, who agreed with Harry.

"You weren't close enough to hear anything, were you?" said Moses.

"No, I was in my car across the street, parked behind a Packard. The street lights were on. I took plenty of photos."

"Good work, Harry," said Moses. "I'll head over to Leroy's corner and track him today. I'm not sure about our next move. Should we quit the stakeout or keep going."

"Wait, Moses. I've got more. I told you yesterday about that woman who roughed up Leroy. Well, he got a triple dose last night from Owen. He took Leroy over to a shadowed nook, and the next I could make out, Leroy was on the ground, and Owen was kicking the shit out of him. Owen yanked Leroy to his feet, straightened the weasel, and dusted him off. He poked his finger at Leroy's chest and then walked over to his car and drove off."

"You didn't think to follow him, did you?"

"I did, and you could never guess where he went."

"I'll bite, where?"

"He took about ten turns to be sure he wasn't followed, but I just had a feeling where he was heading, so I hung way back. He ended up at the Shakespeare Administration building. The building was dark except for a light in a room in the northeast corner."

"Anything else?" said Moses.

"Kressbach left the building about fifteen minutes later. Then, the light went out in the room where they met. The building perimeter lights were also turned off, and I imagine whoever Owen met left the building by a rear exit. I don't know, I never saw the person. I pulled a garbage can outside the room with the high windows where our suspects talked. With my flashlight, I could see that the room was set up for conferences, not an office. So we don't know yet who met with Owen. Sorry, Moses."

"Are you kidding? We're getting close. Tell you what. I'll watch Leroy today. Take a day off from the stakeout. I'd rather you develop the photos we've taken so far. We will have enough to take to Ross Kirkpatrick and Chief Hoyt,[36] maybe tomorrow. It's time to turn Leroy Simmons and Owen Kressbach over to them."

During Moses' watch, he took a dozen photographs of Leroy dealing marijuana to five different customers. Friday must be the time to stock up on weed for the weekend. Moses walked on to work, confident that he and Harry had accomplished much for Eileen. They had also acquired answers to the questions circulating in the Gazette about the strike, riot, and subsequent property damage.

Moses could feel the bolt start to turn. He eased off, not wanting to strip the threads. Then, the mechanic continued, unscrewing the last bolt in the block. As he suspected, the head gasket was shot. Ford parts were well stocked at the garage, and Moses went to the racks carrying the shot gasket. He found the matching piece within five minutes and returned to his bench, glancing at the wall clock. It was 9:30 p.m., a half hour after his standard quitting time.

Moses planned on working another hour as agreed with his supervisor to compensate for the time lost tailing Leroy. The mechanic shoved the block aside, ready to be installed in the 47' Desoto Deluxe, with help from Brent, another mechanic on his shift.

Instead, Moses took the keys of a five-year-old Chevy from the key rack, found the car in the parking lot, and drove it over the pit next to his bench. He raised the lift five feet and descended the stairs into the hole. The undercarriage was now in easy reach. Moses reviewed the work order: A simple exhaust system replacement from muffler to tailpipe. It would probably take a good hour to complete the job, but Moses thought he might stay and finish it to repay his boss for giving him so much leeway these past few weeks.

The bolts holding the strap of the tailpipe were severely rusted. Moses took sandpaper to each bolt to get his box wrench seated on them. Next, he squirted 3-in-one oil on the exposed bolt thread. The bolt loosened pretty quickly at that point. Soon, the rusted tailpipe was sitting on the pit floor, and Moses attacked the muffler, rusted and useless, similarly. Wiping dirt out of the corners of his eyes, Moses, spitting rust, threw the useless sound damper alongside the old tailpipe. He heard a voice ask if anyone in the garage could help him.

"I'm over here In the pit," said Moses. He heard steps approaching his workbench.

"Hello, my name is Ron Dundon. I've got a problem with my car."

"Not sure I can help you tonight. I'm the only one here, and I'm heading home pretty quick," said Moses.

"If you could just take a minute to look at my car. It conked out a couple of blocks east on Kalamazoo Avenue, and I pushed it here. I realize it can't be fixed tonight, but if you could give me a hint as to what the problem might be, I'll wire money tomorrow from my bank in Grand Rapids.

"Alright," said Moses, wiping his hands on his shop towel and climbing out of the pit. "Be right with you."

The man standing before Moses did not look like he could afford an automobile. He looked more like Leroy, wretched. Behind the man, fifteen feet away, Leroy stood unhappily rubbing his chin. Moses felt cold steel on his neck below his left ear.

"Don't turn around, Mr. Webb; we have you at a disadvantage." Moses looked down and, without turning, recognized Shitkicker's boots. The voice was that of Owen Kressbach, and now he was laughing.

Owen's gun never left Moses' neck.

"Billy, bring that chair from the dispatch desk over here," said Owen.

Moses, to stay calm, looked over at Leroy. After three days of beatings, he was a mess. Marvin had given him a purple shiner that had nearly closed his left eye. There was a nasty jagged scratch from ear to chin on the right side of Leroy's face, probably from the woman who had accosted him two nights ago. Last but not least, Leroy held his right side and hunched over to lessen the pain of sore, kicked ribs and gut.

Billy deposited the chair behind Moses, who was instructed to sit quietly with his hands clasped behind the back of the chair.

"Here's a pair of snips, Billy; there's also some baling wire by the garage door. Cut a length to tie Mr. Webb's hands. Feet, too, while you're at it."

Moses was at a loss.

What in the hell do they want with me? Stay calm.

Billy made fine work of tying Moses to the chair. No one works their way out of wire. It was already cutting into Moses' wrists. *Stay calm.*

Owen put the gun down on the workbench far enough away that even if Moses got loose, he couldn't get to it fast enough before being subdued.

"Shall we get down to business, Mr. Webb? May I call you by your biblical name, Moses? Thank you."

Moses remembered his old adage: ignore, run, or fight. Run and fight were already off the table. Moses chose to ignore the smug toughs in the garage.

"I have a few questions for you, Moses," said Kressbach. "Answer them quickly and honestly, and you can go home."

Moses decided to risk one small question. "What led you to me?" he asked.

"Ah, conversation. I like that, Moses. Leroy, over there, happened to mention that a nigger was looking for me. After the money I owed you, you said. Name: Moses Webb. You told Leroy that you work at Cities Service Station. When Leroy told me this morning, I initially didn't believe him. After considerable persuasion, I determined he was telling the truth.

"My work involves a need for discretion and caution, and I know exactly to whom I owe money. I visited the garage this morning and inquired about the best negro mechanic in town. The day supervisor had glowing remarks about your abilities, Moses."

Leroy had shrunk further into the unlit bay beyond Moses' workbench. "I guess I'll take off, Owen," said Leroy. "I've told you everything I know. You don't need me anymore. Time for me to go."

"You're right about being useless, Simmons," said Owen. "You've been useless as tits on a bull throughout this affair. But don't go; I'll get to you as soon as Moses heads for home. We'll figure out if I owe you any money or if you owe me."

Moses could see that Leroy was petrified, shaking in pain, and might break and run for it at any moment. The radio was tuned to WKZO and turned up pretty loud to keep Moses company while he worked late, alone. Loud enough that if Moses called for help, no one in the neighborhood would hear him over the music. But if Leroy ran, chances were good Owen or Billy would shoot him down. The sound of a gunshot or multiple gunshots might wake people up.

The chances of that scenario happening were slim to none. It probably wouldn't help Moses anyway.

"Let's get back to you, Moses," said Owen. "Why did you think I owed you money, and why were you asking about me in the first place."

Moses thought quickly and said, "I don't give a shit about you. You go your way, and I'll go mine. I care about that scum sucker over there. I'm helping out Mrs. Simmons, his wife, who is a friend of mine, looking to divorce the creep.

"I tailed him for a couple of weeks to ensure the settlement went in her favor. That is all I'm about. Now, cut me out of this chair, and let's get some sleep. I've been taking pictures of Pot selling his dope at the train station for a long time. I can get rid of him for both of us."

Owen laughed, and Billy joined in for no reason but to show his devotion to Owen. Owen looked over at Leroy, skulking even further away. Then Owen did something Moses couldn't understand at all. He looked over to the opposite corner of the dark side of the garage. Moses decided someone else in the garage wanted to remain invisible. Moses thought he saw the glow of a cigarette wave in the air.

Owen took that as some sign or signal. "I buy most of what you said, Moses," admitted Owen. "Leroy is a friend of mine, and I trust my friends. I'll ask you one last time. Who have you spoken to about me?"

"No one, I don't know you from Adam," said Moses.

Owen nodded at Billy, who stepped forward and slapped Moses viciously on the left side of his face.

"Let's try that again, nigger," said Kressbach as he backhanded Moses on the other cheek. Moses' lip was already bleeding from Billy's blow, but the pain from Owen's backhand now superseded all thought.

It had been a long time since Moses had been in the ring, but he knew how to take a hit, swinging his head in time with the blow to lessen the impact. His eyes were watering from the bare-knuckle blows, but his head was still clear, and he knew he could withstand more if that was what it came to. As long as they didn't use the gun to kill him.

Owen went off the rails. Laughing, insane with a lust for inflicting pain. He hit Moses twice, joyfully, with no mercy, just as he had kicked him the first night he had encountered Moses. Just like he had been photographed by Harry the night before, gleefully kicking Leroy.

"The best thing for me, if you don't start talking, nigger, is to kill you here. Billy can drag one of those tarps over here, wrap you up, and dump you by the river in one of the celery swamps north of here."

Moses heard Owen but didn't react, couldn't react. For the first time in his life, he felt like taking a dive and going to sleep. Yet, out of the corner of his eye, he saw someone flash across the garage to his workbench. A voice shouted from the dark corner of the garage, "Look out, Owen!"

Billy and Owen both turned away from Moses toward the bench. Harry Martensen picked up Owen's gun and backed away to a tool cabinet where he could see all the players: Owen, Billy, Leroy (in the shadow of the next bay), and whoever shouted the warning to Owen.

"Stay where you are, fellas. Don't move," said Harry. "Moses, I'll get you out of that chair in a minute."

Owen looked at the tall stranger holding his gun. He wasn't shaking, and he was protected by the cabinet. "Take it easy, Mister," he said. "We was just having a little fun with the nigger here. You're not with the police, are you? Can you even use that gun?" Owen took a tentative step toward Harry, and Billy followed suit.

Harry extended his arm full length, turned slightly, and fired the Colt M1911. The July '48 Vargas pinup stapled to the wooden column twenty feet away from Harry now had a bullet hole next to the model's nipple.

"By the time I got to the Pacific theater, target practice on Iwo Jima was as much a pastime as basketball. Now, don't move."

Leroy saw his chance during the echo of the shot reverberating in the garage and left the building. The man in the dark at the rear of the garage also seemed to be gone. Harry directed the two thugs to back away from Moses. He found the snips on the workbench and cut the wire around his wrists. Harry handed the snips to Moses while he kept the gun pointing at Owen and Billy.

"Now what?" asked Harry.

Moses stood, massaged his wrists, and looked over at Owen. "I bet you've forgotten we met once on Rose Street in September," he said. "You enjoy kicking people when they are helpless on the ground, don't you, Owen?"

Moses walked toward Owen, working his jaw back and forth with his right hand, scowling. "Well, I haven't forgotten."

"Moses," said Harry, "This is not the time. You don't want to give these jokers cause for a counter suit."

"Yes, I do, actually," said Moses.

A siren sounded not more than a block away. A minute later, a uniformed cop entered the garage and addressed the group. "What's going on here. We had a report of a domestic disturbance. Is there a woman around? Anyone hurt? You there, with the gun, lay it down on the table."

"Officer," said Harry, "We were preventing these two from escaping until the police arrived. If you look at Moses Webb here, you'll see wire cuts on his wrists and ankles and a bruised bloody lip."

"Moses Webb, I've heard of you. You're retired from the force, right?" said the officer, directing Owen to put his hands behind his back to clasp them in cuffs.

"That's right, officer," Moses said. "I will be at the station by 9:00 a.m. to swear out a complaint."

"That works for me," said the officer, "By the look of you, I've got enough to hold them overnight, anyway."

The policeman directed Harry to wrap Billy's hands with the baling wire.

"What's your name, officer," said Moses. "I'll be talking to Chief Hoyt tomorrow, and I'll put in a good word. By the way, isn't your partner, Ross Kirkpatrick, on this shift? Where is he?"

"Alex Madden is my name. I appreciate it. I told Ross I could handle this one solo. I expected a marriage squabble. Thanks for the help."

Harry helped the officer get the two offenders into the squad car. Billy sat behind the officer, and Owen sat next to him. The officer drove away the short distance, a few blocks, to the police station.

"My car is over here, Moses; I'll give you a lift home," said Harry.

"Let's go back in the garage a second," said Moses. "I want to look at where that man in the dark was hiding."

They found a chair and four cigarette nubs squashed on the floor. Moses recognized the brand as Chesterfield. Perhaps at least one clue to the man's identity.

***

Moses entered the police station lobby at 8:50 a.m. Saturday. He pushed through the oversized double swing doors leading to the offices and holding cells and stopped at the duty desk manned by Sergeant Arlen Whetlend.

"Is either Ross or Chief Hoyt on duty today?" Moses asked.

"Moses Webb, how have you been?" said Arlen. "To answer your question, they're both here along with just about every officer and support personnel on the force."

"What's up? Why so serious."

"Guess you haven't heard yet. Alex Madden was killed last night about a block from here. Strangled. Ross is waiting for you in Chief Hoyt's office."

"That's terrible, Arlen," said Moses. "Was Alex married?"

"Married with a kid on the way. Go on into the chief's office. He and Ross have questions. I've mimeographed the details for donations on the sheet there. You're welcome to take one." Moses picked up the donation instructions, folded it, and put it in his back pocket with his wallet. He knocked on the Chief's door and walked in.

"Moses," said Chief Hoyt. "What the hell are you up to, getting my man killed."

"I'll give you everything I've got, Chief," said Moses. "Madden was fine and in control when I last saw him. What happened, do you know?"

"We're hoping you will fill us in, Moses," said Ross. "Here is what we have so far. Alex logged a call about a domestic disturbance at 10:18 p.m. last night. The duty sergeant who answered the telephone said the caller wouldn't give his name but requested to speak to Alex Madden to explain the situation.

Alex took the phone from the duty sergeant and in three minutes wrote the time and the words 'domestic disturbance' in his log book."

"I started worrying when he didn't return in an hour. I signed out another squad car and decided to head out, not knowing which way to go. A half block from the station, I spotted Alex's squad car that had jumped the curb. Alex was dead, strangled in the front driver's seat. We found another body near the vehicle at the edge of the parking lot. A big man, shot in the back, also dead.

"OK," said Moses. "Let me fill you in. The disturbance was much more than a domestic disturbance. Four men surprised me as I was coming off shift, and one of them, Billy, tied me to a chair with baling wire. Billy was Owen Kressbach's henchmen. Their goal was to get me to tell them who I had spoken to about the name and activities of Owen Kressbach as they pertained to the strike and riot on December 1st.

If not for my friend and associate Harry Martensen, I'd be a dead body buried in a celery swamp. He swooped in, grabbed Owen's firearm, backed the thugs into a corner, and cut me out of the chair. Officer Madden showed up as I was about to repay Owen for this split lip.

"Who do you think called the station, Moses," said Ross.

"Well, two others were in the garage when I was getting worked over. Leroy Simmons, who I have reported on previously, and an unseen mystery man who I haven't identified. My bet is that he is the man who spoke directly to Alex Madden, calling from the Cities Service Station telephone.

"Ross, were you with Alex when that call came in? When Officer Madden came into the garage, he said you had a family emergency, and that's why he was handling the suspects by himself."

"Not true, Moses. I was in the bathroom when the call came in, and Alex left without me. The Rookie did not follow protocol. Got him killed."

"I don't know about that, Ross. Looking back, I would say Madden handled the situation very strangely."

"What do you mean, Moses," said Chief Hoyt.

"Well, Ross, you or I would have used the garage telephone to call for backup. Another officer would have brought a second pair of handcuffs. Madden could have at least cuffed Owen to the car, but he didn't.

"Also, Madden was content to take these two creeps away. He didn't look around at the scene, didn't tell us not to touch anything, and let us go about our business on a promise that I would stop this morning and explain the charges against Owen Kressbach and this Billy character."

Chief Hoyt broke in. "What you are suggesting, Moses," he said, "is that you think Alex Madden may have colluded with this person on the telephone to process the suspects without following procedure.

"The more I consider it, that is what I believe, Chief. If he was in league with the unidentified man in the garage, he may have intended to let those two escape all along. Owen was handcuffed, but both were loose in the squad car's back seat. Billy was sitting behind Madden.

The police car pulls up to the stop sign at the corner a block from the station. This Billy character reaches over the seat and strangles Officer Madden from behind. They find the keys to the cuffs, and Owen is free. Now, I'm guessing, but what if the unidentified mystery man follows them from the Cities Service Station, and when the group gathers outside the car, the boss directs Owen to deal with Billy, the only witness who knows both Owen and the mystery man.

Most of that is supposition, but it fits the circumstances and the evidence.

Chief Hoyt's mood was as sour as it gets. "Ross, take Moses to the interrogation room and get a minute-to-minute account of everything he has been up to. You told me he was an observer of the riot. Get that down as well. Moses, you say you took photographs. I want to see those as soon as they are developed.

"The governor has appointed a special prosecutor and formed a grand jury to investigate who is at fault for that riot. I am confident the special prosecutor will want to meet with you, Moses.

"You're going to be a busy man from now until Christmas. Leaving town is out of the question, understand?

"Ross, I'm going to call in our men. When we can distribute Moses' complete statement, I'll call another meeting, and we'll consider our next move in hunting down Alex's killer. Until I see that report, we operate under the assumption that Alex made rookie mistakes that proved fatal.

Sunday, Moses hung around The Michigan Central Railroad and Bus depot for over two hours, but Leroy was nowhere to be found. The Rat had found a hole and crawled in. Moses bought the Sunday edition of the Kalamazoo Gazette. He carried the folded paper under his arm back to his apartment. In the comfort of his easy chair, Moses read the articles from the front page to the last, but nothing about the murder of Alex Madden was in the paper. Too soon.

The vision of Eileen in her garter belt, undies, stockings, and heels kept worming into his thoughts. He cursed Nadine again, trying not to blame himself for possibly starting her down her morphine path. She had helped him investigate the strike and had given him access to pain medicine she later tried and abused.

Moses wondered if some people are more prone to addiction than others. Nadine was a pretty, efficient nurse/receptionist. It can't be too late for her to straighten out. He spent time planning his approach to Dr. Alexander, who had also helped him immensely over the past two years.

Turning his thoughts to Owen Kressbach, Moses wondered how far and how fast he might have traveled to avoid the dragnet and national All Points Bulletin Chief Hoyt teletyped to the FBI. Moses realized that Owen, for all of his murderous, sadistic traits, was one clever criminal. Moses was sure he would turn up again.

Unless the mystery man who met Owen at the Shakespeare Administration building conference room had eliminated Owen somehow. Had Owen shot his friend Billy in the back? Or was it Mystery Man? Moses decided to check in at the police station on Monday for an update. Had the police recovered the bullet that had killed Billy?

That brought Moses back to Leroy Simmons. Pot may be the last surviving accomplice and eyewitness to the events that occurred during the riot. Even if Owen had been eliminated, Leroy had the same target on his back as Billy.

***

On Monday morning, a warm, sunny December day, Moses, rested and refreshed, decided to walk to Riverside Greenhouses at 1523 Riverview Drive. He ordered a half dozen roses to be delivered to 416 Parsons Street, Eileen's address. The card would say, 'Apologies, Moses Webb.' At the same time, he ordered another half dozen red roses to be delivered Wednesday to Borgess hospital with a card addressed to Nurse Simmons, to read, 'Thinking of your smile, Moses.' Lastly, Moses ordered a dozen red roses to be delivered to Eileen's house on Christmas Eve, with a note that said, 'Merry Christmas, Moses.'

***

Moses walked back to Dr. Alexander's office. Nadine had called in sick. A temp nurse greeted him, looked at his swollen lip, and asked him to wait. Apparently, no appointments had been scheduled for Monday morning to give the doctor time to write up his notes on the previous week's patients. The doctor came to the reception room and called Moses back to his office.

'Doctor," said Moses. "My lip is no big deal. I just needed to see you about Nadine."

"Well, you're here; let me look at it," said the doctor. "That bruise on the side of your face concerns me more. How many concussions did you suffer in the ring before hanging up the gloves."

"Only one doc," said Moses. "I'm OK. It's Nadine I'm worried about."

Dr. Alexander shrugged. "She called in sick today," he said, "third time this month. She's been skating on thin ice. I'm thinking of letting her go."

"I think she got hooked on Morphine due to home nursing me."

"What?" said Doc, shaking his head. "I never approved house visits for your condition."

"That's why I feel responsible," said Moses.

"What do you mean? What did you do?"

Moses started with his first visit to the doctor's office in September. He leaned heavily on his attraction to the nurse and contribution to her addiction, which ended with her becoming somewhat obsessed with him.

"Can you refer Nadine to one of your drug rehabilitation clinics that will keep her on-site until she is clean? I'll pay as much as I can toward the fees."

"First of all, Moses, I could have you arrested for acquiring the Kadian tablets.

"I had no idea, Moses. She has kept the problem well hidden and seems fine at work."

Dr. Alexander fell silent while he rubbed the top of his bald head. "I suppose I might be partially responsible for the accessibility of the drugs. I believe you are right. For some individuals, addiction temptations are more challenging."

"Morphine should be locked in a cabinet," said Moses. "Only you should have the key. Records should be reviewed once a month."

Dr. Alexander nodded. "So we have agreed on a plan of action as far as Nadine is concerned.

"OK," said Moses. "I will outline it for her this afternoon. Then it's up to her."

***

Moses asked Harry to bring all the photographs he had developed to his apartment on Wednesday so they could discuss the case over lunch. Harry had read about the murder of Patrolman Alex Madden in the Gazette.

"That could have been us in the paper," said Harry. "When I read it, I couldn't quit shaking and feeling mad at that Owen jerk and sad for Madden's pregnant wife when I think about it."

"I haven't thanked you for saving my ass that night. You're right. I'm sure I wouldn't be sitting here if you hadn't come along."

"You said these photos were important, so I got excited when they turned out. I hopped in the car and drove to the garage, hoping to catch you. You said you'd be working late."

The telephoto lens had captured indisputable evidence of money for drug exchanges. There were clear pictures of Owen Kressbach kicking Leroy on the ground and his contorted face as he delivered blows. The alligator belts pinned to the inside of Leroy's coat were self-explanatory.

Moses pawed through the pictures, setting them in piles according to relevance to Eileen and Leroy or Owen. He paused in his shuffle to examine a series of three photos. The woman stayed in the shadow, but the woman's features were distinct.

"You captured her scratching Leroy," said Moses. "He's standing in the light, and her hand, arm, and coat are clearly identifiable. The woman is hiding in the shadows, but I can see it is a different woman than the one who met Leroy a few days before."

"Really, you can tell?" said Harry. "These are pretty dark."

"I can tell," said Moses. "The woman's hair in this picture is long and wavy. A gentle perm. The woman I saw had straight hair to the base of her neck. No, this is definitely a different woman. I'll show these three pictures to Eileen. Maybe she will recognize her. I wish I had photographs of the woman I saw meeting with Leroy."

Harry inquired about the meeting Moses, Chief Hoyt, and Ross Kirkpatrick attended. Except for the two-hour interview and recording of events with Ross, Harry already knew most of the information transferred during the discussion. They agreed to watch Eileen and Marvin closely until Owen, Leroy, or both were found and arrested.

"That may be a little difficult for me," said Moses. "Eileen and I have had a falling out."

"She found out about the receptionist, didn't she, Moses," said Harry.

"Yes, in the worst way possible."

Harry rose, put on his coat and hat, ready to return to Nusbaum's and work. "I wish you luck on patching that up," he said. "If you lose Eileen, at least you're still breathing. Count your blessings. Though she is a beauty, that one."

***

Moses made the short walk to the police station on Thursday before work, deciding to deliver a selected group of photographs to Ross Kirkpatrick or Chieft Hoyt, whichever was available. As he walked, the clouds rolled in from Lake Michigan, and the temperature dropped. The Michigan gloom returned. A snowstorm was projected for the next day, Friday, Christmas Eve. Radio listeners were encouraged to purchase supplies today, avoid unnecessary travel tomorrow, and stay out of Santa Claus's way.

Chief Hoyt was thankful for the pictures. "Governor Sigler appointed Judge John Simpson to investigate criminal activity related to the riot. I've given him your name as a possible witness for the grand Jury. I'm sure he will contact you."

"Any sign of Owen or Leroy?" asked Moses.

"We've turned over every rock in the county," said the chief. "Nothing yet."

"What about the FBI," said Moses.

"They want him for questioning in connection to a union riot in Syracuse, New York. They will come on the double if Kressbach shows up here again. I think your photos should provide them enough evidence for an arrest. Watch your back, Moses, and anyone else's back you've done a recent favor for."

"Sure, Chief," said Moses. "I've got to get to work. I'll keep you posted."

"Right, Do that," said Chief Hoyt.

When Moses arrived at the Cities Service Station, he donned overalls and reviewed his work orders and workstation. He spent fifteen minutes cleaning and straightening his workspace, then turned the workbench 180 degrees. Standing on the side nearest the pit, he could see the front and rear entry doors. Neither Owen nor Leroy came through those doors, and eventually, Moses became absorbed in his work and lost track of who was coming and going into the garage.

18|Twas the Night Before Christmas

Moses agreed to work half the day shift with three other mechanics on Christmas Eve. Often, Moses went over to the windows on the south and watched the heavy flakes of the storm burying the parking lot. The windows on the north side of the building revealed the northeast wind gusting and obscuring the building across the street.

At noon that Friday, Moses threw his overalls in the bin and entered the shower, already becoming nervous about his intended next move, knocking on Eileen's door.

I should call her first.

Moses decided not to call ahead but not to push his presence on Eileen if she was still angry over Nadine. He slogged home in the darkness caused by the heavy snowstorm. It was one of those wet, sticky affairs because the temperature hovered close to freezing.

He was spruced up and ready by four o'clock, having crudely wrapped his presents for Eileen and Marvin. Moses called for a taxi. The cab came along on Burdick Street forty minutes later, slipping and fishtailing in the deep snow. Another two inches of snow had fallen since Moses left the service station.

Snow was still coming down in buckets when the taxicab pulled up in front of Eileen's house. Moses carried the presents onto the porch and set them on the porch swing. He knocked on the door and held his breath. Eileen opened the door. After three seconds of surprise, she smiled broadly at Moses.

"I think you better come in, Moses. I was hoping you weren't still upset with me," said Eileen.

"Are you sure," said Moses. "Can I stay a while?"

"Yes, stay."

Moses went back down the walk and paid off the cab driver. Then he returned to the porch, gathered the presents, and brought them into the house.

"Merry Christmas."

Marvin had joined Eileen in the front hall. He took the presents from Moses and brought them into the living room. After hanging his coat and hat in the front closet, Moses and Eileen followed Marvin into the living room, standing next to the Christmas tree, shaking the big present from Moses like a six-year-old on his first Christmas.

"Should I open this one now, Mom?" he said.

"I've got to get back to the stove, Marvin. Open it after dinner. When is Curtis coming by to pick you up?"

"7:15 p.m., then we pick up Sheila.," said Marvin.

"Good," said Eileen. "We'll have time after dinner to open presents."

During dinner, Moses was anxious to discuss the week's events but decided it was inappropriate on Christmas Eve. He focused on basketball instead. High school teams play on Tuesdays and Fridays during basketball season. Marvin played with the team on the 17th, the evening Moses had been tied to a chair with baling wire.

"I couldn't understand," said Eileen, "why Marvin didn't get more playing time. He made so many points in that game you watched, Moses; I thought the coach would want him to start." Eileen reached over and rubbed Marvin's shoulder.

Moses wondered if rumors about the confrontation between Marvin and his father had reached the coach. The JV coach seemed reluctant to play Marvin at all. It had been the varsity coach that had given Marvin a chance in the game Moses watched.

"The game was never close," said Marvin. "We slaughtered Benton Harbor. We could have played everyone at the end of the bench, and we would still have won."

"When is your next game," asked Moses.

"After Christmas break, said Marvin. "I think January 8th. Practices start again on the 4th."

"Keep your chin up, Marvin," said Moses. "They will need you again soon, I'll bet."

Marvin, who never stopped smiling whenever basketball was part of the conversation, said, "I wasn't going to say anything until after the game on the 8th, but Coach Quiring talked to me on Wednesday. He wants me to practice with the varsity starting on the 4th."

"Wow," said Eileen. "Why didn't you tell me."

"I was going to tell you just before the game on the 8th. If practices didn't go well and they sent me back to the JV, I could live with that, but Mom, I know you would be disappointed."

"Disappointed in the coach, perhaps," said Eileen, "but never you, Marvin."

Moses tried to reassure Marvin. "From what I saw of the varsity team on the 10th, you will fit like a glove with Quiring's offense as long as the players go along."

"I know a couple of the starters already. It should be a good experience regardless."

After a few minutes of rustling around in the kitchen, Eileen brought three bowls out and placed them in front of Marvin, Moses, and herself.

"A scoop of vanilla ice cream and two fig newtons," said Eileen. "Marvin, you'll probably have cake at the dance tonight, so I gave you a smaller portion of ice cream."

"Yeah, Mom," said Marvin, "We'll probably go to the pizza place after the dance, so don't wait up for me."

"No later than twelve-thirty if you want to play in that game next week," his mother commanded. Marvin coaxed Moses and his mother into the living room and picked up the box from Moses, shaking it one last time. He looked at his mother, who nodded, then tore the package open. It was a premium Spalding leather official basketball. Marvin twirled the ball, spinning it and then making it run down one arm up the other, defying gravity.

"Great present, Moses, thanks," said Marvin.

"That's to keep you out of trouble. Busy hands and all that."

Marvin passed the ball to Moses, saying, "The grip of a new ball, man, it feels like I could make every shot."

"You just about do now," said Moses, passing the ball back to Marvin

"Mom, why don't you open up your present," said Marvin.

"Would that be OK, Moses," said Eileen, already reaching for the package with her name, not waiting for a response from Moses.

The small flat box held an orange silk scarf from Gilmore's.

"Oh, this is beautiful. Thank you, Moses," said Eileen.

"Unless I'm mistaken, that scarf should compliment the purple gown you wore the other night." Thoughts of the good part of that evening warmed his forehead.

"I agree, Moses," said Eileen, winking at Moses. "It is similar to the yellow one I have. I bet I could wear both scarves together sometimes. And it will go with my blue Sunday suit too.

Marvin went upstairs to change into his suit. As he had hoped, Eileen quietly walked to Moses, standing by the Christmas tree, and kissed him gently. Moses gathered Eileen for a hug and kissed her again eagerly.

Marvin, smelling like Aqua Velva, entered the living room. Moses, sitting on the sofa next to Eileen, smiled. Marvin had no stubble to shave. Eileen retrieved a boxed corsage from the refrigerator in the kitchen and handed it to Marvin.

Eileen heard a truck honking. "That must be Curtis."

"Stick to the main roads," said Moses. "The streets are treacherous. Kalamazoo Avenue is your best bet.

"At least it stopped snowing, although the wind was picking up. Where's the dance?"

"Walwood Hall Ballroom," said Marvin. "At Western Michigan College."

"Marvin, be polite to Sheila's mother, you hear me?" said Eileen."

When Marvin opened the back door, the wind caught the screendoor and banged it against the outside of the house.

Eileen and Moses went back through the kitchen and down the hallway, past the stairs, and into the dining room on the left. They carried the dinner table service into the kitchen, and Moses picked up a dish towel. "I'll dry and stack," he said.

"Alright, I'll wash," said Eileen. She ran water into the sink and sprinkled the surface with Chipso. She poured hot water heating on the stove into the sink and stirred with one of the forks to make suds. The dishes were rinsed, dried, and put away in twenty minutes. Eileen led Moses past the dining room and turned right through a wide archway to the living room. Straight ahead, Moses noted that the four small windows in the front door were now iced over from the storm.

Moses sat down on the sofa while Eileen turned on the radio. The *Adventures of Sam Spade* was starting. Eileen came over to the couch and curled up next to Moses with her head on his shoulder, knees tucked under. Eileen fell asleep as Moses held her. He listened to the radio show, one of his favorites. When the ads came on at the show's end, Moses shifted Eileen's head to the back of the sofa. He got up and looked out the window toward the front of the house. The snow had drifted over Parsons Street to the point where it was indistinguishable from the lawns on either side.

Moses went to the rear of the home and looked out at the garage, thirty feet away from the house. Snow had drifted up five feet on one corner. Opening the garage door would take a considerable amount of shoveling.

Eileen called to him, "Moses, are you here?"

"Coming," he said. When he reentered the living room, Moses indicated to her how deep the snow was getting.

"I hope Marvin and Curtis are keeping an eye on the storm," said Eileen. "I don't want Marvin to get in trouble with Sheila's parents."

"Marvin cares for Sheila a great deal. He won't let anything happen to her," said Moses. Moses debated telling Eileen about the incident at school with Leroy and his gun. Again, he decided Christmas Eve was not the time.

"As I care for you, Moses," said Eileen, looking out the living room window. "You'll stay here for the night. I'll get blankets, a sheet, and a pillow for the couch." When she returned, Moses laid one of the blankets on the floor before the coffee table. He neatly folded the sheet and positioned it on top of the blanket. The second blanket and pillow went on top. The makeshift bed would fit Moses' large frame. The couch, not so much.

The couple sat back down on the sofa. Moses kept his arm around Eileen's shoulders and held her close. They listened to *Suspense* on the CBS network. The story scared Eileen into cuddling even closer to Moses.

Moses looked out the windows again when the program ended. Eileen excused herself to visit the bathroom. When she returned, Moses went to the toilet while Eileen looked apprehensively out at the storm.

Moses glanced at the hallway wall clock as he entered the living room. The time was 9:30 p.m., and the dance was probably over.

Eileen surprised Moses in the living room. She kissed him and ran her hands across his chest, shoulders, and arms, caressing and intermittently kissing him. Eileen stepped back and slowly unbuttoned her blouse. "I think it is time for your birthday present, Moses," she said.

Moses climbed the stairs hand in hand with Eileen. She led him into her bedroom and threw her blouse on a chair. She reached behind her back with a quick, practiced motion and unclasped her bra. Moses had shed his shirt and undid the belt and zipper of his pants.

Maybe the wind whistling through the gaps around the windows in the fifty-year-old Victorian home, or perhaps it was the ice building up on the inside of the windows displaying icerink etchings of skating patterns. Still, the quiet and solitude of the house helped the couple relax and go easy. The couple moved slowly, casually together, smiling with anticipation and need. It was Eileen's house, and she was comfortable.

Moses lifted the naked woman with the lustrous cocoa skin as if she were weightless, carrying her to her double bed. A fleeting thought of Marvin and his reaction to Moses' intimacy with his mother blew through him. He decided that by the time Marvin returned, Moses would be feigning sleep down on the living room floor.

Eileen's touch on his chest sent electric prickling to his stomach and groin. Before him lay the beauty of Nigeria with an all-American smile. He was ready, and Eileen accepted him with a continuous kiss.

Later, Moses fetched his pack of Camels, returned to the bed, and blew rings toward the ceiling. All seemed right with the world and his girl. Eileen seemed content, the sheet and cover draped unceremoniously over one leg and breast for warmth. The weather outside had not let up. Eileen began to again worry about her son reaching home.

Moses sensed her distraction, squashed his cigarette against the bed's metal frame, and returned to repeatedly kissing Eileen. This time, Moses decided it would be all for her, and he began gently stroking her left side from armpit to belly button and down to her thigh. It worked. Eileen pulled at his shoulder, but Moses kept trailing two fingers in that repetitious pattern, occasionally dragging a light touch over her left nipple.

Suddenly, Eileen put a finger to his lips, signaling Moses to silence. She whispered in his ear, "I hear something." For a moment, they both stayed statue still.

"There," said Eileen, "I heard it again. Marvin must be home."

"Yes, I hear someone as well," said Moses. "They must have ended the dance early to be sure the kids made it home in the storm."

"Shh… Let me think," said Eileen.

For three minutes, they waited in silence. Moses figured Marvin, seeing the arrangement of the blankets and pillow in the living room, would be discreet and just come upstairs to his room and go to bed. Marvin was old enough to determine what his mother and Moses were up to. Moses and Eileen continued to wait in silence. Long minutes passed, and there was still no sound of Marvin on the stairs.

Moses' arm ached from staying still, propped on an elbow for so long.

BAM!

The gunshot sounded like a grenade exploding below Moses. The couple froze. A few seconds later, they heard the front door open and slammed shut, and the screen banged loudly.

Moses jumped out of bed, madly scrambling for underwear and pants.

Eileen, sitting up in the bed, yelled, "MARVIN." She had such an expression of panic that Moses sat back on the bed and clutched her in his arms.

"Get dressed, Eileen. Now," said Moses. "Get dressed. I'll go down. You stay here and lock the door. Get dressed, I tell you. If someone is down there, I'll handle it."

Moses had heard no sounds from below since the screendoor had slammed. Since he may have to go outside, Moses took a minute and dressed entirely in his socks, shoes, and shirt.

"What was that?" said Moses, standing still and motioning Eileen to listen. "I think I heard the front door again." In the hallway, Moses closed the bedroom door behind him and spoke through the door. "Lock the door, Eileen. I'll come back for you when the coast is clear."

Moses glanced into Marvin's room to ensure no one was there. He spotted a baseball bat leaning against the dresser, grabbed it, and noiselessly crept down the stairs. Halfway down, he saw the body on the front hall floor, face down, blood pooling underneath. Careful not to step in the blood puddle, Moses squatted for a better look. The hole in the middle of the body's back also gurgled blood. The hall light illuminated the profile of the dead face. Leroy, the rat, would no longer be hawking fake gold watches. He looked around for the gun. Whoever went out the front door took the weapon with them.

Moses turned around when he heard Eileen scream. She was standing midway down the stairs. Moses took the stairs two at a time and enclosed her in his arms. "It's Leroy, Eileen. He's dead."

Eileen was shaking, but she calmed quickly in Moses's strong hug. Then she grabbed Moses' arms and looked up at him, fearful.

"Marvin?"

"Not here," said Moses. "I'll check the rest of the house, but someone outside shot Leroy. I'm going after them."

"In this weather, Moses, what can you do?" said Eileen.

"I can at least see who it is if I catch up with them," said Moses. "Listen. Here's what you have to do. When I leave, lock all your windows and doors. Don't you dare touch anything? Avoid the hallway. PLEASE DON'T TOUCH ANYTHING. Call the police station. They'll be here in minutes. If Marvin makes it home, don't let him touch anything. If you have time, fold the blankets and sheets in the living room and put them away."

"Alright, Moses, I can do all that," said Eileen.

"It's up to you," said Moses, "but my being here only complicates your life. I can explain that I was on a stakeout outside when I heard the shot and rushed in to help you."

Eileen nodded.

"OK, I'm going," said Moses.

"Wait. Marvin has extra boots in the front closet, and take the wool scarf hanging there as well." Eileen ran upstairs, brought down a flashlight, and handed it to Moses.

The woman made sense. Moses pulled on the rubber boots and closed the four metal buckles. He wrapped the scarf around his neck, pulled his fedora tight to his head, and buttoned his leather jacket. He turned to Eileen, took her by the shoulders, and kissed her. "I'll be careful. I'll be back when I can. Don't worry. I'll look for Marvin as well."

Tromping through two and a half feet of snow, sometimes drifting even higher, Moses made steady, if not slow, progress. At times, a wind gust would swirl snow and obscure his goal, which was the end of the next intersection lit by a street light. He had only traveled three city blocks. Moses caught glimpses of someone ahead, making about the same progress as himself.

Edwards Street was just as snowed under as Parsons, but a lull in the wind allowed Moses to see that he was gaining on whoever was trudging ahead.

BAM! Another gunshot. Moses hurried forward.

Through the haze, Moses observed a police patrol car, possibly on Burdick Street. Another lengthy gust of wind blinded Moses, but when it calmed, he was seventy feet from the Burdick intersection with Parsons Street. Two policemen holding batons were on either side of a man leaning against the patrol car at an awkward angle, back to Moses. The man's hands were spread wide apart, as were his feet. The pouring snow, wind, and dark city made identifying the man difficult. Moses moved right, the streetlight illuminating that side of the captive.

"Get back, sir," said the patrolman closest to Moses. "We'll handle this."

"I know this person," said Moses. Marvin turned partially toward Moses. The policeman standing next to Marvin whacked him across his back with a full swing of his baton.

"Argghh," cried Marvin, crumpling onto one knee next to the patrol car.

"Hey," said Moses. "Take it easy. The boy won't give you any trouble. He's not dangerous."

The cop nearest Moses took quick, threatening steps toward him, one hand on his holstered gun. Moses backed away two steps.

"Listen, Mister," said the cop. "This nig… man is a suspected fugitive from a shooting. He was armed, and that makes him dangerous. So move along or be hauled in with the suspect."

The other officer wrenched Marvin's left hand behind his back and handcuffed his wrist. Marvin voluntarily put his right hand behind his back to be cuffed. The officer grabbed Marvin by the arm, pulled him up to stand, and pushed him face-first across the Patrol car's front fender.

Moses bit his lip, keeping his distance, hands at his side against all the churning inside him.

Tears streamed down Marvin's cheeks as the officer roughly stuffed him in the rear seat of the patrol car.

"Officer, I should go with the boy," said Moses.

"That ain't happening," said the officer, getting behind the wheel. "We've got enough to handle with this one in this storm. You move along now."

Moses felt utterly helpless as the police car started out, fishtailing in the snow. A plow had attempted to keep one lane of Burdick clear as it was a major north/south street. Moses ran to the car, pounded on the door to get Marvin's attention, and shouted through the window, "I'll see you at the station. Hang in there."

Moses began walking south on Burdick the three-quarters of a mile to Police Headquarters. He could barely feel his toes in the thin rubber boots. The officer had said that Marvin was armed.

Leroy's gun?

Moses tried to gauge how long ago he had told Eileen not to worry. Moses was worried. He figured Leroy had come to Eileen's for money. What had Leroy done when the cash wasn't in the cookie jar? Search for it, probably. And who was with Leroy. Moses doubted that it was Marvin. Marvin knew that Eileen had deposited her extra cash in her bank account. Or was Marvin just trying to show Leroy that the house had no money.

What about the second front door closing. Was that Marvin? That made the most sense. He would have assumed Moses had gone home if he had not seen the blanket bed in the darkened living room.

If it was Marvin, he had taken it upon himself to follow the other person out the front door into the snowstorm. Why? He could have left that for the police. Marvin should have awakened his mother, called the police, and stayed put.

The kid wanted to get the man who shot his father.

When Moses arrived at the police station, he stomped off the snow from his boots and brushed off his pants and shoulders. He warmed his hands over the radiator, went through the vestibule inner doors, and headed for the duty station. Moses didn't know the night duty sergeant.

"Is Chief Hoyt here, Sergeant, or Ross Kirkpatrick?"

"Ross ain't here. It's Christmas, for Christ's sake," said the night duty sergeant.

"Chief Hoyt?" asked Moses again.

"He left when we caught the man responsible for killing the white man over on Parsons Street," said the sergeant.

"OK, then I need to see the BOY they caught tonight. Where is he?" said Moses.

"None of your business, Mister," said the sergeant. "Maybe he's a boy to you, but he's old enough to carry a snub-nose .45 and kill a man."

"Listen, Sergeant, I'm his basketball coach and care for the boy. I'm sure by now that his mother is worried sick."

"We're not taking any chances with this one. I'm sure this Simmons scum is looking at a 1st-degree murder charge. Shot a white man in the back. Plus, resisting arrest. That is one bad mother fucker."

Moses turned and walked to the other side of the room, controlling his anger and frustration by distancing himself from the bigot behind the desk. His hands had involuntarily formed fists, ready to jab and punch. He kept both fists in his jacket pockets until he could settle down.

If Moses hadn't been a professional boxer, his anger might have overcome his ring smarts, and after being overpowered, he would have been thrown in a holding cell next to Marvin's. As it was, Moses played the game. He went back over to the sergeant's desk.

"Who is the detective assigned to interrogate the suspect," said Moses. Can I speak to him, please?" said Moses.

"That would be Tom Garten. I will tell him you'd like to speak to him when I see him. Until then, I guess you can wait here."

Moses waited.

Around 1:30 a.m., a policeman walked in, holding Eileen by the elbow. Startled awake, Moses jumped up and intercepted them before they entered the inner offices. He stood before the door and read the officer's name tag.

Looking at Eileen, her lower lip trembling, Moses observed a woman of strength able to play the same game he was accustomed to in the white world.

"Officer Barrett," said Moses, "my name is Moses Webb, retired from the force here in town. Mrs. Simmons is a good friend of mine. Could I have some time to speak to her? I know she's worried about her son, and I have some news for her. Would that be possible?"

"I don't see why not," said Barrett. "Why don't you both come on back."

Officer Barrett led Eileen and Moses through what Moses knew to be the detectives' desks and to a small waiting room next to the interrogation rooms. Barrett left to report to his superior.

The room held a couch positioned against the long wall and two easy chairs arranged against the wall at the end of the room. An end table fit in the corner between the couch and two chairs.

When Officer Barrett closed the door, Eileen leaped into Moses' arms and began to wail. "O, Moses, what is happening? I keep trying to wake up from this nightmare."

"I know, darling," said Moses. "We have got to stay strong. I don't know how much time they will give us. Probably only minutes. What happened at the house?"

"About ten minutes after I called the police station, two police cars came up Walbridge Street and plowed over to the house," said Eileen. "Moses, I still haven't heard from Marvin. I was desperate and wanted to call Sheila's parents, but the police discouraged me."

"Marvin is here and a bit roughed up, but OK as of the last time I saw him." Moses sighed, deciding to fill Eileen in on Marvin's arrest. "Eileen, I believe Marvin is in a cell at the station. They are holding him on suspicion of murder. I strongly feel that all three of us are in for questioning about Leroy's murder."

Eileen began to cry. Moses held her tightly for a full minute, then said, "Eileen, we'll get this straightened out. We both know Marvin wouldn't, couldn't shoot his father." They don't know him here. He is another suspicious-colored face to these people. We must keep our wits about us, but we'll beat this.

"Tell me what else happened at the house."

"I unlocked the door, and Officer Barrett backed me against the kitchen wall and asked me who was in the place and where the body of the murdered man was located. For the next few hours, men searched and examined the house.

"I heard them going through every room while I sat at the kitchen table. Eventually, Officer Barrett called the station and spoke to someone there at length. Then he said I would need to make a statement at the station, and I put on my coat, and we came here. When I left, officers were still working in the hallway.

"An ambulance passed us on Kalamazoo heading to the house."

"Alright," said Moses, "they haven't asked you any questions yet?"

"I told them I heard the shot, put on my clothes, came downstairs, saw the body, and called the police station."

"Good," said Moses. "All of that is true, but with Marvin under suspicion, I don't think you or I can afford to hold anything back. We have to concentrate on Marvin. That means we must accurately divulge the events from the start to when I saw him at the Burdick intersection."

'I think you're right, Moses," said Eileen. "Marvin is grown up enough to understand you and me being in the bedroom."

"Good, what about a lawyer? How much can you afford? I can contribute a little," said Moses.

"Next to nothing. I could sell the car; that might give me 400 to 600 dollars," said Eileen. Tears welled up at the edges of her eyes.

"There, girl," whispered Moses, trying to soothe her. "You've got to hang in there for a while longer. Let me make a couple of calls in the morning to public defenders I respect. One in particular, Jeremy Fulton, is as good as they get for a defense lawyer. I know because he got a few of my arrests knocked right out of court.

There was a knock on the door. Officer Barrett entered and said, "We're ready for you now. Mrs. Simmons, allow Miss Larraway to take you to room B down the hall. Mr. Webb, if you will come with me." Moses followed the officer to interrogation room D, which Moses had used dozens of times while on the force.

Moses sat on the center chair of the five that surrounded the small rectangular conference table. At one end of the table was a reel-to-reel tape recorder with a cord leading to an outlet on the wall. A red light blinked on the top edge next to the control buttons. Four-inch diameter reels were mounted, and tape was threaded to the empty spool through the machine. Moses waited about eight minutes until two suited men entered the room, closed the door, and sat opposite Moses at the table.

"Hi, Lucas," said Moses. "It's been a while." Lucas Shotmire had joined the police force four weeks before the drugstore robbery that had put Moses in the hospital. They had worked on one case together. Moses respected the man, a straight shooter.

"Yeah, Moses," said Lucas. "I'm sorry it has to be like this." The officer who came in with Lucas pressed the record button on the tape recorder.

"It's the job," said Moses.

Lucas shuffled a few papers, searching for his notes. "Lucas," said Moses, hoping to speed things along. "I spoke to Chief Hoyt just a few days ago about Leroy Simmons, even gave him photographs. Ross Kirkpatrick interviewed me as well. Leroy was a conman and teenage girl abuser. I observed him during the riot at the Shakespeare fact…"

"Hold it, Moses. Stop. I ask questions. You need to answer. Simple. I prefer that you didn't speak unless you answer my question."

Moses went quiet.

So that's how it's going to be.

"Good, we understand each other," said Lucas

No, we don't.

"Can you tell me where you were between nine and ten last evening?"

"Yes, I was in the upstairs bedroom of my girlfriend, Eileen Simmons. We heard one gunshot, and the front door and screen slammed shut. I heard the front door close again as I picked up a bat in the second bedroom for protection. I went downstairs and found Leroy Simmons lying face down in the hallway. After determining that he was dead, I calmed Mrs. Simmons. Then I retrieved my hat, coat, boots, and a flashlight that Eileen handed me. Out in the snow, I followed tracks and the vague figure of someone walking west on Parsons."

"What were you doing in Mrs. Simmon's bedroom?" asked Shotmire. The other officer smirked.

"None of your business," said Moses, turning toward the officer operating the tape recorder. "Definitely none of **your** business either, rookie, so be careful."

"Alright, Moses, thank you," said Lucas. "Just a couple more questions." He finished a note he was writing in his notepad.

"So, you never saw Marvin Simmons leave the house after he shot his father, but you did go out into the storm after discovering Leroy was dead?"

"Yes."

"And you eventually caught up to Marvin being arrested and taken to the station?"

"I followed someone. The snow, at times, was blinding. I couldn't tell if it was Marvin, someone else, or the man on the moon ahead of me in that storm. All I know is when I came upon the officers and Marvin, they were manhandling him. The boy was near hysterics after one officer hit him from behind with his billy club."

"Alright, Moses," said Lucas. "That's all for now. Obviously, stay close; we may have more questions later."

"How about Marvin," said Moses.

"Oh, we're holding him while we investigate his account, your story, and Mrs. Simmons. We have a couple of interviews to conduct in the morning."

"What has he told you."

"He has a story, all right. You won't hear it until we finish our investigation."

Moses wasn't surprised by Lucas's reticence. Standard procedure at this stage of a homicide case.

"The reason I ask is I've been a mentor to him for basketball and such. He's a good kid and a minor. If he were released under my supervision, I would ensure he was available at the station if you had more questions."

The officer working the tape recorder laughed. Moses glared at him, leaning closer and gathering his right hand into a fist. Then he let out his breath, smiled, spread his right-hand fingers out on the table, and turned back to Officer Shotmire. "What about Mrs. Simmons?"

"I'll check on that interview, but probably. You can wait in the lobby again," said Lucas.

Twenty minutes later, Eileen and Officer Shotmire met Moses in the lobby. "Stay close," Lucas repeated and returned to the offices.

Eileen looked like she had been on nursing duty twenty-four-seven for a week straight. Her eyes were puffed, nearly closed. She pulled out a handkerchief from her purse and blew her nose. "It was horrible, Moses. I thought they were going to arrest me for Leroy's murder. I told them everything like you said to. I don't know if they believed me or not.

"I kept asking to see Marvin. I asked them to tell me what he had told them. I inquired about you. They just kept repeating that it was an ongoing investigation. I asked when I could take Marvin home. They said I couldn't. Then the man who questioned me left, and I waited ten more minutes until Officer Shotmire came in and led me to you here."

"Eileen, you have to stay strong," said Moses. "They may still arrest you, me, or Marvin. They are holding Marvin, but they have three suspects right now, and one or more of us could be guilty in their eyes.

"The snow has stopped. I've been hearing the plows working," said Moses. "I'll have the duty sergeant arrange a ride to your home or my place, whatever you want. At 9:00 a.m. this morning, I'll call Jeremy Fulton and beg him to take the case.

"If he does, he'll be able to see Marvin immediately and learn why the cops are holding him."

Moses lifted Eileen's chin and offered a polite kiss. Eileen melted into his arms for a firmer kiss. When they broke apart, Moses said, "Merry Christmas, darling, keep that chin up." Eileen managed a slight smile.

A patrol car dropped Eileen and Moses off at his apartment (her choice). Once inside, Eileen couldn't stop shaking. Moses gave her a pair of his pajamas to put on, put her in his bed, and piled on another blanket. She was still shaking, so Moses stripped off his clothes to his boxers and climbed under the covers with her. Eileen eventually stopped shivering, and Moses gave her two aspirins, and they both dropped off to sleep.

20 | Eeny, Meeny, Miny, Moe

Marvin continued to sit in a holding cell on Sunday, the day after Christmas. Fortunately, Moses had been able to persuade Jeremy Fulton to defend Marvin.

When Fulton met briefly with the assistant prosecutor, he demanded that Marvin, a juvenile, be released into the custody of his mother. The Assistant D.A. told Jeremy that due to the heinous nature of the crime (Leroy being shot in the back at close range), Marvin would most likely be charged as an adult and would definitely stay in jail, pending arraignment. The prosecution had already applied for an extension to the 24-hour limit for indicting Marvin because of difficulties completing their investigation during the holiday/weekend.

By Sunday afternoon, Eileen felt well enough to check on her house. She took a cab to the Parsons Street address, but the front and back doors had wide boards nailed to the frames to discourage entry. A sign was stapled to the center board that said: No Admittance – by order of the Kalamazoo Police Department. Luckily, the taxicab had not left, and Eileen returned to Moses' place.

On Monday morning, Eileen was still going out of her mind. Moses was urging patience while the wheels of injustice turned. By nine o'clock, Moses was waiting outside Police Chief Hoyt's office. Howard Hoyt arrived for work and asked Moses to step into his office.

"Chief," said Moses. "I'm hoping you might expedite the release of Marvin Simmons into my care. He's being held as a suspect for the murder of Leroy Simmons."

"I'm well aware of the situation, Moses," said Howard.

"Good, Marvin is a sixteen-year-old minor. He's never been in trouble at school or in the community and is dedicated to basketball. Coach Quiring moved him up to the varsity; he's that good. Marvin has been in a holding cell since Christmas Eve. His mother, Eileen Simmons, wants her boy home."

"Look, Moses," said the Chief. "This is the police department. We catch criminals and suspects. You know that. We gather evidence, which, in the case of the Simmons murder, we've done pretty quickly. The prosecuting attorney's office is pushing for the boy's arraignment and elevating the kid to adult status. There is nothing I can or will do in the matter."

Moses remained calm. "I understand your position, Chief," he said. "I have given you evidence of Leroy's involvement with the strike and riot at the Shakespeare plant. I believe there are others involved in Leroy's activities that have a greater motive than Marvin for Leroy's murder."

"A strike conspirator would shoot Simmons in the foyer of his home?" said Howard. "Moses, that is far-fetched.

"Listen, I've given your evidence to the attorney in charge of the grand Jury probe into the Shakespeare riot, but that is a separate issue to this one of a son shooting his father."

Moses could see that Leroy's scams, drug dealing, riot instigation, and abuse of a teenage girl would be costly investigations. Leroy wasn't worth it. Not when they had a suspect in custody with a motive, and they had the weapon with the son's fingerprints on it. Marvin was from Northside; he was not worth further effort.

When he returned from the police station, Moses explained his frustrations to Eileen.

"I almost prefer it this way, Eileen," said Moses. "I see them staying out of the way of my efforts until the Grand Jury in the Shakespeare Company riot calls on me."

"What can you do?" said Eileen.

"Start over, from scratch. Narrow the possibilities."

Moses hugged Eileen. "Hell," he said, "I've already eliminated Marvin as a suspect, that's progress."

***

They both decided that work might be a welcome distraction and left for work mid-afternoon. Eileen received a call from the prosecuting attorney's office just before five. She was informed that Marvin would be arraigned the following morning at 10:00 a.m., Tuesday, December 28, 1948, in the 9th Circuit Court of Kalamazoo County. Eileen called the Cities Service Station, asked for Moses, and cried the news into the telephone. Moses stayed on the phone for ten minutes until Eileen settled down. Moses asked if he could call Curtis Knapper and Sheila Rohan to attend as character witnesses for Marvin when seeking bail.

Moses left a message at the Kalamazoo Central High School administration office to pass on to Curtis. He was informed that Sheila was absent from school. Moses reached Sheila's mother at home. He heard Sheila in the background insisting on speaking to him. When Sheila took the handset from her mother, Moses told her of the importance of character witnesses at the arraignment.

At around seven in the evening, a police car pulled into the Cities Service Station. Lucas Shotmire and his partner walked into the shop and over to Moses, who was dismantling a carburetor at his workbench.

"Moses," Shotmire said, "we need you at the station to review the Simmons murder case. We'll bring you back after the session."

Again, in interrogation room D, Moses sat opposite the two officers. The tape recorder was turned on, and Shotmire's partner hit the record buttons.

"This interview is really a courtesy to Chief Hoyt," said Lucas. "He has made it clear that we should give you every courtesy. So, I will present the evidence we have collected to date. If you wish to add or alter the facts I laid out or if you have additional information or evidence, I'll listen. Fair enough?"

"Of course, Lucas," said Moses.

"Marvin stated that the dance ended early due to the snowstorm," said Lucas, referring studiously to his notes before continuing.

"The three companions planned to go to Louie's Trophy House for pizza after the dance and brought clothes appropriate for the weather. A couple of blocks from Wallwood Hall, the snowstorm changed their minds, and the three friends decided to head home. Curtis Knapper, a teammate of Marvin's and the driver of a '42 Ford F-100 pickup, provided rides for Marvin and his date, Sheila Rohan.

"Curtis first drove to the corner of N. Westnedge (plowed) and Bosker Ave. He waited for Marvin to walk Sheila to her house halfway down the block. Then Curtis drove south on Westnedge, east on Kalamazoo, and north as far as the truck would go on Walbridge to drop off Marvin.

"The time was approximately ten minutes to ten."

Moses had pulled out his own notepad and was madly taking notes the whole time Lucas spoke. Lucas waited a moment for Moses to finish recording his thoughts.

"Moving on," said Lucas. "Marvin stated that he walked to his mother's garage and hunted down a flashlight, intending to use it in the house to not wake up his mother if she had gone to bed. He thought it took him five minutes to get to the garage and find the flashlight.

"While in the garage, Marvin says he heard a gunshot. He ran to the back door and through the kitchen and found his father face down in the hallway. His father's gun was a couple of feet from the body. Careful not to step in the blood pooling around the body, he stood over the body for a minute or two. Then he picked up the gun and went out the front door, following footsteps in the snow drifting over in the wind."

Moses interrupted, "Did Marvin say why he went after the killer?"

"He said he wanted to catch the person that killed his father, Moses," said Shotmire. "I don't buy it, but that is for a jury to decide.

"From that point, Moses, you know the rest except for this. Marvin says he got within range of whoever he was following and fired the gun to disable the runner. Of course, he missed. The runner hopped in a car that sped away to the north on Burdick.

"When we received the call from Mrs. Simmons, it seemed prudent to send out patrol cars to surround the address on Parsons Street from the east and the west. The police car traveling north on Burdick saw Marvin and detained him for questioning. He was ordered to put his hands in the air, which he did. The officer who searched him found the gun in Marvin's coat pocket, recently fired, and ordered Marvin to assume the position against the patrol car.

"Once at the station, Marvin was given a paraffin test confirming he had fired the gun."

Moses interrupted, "Why didn't the officers pursue the car fleeing north on Burdick Street."

"What car, Moses? The patrol car came up seconds after Marvin reached the intersection on foot. There was no car. The slush made it impossible to track if there ever was one."

"They should have tried," said Moses.

"No! They had their man. There were no fingerprints on the gun, by the way, except for Marvin's. The case is closed as far as I'm concerned.

"Now, if you or Mrs. Simmons want to confess to shooting Leroy, I'll listen. Eeny, meeny, miny moe. Confess, and I'll go in that direction. Marvin could have been one big blind red herring.

"What, no confession? Then keep the girl, Moses, and we've got our man."

"Except that you don't," said Moses. "far from it. Marvin is a good kid. He is not going to shoot anyone."

"What about the shot in the dark to stop the ghost?"

"A warning shot. Your men should have followed that car."

"By the way," said Lucas. "We spoke to several students at the high school this morning who witnessed an argument between Marvin and Leroy. We understand Leroy pulled a gun out and threatened Marvin, who slugged him to the ground. Apparently, Leroy was bothering Marvin's girlfriend, and Marvin exploded. That's a motive right there. Motive and capability.

"Don't tell me Marvin is a good kid. He murdered his own father." Detective Shotmire reached over and shut off the tape recorder.

21 | Arraignment

The Leroy Simmons murder case was the opening appointment on Judge Sinclair Mcdonald's docket for the morning, and the room was sparsely populated. The court clerk and one police officer wandered the room, preparing for the arraignment. The court stenographer sat at a desk left of the judge's bench. Marvin sat at the defendants' table. The assistant prosecuting attorney was shuffling papers at his desk on the opposite side of the room. Right behind the defense desk, Eileen sat beside Moses, gripping his hand. Sheila, wearing her best Sunday dress, sat with her mother in the next row of chairs. Curtis was sitting alone, three rows further back.

Moses rose and spoke to Sheila, thanking her for attending. Sheila's mother glared at Moses. She was obviously unhappy with her daughter and, by extension, Moses, Eileen, and Marvin.

Eileen was composed, sitting still in her seat. She leaned forward and gripped Marvin's shoulder. He put his hand over hers, turned, and smiled reassuringly at his mother and Moses. Jeremy Fulton, Marvin's attorney, pulled Marvin's attention back to the matter at hand, and Moses heard him review the sequence of upcoming events when the judge arrived in the court.

Three minutes passed, and the door behind the judge's podium opened. The judge appeared, wearing a dark blue pinstripe suit. His hair glistened black with Wildroot Cream Oil except for his graying temples, but he had an efficient and commanding presence.

The court clerk asked everyone to rise as Judge McDonald entered the room. When seated, the judge asked the clerk to proceed. The statement read by the clerk stated the facts in the case involving the alleged murder of Leroy Simmons and named Marvin Simmons as the defendant.

The clerk ended by saying, "Will the defendant please rise." Mr. Fulton stood and touched Marvin on the shoulder. Marvin, wearing the same suit he wore to the dance on Christmas Eve, stood, taking a stance that he might have used being introduced before a game. His hands clasped together but relaxed, shoulders back, eyes intent on the judge, calm.

"How do you plead?" said the judge.

"Not guilty," said Marvin.

The judge nodded to the stenographer. "Let the record show that the defendant, Marvin Simmons, pleads not guilty.

"Mr. Simmons, you requested Mr. Jeremy Fulton of the public defenders' office to be your attorney. Is that your wish?

"Yes," said Marvin.

"Your honor," said Mr. Fulton. "We respectfully request that Marvin be released without bail under the supervision of his mother, Eileen Simmons, and Mr. Moses Webb, a former police detective with the Kalamazoo Safety Department. We have character witnesses in court who will testify to Marvin's upstanding character in all of his endeavors."

"That won't be necessary, Mr. Fulton," said the judge. "The prosecutor has requested that Mr. Simmons, here, should be tried as an adult. In reviewing the facts and evidence collected by the police, I am in complete agreement. By his size alone, the man standing before me should be considered a man. An alleged back shooter, I'm not taking any chances with this defendant. A request for no bail or bail of any amount will not be acceptable. My clerk will advise you of my schedule and the trial date.

"I have been brought to Kalamazoo temporarily from Ann Arbor as an impartial outsider to adjudicate the matter of the Shakespeare Company strike and riot. I am waiting for indictments in that case before scheduling an arraignment. We should work this case into the schedule as soon as possible. Does the defendant have any questions at this time? If not, the court is adjourned until the trial date."

The judge left. The court police officer handcuffed Marvin and started for the side entrance. Sheila broke from her mother and ran to Marvin. She embraced him, kissed his cheek, and laid her head on his chest until the policeman pulled her off and escorted Marvin from the courtroom.

Moses was struck by the passion Sheila exhibited. He concluded that the teenage couple's relationship was more profound than merely dating. The two were deeply in love.

Eileen observed her son's stoicism and acute regard for Sheila as well. Moses hugged her and asked her to wait while he spoke to Curtis, who was leaving the courtroom.

"Curtis, got a minute?" Moses asked.

"I guess, but I gotta get back to school soon," said Curtis. "It looks pretty bad for Marvin, Mr. Webb. He didn't do it. I believe that. I've only known him since he joined the varsity, but besides being an amazing player, he is also a great unselfish teammate. Two things are important to him, and he stays focused 100% of the time. Basketball and Sheila. He'll do anything and everything for either one."

Moses rubbed his chin in thought. "I read your statement about the Christmas Eve dance. You are a senior, right?"

Curtis nodded.

"Marvin's a sophomore, is Sheila?" asked Moses.

"She's a junior, Mr. Webb. Why does that matter," said Curtis.

"It doesn't, but their relationship seems pretty intense. Something is nagging me about Marvin's behavior in all of this. You say you dropped Marvin and Sheila off quite a distance from her house, and Marvin walked her the rest of the way home, right?"

"That's what I said."

"What about her evening gown and accessories? Did she leave it all in your car? It seems like Marvin could have helped get her stuff to her house."

"Naw, we talked about it. I told Sheila I'd drop it all off after the next melt. It looked difficult enough to walk in the snow. I couldn't get very close in the truck. That's the way Marvin wanted it, Sheila too."

Curtis turned and left for school. Moses was still nagged by the sequence of that night. He wanted to check with Sheila, but she and her mother were no longer in the courtroom. Eileen was talking to Jeremy.

"Moses, I just asked Mrs. Simmons to come to my office for a strategy session. Could you come as well, Moses?"

Jeremy's office was around the corner from the courthouse. They walked, leaving Eileen's car in the courthouse parking lot. Jeremy's office was in a suite of cubicles for other lawyers, community advocates, psychologists, and activists. The offices shared resources, typewriters, telephones, a conference room, and a receptionist. The conference room was empty. The receptionist brought a tray with cups of coffee, cream, and sugar packets.

"Mrs. Simmons," said Jeremy. "You have a fantastic son. He must do pretty well in his studies."

"Please call me Eileen, Mr. Fulton," said Eileen. "I am trusting you to help us out of this mess. Moses thinks you can. Yes, Marvin is an 'A' student."

"Well, let's get started then," said Jeremy. "Moses, I understand that Detective Shotmire has informed you of the evidence and statements they have collected regarding the murder?"

"And everything I know, Eileen knows," said Moses.

"So, in all candor, how do I fight this one, Moses," said Jeremy. "You're a detective. The facts and evidence stack up to an open and shut case against Marvin. The fact that he is a stellar student with dozens of character witnesses will not be enough. The altercation with Leroy on school grounds, witnessed by over thirty students, will weigh just as heavily on the jury."

Moses looked over at Eileen, then grabbed her hand. "Eileen," he said, "Jeremy is giving us a realistic viewpoint on the case. It's a starting point. That's all."

"I understand," said Eileen, "but I know he didn't do it. There must be another explanation."

"That's my starting point," said Moses. "Someone else shot Leroy, wiped off any fingerprints or was wearing gloves, and dropped the gun in the hallway.

"But why did Marvin pick up that gun and go out in that storm. It doesn't make sense. It's a stupid thing to do. It's out of character."

"But Moses," said Eileen. "If Marvin panicked or was in shock, he might have had some vestige of loyalty left to his father. Enough to try and stop the real killer."

"Could that be it, Moses," said Jeremy. "Might that be a direction? I don't see how that helps us. Temporary insanity might be better. Or maybe Marvin tried to make a citizen's arrest of Leroy for abusing his girlfriend. The gun accidentally discharges when Leroy tries to escape."

"No," said Moses. "I think you're both wrong. I am positive that I heard the front door close twice. Once, twenty seconds or less after the gunshot. Again, a minute and a half later. That points to Marvin telling the truth about someone else being in the house helping Leroy search for money. That man would have gloves on so as not to leave fingerprints. Leroy sets his gun down on the table while searching cupboards, and the gloved man picks it up, shoots Leroy, drops the revolver, and runs.

"Marvin enters the kitchen from the garage, finds the body, picks up the gun, and puts it in his coat pocket. Now the gun has his fingerprints on it. He chases the murderer just as he has told us. That all fits, but I still say it's not quite right."

"So what's next, Moses," said Jeremy.

"I want to talk to Sheila," said Moses. "I'm not at all certain Sheila's mother will let me. Jeremy, if you initiated the interview, I could ask my questions; I think it would be better."

Jeremy set up the interview for the following day on Sheila's lunch break at the high school. Mrs. Rohan would be working but permitted Mr. Fulton to interview her daughter. Moses and Jeremy waited in a small conference room connected to the principal's office at the high school. Sheila walked in, accompanied by Mrs. Jessup, her guidance counselor. Mr. Fulton introduced himself and Moses to Mrs. Jessup.

"Sheila, thanks for meeting with us," said Jeremy. "We're double-checking the evidence the police gathered in their case against Marvin. We want to review that evidence and ensure it is complete and accurate."

"I hope I can help," said Sheila.

"Marvin is a good student," said Mrs. Jessup. "He is under my wing as well here at the school. He is an outstanding student. If there is anything the school can provide the police to reinforce his good behavior, please let me know."

"Thank you, Mrs. Jessup," said Jeremy.

Jeremy turned the questioning over to Moses.

"We do not want you to feel uncomfortable during this meeting," said Moses. "If you or Mrs. Jessup request to stop our questions or do not wish to answer any or all of my queries, say 'No Comment,' or raise a hand."

"Alright," said Sheila. "I just want to help Marvin as much as I can."

"That's great, Sheila," said Moses. "The more information we have, the sooner we can get Marvin out of this nightmare.

"You like Marvin more than just a boyfriend, right?" said Moses.

"I'm in love with him," said Sheila. "Marvin's the most sensitive, kind, strong person I have ever known," said Sheila.

"He feels the same way about you, doesn't he?"

"Yes, he's told me more than once that he is also in love with me."

"OK," said Moses, "I think I understand. I'm learning that Eileen is as caring a person as Marvin. Leroy, however, was a different sort.

"I don't know if Marvin told you, but I shadowed Marvin for two weeks at the request of his mother to see that he wasn't getting into trouble. He never disappointed me or his mother. On one of those days, I was fifty feet away from him when Leroy accosted you outside of Central High School. I witnessed the whole thing and would have intervened on your behalf if Marvin hadn't appeared and taken care of the weasel."

"That was unbelievable, Mr. Webb," said Sheila. "Just looking at that man or even thinking about him now makes my skin crawl. I couldn't believe how Marvin faced him down while Leroy's gun was pointed at him. When Marvin knocked him down, I thought I'd melt with relief and pride at how he handled Leroy."

"That's fine, Sheila," said Jeremy, "because the prosecution will grill you about that episode repeatedly to show that Marvin has a murderous nature. I predict that the prosecuting attorney will have you describe where Leroy touched you to rile Marvin into an outburst in court."

Moses let Jeremy's comment sink into Sheila. Moses knew that she still didn't realize what that day in court would be like. She was a teenager, optimistic, naïve?

"Our team hopes to avoid that situation by never getting to court," said Moses. "Do you need a break, Sheila? We could get a roll from the lunchroom?"

Sheila shook her head. "I want to know what you will do, Mr. Webb. Let's keep going."

"Alright,: said Moses. "Now, I want to review what happened on Christmas Eve.

"Sheila, Curtis made a statement to the police that after the dance, instead of going to Louie's Trophy House, he drove as close to your house on Bosker Avenue as the storm allowed and that you and Marvin walked the rest of way to your home and then Marvin walked back to the truck.

Until then, Sheila had been attentive and interested in what Moses was saying. Now, she lowered her eyes and rubbed her hands on her skirt.

Jeremy noticed. "That's right, isn't Sheila," he said.

Moses kept going. "Curtis then drove as close to Marvin's house as he could get, dropped him off, and Marvin walked home. After finding a flashlight in the garage, He entered the house and found Leroy dead.

"That meshes with your recollection of the drive home, right, Sheila? Curtis said it was about 9:45 p.m. when Marvin located the flashlight in the garage and heard the shot."

Sheila was silent. Moses could almost hear her thinking through her answer to his question. Jeremy and Moses could tell that whatever Sheila was about to say would probably be a lie, but Moses did not want to pressure her.

Finally, Sheila spoke. "What has Marvin said about how we got home?"

"Well," said Jeremy. "He hasn't contradicted Curtis."

"Can I talk to Marvin?" Sheila asked.

"I doubt it, Sheila," said Jeremy. "As his attorney, I can pass a message from you to him. Client attorney privilege means I cannot reveal anything you wish to tell me about Marvin unless you give me permission. Moses would have to leave the room. Is that something that you would like?"

Sheila kept getting more upset. She thought again, then spoke. "Whatever Marvin says happened, happened. I believe in him and that he is innocent. I need to go home now."

Sheila was almost crying. Moses stood up.

"You did fine, Sheila. Mrs.Jessup, thanks for your time." Mrs. Jessup nodded, glanced at her watch, and hurried off.

"Why don't you go with Mrs. Jessup back to her office?" said Moses. "Take a minute or twenty to settle down, as long as you need, then return to class. Thank you for talking to us. We'll get Marvin cleared, I promise." But Sheila seemed reluctant to leave. She gathered herself and looked directly at the attorney.

"I can say for certain," she said fiercely. "That if Marvin did shoot that bastard, it was to protect me from him. So that he would never touch me again." Then she left for class, closing the door behind her.

Jeremy searched through the file in his briefcase.

"Here it is," he said, "Curtis Knapper's statement. What could Sheila be alluding to in his testimony that made her clam up?"

"I don't know, but I have my suspicions. I want to talk to Marvin. Can you arrange that?" said Moses.

"Let me make a call," said Jeremy. "If I can schedule it with the jail for early afternoon, could you make it before you go to work?"

"The sooner, the better," said Moses.

"Give me twenty minutes," said Jeremy.

The attorney stepped out to call the jail. Then he zipped down the stairs and out the school's front door. Fifteen minutes later, he was back, sitting beside Moses in the conference room.

Jeremy took his billfold from his hip pocket, plucked out a dollar bill, and placed it on the table. "Standard contract for service to assist me, the attorney for Marvin Simmons. And a receipt from you for the money. You can sign under my name, Jeremy Fulton, J.D., M.B.A..

Moses signed beneath Jeremy's signature. He stuffed the dollar in his shirt pocket. It would buy a bottle of Coca-Cola for lunch for a week.

"The contract means that anything Marvin tells either of us is covered under client/attorney privilege," said the attorney. He put the signed papers in his briefcase, rose from the table, and put on his coat.

"Let's go. The jail awaits. When we're settled in the visitors' room, a corrections officer will bring Marvin out.

***

The officer stepped aside to let Marvin enter. He was not wearing handcuffs or ankle shackles. Moses thought he looked well and energetic.

Jeremy asked Marvin to sit across from Moses, and he sat beside Moses. They both shook Marvin's hand before sitting.

"You don't look any worse for wear," said Moses. "How is it in here."

"It is what it is," said Marvin. "When you know you are innocent, I guess you can put up with anything."

'That's a good attitude, Marvin," said Jeremy. "I apologize for handling you've experienced by the police and the court. From what Moses has told me about Leroy, it looks like the law's rush to judgment, in this case, contradicts our justice system. They think they can prove their case but have made a major mistake by not investigating other possibilities. We're here today to start to counter their supposition. I have retained Moses to investigate the events leading up to and including Christmas Eve. Will you be comfortable with our arrangement? I understand he is seeing your mother romantically."

"I am comfortable with that arrangement," said Marvin.

"Alright, Marvin," said Moses. "I may brush you back with my questions today. Please remember that I am on your side, as is Jeremy. Your mother is even more important to me. I only have an hour before work, so I will get right to the point."

Marvin smiled. Moses decided Marvin was setting his feet guarding the basket from a drive down the lane. Moses was instantly wary. If the kid was as good at fending off his questions as he was at blocking shots, Moses had his work cut out.

"Review for me what occurred after you heard the gunshot."

"I ran to the house, went through the kitchen, and saw Leroy dead on the floor. His gun, at least it looked like his gun, was lying on the floor about three feet from his left hand. I guess I couldn't believe it at first. In seconds, I decided to pick up the gun and put it in my coat pocket. Then I ran out the front door. In the distance, through the heavy snowfall, I could see a figure trekking down Parsons Avenue hurriedly, so I followed them and tried to catch up.

"Almost immediately, I lost sight of the figure ahead of me, but when the snowstorm lessened in a minute, I spotted the figure pretty far along in the next block. I slipped and slid in the snow, running to get closer. I was still fifty feet away when I saw a car idling on Burdick Street, so I took aim and fired. I knew I wouldn't hit him, but I hoped the gunshot would scare him into surrendering. As I approached Burdick Street, I saw whoever it was hop in. The car spun its wheels, trying to get away to the north on Burdick. The snowstorm picked up again, and the car vanished from sight, but a police car pulled up.

"Should I keep going?"

"Not necessary," said Moses. "Let's go back to the time you heard the shot. How long would you say it was before you saw the body in the hallway?"

"About one minute. No, less than a minute. Twenty to thirty seconds." Marvin looked at the ceiling, silently counting the steps from the garage to the kitchen. "Probably less than twenty seconds," he corrected.

"Now, this is important," said Moses. "Did you see or hear anything in the house before you saw the body?"

Marvin looked away, hesitating. Moses wanted an answer, "Don't think about it; what did you see or hear."

"When I got to the kitchen, I heard the front door close and the screen slam," said Marvin.

"That's better; why did you leave that out when you described your actions after the gunshot?"

"I don't know, I forgot, I guess."

"I was upstairs when that gunshot occurred, Marvin," said Moses. "I heard the front door and the screen slam shut about fifteen seconds after the gunshot. That just about meshes with your estimate.

"You say you forgot. That is a pretty significant detail to overlook. How long did you stand over Leroy before you picked up the gun?"

"I told you, not more than ten seconds."

"It seems you would have decided as you entered the hallway and saw the gun that you intended to capture the assailant on an impulse, and seconds could have been crucial. Picking the gun up immediately and rushing out the front door might have made the difference."

"I've never been a policeman like you, Moses; I wasn't sure what to do. I guess I was scared, too."

"Alright, I get that. I do have the experience, and I get scared every time."

"So, when you went out the front door, why did you have the gun in your coat pocket? You could have walked right into the assailant. You might have had a chance if you had kept the gun in hand."

"I guess I can't answer that. I am not a policeman; I haven't had your training."

"Exactly," said Moses. "Why did you pick up the gun in the first place. Why didn't you leave the scene untouched and leave catching the bad guy to the police?"

"I wanted to help. I thought I could…"

"And look where that has gotten you. Your fingerprints are the only ones on the gun, and the gunfire residue on your clothes from the second gunshot reinforces the possibility that you shot Leroy."

"OK, Moses," said Jeremy. "That's enough."

Jeremy let the room rest in silence. A minute of quiet helped ease the tension.

"Marvin," said Jeremy. "What Moses just put you through is a tenth of what the prosecuting attorney will do when he grills you on the stand."

"I guess that's all for now," said Moses. "I've got a few things to work on. I'll never pull my punches, Marvin, and I want you to think about what you said today. I honestly believe there is more to your story than what you have told us. Do you have a problem with me speaking to Sheila again?"

"I don't see why that's necessary. Moses. I'm the one in a jam, not Sheila."

"Sheila cares about you and wants to help. In fact, she is desperate to help you."

"Well, OK, Moses, but please don't be hard on her."

"Agreed," said Moses.

I've almost got it worked out. Sheila is the key.

23 | Truth Be Told

When Moses walked into the gym at Central High School the next afternoon, the Varsity was scrimmaging the JV team. When the Varsity reached twenty-four points, Coach Quiring whistled the boys in. The coach reviewed a few things they did well and the areas they needed to work on. At that point, the Varsity was done with their practice. The JV team would have the court for the next hour and a half.

Moses walked over to Coach Quiring. "How's it going, Coach," said Moses.

"It would go much better if we had Marvin," said Coach.

"He wishes he were here, that's for sure," said Moses. "I'm here to see Curtis. Would it be OK if I talked to him for a few minutes?"

"If it helps Marvin, I'm all for it," said the coach.

Moses entered the locker room, singled out Curtis, and asked him if he was available after getting dressed for additional questions.

Minutes later, Moses got to the point in the hallway. "Curtis, I'm spinning in circles. Sheila won't explain things unless Marvin says it is OK. Marvin won't tell me anything and doesn't want me to bother Sheila. You're holding the line as well."

"I'd like to help, as I said before, but I don't think it's my place."

"Curtis, I've had it with this all for one and one for all bit. That tactic is going to put Marvin in jail, possibly for life. Now, come on. What have you left out? What is Sheila scared to talk about. I will try my damnedest to fix this mess, but I need the walls broken down."

Curtis rubbed his chin. "I'll trust you, Mr. Webb; I know Marvin does. I think he should have told you and his mother right off.

"I didn't drop Marvin and Sheila off near her house. They wanted to be alone after the dance. Get me? Marvin had arranged a place in the garage at his house and a kerosene heater. I dropped them off there at 9:15 p.m."

"Thank you, Curtis. I was pretty sure it was something like that."

Every turn of the wrench that night triggered daydreams of doom in Moses. Marvin and Sheila were basically good kids. Perhaps they were getting ahead of themselves. But who could blame them? Sheila could be a seventeen-year-old exquisite colored model. Marvin is already a basketball star. A better magnet was hard to imagine.

Teenagers! Why do they act like guilty children at times?

Moses considered his own tangled younger days. In the south where he lived, black or white, a menace waited around many corners. Moses developed a singular thought. He worked at being the best fighter, the strongest kid on the block, to the exclusion of studying and learning. That would come much later, after boxing. Boxing probably kept Moses alive. For Marvin, it was basketball.

For all of Marvin's bravado, the mousetrap seemed to be snapping shut. Marvin's color and the innuendos of his status weighed him down almost as heavily in Kalamazoo as it would if he were growing up like Moses in Baton Rouge.

Eileen would not be happy with the truth. Sheila's mother might send Sheila to a convent. What would Eileen think of him exposing Marvin's charade?

The bandaid had to be ripped off; the sooner, the better.

***

Jeremy waved a hand at Moses to sit across from his desk. He was speaking into his Dictaphone. Moses heard him dictate notes on the Simmons case. Jeremy finished his thoughts while Moses waited patiently. Then he turned to Moses. "What's up, anything new?" he asked.

Moses gave Jeremy the highlights of his conversation with Curtis. "You kept saying there was something screwy with their story, Moses."

"Yup," said Moses, "and you can bet Shotmire and Glen Cornell, the prosecuting attorney, will also dig it out of them. We have to get back to Sheila before they do."

Jeremy called the school. Forty-five minutes later, the attorney and investigator sat in the principal's conference room with Sheila and Mrs.Jessup.

"I was able to get a hold of Sheila's mother at the Gibson factory,"[37] said Mrs. Jessup. "She forbade this interview at first. I assured her this would be the last one, less than twenty minutes long."

"Thank you, Mrs. Jessup," said Jeremy. "Sheila, Moses, and I have spoken to Marvin. He has not betrayed your trust or integrity. Unfortunately, he is adamant about it, which might put him in prison for a long time."

The girl, serene in a violet Angora sweater, her hands clasped together on the table. Moses could see that she would answer his questions. "That's right, Sheila, Curtis decided to help us get closer to the truth, not Marvin."

"I know," said Sheila. "Curtis came to my locker before 1st hour. He said he had told you about dropping us off close to Marvin's house. I want to help as well."

"That's great," said Moses. "After the dance on Christmas Eve, Curtis drove you and Marvin as far as he could go on Walbridge Street, and the two of you made your way to Marvin's garage."

"That is correct and the truth," Sheila said. "There were candles that Marvin lit, and in five minutes, the heater had warmed the area around an old mattress Marvin tipped down onto the floor. He had two blankets ready to spread out. The storm was blowing snow through the cracks around the garage door, piling up inside, but the mattress was warm where we were.

After about twenty minutes, I began to get nervous about getting home. It's a twenty-minute walk in good weather, and I promised my mother I'd be home by ten-thirty. We bundled up. Marvin said he would walk me home. The outside lights were on, and we walked around the house. The snow and wind increased again. It was hard to see the way down Parsons Street. Marvin returned to the garage for a flashlight. He told me to wait up on the porch, out of the wind, by the front door that was leaking heat.

"I stood there, getting colder by the minute, waiting for Marvin. I figured he was working more on the garage, making it look like we were never there. Then I heard the gunshot and just about died. I knew Leroy was expected to come and beg money from Mrs. Simmons or Marvin, and I had seen the gun at school.

Mr. Webb, I was so scared I began to shiver. The freezing weather didn't help. I thought Leroy had shot Marvin, and if I went in to help him, Leroy would shoot me. And then I thought that maybe Marvin had somehow taken the gun away from Leroy and had shot him.

Whichever was the case, I was so scared I ran, slipping and sliding, off the porch and into the night. I had no flashlight, afraid my Marvin was dead, and Leroy was after me next. I'm ashamed that I just left Marvin to face that despicable man, but there you have it. That's what happened."

"Did you ever see anyone following you or anyone up ahead as you tried to make it to your house," said Moses.

"I never saw anyone behind me," said Sheila. I saw a car on Burdick Street over to my left. I kept wandering off the road in the dark. I didn't have a flashlight."

"Could you tell me the model of the car or the manufacturer?" said Moses.

"Are you kidding? No," said Sheila.

"Well, since you didn't have a flashlight, I bet the men in the car never saw you. There wasn't anyone outside the car?"

"No. I just kept going. I heard sirens as I walked the last three blocks, but I reached home before my curfew. My mother asked from her bed if I had had a good time, and I said yes. I was shaking so badly that I couldn't bring myself to go in and talk to her. I went to bed. I was up for another two hours, shaking under a pile of blankets.

"Eventually, I fell asleep."

"When did you know Marvin was OK," said Moses.

"I found out from the news on the radio that Leroy Simmons was murdered, but they did not mention Marvin at all. I was sick, worried about Marvin, and stayed home from school. Mrs. Simmons called me about the arraignment, and I told Mother I was going whether she came along or not. She made me go to school after that."

"So, from the commotion you heard inside the house, you think Marvin killed Leroy?" said Jeremy.

"I thought so, I guess," said Sheila. "As I said the other day, I was OK with that because I know he would have done it to protect me. In the courtroom, Marvin pleaded, 'Not Guilty.' If Marvin had done this, I think he would have pleaded guilty. I will stay by his side no matter what, Mr. Webb. I love him."

***

Moses and Jeremy went directly to the jail from the school. They had to wait an hour for Marvin to join them in the visitors' room while lunch was delivered to the inmates.

"Hello, Marvin," said Jeremy, "a couple of notes. Your trial date still has not been scheduled. I have appealed the judge's decision to treat you as an adult. Your mother is doing well, going to work, etc., and she sends her love. I thought we would have your mother and Sheila visit you tomorrow. Would that be OK?"

"Sure, that would be great," said Marvin.

"Moses, how do you want to proceed today," said the attorney.

"Well," said Moses, "I want to cut through the bullshit. Marvin, we know Sheila was with you at your house on Christmas Eve. Jeremy and I could have saved time if you had told us first, but there it is. Now I want to clear up some details.

[196]

"According to Sheila, you left her on the front porch while you returned to the garage to retrieve a flashlight. Don't look so upset. Believe me, she never would have told us out of loyalty to you if Curtis hadn't set us down the right path. You heard the gunshot and rushed into the house.

"You were in the kitchen heading for the hallway and heard the front door and screen close. Who did you think it was?"

"I had no idea," said Marvin.

"Bullshit, you thought it was Sheila."

"I… Yeah, I did. Leroy was there on the floor. All I could think about was Sheila. I watched her throw up when we got to her house that afternoon after Dad touched her. She hated him and kept telling me she wanted to press charges. For days, she kept repeating that she was going to kill him.

"She must have heard Leroy rustling around in the house while she was on the porch. She went inside, thinking it was me. Panicking, Sheila picked up the gun and shot Leroy. She threw down the pistol, ran out the door, and didn't stop running. I couldn't catch up to her.

"When I saw the gun and thought of Sheila, I knew the only way to protect her then was to wipe the gun clean of her fingerprints and try and help her secretly get home. Outside, I saw her in the distance but lost sight of her in a snow squall. I had the flashlight, and I knew she didn't. Then, I saw the car over on Burdick Street and a figure approaching me. I figured it had to be someone waiting for Leroy to hand them the money he owed. So I fired the gun. I knew about gunfire residue from listening to Dragnet, so that was the icing.

"You're my lawyer, Mr. Fulton. Don't you have to do what I say? If it comes down to it, I will confess to killing that son of a bitch."

Moses shook his head and looked over at Jeremy. "Maybe that's for the best," said Jeremy. "I can change your plea to guilty of murder due to temporary insanity. The sooner we do that, the more believable it will be. I'll have to get at least two psychiatrists to test you. The prosecutor will also want you examined by their experts."

Moses had been thinking of Eileen and Marvin's future. An insanity plea would scar the boy for life if he got away with it. He could forget about playing basketball for anyone, anywhere.

"Hey," said Moses. "It seems like you two are rushing to judgment now."

"I won't let Sheila go to jail," said Marvin. "It has to be me."

"You don't have to worry about that," Moses said. "Whether you plead guilty or not guilty, sane or insane, you're practically there already. Let's all calm down."

Silence lingered around the table for a full minute.

"Marvin, when we spoke to Sheila, it was evident that she thought you had shot Leroy. She said it was justified in her eyes if you did, and she would stand by you, whatever. I believe she sincerely thinks you eliminated her predator."

"You think she entered the house, picked up the gun somehow, and shot the man. Think about it, though. What was the body's position when you entered the hallway fifteen seconds after the gunshot?

"Leroy was face down," said Marvin.

"That's right. Face down, shot in the back, Leroy's head pointing at the front door, his feet near the kitchen. That is significant.

"If Sheila opened the front door, picked up the gun, and shot the man, his body would be lying pointing away from the front door toward the kitchen. She wouldn't have had the time or the strength to turn him around if, when she shot him, he was in front of her heading toward the kitchen. Sheila literally couldn't have been the person that shot Leroy Simmons."

Marvin stood, found a clear spot in the room, and paced off the murdered body, pointing to an imagined front door and turning back toward an imaginary kitchen.

Jeremy followed along, watching Marvin closely. "You're absolutely right, Moses. Sheila couldn't have done all of that. Let alone the hutzpah to pick up the gun in the first place."

"The way I figure it," said Moses, "since Marvin and Sheila didn't do it, there must have been someone else in the house with Leroy. I can see Leroy, gun out, searching the kitchen where he knew Eileen kept her savings. He didn't realize that Eileen had deposited her cash in the bank.

"He is holding the gun ready in case someone else in the house (Eileen, for instance) surprises him. He's opening drawers and looking into closets and cupboards. At some point, he sets the gun down, and the murderer seizes the opportunity, picks up the weapon, and shoots Leroy in cold blood. Both burglars are wearing gloves, so fingerprints aren't a problem. But what if Leroy had some funds to repay the person waiting in the car at the Burdick Street intersection. The assailant takes several seconds to rifle Leroy's pockets, find whatever cash is on his person, and exit through the front door. That would give Sheila, who never came into the house, a head start in the dark to get away and out of sight of the burglar, just like she said."

Jeremy rose and stood between Moses and Marvin. He clapped them both on the back and said, "Moses, what you outlined fits the sequence and the evidence. The crucial point is that Leroy handled the gun until he set it down to open a drawer to rifle papers and such.

"Marvin," said Jeremy. "There is a lot to hope for in Moses' theory. I can face a jury, confident in explaining your commitment to Sheila and her reputation, so that is why you…"

"Lied during the early days of Marvin's arrest," said Moses, finishing Jeremy's thought. "Unfortunately, that is about the weakest defense imaginable. The prosecution will shred Marvin, whom you have painted as an honest, upstanding citizen. They will ask the jury which version of the shooting is the most realistic. The one where Marvin is taking the blame for shooting Leroy to protect Sheila or the version where he actually did shoot Leroy as all the evidence proves beyond a shadow of a doubt."

"What am I left with," said Jeremy. "I don't dare put Sheila on the stand. She heard the shot but did not witness the murder, and under pressure, she would have to admit that she believed it was Marvin who used the gun."

Moses eyed Marvin, stoic but losing ground even as he seemed relieved to have told the truth. "Jeremy," he said. "Get Eileen and Sheila in here tomorrow and make sure Marvin and Sheila's stories are laid out, one to the other. They both must be convinced of the innocence of the other. I hope that will make Eileen feel better as well."

"That makes sense, OK with you, Marvin?" said Jeremy.

"Sure," said Marvin. "Tell Mom to bring a book for me to read."

"You'll get a load of school books if I know Eileen," said Moses.

"Fine," said Marvin.

Jeremy had been pondering what he could do to help.

"I'll work on the appeal to treat Marvin as an adult. Moses, I know you're doing all the work on this case free of charge, but I guess it is up to you to prove your theory of another thief being in the house that night."

Moses sat back in his chair and said, "My hands were tied up until now, but I'm convinced we're on the right track.

"I won't kid you, Marvin; it will be tough," said Moses. "Leroy wore gloves, and I'm assuming his accomplice also did. There are no fingerprints to trace. I'll need help tracking Mr. X down. I'll call Harry Martensen to give me a hand."

"Keep track of your hours and Harry's. They're reimbursable by the public defender's office."

***

That night, New Year's Eve, Moses hired a taxi to pick up Eileen and take them to The Paradise Club for dinner.

Entertainment consisted of dueling pianos. The pianists began playing at 9:30 p.m. Moses and Eileen sat down to dinner ten minutes later. Eileen wasn't sure she wanted to go out, but Moses told her he had much to report.

Eileen told Moses that Mr. Fulton had called and asked if she could meet with Marvin, Sheila, and Jeremy in the morning. Moses let her know what the meeting would entail. He warned her she would hear the events on Christmas Eve, at least Marvin's, Sheila's, and Curtis' covert activities that had gone awry. He downplayed the mattress rendezvous as much as possible. Eileen smiled wryly. "I guess we can't throw stones, can we, Moses," she said.

"I should say not," said Moses. "Give the boy a package of rubbers as a present when he's released."

"I wish I could laugh about that, but I can't," said Eileen. "I know he didn't murder my scum husband, and I think you know it now as well, but he's still in terrible trouble, isn't he?"

"That sadly is very true," said Moses. "The prosecution can prove beyond a reasonable doubt that Marvin did commit murder. MARVIN WILL BE CONVICTED unless I can find the person who shot Leroy in the back."

"It seems nearly impossible, Moses. Dance with me. I don't want to make a scene, but I need to hold you. They're playing *Nature Boy*, a nice slow number.

Dinner arrived at the table and was as enjoyable as the dance. Council Hawes approached the table as the couple waited for dessert. "How was dinner, Mrs.Simmons?"

"Very tasty, Mr. Hawes, thank you," said Eileen.

"How is your son holding up?" said Council.

Eileen pressed her fist to her mouth, nearly choking. "You know about Marvin?"

"The star basketball player on the team at Central High?" said Council. "We can't wait until he gets back on the court. How is the case coming along, Moses?"

"There is a lot of unfavorable circumstantial evidence against Marvin," said Moses. "If you read about it in the

Gazette, you should consider it carefully, with a grain of salt."

"One circumstance that never should have occurred," said the club owner, "is that this fine lady should have ever gotten mixed up with Leroy."

"They have been separated a while," said Moses. "Eileen recently filed for divorce before he was killed."

Council nodded to Moses, then shook his head from side to side. "I've seen enough during the war that now I try to live a charitable life. I gave Leroy more than a few meals when he came around for a handout. Black or white; people got to eat."

"Leroy was a pretty good father to our son when Marvin was small," said Eileen. "They had a falling out as Marvin became a teenager, and Leroy left the house, but Marvin would never have wished him dead."

"Let me assure you, Eileen," said Council, "all of Marvin's classmates that work here part-time support him. They talk about his achievements at school and on the basketball court.

"They asked if they could take up a collection for his defense fund. I emptied the jar on your table before opening the club tonight. Looking around, you'll see dollars and change in most of the jars on the tables. The big jar at the cashier's counter is also filling up. We're a community and must look out for our brothers and sisters."

Eileen cried into her napkin. Moses put an arm around her shoulder. Eileen looked up at Council but could not speak. Council Hawes raised his arms to get the diners' attention and started clapping. People stood and joined the applause for Moses and Eileen. Even some of the white folks participated. Eileen stood, steadied herself, and waved to the tables, mouthing "thank you" to the diners.

Eileen dragged Moses back onto the dance floor, and they danced until midnight when the pianists struck up a duet of *Aude Lang Syne*. Moses kissed Eileen's trembling lips. "I wish this ordeal was finished, and Marvin could celebrate with us," said Eileen.

"Patience, Honey," said Moses."

And a whole lot of prayer.

24 | The Bug

"How's it going, Harry? Does Sarah like the new automatic washer?" Said Moses on the phone with Harry Martensen.

Harry was a gadget man, a tinkerer. Moses could hear the excitement in his voice. "We went with a GE All-Electric Washer and Wringer. It's a dream. You fill it with clothes, add hot water to the line, add the soap flakes, and turn it on. When the cycle completes, you run the clothes through the attached wringer on the machine and hang them up to dry."

"That's great. It didn't take you long to spend that check I sent you," said Moses

"Long enough, Sarah has a long memory of the difficult time her parents had during the depression. My father-in-law was shot protecting the railroad yard in Chicago from poachers, the only job he could get. Sarah is one frugal woman as a result."

"The surveillance and photographs of that Shakespeare executive's dalliance paid off for the wife and us. You were a big help. Thanks," said Moses.

"There is only one problem with the washer," said Harry. "I'm now the chief laundry man in the family. Sarah attends graduate classes. I was hoping the washer would help with her time crunch. But no, laundry came over to my list, even though I'm also taking correspondence courses in accounting and bookkeeping."

"Who is babysitting the boys during Sarah's time in class?" said Moses.

"We hire Joanne, a negro teenage girl, to babysit. Her family owns the farm next to ours here in Gobles. She is saving to attend nursing school after high school."

Moses took no offense. If anyone treated someone of his race fairly, it would be Harry and Sarah.

"Things have turned serious for Marvin. The prosecutor established the murder of Leroy at the preliminary hearing and presented the physical evidence against Marvin. The hearing took twenty minutes. Marvin was bound over for trial.

"Jeremy's appeal to have Marvin moved back to juvenile status has failed. His trial is scheduled to start with jury selection. Jeremy hopes we'll have something new to present at the pretrial hearing."

"There's no need to twist my arm, Moses," said Harry. "I want to help any way I can, for free if that is what it takes."

"We'll bill the public defender's office," said Moses. "You're on the clock. Track your expenses as well."

"Now you're talking, Moses. I'm eyeing an electric mangle. If I'm going to be doing the wash, I want my slacks and shirts to make me look like a lawyer instead of a parts salesman."

"Enough on the telephone," said Moses. "Let's quit racking up long-distance charges and meet at my place tomorrow for breakfast; I'll make the eggs. How do you like them?"

"Over easy," said Harry, "I'll stop off at the bakery and pick up a couple of sweet rolls. See you at seven so I can get to work by eight."

***

Moses walked around the corner from his apartment on the way to work and stopped at Police Headquarters. The duty sergeant indicated that Ross Kirkpatrick might still be dressing in the locker room. Ross' shift corresponded to Moses's 2nd shift work schedule.

"Hi, Ross," said Moses. "Another day, another dollar?"

"So it seems," said Ross. "Gonna be cold tonight, in the teens."

"Plenty of heat in the squad car. Maybe it will be a quiet night for you," said Moses. "Any progress on locating Owen Kressbach?"

"I'm afraid not," said Ross. "Apparently, he was spotted in Philadelphia but eluded police. Last week, we received a report from Dayton that he was there. No luck catching him, though."

"He's a slippery bastard, for sure," said Moss. "Heading this way. Hopefully, he'll stop in Kalamazoo to get paid."

"Watch your step," said Ross. "A guy in Iowa that Owen beat up lost an eye. No witnesses and charges were dropped for lack of evidence.

"According to you, Kressbach is probably armed and even more dangerous now. Call my home if you can't reach me at the station for backup."

***

That evening, Moses spent most of his shift replacing a connecting rod in a '46 Chevrolet Style Master Sedan engine.

In the morning, Moses answered the knock on the door and let Harry in. The egg carton was open next to the hot plate, and the table was set. The frying pan and the butter were ready to go.

"If you don't mind, Moses, I'll fry the eggs," said Harry. "I don't trust a boxer to turn an egg. I was a short-order cook for my stepfather's resort in Chatanooga before the crash in '29."

Harry was so fast at cooking the eggs that Moses barely had time to finish making the coffee and butter the toast to put on their plates. The two friends talked while eating their sweet rolls.

"We only have a few weeks to find Owen Kressbach," said Moses. "That's the new goal. Leroy's out of the picture, but I'll see what I can discover at his flop house. He must have had dealings with other users staying there. We also have two women to find and interview."

Harry shrugged, "Kressbach will be tough to find. We don't know where to look. Are you talking about traveling out of state to Philadelphia or Dayton to pick up his trail?"

"I can only do so much without a car," said Moses. "My gut says that he will come to get me. We're both loose ends in his mind."

"Yeah," said Harry, "But when will he get here. You say we're short on time."

"Maybe we can entice him," said Moses. "Let me think about that."

"Don't take too long. You think Owen was with Leroy at Eileen's house?" said Harry.

"Not really. Leroy was dumber than stone. He was a fair grifter but a terrible conman. Owen Kressbach has made a name nationwide without imprisonment. He's intelligent. Owen gets others to do the dirty work, like Billy and Leroy.

"I can explain what happened in the house that night based on my observations and Marvin's statement. Someone was in the home with Leroy. The burglars must have come in through the back door while Marvin and Sheila were bouncing on the mattress in the garage. They wore gloves and were looking for cash everywhere because the hiding place Leroy knew about was empty. At some point, Leroy sets down his gun to open a drawer. The other burglar picks up the weapon and shoots Leroy in the back.

"When Sheila hears the gunshot, she panics and runs off in the snowstorm toward her house to the west without a flashlight. Leroy's accomplice (murderer) throws the gun down and takes off through the front door."

"So, was it Owen Kressbach?" said Harry.

"I doubt it, seriously. Maybe. We won't know until we hear Owen confess. I don't think Owen was in the house because Owen and Leroy got along like oil and water. I think they each hated the other, which is hardly conducive to cooperation.

"Owen sent the two burglars to Eileen's house, hoping to recoup the money Leroy had conned out of Owen and the Strike Security Committee."

"Either way, we have to hear Owen Kressbach's story."

Harry poured more coffee into their two mugs while he pondered Moses' report. "That all seems possible, Moses, but what about after everyone left the house."

"OK, take Sheila. She was in the lead, without a flashlight, freezing, and just wanted to get to her house. She saw no one except the man waiting outside the car parked at the Burdick/Parsons Streets intersection. She was on the north side of the street, and because of the storm, the man in the car never saw her., which is probably the only reason she made it home safely.

"Then the murder comes next. We only know about that person from what Marvin has reported. When Marvin left the house, he saw a figure in the distance, but it vanished as the snow and wind intensified. Marvin saw a figure near the car and fired Leroy's gun, hoping the person would surrender and also to distribute gunfire residue on his coat to cover for Sheila, whom he assumed had shot Leroy."

Harry nodded in agreement. "I follow you, Harry. Why didn't the police follow up on any of these possibilities?"

"Three reasons I can think of, Harry," said Moses.

"One, the patrolmen who detained Marvin never saw the car that Marvin and Sheila claim was ever at the intersection where they arrested Marvin.

"Two, They have overwhelming evidence against Marvin. The burglars were careful and quiet. Eileen couldn't point to anything being out of place in the house.

"Three, Marvin fits the profile of a killer in their minds."

"By that, you mean Marvin is the wrong color," said Harry.

"You said it, Harry, not me, but history backs up the premise, even up north here in Kalamazoo."

Harry sat quietly with Moses until he finished his coffee. "I better get going, Moses," said Harry. "What's our strategy."

"We used a wiretap in a few cases when I was on the force. Can you outfit a kit for us? Our only connection with

Owen Kressbach is the meeting he attended with someone in management at the Shakespeare Offices.

"From the police sightings of Owen, we have to assume he is heading this way. He'll probably meet with his superior when he arrives, and we need to be in on that meeting secretly."

"Mmmm," said Harry, "That will take some doing. The police would assign men to listen to conversations in that conference room 24/7. Since it will just be you and me, we'll have to recruit more help."

"Too risky," said Moses. "We can assume that the meeting will occur at night after the office personnel has gone home."

"Alright," said Harry. "So, anytime between 6:00 p.m. and midnight, we want to capture a conversation. We will gather what we've recorded daily and reset everything for the next night. I'll work on it and let you know what I come up with.

"Regardless, I'll have a list of equipment for you by tomorrow."

"Good," said Moses. "We can do it. You'll have to take the six to nine shift. I'll take the ten to midnight shift.

***

Harry stopped in at the apartment the following day. He told Moses, "The tape recorder needs to be ordered from the company in Chicago with a rush delivery charge of $85.00."

Equipment list:
    Magnecorder PT6 reel-to-reel recorder $235
    Magnecord Amplifier A20 $185

200 feet two or four wire cable	$25
Headphones - Miniature Microphone	$110
Misc connectors	$15
Delivery Charge	$85
Total:	$570

Moses dialed Jeremy Fulton's office, which approved the equipment list billed to the public defender's office.

"Harry, can you handle ordering the equipment?" asked Moses.

"Yes," said Harry.

"Try to get that tape recorder and amplifier here by tomorrow, even if they drive it. I'll scout the place this afternoon before work. If we get the equipment list gathered by tomorrow, we should meet at 10:00 p.m. for the installation. Then we'll be ready for the meeting. Fingers crossed, Owen hasn't been and gone before then."

The Shakespeare Administration building[38] was four blocks north of Moses' apartment. From there, the Cities Service Station where Moses worked was only two blocks southeast. Moses left an hour early for work and walked around the block containing the Shakespeare Factory and Administration Offices. The railroad tracks in the back of the factory ran right along the shipping dock, fifty feet away. Moses walked around the front of the factory, wondering about the four-story office building sandwiched between the Admin building and the factory, clearly not associated with either Shakespeare facility. Moses walked into the lobby. The marquee listed ten companies and their suite numbers. Several of the suites were listed as vacant. Then the receptionist asked if she could help.

"Do you have a maintenance department that takes care of the building? Everything looks clean and neat."

"Cybil Coates comes in every night to empty wastebaskets, sweep and mop the floors, and shovel the walk when necessary," said the receptionist. "She starts on the fourth floor and works her way down. She's probably handling the trash upstairs now."

Moses put on his best swagger. "I'd like to see the vacant office on the fourth floor and maybe the one on the first floor. Can Cybil let me in to look around?"

"Those two suites are each listed at $350.00/month, unfurnished. That's probably beyond your price range."

"That is a bit steep for today's market, but I would still like to see those two offices."

"Cybil has keys; I'll leave it up to her."

On the fourth floor, Moses found the cleaning lady working in Suite 440. Cybil looked up and grinned. "Moses Webb, this is an honor. You look lost. Can I help?"

"Do we know each other?" said Moses.

"You went out with my sister, Denise, about a year ago. Denise Coates, remember?"

Moses remembered. Denise had the longest nails that had ever scratched him. She dug into his back so hard he had bloody scabs the next day. Lovemaking was not supposed to be painful, in his opinion.

"Say," said Cybil. "Is that boy Marvin Simmons still in jail? I had him in my Sunday School class. Sweetest boy in the city, if you ask me. I don't believe he killed that white man. No siree. That is not his nature."

"I agree with you, Cybil," said Moses. "I'm working to get him out of jail."

"A favor, right," said Cybil. "I've heard about your Northside favors."

"You could help me by letting me into the empty suite on the 1st floor. Can we go take a look?"

When Moses entered the room, he knew it would work as a base of operations. "How long has the office been empty?" he asked.

"I'd say seven months or so," said Cybil. "There has been no action on it for the last two months. The price is too high."

"That vent near the ceiling over there. Is that hooked into the heating system?"

"Naw, it's just a vent to the outside. The heating system is in the core behind you."

"How about utilities."

"Air conditioning and electricity are covered for the whole building, so there is nothing to turn on or off. All of that is included in the rent. I bet they would come down in price to help with the fuel and electric bills."

"Keys?"

"I have an extra set. Look, Moses, I think all these questions are not because you want to rent this place. What exactly are you up to, and who is the favor for?"

"I am working on Marvin's defense and require this space as a headquarters for at least two or three weeks. I need after-hours access to this room between 6:00 p.m. and 8:00 a.m. Does anyone work long hours at night in the building?"

"No, Moses, half the building is rented out to insurance agencies, two suites are Marketing agencies, and the rest are vacant. I've never seen anyone in the building except me after 5:30. How much trouble can I get into helping you?"

"Honestly, there is a small risk to you if you help. I would ask you to measure that against the assistance you would provide for that highly thought of Sunday School student we both know."

Cybil went to the window facing the street and ran a finger along the sill. Then she turned back to Moses. "I'll help Marvin. That's the thing about the jobs us folks get in this city. There is always another one around the corner that no one else wants."

Cybil loaned Moses the key to the office suite and the back door leading to the building parking lot next to the tracks. Then Moses walked on to work.

***

Moses called Nusbaums on Harry's lunch break and told Harry about the Hamilton Building office suite he had hijacked from an agreeable supporter of Marvin Simmons. Then he asked Harry if the equipment would be ready when he finished his shift.

"I need to pick up a few more things from the hardware store and Radioshack in the morning. The good news is that the tape recorder will arrive tomorrow around two o'clock. They had another delivery planned for Detroit, so we are piggybacking off that shipment."

"I guess we'll have to put off the installation until tomorrow night," said Moses.

"Actually, Moses, we need to do most of the setup during the day when we can access the conference room in the Shakespeare Admin. building."

"Oh, you're right," said Moses. "I'll bring home a second pair of coveralls for you. Maybe we can pose as maintenance men for the telephone or electric company and ask to use the conference room. How much time do we need to hide the mike and such."

"No more than a half an hour, tops," said Harry.

"OK," said Moses. "Let's meet at noon in the Shakespeare parking lot on your lunch break before I go to work. We'll walk in, plant the mike, and get out. Tomorrow night, we'll hopefully hook up the other end in the office I didn't rent today.

***

The cable coil hung over the shoulder of the man in blue overalls carrying a large toolbox into the Shakespeare offices. A bulky negro, also in coveralls with a lunchbox, trailed behind. The receptionist interrupted her typing to glance at Harry, then continued typing.

Harry addressed the receptionist. "We're here to install the new circuit, repeater, and handset in the conference room."

The typist looked the two men over, annoyed that they weren't the usual flirtatious, well-dressed businessmen who stopped at her station. One of them looked big, dumb, and dark. "Down the hall, third door. Knock, if anyone answers, you'll have to wait or try later. Everyone is out to lunch; you should be OK."

Harry scanned the room quickly once Moses closed and locked the door. The light fixtures over the conference table were fancy enough that the miniature microphone could be mounted inconspicuously. The room had a soffit around the perimeter and two light fixtures above the table. The soffit also contained fluorescents behind a baffle that gave the room a soft glow, perfect for hiding the cable running from the microphone.

The two went to work. After attaching the leads, Harry used electrical tape to secure the microphone to the light fixture nearest the window. As Harry worked on the microphone, Moses tucked the cable down in the baffle until he came to the corner above the window. Harry hooked up a drill machine and locked in a drill bit large enough for the cable. He opened the high awning window and drilled a hole through the aluminum frame.

Moses, meanwhile, used white electrical tape to neatly mask the cable running from the baffle down the soffit and over to the corner of the room and down to the window where Harry was drilling.

Harry cut the cable, leaving twelve inches, and fed the excess through the drilled hole, letting it hang outside the building.

Finally, both men packed up the toolbox and wiped their footprints off the tabletop. Moses looked over Harry's handiwork and his tape job. He picked up his lunchbox and slapped Harry on the back. "They'll never see it," he said.

They walked out of the building. Moses waved to the receptionist. She didn't look up from her typing or acknowledge him at all.

"Sometimes being invisible has its advantages," said Moses as they stripped off their coveralls, folded them, and put them in a bag for Moses to carry to the Cities Station.

"See you at ten tonight, Harry," said Moses. "Thanks a million."

"Moses, my friend," said Harry. "I did a lot of improvising on Iwo Jima, piecing parts together to get the planes off the ground with working radios. That was great training for this spy business. My pleasure."

***

After his shift, Moses walked over to the Hamilton Building. Harry was parked in the back. The Hamilton building was ten feet apart from the Shakespeare Administration offices on the west side. A driveway on the east side of the Hamilton led to the parking lot in the rear, separating it from the Shakespeare factory.

The two waited half an hour, but no one seemed to be patrolling the Shakespeare complex. The court order restricting the picketing of the union was being honored.

They used Cybil's spare set of keys to access the rear entrance of the Hamilton building and suite 104. Cybil had supplied a table and two chairs. Moses set the box of accessories on the table. Harry opened the tape recorder and put it on top of the amplifier. Moses showed Harry the vent in the wall leading to the ten-foot space between the Hamilton and the Shakespeare Administration building. Harry went outside and pulled the cable that Moses fed through the vent. A floodlight was mounted under the eave at the front southeast corner of the Shakespeare Administration building. Another flood light under the eave of the northwest corner of the Hamilton building illuminated the parking lot. The space between the two buildings stayed dark.

It took Moses twenty minutes to locate a closet in the Hamilton building basement that contained a step ladder. He brought the ladder out to Harry, waiting beneath the window of the Shakespeare building where the two men had left cable hanging in the afternoon.

Harry connected the cable from the Hamilton building using the step ladder, ensuring the contacts were well twisted together and wrapped with electrical tape to waterproof the splice. Moses used flexible putty to stick the cable to the Shakespeare building, running the cable along the crevices in the brick in a zig-zag pattern down to ground level. Loose gravel and scrub weeds grew in the sun-starved area between the buildings. Moses kicked gravel over the cable along its path to the Hamilton building. Harry used the putty to hold the cable to the brick wall of the Hamilton building.

The black cable stood out in contrast to the light color of the brick on both buildings. Harry suggested they cover the cable snaking up both building walls with the dull grey putty. They would have to see how their camouflage worked in daylight.

Next, Harry mounted the 7" reel on the tape recorder and showed Moses how to thread the tape through the recording heads to the empty 7" reel. After explaining how to start the recorder, Harry put on the headphones and tested the setup.

"That should do it," he said. "I'm ninety percent sure the system will work, but it would be nice to test it."

"How about if I sneak in here tomorrow on my way to work. I'll start the recorder, go around to the front entrance of the Shakespeare Admin. building, and give the receptionist some excuse about leaving a tool behind. Once I enter the conference room, I'll recite the pledge of allegiance. That should give us a test run."

"Good, Moses," said Harry. "Move around the room while you're giving the pledge. If we have to adjust our setup or add a second microphone, it will be best to know that now."

Moses arrived back at the Shakespeare Administration building ten minutes after twelve noon. Again, the place was deserted as the office workers had left for lunch. The receptionist glanced at him and frowned as he started to explain. She didn't wait for Moses to finish his explanation but just flipped her hand toward the conference room and continued typing.

After returning to the Hamilton building, Moses replayed the taped pledge. The volume of the sound varied as he moved around the room, but his voice was intelligible throughout the recitation.

25 | Grand Jury

Caliper mounting brackets, attaching hardware, bearing adapters, rotors, and calipers for the '44 Chevy. Moses aligned the parts and hand tools he needed on his workbench. Then, he used the lift to raise the car four feet and descended into the pit to work on the rear brakes. He finished the left rear brake and turned to start on the right brake when the supervisor's voice announced over the loudspeaker that Moses needed to report to the office.

Two policemen were waiting with the supervisor. Moses didn't know either one. They were both young, possibly new recruits. The taller one looked Moses over. "Moses Webb?" he said. Moses nodded. "We have a subpoena. Your presence is requested before Judge Theodore Smith, appointed by Governor Sigler as a one-man grand jury, to investigate the riot on December 1st at the Shakespeare factory. We'll take you to his temporary office in the courthouse and bring you back."

Moses looked at his supervisor. "I guess they've got me, Boss. I'll be back as soon as the judge lets me leave.."

"Not to worry, Moses," said the supervisor, Frank.

Moses sat in the back seat of the squad car. When the car began to move, he tapped the shoulder of the officer in the passenger seat. "We should stop off at my apartment. I can pick up the documentation the judge will want. My apartment is literally a block from the station. Take me five minutes to collect. Stop in front of the Paints and Oils store on Burdick."

The driver nodded and obliged Moses, who spent eight minutes sorting all the photographs Harry had supplied in his apartment.

The policeman parked on Church Street next to the Michigan Avenue Courthouse. Moses was led downstairs to the basement level in the courthouse and along a corridor to a conference room containing a ten-seat conference table. A fair-featured man in his fifties wearing a dark blue pinstripe double-breasted suit motioned Moses to a chair to his right. The table was covered with papers, and the whole left side contained neat stacks of documents.

To the judge's left sat a stenographic court reporter. She had wavy, shoulder-length blond hair and sat stiff-backed and ready to type. The judge nodded at the reporter and began the interview. "Record the date. The time is 5:20 p.m. Present in the room is Judge Theodore Smith, municipal judge for the city of Jackson and acting head of the Grand Jury investigating the Shakespeare Company riot on December 1st, 1948.

"In the room is Moses Webb, a Cities Service Station mechanic. Mr. Webb works at 355 E. Kalamazoo Avenue and resides above the Paint and Oils Store on Burdick Street.

"Mr. Webb," said the judge. "Do you solemnly swear or affirm that your testimony will be the truth, the whole truth and nothing but the truth, so help you God?"

"I do," said Moses, his right hand resting on the Bible the judge slid before him.

"Then I will proceed. My name is Theodore Smith. Governor Sigler decided that a judge outside of Kalamazoo County would be more impartial in considering the criminal conduct of persons involved with the strike and not biased by the local political crossfire.

"I know a little of your background, Mr. Webb. A policeman from 1942 to '45. Elevated to detective in late 1945. In October 1946, you were shot foiling a drugstore robbery in the Eastside neighborhood. You retired from the force and now work as an automobile mechanic. Do you have anything to add?"

Moses shook his head.

"Let the record show Mr. Webb has nothing to add to the summary of his recent biography," said the judge.

The Honorable Theodore Smith reshuffled the papers directly in front of him. "So, let's begin," he said. "I am holding ten photographs marked with your name that I received from Kalamazoo Chief of Police Howard W. Hoyt.

"The photos primarily feature a man standing on a street corner in front of the Michigan Central Railroad Station, participating in the illegal street sales of wristwatches and belts, and what purports to be drugs."

"That is Leroy Simmons," said Moses, "a known grifter, conman, and drug dealer that worked that corner."

"How is this man connected with the Shakespeare factory riot?"

"He was there, your honor," said Moses. "Leroy worked for a short time at the factory and had a union card that allowed him into the union meetings leading up to the riot."

"I see," said the judge. "Then I'll issue a subpoena for this man to appear, and we'll find out who directed his activities."

"Unfortunately, your Honor," said Moses. "Leroy was murdered on Christmas Eve. His son is being unjustly held for the…" The judge interrupted.

"The person primarily represented in these photographs is dead. Testimony, photos, and any evidence regarding his activities can no longer be corroborated. These photos were not taken at the site of the riot and would most likely be inadmissible as evidence in court.

"A couple of these photos are marked as significant. Why Mr. Webb?"

"Photo No. 7 shows a woman scratching Leroy Simmons. Photo No 8. Shows a man kicking Leroy as he lays on the ground. They are significant because the second person in each photo is not buying or selling anything. They interact violently with Leroy Simmons and should be investigated as possible murder suspects. Marvin Simmons, the teenager being held for the murder of Leroy Simmons, should be released pending the investigation of the pictured suspects.

"Even if what you say is true, Mr. Webb, these persons must be investigated by the prosecuting attorney and police. I do not see where they are pertinent to the case I am researching, the Shakespeare Riot. I was tasked with determining guilt for property damage and personal injuries that day.

"I can clearly tie the Union plans and sequence of events that caused the factory's destruction to the union leaders. It has been challenging to acquire testimony about individuals onsite who caused the violence or are willing to testify against fellow union members that they observed destroying property. The plans of the CIO union leaders, the flying squadron from River Rouge, the evidence of destruction, and the medical records of the injured clearly point to a conspiracy to cause havoc by the leadership of the CIO and local union. That is indictable, and I intend to charge the union leaders, even if I cannot gather evidence of individual participation in the crimes."

The judge gathered the photos and squared them into a neat pile. Moses guessed the pile would be aligned with the other document stacks on the table and immediately forgotten.

"Your Honor," said Moses. "If you look again at photo No. 8, the man in that photograph kicking Leroy Simmons is Owen Kressbach. He is currently wanted on suspicion of the murder of a local policeman named Alex Madden.

"I witnessed Owen Kressbach instigating much of the violence during the riot.

"My associate is also willing to testify that he witnessed Owen Kressbach entering the Shakespeare Administration building late at night days after the riot. Kressbach possibly met with an executive to review and plan the next set of disruptions to be blamed on the union. The police have reports from multiple regions where this mercenary for hire has used disruptive tactics to discredit peaceful union protests."

Judge Smith pulled out photo No. 8 and studied it, rubbing his brow. "I would be interested in interviewing this individual."

"When the police catch Owen Kressbach, I'll make sure you are informed," said Moses.

"Good," said Judge Smith. "You may also be called to testify in court. In the meantime, I'll continue to pursue the union leadership and the communist influences that led up to the riot."

"But, Your Honor," said Moses. "Owen Kressbach and the person he met at the Shakespeare Administration building are the furthest from communists you could imagine. Kressbach is a psychopath, and the executive, whoever he is, is profit-motivated. I believe their objective is to discredit the peaceful union protest of conditions at the Shakespeare factory, and so far, they are succeeding."

Judge Smith stood and threw down the pile of photographs. "There is no evidence on this table that supports your supposition regarding the events on December 1st.

"The red scare in this country is real, Mr. Webb. Like it or not, communists are working to break down our institutions and foment chaos.

"I have documentation that William Shakespeare Jr., president of the Shakespeare Company, is a declared socialist. Hearsay has been provided to me that he has communist leanings. He may be the executive meeting with this Kressbach person."

"Do you really think," said Moses, "the company owner would sabotage his own company to provide an avenue for socialism to take root in this county?"

"The mindset of communists can't be rationalized. We must be wary and ready in a lawful manner to counteract their tactics. You're dismissed, Mr. Webb. Thank you for your candor and former service on the police force."

On the ride back to the Cities station, Moses considered the testimony he had just given to the one-man grand jury headed by Judge Smith. The judge was right. Moses needed evidence.

Owen Kressbach had better show up.

***

Moses asked the officer who drove him back to the service station to get a message to Ross Kirkpatrick to get in touch with him, hopefully in person, ASAP.

After work, Moses hurried over to the Hamilton building and found Harry using a flashlight in the darkened room, reading the latest Rex Stout - Nero Wolfe novel "And Be a Villain."

I didn't expect you to still be here, Harry," said Moses. "I thought you would just set the machine to record and leave it for me to turn off when I got here."

"I just wanted to ensure everything is working as you want," said Harry.

"Anything happening?" said Moses.

"Not a whisper or a pin drop, Moses."

Moses brought Harry up to date regarding the grand jury interview.

"I better get going, Moses," said Harry. "Janet's eyeballs are filling up." (Janet was Harry's milk cow that needed to be milked twice daily.)

Moses slipped on the headphones, read five pages in the detective story Harry had left on the table, and fell asleep.

***

The next evening, Moses finished adjusting the brakes on the '44 Chevy with a brake spanner, turning the spanner clockwise to bring the shoes closer to the drum. He climbed out of the pit and found Ross Kirkpatrick and a second policeman waiting patiently.

"Hi, Moses," said Ross. "Meet my new partner, Craig Sheid. I've been riding solo since Alex Madden. You wanted to see me?" said Ross.

Moses shook Craig's hand, another rookie. Ross seemed to get stuck mentoring rookies.

"Thanks for stopping by, Ross. Nice to meet you, Craig. Watch this guy's back, will you?" said Moses as he gently punched Ross' shoulder in jest. "I testified before the one-man grand jury yesterday. I'm still not getting any traction with my effort to attain the release of Marvin Simmons.

"Yeah," said Ross. "It's a shame. Detective Shotmire, The D.A., Judge Smith, and U.S. Congressman Clare Hoffman all seem deaf regarding the innocence of Marvin Simmons and the guilt of Owen Kressbach."

"If we can apprehend Owen Kressbach, maybe they will be convinced by his confession," said Moses.

"If you get a confession," Ross noted.

"That's why I wanted to talk to you," said Moses. "I am hoping that Owen will appear here in Kalamazoo and meet with the same person he did before the riot at the Shakespeare Administration building."

"Hold on a minute, Moses. Craig, use the phone in the office and ask the duty sergeant for any updates on Owen Kressbach's apprehension. Thanks."

Craig walked over to the office.

"What are you and your favors up to Moses," said Ross.

"If Kressbach does show up," said Moses. "I'll record the conversation and call you to nab the bastard."

Ross looked shocked. "Now, wait a minute, Moses. Are you telling me you're operating a wiretap and recording conversations at the Shakespeare Administration offices?"

"Who said anything about a wiretap," said Moses. "I'm just trying to help you arrest a fugitive, and you better come-a-runnin' when I call."

Ross Kirkpatrick scratched his chin. "You know that any evidence you obtain will be thrown right out of court, but we'll be there. Count on us. Leave your gun at home, Moses. I don't want to put you in a cell next to Marvin's."

"You know I never carry that gun," said Moses.

"I know, Moses. We'll be there."

***

After work, Moses walked to the Hamilton building, used the hidden key to let himself into the building, and then found the key Harry had left on the first-floor suite door header to enter the office. As arranged, the tape recorder reels were turning. Moses reversed the tape and then played it forward until Harry's voice sounded, giving today's date and time, 6:00 p.m. After Harry's date announcement, the tape wound ahead in silence.

Moses settled back in the chair, ready to hit the record button if the headphones indicated a conversation in the Shakespeare administration conference room. Forty minutes later, he laid the book on the table and closed his eyes. The detective story was good, but it had been a long day, and the quiet in the building made for heavy eyelids.

At 1:30 a.m., Moses shook himself awake, turned off the lights, locked the office and back door, and walked home.

***

Eileen lay quietly next to Moses in his bed. She wanted to shake Moses and tell him to get up and investigate. He should look for Owen on the streets of Kalamazoo or borrow her car and drive down to Elkhart, Indiana, a known haunt of Owen Kressbach, according to research provided by Ross, Moses' friend in the police department. She wanted to yell, *Get my boy out of that jail.*

When Moses stirred, he looked over at Eileen, sitting on the side of the bed. She had discarded the tank top, one of Moses' undershirts. Moses took her left hand and pulled her around to face him, admiring her right breast and taut nipple.

"I'm getting dressed for my scheduled visit with Marvin," said Eileen. "Are you coming?"

"I'll walk over to the station with you, but instead of seeing Marvin, I'll check on any updates in the search for Owen Kressbach. Then, I want to work out at the 'Y.' It's Saturday, and there won't be anyone in the Hamilton building. After my workout, I'll stake out the Shakespeare conference room."

"Alright," said Eileen."Sheila is meeting me at the station. I'll leave early to give them some time. I'll do some grocery shopping and bring them to your place. Is that OK?"

"That's more than okay. I hope you don't feel I have kidnapped you. You have no obligation. As much as I want you, I realize the time we have had together is unusual, to say the least."

"Oh, Moses. If you only knew how much I want to be with you. I haven't felt this way in fifteen years. I know it's a dream, a bubble that will burst. Let's put it this way. I believe Marvin's troubles are keeping both of us balanced

[230]

between our dream time together and the horror we're trying to fight."

Moses looked at her, admiring her strength, her chin up, her shoulders straight, even though he knew she cried often for her son. He swung his legs over the side of the bed and embraced her. He pulled Eileen to her feet, so his hug took full advantage of their chest-to-chest contact, and he kissed her. When he pulled away, he smiled and said, "I'll make the coffee."

***

Moses beat on the punching bag in the weight room of the YMCA. He didn't alternate between fists, as is the standard method of exercising the timing of jabs. Moses knew his left hand could never keep up the rhythm. Instead, he worked on increasing the speed of his right-hand punch. The staccato sound of the bag bouncing against his fist became ever faster and louder. An observer might swear he was using both hands. By necessity, Moses had developed the speed and strength of his right arm and shoulder to compensate for his indefensible left side.

Moses looked at the stationary bikes with fleeting disdain as he climbed the stairs to the gym. He just never got into pedaling a bike that went nowhere. On the court, a pickup basketball game was in progress.

Basketball worked every muscle with a purpose. Basketball: a thinking man's sport, a team effort, and a reward no matter the player's role. Shooting, passing, blocking, rebounding, or dribbling. Moses lined up with four others to take on the winners, and soon, he was running and finding his niche on his team.

Exhausted from three winning games in a row, Moses showered and dressed. He headed to the Hamilton building; the itch at the nape of his neck gave him a sense of foreboding.

26 | The Recording

There was a man in dark slacks and a tan sweater climbing the back stairs in the Hamilton building when Moses entered. The office worker must have had weekday work to finish. He was upstairs when Moses replaced the building key under the rock outside the back entry door.

While unlocking the office suite door containing the taper recorder, Moses decided to scrounge up another chair, so he took two more comfortable chairs from the reception area. No one would notice on a Saturday, and he would return them before leaving for the night. Once in the room, Moses removed his cribbage board from his leather jacket and set up the pegs for two players.

At six o'clock, Harry arrived. Moses was glad to see him. No sounds had emanated from the amplifier all afternoon. "Hi, Harry," said Moses. "How's Janet (the guernsey), Sarah, and the kids."

"All are fine. I see you are prepared to lose at cribbage. Cut for the first deal?"

Harry won the first three games. It seems he played a lot of cribbage overseas during his free time. In the fourth game, Moses pulled ahead. His peg was a good four inches out in front when he thought he heard paper rustling over the amplifier speaker. Harry also listened to the sound and punched the record button on the tape recorder.

The conference room was carpeted, with very little noise from chair movement. For a while, there was silence except for an occasional throat clearing. Moses looked at his watch. The time was 9:05 p.m.

Moses heard someone shut the conference room door.

The two investigators stationed in the Hamilton building bent over the amplifier speaker, listening. They heard:

"You're late."

"I made it. That's what counts."

"You're probably lucky. I hear there is a wide net out for you."

"But not for you, I take it."

"No."

"You've got the rest of the money?"

Moses and Harry heard a dull smack as if a stack of bills had been thrown on the conference table.

"Give me a minute to count it, not that I don't trust you, but this is my living. I run it like a business."

Harry looked at Moses while they distinctly heard two bills thumbed to the table, and Owen Kressbach counted, "One hundred, two hundred,,," Eventually stopping at $2,500.00.

The other voice dripped with sarcasm, "If you didn't have such an expensive companion, you'd be living easy with that much money."

"She's helpful in more ways than one."

"Your problem."

"Right, I guess that does it. Everything we did worked like a charm. The papers are all convinced the Red Scare is alive and well in Kalamazoo."

"It would appear so."

Another period of silence.

"Is there something else?" said Owen.

"Loose ends."

"Simmons is dead," said Kressbach. "He's not talking. Convenient that. His son takes the fall. He's heard threatening his old man and leaves his fingerprints all over the gun. Poor Leroy. Shot with his own gun in the back. Someone played him good."

"It wasn't you?"

"Nope," Owen said, "and before you ask, I don't know who it was. Leroy told me he was taking someone along to watch his back and help him search for the money, if necessary."

"He never returned the money I shelled out to him. That was unfortunate. The union committee was careful to keep the date of the Detroit faction's arrival here a secret."

Owen laughed.

"Someone must have known he carried his money in a money belt. That would have been a nice haul with what his wife saved up."

"Did Melissa know about the money belt?"

"That's how I found out about it."

"Was Melissa watching Leroy's back that night?"

"Maybe. Come to think of it, if Melissa was with Leroy, she must have kept the money for herself."

"I should have deducted that expense from your fee."

"No."

"Isn't she a loose end if it was her?"

"She'll be with me, and don't get any ideas that I'm a loose end. You don't have an army big enough."

"What about Leroy's wife. This lawyer she's hired is green but persistent."

"Are you kidding? They have an open and shut case against the kid. Everyone's convinced Commies were behind the riot. With Shakespeare Jr.'s ties to the socialists, he'll be out, and you'll be a shoo-in."

The minute he heard Eileen's name mentioned, Moses stood up. "I'm calling Kirkpatrick." He rushed from the room, heading for the receptionist's desk and telephone.

Meanwhile, over the speaker, Harry heard the voice of Owen's co-conspirator.

"What about this Webb person?"

"Now, that is a different story. How much is Webb's dead body worth to you. I owe that nigger a kick in the balls and a celery bog burial."

Silence for another minute.

"$500.00, but you'll need to include that bastard who got the drop on you at the service station."

"Why don't you take care of Webb. I noticed you had no qualms telling me to give it to Billy-boy after he choked the life out of Alex Madden."

"He outlived his usefulness.

"Alright, $1,000.00, and you've got a deal."

Harry, now white as snow, heard another stack of bills hit the table.

"There's three hundred on account. Finish the loose ends."

***

"Kalamazoo Safety Department, how can I help you?" said the dispatcher.

"Moses Webb, here, I need Ross Kirkpatrick, and I need him now."

"OK, Moses, Ross gave me a heads-up. He's been checking in every thirty minutes, as you two agreed this afternoon. The last time was nine o'clock. It's 9:23 now. He should be calling in any minute. He knows where you are? The Shakespeare Administration building, right?"

"Yes, tell him to block the front and rear entrances."

"OK, I'll call you back as soon as I give him the message. What's the number there?"

"FI9-3304, I'll stick close to the phone."

Moses hung up and ran back to check with Harry. As he entered the room, he heard a voice say, "How do I get a hold of you now that you're back in town."

"Forget that. I'll be here one week from today, at the same time."

Moses was frantic. Was Ross on his way? Should he and Harry go over and delay Owen's departure?

"I'll be right back, Harry," said Moses. He tore through the hallway to the receptionist's desk, where the telephone began to ring. He picked up the receiver.

"Moses, Sergeant Whetlend here. Ross stopped in at the station. I was able to give him the message a few minutes ago. I told him the situation. His partner, Craig Sheid, grabbed the keys to a second squad car. He will block the rear entrance to the building. They should be there in less than five minutes."

Moses ran back to update Harry.

When he entered the room, he heard a telephone ringing. Moses looked around the room but quickly realized the phone in the conference room of the Shakespeare building was ringing.

He heard a voice say:

"Impossible, you're certain?"

"What's up?" Owen said.

Harry and Moses heard the receiver being banged back on the telephone set. Then they heard paper shuffling and a door open and close. Silence.

Moses heard sirens from two squad cars roaring up to the Shakespeare building four minutes later. Ross exited the vehicle and met Moses at the front door. The second squad car arrived a minute later and used the Hamilton building driveway to reach the back of the Shakespeare Administration building.

Moses picked up one of the large rocks near a bush by the front door and hurled it through the glass door. Ross used his nightstick to clear the glass in the frame so the policeman and Moses could safely step through. Ross, gun drawn and with direction from Moses, ran to the conference room. Moses threw the door open and stepped back as Ross crawled into the room. Moses reached around the door frame for the light switch.

Craig Sheid stepped around Moses and offered backup to his partner. The room was empty.

For the next twenty minutes, the two police officers searched one-half of the one-story Shakespeare offices while Harry and Moses searched the other half. No one, other than the searchers, was in the building.

Next, the group searched the back parking lot. At the north border of the parking lot, Harry noticed tire tread marks heading toward the railroad tracks running east to west behind the buildings on Kalamazoo Avenue. Walking toward the train tracks, Moses determined that the car had swerved to the right to take advantage of a roadmaster maintenance bridge, level with the height of the rails that allowed the vehicle to get across the tracks and disappear before the squad cars arrived.

The timing of the escape must have been within seconds of the arrival of the police. Someone, somehow, had warned Owen Kressbach's boss.

Moses was sick over failing to apprehend Owen Kressbach. According to the recorded conversation, Owen did not shoot Leroy Simmons. Moses was now back to square one. The whole Shakespeare strike probably did not result in the death of Leroy Simmons. Something else, someone else was involved.

Ross interviewed Moses and Harry for another hour, recording the incident in his notebook; he wanted nothing to do with the illegal tape recording. While Ross and Craig interviewed Moses, Harry removed the microphone and cable in the conference room.

Ross released Harry and Moses, who ripped up two cardboard boxes from a storage room and the tape they used on the cable to cover the broken front door. Ross suggested he would inform Shakespeare's management of the intrusion and breaking the front door glass.

After the policemen left for the station, Moses and Harry returned to the Hamilton building, and Moses replayed the tape recording three times, taking down notes of the key revelations. Owen had probably been sitting directly under the microphone. His voice was clear and distinct, easily recognizable. The other man's voice was barely comprehensible, almost at the level of a whisper. Moses doubted that if he met the man in person, he could equate his voice to the voice on the tape.

Eileen, Harry, and Moses, the loose ends referred to on the tape recording, would need to be vigilant and cautious until Moses or the police could again find Owen Kressbach, identify the mystery man, and disable them both.

Harry and Moses cleaned up the office suite in the Hamilton building. The tape recorder and amplifier were carted out to Harry's car. The cable was wound up and thrown in the trunk as well. Moses replaced the chairs in the reception area and left all the keys on the table with a thank you note for Cybil.

Harry handed Moses the tape reel of the recorded conversation. Moses told Harry he would meet with him soon to determine what came next. Harry dropped Moses off in front of the Paints and Oils store.

In his bedroom, Eileen stirred and asked what Moses had learned, but Moses told her he was too tired to explain and would do so in the morning.

27 | Funeral Arrangements

While Eileen made scrambled eggs for breakfast, Moses reported on the previous night's activities, including what was on the tape recording of the conversation in the Shakespeare conference room. Referring to his notes, Moses listed the highlights for her:

1. Owen probably didn't shoot Leroy, although Moses only had his word.
2. According to Owen, Leroy had commandeered someone to help him search Eileen's house and keep watch in case Eileen, Marvin, or the police tried to surprise him.
3. The other man in the conference room never identified himself, and Owen never called him by name.
4. Because the man's voice on the tape was so soft, identifying it would be nearly impossible.
5. Someone warned the two men in the conference room of the impending arrival of the police. They escaped scant minutes before the police arrived to arrest them.

Moses did not mention the loose ends that Owen would be 'cleaning up.'

Moses wolfed down his eggs and poured another cup of coffee to eat with his toast. Eileen toyed with her eggs and pushed her plate away after a minute.

"I really thought this Owen person would be Marvin's get-out-of-jail ticket," said Eileen.

"I know, honey," Moses said. "I thought Owen was the answer. Maybe my logic was clouded by my personal need to beat the shit out of that guy.

"Sometimes this is the way it goes with an investigation."

"Shouldn't we turn the tape over to the police?" said Eileen. "Marvin is mentioned as a fall guy. Isn't that someone unjustifiably accused of a crime?"

"Two problems with that strategy. The tape I made was illegally obtained. That nullifies its credibility to a large extent. Secondly, I think the lead detective, Lucas Shotmire, would still hang the murder on Marvin. Leroy's accomplice isn't indicated on the tape. It could have been Marvin; that's what they'll say."

"I was just so hopeful; what more can you do, Moses."

"Start again," said Moses. "Don't forget we've eliminated Marvin, Sheila, Curtis, and now Owen and a mystery man as suspects. It may not seem like enough, but we have made progress."

"OK, is there any way I can help?"

"Yes," said Moses. "Eat your eggs, stay strong. Visit Marvin and take Sheila along. Stay hopeful. I'll update Jeremy Fulton and head to the police station on Monday to check in with Chief Hoyt."

"You can have my eggs, Moses," said Eileen. "I'll have a toast and peanut butter. Then I have to get ready for church. Will you be coming?"

"Not today. I'm a bit exhausted from last night's debacle. I need a basketball game at the 'Y' to clear my head."

"Good idea. I have to meet with Leroy's sister after the service and go over the funeral arrangements for Leroy. She wants to discuss Leroy's possessions and what she may be entitled to.

"Oh really," Moses said. "Is there anything of value she is looking forward to?"

"I have no idea. I guess I'll know when we meet."

"OK, I'll walk to your house and meet you there.

***

After forty minutes in the weight room and ten minutes in the sauna, Moses went upstairs to the gym. Soon, he was running with Magic, John, Shooter, and the 'Old-Guy,' against the other Sunday morning regulars. Showered and dressed, Moses walked to Eileen's house. He knocked on the kitchen door and entered, passing through the mudroom and hearing Eileen's voice in the kitchen.

"Bev, the ring is the only thing Leroy ever mentioned giving to Marvin one day."

As far as Moses knew, Beverly Simmons was the older sister of Leroy. The brunette looked his elder by at least ten years. Her face and neck were wrinkled and sun worn. Moses wondered what work had taken that kind of toll. The only thing that came to mind was picking cotton down south.

Beverly's Sunday dress had squared-off shoulders and reached six inches below her knees, not the prevalent hem length of the times. The dress had long sleeves, and Beverly wore dark black stockings. She had a decent figure, slim at the waist. Moses would have called her attractive if it weren't for her oak tree skin and frumpy dress. Moses guessed she was hand-to-mouth like Leroy had been.

There was a thread-bare man's suit lying across the kitchen table. Three shirts, neatly folded, including one yellowing white one, lie atop the suit. A couple of ties hung across the back of a kitchen chair. Moses wouldn't be caught dead wearing either tie, and he doubted Marvin would want them either.

"Marvin can have the suit," said Bev. "Every man can use an extra suit. The ring might be worth something."

Eileen remained calm. "That suit would have fit Marvin when he was in seventh grade. The ring is probably worth only ten dollars, but it may be the only thing Marvin can one day look at and think kindly about his dad."

"I'm sure it is worth at least a hundred dollars," said Beverly. "I'll take fifty dollars for the ring, and Marvin can keep it in the family."

Moses thought Eileen would explode. Moses could tell that the jewel was glass and guessed the gold making up the band was probably ten carat. Eileen's ten-dollar estimate was more than generous.

Eileen opened her purse and wallet and extracted a ten-dollar bill. "This is all the cash I have today."

Moses jumped to the rescue, grabbing his wallet from his back pocket and placing two five-dollar bills on top of Eileen's ten spot.

Eileen looked up at Moses, tears forming, and then turned to Beverly. "Twenty dollars and everything else on the table," she said. "Whatever you find in Leroy's apartment is yours. I don't even want to know what's there."

Beverly wadded up the suit and shirts and stuffed them in a paper grocery bag.

[244]

"His underwear and a pair of worn-through shoes went in the garbage," said Eileen.

Beverly placed the bag on the kitchen chair and spread both hands on the table. "Now, we need to talk about the house. Will you be selling? What would you expect this place to be worth, or could you pay half its worth directly to me in cash?"

Eileen finally did explode. "Beverly Simmons, you are crazy if you think for one second that you'll receive any money involving this house. This is my house. My name and only my name are on the deed and the mortgage. Leroy had nothing to do with it. I intend to keep the house, and that is final."

"Beverly rose to her full height and glared back at Eileen. "We'll see what a judge says about that. Make me an offer, and we can avoid all that," she said.

Moses couldn't believe his ears. Michigan spousal law provides that Eileen inherits all of Leroy's assets, including the ring. Beverly had nothing to stand on without a will signed by Leroy and witnesses. No judge would look at Beverly twice before deciding in favor of Eileen.

Moses stepped between the two women, but Eileen yelled at Bev over his shoulder, "You couldn't even be bothered about a coffin and gravesite. Just get out of my house. I've had it with you. The funeral is four days from now at 1:00 p.m. at Mt. Zion Baptist. Show up or not. I won't miss you if you don't."

Beverly Simmons gathered the grocery bag of clothes and stormed out the back door. Eileen sat down and cried. Moses rubbed her back and shoulders until Eileen settled down.

Moses helped with the clean-up of the supper dishes that evening. "Eileen, there is another suspect I didn't mention yesterday,"

"Tell me," said Eileen. "Maybe I'll have a chance at sleep tonight."

"Probably so, especially if I don't stay the night. The suspect is Owen's sometimes girlfriend, a woman named Melissa something. Owen may be with her, and I may be able to handle two birds with one stone."

***

Sleeping in on Monday morning, Moses awoke to a knock on his door. A familiar knock. He opened the door dressed in his boxers before realizing it was Nadine on his doorstep.

This time, Nadine waited patiently to be invited in. Moses recognized Nadine as the cheerful girl from Dr. Alexander's office. She seemed alert and obviously apologetic.

"Good morning, Moses," she said. "Is Eileen here? I won't be but a minute."

"Come in, Nadine," said Moses. "Let me get my pants on. Then I need coffee. Can you wait that long?"

"Yes," said Nadine, and she sat down in the kitchen without taking off her coat.

Moses returned to the kitchen wearing pants and a sweater and began making coffee. "How have you been, Nadine? I understand you've been in treatment."

"Yes," said Nadine. "I credit you for helping me get over our thing and the morphine problem. I'm dating an anesthesiologist from Borgess Hospital who knows of my condition. He has been very supportive. I think I'm falling in love with him."

"Nadine, we were both coming off a rough patch when we met. My injuries and you… Well, we made it through. Here's your coffee. Sugar, right?"

Nadine couldn't help noticing the photographs on one side of the table. She pretended not to be looking at them.

"That's why I came here today, Moses, to apologize. I still have a job, thanks to you. Dr. Alexander paid for my treatment. I'm mending, and I hope, as friends, you'll meet Jerome one of these days. Maybe we could even double-date sometime."

"I look forward to it, Nadine," said Moses.

Nadine glanced at the photographs again. "Moses, have you gotten the charges dropped on Mrs. Simmon's boy?"

"Not yet," said Moses. "Why? Do you see someone you recognize in these pictures?"

Moses noticed Nadine shudder. He decided not to pursue the point. Nadine might still be too fragile to talk about her drug-craving days. She seemed to shake off her anxiety and straightened her shoulders.

"This woman was my dealer once my access to Dr. Alexander's cabinet was cut off. I also recognize this man kicking the man on the ground. He was at Melissa's place once in a while. Melissa and Owen, I think is his name, had a thing going on."

Moses couldn't believe his luck. "What's her name?" he asked.

"Melissa Soebbing. S.O.E.B.B.I.N.G. She's a bitch, by the way. A bitch with claws," said Nadine.

"Do you know her address?" said Moses. "She may be the key to getting Marvin Simmons out of jail."

"I don't know her address," Nadine said. "I was often in a fog, so I couldn't even show you on a map. I may be able to take you there."

"That won't be necessary, Nadine. I can do a background check and find her address."

Nadine and Moses finished their coffee. Nadine described the new security system protecting the drug cabinet at Dr. Alexander's office. She rose to leave, and Moses thanked her for stopping by.

***

By late morning, Moses had exercised at the 'Y.' He walked to the police station and asked to see Chief Hoyt. A few minutes later, the chief leaned out his office doorway and motioned to Moses to enter and sit down.

The chief held up his hand, indicating a small gap with his thumb and finger. "I hear we came this close to nabbing Owen Kressbach."

"That's correct, Chief," said Moses. "I called in the signal for the police raid myself. Within minutes, Owen and his accomplice were warned by telephone and skedaddled, just before Ross and his partner showed up for the collar."

"You are implying that warning came from this station," said Hoyt.

"Sorry, Chief," said Moses. "That is the only explanation that fits the timing."

"Ross and I have been investigating the possibility," said Chief Hoyt. "When Alex Madden was murdered, I was reluctant to acknowledge he may have been an accomplice in Kressbach's escape. This latest breach will be choked out.

"Ross reports directly to me, and we will find the leak. Please use the code word 'Encyclopedia' when starting a relevant conversation with Ross or myself. Only the duty sergeants, who have been here longer than ten years, are privy to that code word."

"OK, Chief, thanks," said Moses. "This fugitive has threatened my friends and me. We need him stopped. You have my full cooperation."

"Just remember, Moses, you are not the police. Trust that we will get this done.

"Now, as to the other night, the duty sergeant made an announcement that night when your call came in. He scrambled resources to rush to the Shakespeare offices. Ross has narrowed his inquiry to seven officers within earshot of that announcement."

"When he narrows the field to one suspect, I will request your under-cover assistance."

"I'll help any way I can," said Moses and stood to leave. "I'm heading over to records. I need to check on a suspect, Melissa Soebbing, for priors and an address."

"Right. Keep me updated. Good luck."

***

Moses discovered that Melissa Soebbing had priors for solicitation and drug possession but had not been arrested or brought in for questioning during the past eight years. Her address was 1329 Hillcrest Ave. in the Westnedge Hill neighborhood, which made Moses shake his head. An independent woman with no means of support listed in her file would be hard-pressed to afford a place in that exclusive neighborhood. From indications Harry had photographed and Nadine's historical account, it seemed evident to Moses that Melissa Soebbing was now a major drug supplier.

It was close to his shift start time at the Cities Service Station. Moses went on to work. He had no idea how he would approach Melissa Soebbing. A man of color, strolling through the Westnedge Hill neighborhood during the day or under cover of night, faced the possibility of being shot or arrested as an intruder.

In the end, Moses decided he had to risk a direct approach. Marvin's trial was now just days away, and he still had no evidence to present that would let Marvin off the hook. Tomorrow, he would pin Melissa Soebbing down and eliminate Owen if he hid in her home.

The following morning, Moses stopped in at Jeremy Fulton's office. Jeremy was glad to see Moses and looked hopeful that Moses was bringing good news. "Eileen has kept me apprised of your activities. She mentioned a tape recording of a conversation between Owen Kressbach and another person. It's inadmissible, but I should probably listen to it for reference."

"I'll bring the tape in. Do you have access to a reel-to-reel recording machine?" said Moses.

"I can borrow one from the police media department," Jeremy said. "I won't tell them what I'm up to."

"That's fine," said Moses. "Be highly guarded. Ross Kirkpatrick, Chief Hoyt, and I are investigating an information leak from the police force. Someone in the station is signaling the bad guys that the police are on the way."

"Corruption in the police force?" said Jeremy. "In Kalamazoo, hard to believe."

"Evidence to the contrary. By the way, can I give you a retainer? I might require your services."

"Certainly. Have you got a dollar on you? I'll make out a receipt."

Moses slid a dollar bill across Jeremy's desk.

"Civil or criminal," said Jeremy.

"The latter, but I'll try to avoid either," said Moses. "Do you have anything new that you can tell me? Marvin's trial is coming up."

"I was hoping you would have something for me, Moses," said the attorney. "Things look pretty desperate at this point. I could try for a continuance, but this judge will probably reject it. He is determined to send a message to the people on the northside that the city will not tolerate such violence against a white man."

"Desperate times may mean desperate measures, Jeremy,"

"You know, Moses, the day of Marvin's trial is close to the date that the CIO Union management men will be indicted on conspiracy charges for the riot on December 1st at the Shakespeare factory."

"Jeremy, that's bullshit," said Moses. "A Shakespeare manager hired an outside agitator to instigate that riot. Yet no one is listening."

"What evidence do you have to support your premise, Moses."

"An inadmissible tape recording and my eyewitness testimony that no one wants to publicize."

"Stay on Marvin's case. When we get him cleared, I'll see that your information on the riot gets heard."

***

Eileen buzzed the intercom of Moses' apartment and, a minute later, opened his front door, entered, and shed her coat and hat. She hung both on the tree next to the door, kicked off her nursing shoes, and flopped on the bed. Moses had been up for an hour. He had showered and shaved down the hall. He's on his second cup of coffee.

Setting his second mug of coffee on the kitchen table, Moses went over to the bed, bent down, and kissed Eileen. "How was your shift," he said.

"Busier than usual," said Eileen. "A heart attack patient came in that we didn't save."

"That's a shame," said Moses.

"It puts a sullen spin on the night. A bus hit two people riding a motorcycle. The bus was returning from a swim meet. Three boys smashed their teeth against the aluminum bar of the seat in front of them. The girl on the bike flew fifteen feet, skidding on the pavement. We patched her up. The boy stayed with the bike but broke his pelvis when the motorcycle landed on him."

"How about a back rub," asked Moses.

Eileen ran her hands over Moses' chest and left her hands resting on his forearms.

"Moses, with everything that happened at the hospital tonight, you'd think I wouldn't have time to worry about

Marvin. But I do, every second of every minute of every hour.

"I don't know how much more I can stand. Marvin should be home with me or at school with Sheila. He should be at basketball practice and playing in the games. It's not only unfair, but it's also terrifying. What if this nightmare is our permanent way of life from now on."

"Eileen, you've got to shut that worry down. We'll find an answer. We have to keep going."

"But we only have seven more days," said Eileen.

"I know, but we still have one more lead to investigate," said Moses.

"But if that woman, Melissa Soebbing, doesn't pan out," said Eileen, "what then? I think it's time to make the tape recording public."

Moses could think of no way to let Eileen down easily regarding his illegally obtained and inconclusive tape recording. He said nothing.

"At least the tape would cause a stir, wouldn't it?" said Eileen. "If the Gazette ran an article about that conversation, that might at least delay the trial while the prosecutor investigates the exchange. Maybe that would give you more time to prove Marvin's innocence."

"That might be what would happen," said Moses, "but it may just provide more ammunition to convict Marvin."

"Marvin is my son, Moses. I'm willing to take the chance that the tape recording will help him by spurring additional investigation or stalling the trial, giving us more time."

"All right," said Moses. "I'll go along with you. How can we get the Gazette interested in the tape."

Eileen paused to think. "I'll start by calling Sarah Martensen, Harry's wife," she said. "When we spoke over dinner at the Pacific Club, Sarah mentioned that journalism was her major in college. During the war, she was an editor for a farming magazine published in Chicago. I wouldn't be surprised if she has written articles for the Gazette. She can help us, I'm certain."

"You know, Eileen, that's quite an idea. It may work. I'll work on pinning Leroy's murder on Melissa Soebbing while you go through Sarah to garner interest in the tape by the editor of the Gazette."

"It's a plan," said Eileen. "It gives me something of importance to think about rather than dwelling on the worst-case scenario."

29 | Calico Cat

Moses left Jeremy's office, pocketed the retainer receipt, and hailed a cab to Westnedge Hill. Moses had splashed on old spice that morning and thought a checkered white-on-white ascot slung around his neck gave him a seedy, sophisticated look. The walkway was paved but interrupted by two sets of three steps before reaching the wide wooden steps up to the porch, running the length of the front of the house. The two-story, four-square '30s home was well-kept, and the porch and rocking chair looked comfortable.

Moses set a jaunty, confident pace to the front door and rang the bell. He lit a cigarette and prepared his spiel in his head, waiting for the front door to open, standing slightly to the side of the door in case Owen opened it. Moses readied a blockbuster blow if he showed his face. The door opened, and Melissa Soebbing said, "I'm not interested in whatever you're selling."

"I'm not selling," said Moses. "Owen and I were talking down in Elkhart a month ago. He thought you might be looking for a street vendor by the train station. Something about the guy working that territory becoming a liability. I'm here to buy, not sell. My name is Torrence. Hershal Torrence."

"I'm sorry, Mr. Torrence," said Melissa. "I'm not selling anything either. Perhaps you have the wrong address. If you step inside, maybe we can straighten this out. Perhaps you're looking for one of my neighbors."

The woman motioned him inside as if she did not want her neighbors to see Moses at her doorstep. A beautiful calico cat ran into the foyer and threaded its way between Moses' legs.

"Aurora, you pest, go eat your food," Melissa said.

Moses reached down and picked up Aurora, pleased that the cat seemed comfortable in his arms.

"Let me get my address book, Mr. Torrence," said Melissa. "We can call around and get you steered in the right direction." She left him standing in the foyer and disappeared down the hallway. Moses glanced into the living room. He spotted a desk in the corner of the room with what looked like a diary or notebook sitting neatly on a corner. If Owen walked into the living room from the den, Moses would be cornered in the foyer with no retreat or cover. Still holding the cat, he moved to a spot in the living room where he could see every entry to the living room and hopefully react accordingly. At least he wouldn't take a bullet in the back.

Melissa appeared from the hallway, carrying a snub-nosed 38 special. "No one I don't know shows up here without my personal invitation," she said, waving the gun at Moses to indicate he should move in the direction of the back of the house, possibly the kitchen.

Instead, Moses pitched the cat directly at Melissa's face with as much underhand force as he could muster. Aurora screamed and landed on Melissa's neck, claws digging repeatedly to obtain a purchase on her shoulder.

Moses was also on Melissa in two strides, grabbing both her hand and gun in his right hand. He bent her arm backward and wrenched the revolver from her grasp.

Melissa transformed into a raging tiger, clawing at Moses' head, neck, and the hand that held her wrist. Moses ducked his head into her chest for protection from her long, sharpened nails. He didn't let go, but the woman went into a frenzy.

Moses had cornered and captured a small terrier once. The dog wriggled and swung its head back and forth, biting air, hoping to chomp on Moses' hands or arms. At the same time, all four of the creature's legs and paws were scratching furiously to get away or injure its attacker.

Moses had not experienced such fury since capturing that dog, either from a woman or a man, not even in the ring. Melissa seemed to find the strength of a pit bull, trying to bite his neck.

Finally, his own adrenalin peaking, Moses pushed her away without letting go and then backhanded her as hard as he could across her cheek. Stunned, the woman shook her head to recover her senses. In seconds, she was at him again and caught the side of his neck with a four-inch gash.

Moses still didn't let go and slapped her with all his strength across her other cheek. Melissa went limp. Moses dragged her into the kitchen and sat her on a straight-back kitchen chair. The woman didn't resist.

Without letting go of her wrist, Moses took a length of rope from his jacket pocket. He looped the rope around her wrist, pulled it behind the chair, and tied Melissa's hands together.

Melissa, beginning to recover, blood seeping out of the corner of her swelling lip, began kicking out as she sat, hoping to find the groin of her assailant with one of her feet.

Moses slapped her. Melissa again went limp, knocked out. He finished tying her ankles to the chair leg, brought a second kitchen chair next to Melissa, and sat down. After a minute, he filled a glass with water and threw it in her face. She woke up sputtering. Moses held a dish towel for a gag if she screamed. She didn't; instead, she licked her bloody lip and said, "Untie me, you bastard. What the hell do you want?"

"A few simple answers, that's all. If your story sounds right, I'll get out of here. Lie, and I'll really make your ears ring. I am running out of time and patience. Where is Owen Kressbach? I thought you two were an item?"

Melissa turned her head toward Moses and spat blood at him. He slapped her again. "Where is Owen," he said.

Coming to her senses again, Melissa said, "Out of town. He'll be back soon, though, and he'll find you and kill you. You're all he talked about this week. *'Kill the nigger and bury him in the celery bog.'* He went on and on about it. I got sick of it. He's in so much trouble now that I called it quits. He's a psychopath."

"Never mind that," said Moses. "I know you fought with Leroy Simmons at the train station. I saw his claw marks. I have photographs of that incident. That wasn't enough for you. You wanted to get rid of him. So you shot him in the back."

"Bullshit," said Melissa.

"You picked up his gun and shot him."

"Why would I? No one paid attention to that scumbag."

"Probably because he would give you and Owen up in a blink. The special prosecutor threatened him over the riot at the Shakespeare factory."

"I had no worries about the riot. That was all Owen."

"Owen, as much as said, you may have been with Leroy Simmons the night he was killed."

"I wasn't, and Owen wouldn't know anything about where I was that night because I broke up with him two days before that night. That was Christmas Eve. I was at a cocktail party three doors down., keeping up appearances in the neighborhood. I was there from 8:30 p.m. to midnight when it broke up. Probably fifteen people would alibi me. Ask Mr. and Mrs. Broyhill. They watched me drown my sorrows in martinis.

"Now, let me loose."

Moses stood and looked down at the disheveled woman. When she opened the door to his knock, she was made up befitting the classy Westnedge Hill neighborhood. Now her hair was a mess, her mascara was smeared, and her lip was swollen to the size of a walnut. Downright ugly. The real Melissa Soebbing sat in that chair, and despite her plea, Moses wasn't about to cut her free.

"Buy me off," Moses said. "A pinch of smack for a friend of mine would do it."

"Alright, just cut me loose."

"First things first."

"Alright," said the prisoner. "Upstairs on my bedroom nightstand. Take the jar and get the fuck out, but cut me loose."

"I'll be right back," said Moses.

He took the stairs two at a time and found the nightstand in the bedroom. The jar of white powder sat next to two razor blades in the drawer. He left everything as it was, took the stairs to the living room, and quietly left by the front door without returning to the kitchen. Not quietly enough. Melissa screamed, "You come back and cut me loose, you fucking nigger. I'll see you dead next time."

Moses knocked on the front door of the third house west of Melissa's, but no one was home. He tried the house three doors from Melissa's to the east. When the woman of the house opened the door a crack, Moses stooped down and huddled in his leather jacket while he told the woman his story.

"Mrs. Broyhill?" he said. "Miss Soebbing asked me to stop by. She thought she may have left her purse here on Christmas Eve. Is that possible? It was around midnight when she left. She said it was a wonderful party and wished to apologize for having too many martinis."

"I'm afraid she'll have to look elsewhere for her purse, young man. She was swinging it while she wobbled down the sidewalk. We all chuckled about it, hoping she would make it home.

"Thank you, Mrs. Broyhill. We'll look again at her house. Sorry to bother you."

Moses was confident Mrs. Broyhill would never be able to accurately describe his height, weight, age, or features other than his color. Sometimes, being invisible has its advantages.

Moses walked east on Howard four blocks to Westnedge Street and hailed a cab. When Moses returned to his apartment, he called the police station and anonymously tipped off the desk sergeant about a stash of heroin in the nightstand drawer of the upstairs bedroom of Melissa Soebbing's house at 1329 Hillcrest Ave.

30 | Congressman

At work that evening, Moses kept an eye out for Owen Kressbach. Ross Kirkpatrick had called the service station and informed Moses of Melissa Soebbing's arrest on drug charges, possession, and dealing. The police found three more butcher paper-wrapped bricks of heroin in a locked trunk in her attic. Melissa Soebbing was out of the picture, at least for a few days, more if bail was denied. Owen would be angrier with Moses if she spoke to him. Chances of that were slim if Owen continued to lay low. Of course, if he did find out about Melissa's plight, that might make him even more reckless and extremely dangerous. Moses kept his large wrench within reach.

The fact was that Melissa Soebbing hadn't murdered Leroy Simmons. Mrs. Broyhill crushed that possibility by giving her an alibi.

Moses had rerun out of suspects. Around six-thirty, Moses was called to the telephone.

"Mr. Webb, Moses Webb," said a man's voice.

"Yes," said Moses, "How can I help you."

"My name is Carlton Miller. I work for United States Representative Clare Hoffman[39] of the 4th congressional district. Mr. Hoffman is preparing his report for the committee investigating the riot at the Shakespeare factory. He has been given a transcript of an interview conducted by Judge Smith, head of the grand jury, in which you gave testimony. He requests a meeting with you at 10:00 a.m. tomorrow. Might that suit you? He is only in town a couple of days."

"Yes," said Moses. "Where is his office?"

"He will be using a conference room on the first floor of the Michigan Avenue Courthouse."

"I will be there at 10:00 a.m.," said Moses. A U.S. Representative warranted a first-floor conference room, whereas a grand jury judge was relegated to the basement.

***

When Moses walked into the conference room, Representative Hoffman was standing in the corner looking out the window, left hand on hip, right hand holding a sheaf of papers. He looked three inches shorter than Moses and wore a grey, conservative suit, starched white shirt, and dark blue tie. Moses thought he looked in his seventies, but he had a full head of well-combed, greying hair cut neatly to his ears. Hoffman's energy radiated throughout the room. He stood well-planted and sturdy, especially for his short stature. Scrappy. He didn't turn from the window. Instead, he glanced at the papers in his fist and said, "Take a seat."

Moses sat at the conference table, folded his hands, and waited. No introductions, no handshake. Moses would not play the game. Instead, He thought about the carburetor he was cleaning at the service station.

"Mr.," said Hoffman. "I've read a report of your history on the Kalamazoo Police force. Quit after only a few years. Never served your country during wartime. Questioned by Detective Shapiro about the murder of a white man, Leroy Simmons. Not exactly exemplary."

"I guess you missed the two commendations and the medal for courage under fire," said Moses. "The advancement to detective within two years also escaped your attention."

"The times were desperate. All the real men were overseas."

"Maybe so," said Moses. "Perhaps you can tell me why I'm here? I spoke freely to Judge Smith. Everything I had to say, I said. I'd be fine with going on to work."

Noting that Moses wasn't about to cry, throw a tantrum, walk out, or plead for mercy, Congressman Hoffman shrugged and sat at the table. He arranged his papers neatly before him and folded his hands, matching Moses.

"One of my duties is the protection of U.S. citizens. A duty I take very seriously. In reading the report of your account of the Shakespeare riot, I can see that you are misinterpreting the events you witnessed. Understandable. The scene must have been chaotic and dangerous.

"Mr., I'm here to educate you and the public. If you listen with an open mind, I think we can put your report in its proper perspective and concentrate on the real culprits here in Kalamazoo. Communists."

"Congressman," said Moses. "The men I identified in my testimony instigated and contributed to the violence that occurred on December 1st. The word communism or the philosophy of the communist party in America was never uttered."

Representative Hoffman clasped the top of his head with both hands. He said, "So you still believe the Shakespeare riot had no connection to the spread of communism across this nation."

"You can pitch that all you want," said Moses. "The evidence of a 'Red Scare' in Kalamazoo is nonexistent. Someone in Shakespeare's management conspired with

Owen Kressbach and Leroy Simmons to start that riot, discredit attempts to form a union among the workers in the factory, and set the community against the union, which is exactly how things are turning out. Kressbach and Simmons were paid to start that riot."

"You're forgetting the company's President, who has socialist leanings," said Hoffman. "He even voted in that direction in the last election. Perhaps he was in league with Kressbach."

"So go pin him down," said Moses. "From what I understand, socialism was a passing fancy for Shakespeare Jr. No, I'm talking about someone in upper management who is trying to maximize company profits by eliminating the bargaining power of a union."

"Let me tell you, Mr.," said Clare, picking up a pile of reports from the corner of the table. "You don't know what you're talking about. I have documentation highlighting several communist plots being perpetrated across our state."

Representative Hoffman picked up the top report, slapping it hard on the table before Moses. He put the knuckles of both hands on the table and leaned in, too close, to Moses.

"You take the city-wide fluoridation effort adopted in Grand Rapids, Michigan, three years ago," said Clare, holding the report. "Several sources in this report confirm that fluoridation is the communists' plan to control the minds of our citizens."

Hoffman thumbed through the report. He stopped at page 38 and showed Moses the underlined section he felt was significant. "I quote: 'This is a Communist plot to deplete the brainpower and sap the strength of a generation of American children.' Dr. Charles Betts charges that fluoridation is 'better than using the atom bomb because the atom bomb has to be made, has to be transported to the place it is to be set off while poisonous fluorine has been placed right beside the water supplies by the Americans themselves ready to be dumped into the water mains whenever a Communist desires!'" Hoffman thumbed a few more pages to another section of the report.

"Similarly," he said, "the *American Capsule News* reports that "the Soviet General Staff is pleased about municipal fluoridation efforts in America. Anytime the Communists get ready to strike, and their 5th column takes over, there are tons and tons of this poison 'standing by' municipal and military water systems ready to be poured in within 15 minutes."

Moses remained quiet. Quasi-scientific studies have been presented ever since the first men and women of color were herded off the slave ships. Control and persecution of minority peoples have been justified under the guise of their inferiority, their wish to be taken care of, and their inherent love of backbreaking manual labor such as picking cotton. Moses wasn't buying any of it.

He was one man trying to ring a bell in the city where he lived and worked. Moses found Kalamazoo better by degrees than the environment he was from in Lousianna, but the man ranting over him, calling him 'Mr.' instead of 'boy,' wore his prejudice on his sleeve. Moses had to deal with that the best way he knew: ignore, run, or fight. This was city hall. You don't fight City Hall with boxing gloves.

"That's interesting," said Moses. "According to the Gazette, Kalamazoo is considering the trend toward municipal fluoridation. If it saves kids going to the dentist with cavities, that would be a good thing. What does fluoridation have to do with the workers' strike at the Shakespeare factory?"

"Everything," said Clare Hoffman. "Everything is connected." Hoffman scattered his pile and picked another report to hold under Moses' nose.

"Take this Jewish doctor at the University of Pittsburgh School of Medicine. Jonas Salk is attempting to create a vaccine to protect people from polio, a disease that has been a fact of human existence for thousands of years. What he might eventually propose to inject into millions of our citizens must be scrutinized and probably outlawed."

"Mr. Hoffman," said Moses. "Are you upset over scientists trying to find cures for horrible diseases causing untold suffering for your constituents? Or are you upset that this Jonas Salk is Jewish?"

"Too much control," said the Representative. "That's what I'm talking about. Russian doctors among us." He picked up a third report, holding it over his head.

"Here is more proof. Rabbi Spitz, in the *American Hebrew, March 1, 1946* issue, states: 'American Jews must come to grips with our contemporary anti-Semites; we must fill our insane asylums with anti-Semitic lunatics.'

"You see, Mr., what will happen when Jews and Communists take control of this great nation. Real Americans will be locked away in asylums. Freedom will blow away in a dust storm."

"Congressman," said Moses. "I realize you were not up for reelection this cycle, but as of January 3rd, the committee you sat on as chair last year is now chaired by a Democrat. We have a new governor, Soapy Williams, a Democrat, and you may have difficulty finding an audience for your final report."

For the first time, the Congressman sat down. "I still have time to submit my report, Mr., and what I have to say may have repercussions for you in particular."

"How so," said Moses. "I have cooperated with the grand jury and your probe. I offered to help the grand jury in any way I could. I have one goal and only one item on my agenda, and that is to get an innocent sixteen-year-old boy released from jail. He didn't shoot his father despite the circumstantial evidence.

"If an official investigation were launched into the background and activities, both historical and current, of Owen Kressbach, I believe the real murderer would be revealed. I've done all I can to explore this matter and ask for help to move forward with the case."

Mr. Hoffman rose again and paced back and forth along the table length, rubbing his chin. Then he smiled as if he had just trapped the fox and was ready to blow his horn to end the hunt.

"So," he said. "You now admit to investigating the lives and actions of people in this city, acting independently as a private investigator. That, Mr. Webb, is illegal in this state.

"Or have you just made a mistake in judgment and see now how the facts line up with a conspiracy to incite a riot by Detroit and Kalamazoo Union management."

"I'm not a private investigator, and I never represent myself as such," Moses said.

"Oh, then how do you get your information?" Hoffman said, hoping Moses would dig an even deeper hole for himself.

"I'm a good listener," said Moses.

"Oh,"

"Look, I have a full-time job as an auto mechanic. I have occasionally done a favor for friends who ask me because of my background working on the police force. I am occasionally reimbursed for my expenses."

"What church do you attend, Mr. Webb."

"Not your concern," said Moses.

"Don't you feel the weight of the Lord on your shoulders?"

"No, my conscience is clear."

Hoffman said, "Hmmfff," and "I've met a righteous man," and dropped the subject. "What do you think of the police force in Kalamazoo," he asked.

"**Chief Hoyt** leads an exemplary force. I've no beef with the chief. Ross Kirkpatrick is an outstanding cop, honest as the day he was born."

"Having said that, there is a worry in the department that a mole is feeding information to the agitators of the riot. In particular, to Owen Kressbach. One mole has already been eliminated, and an arrest warrant is out on Kressbach.

The congressman shuffled more papers and referred to his legal pad. "Alex Madden, right?"

"What happened to Mr. Madden?" said Hoffman.

"He was shot to death in the back by Owen Kressbach," said Moses. "Thus the arrest warrant."

"And you say there is another pipeline to these riot agitators.? You're exaggerating. You just said Chief Hoyt's police force is above reproach."

"There is still a leak. I believe Chief Hoyt will root it out as well."

"If it exists, which I doubt," said the Congressman. "I think it is time to bring Judge Smith into our conversation."

Mr. Hoffman used the telephone and dialed the building operator. He spoke into the phone, "Send someone down to Judge Smith's office and request that he join me in my conference room. Have him bring his rough draft of the grand jury report."

Mr. Hoffman's ability to pull strings became evident. Judge Smith opened the conference room door within ninety seconds of the call.

"Morning, Clare," said the judge. "How can I assist you. I brought the report."

"Summarize for us the report's main thrust," said Hoffman.

Judge Smith opened the notebook he carried, glanced at it once, and then looked at his audience, Clare and Moses.

"The gist of it," said Judge Smith., "is that we will be indicting CIO Union officers for inciting a riot at the Shakespeare factory on December 1st, 1948. Charges may include conspiracy and destruction of property. The report's body outlines several officers' testimony confirming our accusations."

Moses was not impressed. Judge Smith mentioned no guilt by the Shakespeare management team for the riot. "I take it," Moses said, "that my testimony didn't make it into the report."

Judge Smith replied, "Your testimony, Mr. Webb, as recorded by the court stenographer, is included in Appendix G. We didn't feel it credible enough to include in the conclusive summary of the report."

Moses stood up. "Thank you, Judge Smith and Congressman Hoffman, for your explanation. If you have no more need of my presence, I'll head on to work. I have a carburetor to put back together."

The congressman opened the conference room door for Moses. He would get the last word, saying, "I hope you understand how impressed we have been with your testimony and the photographic evidence you provided. We will pass copies back to the proper authorities for further investigation."

Moses smiled. "I see where you're coming from. Your vigilance against communist influences here in Kalamazoo is something to consider."

"That's all we ask."

Mulling over the meeting as he walked back to his apartment, Moses pondered his ambivalence. If he hadn't already dismissed Owen Kressbach as Leroy's murderer, he might have demanded further investigation, possibly by the FBI. Perhaps Moses should have done just that, if only to get more agencies in on the hunt for the man threatening Eileen, Harry, and himself. Luckily, he had checked himself before going in that direction with Congressman Hoffman, whose deaf ears would have tuned him out immediately.

As to his ace in the hole, the tape of the conversation in the Shakespeare conference room, Moses realized the mention would have gotten him thrown into jail. The tape did not disprove that Martin Simmons murdered Leroy Simmons, only that an associate of Leroy's, other than Owen Kressbach, might have.

31 | Funeral Service

Eileen and Beverly Simmons greeted people entering the Mt. Zion Baptist Church as Moses walked up the front steps. The temperature had reached 16 degrees, and the perpetual Michigan winter gloom hung low and heavy overhead. There were only two people ahead of Moses entering the Narthex. Eileen stood to the left, Beverly to the right. Eileen wore a black dress just below her knees, a white silk scarf, and a gold Egyptian pin. Beverly favored a black long-sleeve turtleneck sweater, nylons, and skirt. She kept her black hat on, which had a wide weave veil she peered through. She looked like she had stepped out of a beat bar in Greenwich Village.

Moses sat in the fifteenth pew to observe the guests. There were about thirty people in attendance, which surprised Moses until he gathered that all of the guests were friends or coworkers of Eileen. Council Hawes Jr. was paying his respects (to Eileen more than Lercy.) When Beverly entered, she sat beside a gentleman friend in a dark blue, well-fitted suit seated in the second pew on the right. Eileen coaxed Moses to move to a seat next to her in the second pew on the left.

A tap on his shoulder caused Moses to turn around. Harry and Sarah Martensen sat in the pew behind Eileen and Moses. Sarah reached forward and gently gripped Eileen's shoulder. Eileen patted Sarah's hand.

Leroy's closed coffin was positioned to the far left of the pulpit. The minister was Caucasian and dressed in a black robe with a grey stole. The crisp collar of his white shirt was buttoned at his neck. He was assisted on the organ by a heavyset woman of color.

The minister seemed to be waiting to start the service, watching the rear doors to the sanctuary. Two minutes later, the doors opened, and Marvin Simmons entered with Ross Kirkpatrick in his dress uniform holding his elbow. Marvin's coat was draped over his clasped hands, hiding the obligatory handcuffs. Turning, Moses noted the six-foot-one sophomore guard walking with his head high and shoulders back. Marvin looked ahead to the pulpit until he and Ross reached the pew where Eileen and Moses sat. Moses slid away from Eileen so Marvin and Ross could sit beside her. Sheila sat on the left side of Eileen. She looked over at Marvin once and smiled. During the rest of the service, she looked straight ahead, her lip curled and bitten to keep from losing control of her emotions in seeing her boyfriend for the first time in nearly a month outside the jail.

Eileen spent another minute hugging her son. The boy was crying now upon seeing his mother. When she finally let Marvin loose, he turned and nodded to Moses.

Ross leaned into Moses. "Compliments of Chief Hoyt, who hopes this doesn't get back to the prosecutor," said Ross. "By the way, he thanks you for the collar of Melissa Soebbing. She's turning states evidence against her suppliers, which are another level up the chain."

"She put up quite a catfight," whispered Moses. "Did my name come up?"

"Once at the beginning of the interview, but when she started to bargain, we gave her a chance to forget your name. Unfortunately, we didn't discover the whereabouts of Owen Kressbach. She either doesn't know where he is, or she still carries a torch."

The minister must have been waiting for the police escort of Marvin Simmons. Moses saw Marvin glance over at the coffin for about five seconds. Eileen placed her hand on the coat covering Marvin's handcuffs.

Pastor Daughtry began the service by pointing to an open-top glass jar on the top step next to the podium. "If anyone would like to say a few words on Leroy's behalf or in sympathy with the family, please put your name on a slip of paper and place it in the jar.

The service was predictably short except for the three hymns led by the choir director playing the organ. Before the last hymn, the minister checked the jar and announced, "No one seems to wish to speak about Leroy Simmons. So, we'll take a moment for silent reflection before Mrs. Clemmens starts our final hymn, No. 103.

"After the Hymn, I would request that everyone stay seated while Officer Kirkpatrick escorts Marvin Simmons out of the sanctuary."

Marvin stoically walked out of the church, Ross at his side. Several of Eileen's friends in the pews reached out toward Marvin, but Officer Kirkpatrick brushed them back.

Eileen was surrounded by friends in the fellowship hall next to the sanctuary, where the Women's Missionary Auxiliary served coffee and cookies. Moses leaned against the upright piano, drinking coffee and observing, close enough to hear the conversations.

When Eileen's audience began to filter out of the church, Beverly approached. The blue suit distanced himself from the two of them. Beverly took Eileen by the elbow, huddling close. "Eileen, I need money. I'm so desperate. You owe me for the times I helped you through some pretty ugly nights before Leroy finally left you.

Please. Please see it in your heart to give me just $1,000.00 for all my support over the years."

Eileen rolled her eyes, barely containing her anger. "In the first place, I kicked that man out of my life. Second, remember I have paid for the funeral, coffin, and cemetery plot. Someday, perhaps Marvin can look at his father's grave with forgiveness. For now, please leave me alone."

Beverly's friend in the blue suit approached and led Beverly away, passing by Moses. "Any luck, you're running out of time."

Moses had found his new suspect. The man in the blue suit was too polished. He didn't fit as Beverly's boyfriend. Moses found Harry and Sarah near the coffee machine.

"Harry," he said. "Do you, by any chance, have your camera with you?"

"It's in the car. What do you need," asked Harry.

"I want to get a picture of the man with Beverly."

"Got it." Harry rushed out. Beverly and her friend were heading out of the church. Moses rushed over to them.

"Bev, have you got a minute," he said, stalling for time.

Beverly was raking her arm through the wool sweater she was wearing. Either the wool was unbearable, or something else was irritating her skin. Moses became even more suspicious when Beverly scratched her other arm vigorously before putting on her heavy coat and scarf.

"I hope you have gotten the message, Miss Simmons," said Moses. He looked at the man in the blue suit, reaching out with his hand. "We haven't met. My name is Moses Webb; I'm a friend of Eileen's, and your name is?"

"Beverly, we're late," said the man. "Nice to meet you."

A couple of minutes after the couple left the church, Harry entered and nodded at Moses. Mission accomplished.

"What are you thinking, Moses," said Harry.

"I looked at Beverly in her scarf and coat, and it hit me," said Moses. "She's the woman I spotted through your telephoto lens conversing with Leroy outside the train station."

"How does that help us," said Harry. "She's Leroy's sister."

"I don't know if it does yet. Develop the snapshot. I'll try to do a background check with Ross. I have a feeling we're back in the game. Can you get me that photograph by tomorrow? The trial is just around the corner now."

Moses and Eileen thanked Harry and Sarah for coming to the service. Eileen and Sarah were already fast friends. Moses helped Eileen and then Sheila with their coats.

Yep, things just went north again.

Harry walked into the garage shortly after five the next day and handed Moses a six-by-nine-inch manilla envelope. Moses pulled out two photographs of the man in the blue suit who had attended the funeral service. A third photo captured Beverly Simmons walking down the steps of Mt. Zion Baptist Church.

"That was quick, Harry, thanks," said Moses.

"What are you thinking, Moses," said Harry. "They aren't exactly the couple of the year."

"That's what caught my attention," said Moses. "They definitely don't fit. She looks as trashy as her brother, Leroy, even in her Sunday best. He's a snappy dresser but looks better suited to selling the cars in the church parking lot. Something is up with these two. Anyway, it's all I've got right now. I'm going to play it out."

"Let me in on it, Moses; you look like you swallowed the canary," said Harry.

Moses scratched the back of his head. "I think Beverly Simmons is the woman I saw arguing with Leroy before you joined up and began taking photographs."

"I remember," said Harry. 'You said the woman wanted money from Leroy. He showed her his empty wallet .'"

"Right," said Moses. "This picture in front of the church matches my memory of that woman."

"Ok, what's next."

"Background checks. First thing in the morning, I'll bounce these pictures off Kirkpatrick at the police station and thumb through the mug shots again."

[276]

"Anything I can do," asked Harry.

"Not until I check out these two," said Moses. "Hang loose. Did Sarah get a hold of the editor at the newspaper?"

"Not sure, but I know she has been talking to Eileen quite a bit. They seem like old chums now."

"They're both driven. Tell Sarah how much we appreciate her help, and yours, for that matter."

"No worries, Moses."

***

The following day, Moses waited for Eileen to return from Borgess Hospital before he left for the police station. He felt uncomfortable speaking ill of her late husband's sister, deciding that if he found out anything at the police station, he would fill her in.

"By the way," said Moses. "Where does Beverly live?"

"I don't honestly know, Moses," said Eileen. "I try not to think about her and haven't for over two years. I heard she moved from Battle Creek, but I have no idea where."

"Ok, I better get going," said Moses. "How's Sarah doing with getting the newspaper to help."

"She's working on it. She knows the editor, John Walsh.[40] He's been tied up in meetings when she calls. She said she's coming in for a class at Western Michigan College tomorrow and plans on collaring him then."

"Good; if your idea is going to work, we need to get something in the Gazette by the day after tomorrow."

***

When Moses checked with the duty sergeant, he was told Ross Kirkpatrick hadn't arrived yet and probably wouldn't for a few hours. Moses asked to see the mug books. Starting with the notebook labeled 'A,' He slowly turned each page. Moses made it to 'Belkin' in the 'B' notebook before he thought he would go blind if he turned one more page.

Standing and stretching to ease the knot in his neck, Moses walked to Chief Hoyt's office and knocked on the door.

"Come in," said the voice behind the door.

Moses opened the door and stood in front of the Chief's desk. Chief Hoyt, startled for a few moments, said, "Moses, I've been hoping you would stop in."

There were several piles of documents on his desk. Each pile was squared to the table and neatly aligned. Chief Hoyt went immediately to the stack on the upper right corner of his desk. He extracted a paper three down from the top of the pile.

"Ross and I narrowed the possibilities to three officers. If you find out any of these men have connections to the Shakespeare company or any other major Kalamazoo company, I expect you to contact me immediately. I'll decide on a course of action. Don't act on anything on your own at the risk of you or the department being sued. Hopefully, these three men will never know of your investigation. Do you understand the parameters?"

"Yes, Chief," said Moses, "Discretion. I'll report to you in a week, sooner if I find the leak."

Moses glanced at the names on the list before folding it and putting it in his hip pocket next to his billfold. The name he expected to see was not on the list. He mentally added it anyway.

Halfway through the 'D' notebook, Moses stopped at a picture of Devon Drelles. He had been questioned and held for 48 hours during a drug sting operation in St. Joseph, Michigan. He was never charged. No Kalamazoo address was listed.

It was mid-afternoon when Moses turned his attention to Beverly Simmons. He only had thirty-five minutes before the start of his shift. He pulled the 1st of two 'S' mug books and quickly found Beverly Simmons.

Beverly had been arrested three times five years ago for possession of a controlled substance. She had been picked up three months ago and questioned for loitering in the Westnedge Hill Neighborhood. The arresting officer suspected Beverly was offering sex for money to buy drugs. Police patrolled the upscale area between Westnedge Street and Oakland Drive to prevent riff-raff from taking hold. Beverly was released after being questioned for an hour and a half. The address area under her picture was smudged, erased, and filled in with her current address as of the date she was questioned.

Moses rushed to the Cities Service Station to punch in for his shift. On his lunch break, he ate his sandwich in front of the wall outside the manager's office that held a four-foot by four-foot City of Kalamazoo Avenue map. When called out to pick up a vehicle, the tow truck operators would use the large map to pinpoint little-known streets they weren't familiar with.

Myrtle Street was only two blocks long, running east to west. 407 Myrtle, where Beverly rented, was on the corner of the west end of the street, next to the railroad tracks.

Moses had no doubt Leroy camped out on occasion at Beverly's place, able to keep an eye on his family. From Eileen's house, a person would walk half a block west to Porter Street and one block south to Myrtle, and they would be at Beverly's doorstep.

As his shift wore on, Moses became more convinced he was on the right track. He came up with three possible motives for the murder of Leroy. Desperation for drug money, debts owed by Leroy, and perhaps family psychology. Beverly fitted the bill better than Owen Kressbach and Melissa Soebbing.

When Eileen unlocked the door to the apartment, Moses was waking up from the best night's sleep he'd had in weeks.

At midnight, in bed, he had come up with a plan. A bit crazy. Maybe a lot crazy, but time was running out. Marvin's trial was now only four days away.

A two-pronged approach was in order. Hopefully, Sarah Martensen had made progress with the editor of the Gazette. An article in the newspaper might help with public sentiment, even if short on evidence. Many readers would read the headline, absorb a well-written spin, and ignore the lack of proof. Marvin was a rising sports star in high school. He was a good student and had never been in trouble before. All points were in his favor, except for his mother's skin color.

Moses needed to accomplish the second prong of attack on his own, possibly with Harry's assistance. He couldn't involve Eileen. She must not know his intent. Moses was committed to Eileen; his personal risk was only a minor consideration. If things didn't work out or went south again,

Eileen would be, at worst, an unwitting accomplice, safe from prosecution.

Moses swung his legs over the side of the bed and stretched. When he stood up, Eileen embraced Moses, kissed him, and peeled off her nurse's uniform.

"Do you mind if I take the first shower, Moses?"

"Go ahead, I'll make coffee."

Ten minutes later, Eileen reentered the apartment in her bathrobe and slippers, and Moses shuffled off to the shower. He came back clean and shaved.

Eileen had news to share over breakfast. "Sarah has a class this morning at the college. She plans to camp at the Gazette editor's office at ten-thirty. We'll know if she is successful by lunchtime."

"Harry and Sarah are both gems," said Moses.

"I'll say," said Eileen. "Sarah has already sketched out an article. If she gets the assignment, she'll have it written by the deadline. Sarah was the editor of her yearbook in high school and reporter for The State News in East Lansing as an undergraduate."

"Come to think of it, I need to talk to Harry on another matter," said Moses. He called Nusbaums, where Harry worked, and left a message for him to return the call. Forty-five minutes later, the phone rang. It was Harry.

"Could you stop by the station on your way home to milk the cow," said Moses.

"Sure. Does this have anything to do with Leroy's sister?"

"Yes," said Moses into the phone. "I'll fill you in when I see you."

"So Eileen hasn't heard about this development."

"That's right. Eileen is right here. See you this evening."

"See you then," said Harry and hung up.

The couple had nearly two hours before they thought Sarah might bring them news. Moses was sitting at the kitchen table, and Eileen, standing, reached around his shoulders and hugged his head to her breasts.

"I really think Sarah will help us," said Eileen.

Moses stood up, took Eileen by the hand, and led her to the bed. "I think we should get rid of some of that nervous energy," he said. At the bed, Moses stopped and began to unbutton Eileen's blouse.

"I just got dressed, Moses," Eileen said.

"I know, and now I'm getting you undressed.

After removing the blouse, Moses reached around and unclasped Eileen's bra. She shrugged it off, breasts bouncing and nipples extended in the cool of the apartment.

Eileen unbuckled Moses' belt and pulled his pants down to his ankles while Moses unbuttoned his shirt and discarded it on a kitchen chair. He kicked his pants away while Eileen dropped her skirt to the floor. She smiled up at Moses, relaxed at the moment, leaving her worries in the pile of her clothes.

She loved the strong man beside her, and he loved her and couldn't get enough of her.

***

Moses was tucking in his shirt, and Eileen was buttoning up her skirt when they heard a knock on the door. Moses opened it, and Sarah Martensen entered.

"I'm a bit early," she said. "I hope you don't mind. I only have the babysitter until three o'clock."

"Give us the highlights, and we'll let you go," said Moses.

"Ok, maybe we could sit at the table," said Sarah.

Moses nodded and sat down.

Eileen also sat down. "How did it go," she said. "Will he listen to the tape?"

"I got in to see Mr. John Walsh, the editor-in-chief. He's been around since the great war but would only give me five minutes of his time."

Eileen's shoulders slumped a bit. "Did he listen to you? Will he run an article?"

"Well, he said I could write it. Honestly, I got the impression from the speed at which he shooed me out of his office that we'd be lucky to get four inches in one column on page three."

"That's crazy," said Moses. "Anything connected with the strike at Shakespeare is big news locally. Nationally as well."

"Can you write the story within those parameters, Sarah?" said Eileen. "Maybe he will see the importance when he reads your article."

Moses shrugged. "The story involves a colored boy from the Northside Neighborhood, which most of the city doesn't want to hear about or even acknowledge. Marvin is part of the dark city of Kalamazoo. A too dark city in many white minds."

"How can you say that, Moses," said Eileen. She was turning desperate again. "This isn't the deep south."

"What do you think, Sarah. Where you're from in Chicago, would you imagine the same response?"

"Honestly," said Sarah. "I don't know. Harry and I see things a bit differently than locals. Harry went through officer training at Valley Forge Military Academy. They were running an experimental joint training course that mixed Negros and Caucasians in the classes and in the dorm rooms. That's where Harry became so good at cribbage, playing against his roommate, Jeffery Gardener. They still send each other Christmas Cards."

Eileen was determined to stay positive. "Sarah, I know it is a lot to ask, but how about writing two articles. One should be short like Walsh requested, and the other longer and detailed in the hope that Walsh will pursue a braver path."

"I can do that, Eileen; that's a good suggestion. The article with the tape recording as evidence might do the trick for Marvin."

"The Gazette is a good newspaper," said Moses. "It's the oldest continuously publishing newspaper in Michigan outside of Detroit.

"We'll have to trust Walsh to do the right thing."

Moses refused to show his disappointment but had long since left his naïvete behind in **Baton Rouge.**

Plan B had better work.

33 | Break In

On Saturday evening, Moses and Eileen ate dinner at the Pacific Club. Council Hawes found a table in the far corner of the dining room. They ordered the roast chicken dinner with gravy, mashed potatoes, and green beans. Moses was not about to skip a piece of apple pie for dessert. The stares were becoming more furtive and embarrassing for Eileen. They didn't stay long. After dessert and one slow dance, the couple left. Moses drove Eileen's car back to her house.

Eileen had bagged her soiled laundry to soak before they left for dinner. Moses grabbed his duffel that held his pajamas and shaving kit and carried it to the bedroom while Eileen ran her clothes through the wringer and hung them up to dry. Moses made a pot of coffee.

The phone rang, and Eileen spoke to Sarah Martensen. She promised to stop by on Sunday so Moses and Eileen could read the article. She planned on presenting the article to John Walsh or another of his editors first thing Monday.

The couple was sitting at the kitchen table, finishing their coffee, when they heard a knock on the back door. Eileen went to open the door while Moses remained seated.

Moses heard the back door crashing open with a tremendous bang, rattling the glass in the transom and causing the door handle to bang into the mudroom wall. Moses began to stand as Eileen backed into the kitchen, followed by Owen Kressbach, gun already pointing at Moses' chest.

"Don't get up," Owen said. "Keep your hands on the table." Moses obeyed.

"You," Owen said. "You must be Eileen Simmons. I've seen you from a distance once, talking with Leroy. Up close, you're a much pretty nigger woman than Leroy deserved, that's sure."

Blood rushed to Moses' face. He half rose in his chair.

"Don't," said Owen. "You'll die sooner than I wish if you try it." Moses sat back down.

Kressbach reached behind and closed the door to the mudroom. He backed up against the door, a good seven feet away from Moses sitting at the table. If Moses tried to rush the man, he would be shot in mid-air.

"You must be crazy, Kressbach, coming here. Every cop in the city is looking for you. My friends patrol this place every half hour. Hang around here, and you've had it."

Owen laughed. Eileen covered her ears to shut out the maniacal noise. "Hands on the table, woman," said Owen. He stepped toward Eileen and raised his hand, ready to backhanded slap her. Eileen quickly placed her hands on the table.

"Whatever you do, Eileen, whatever you might try, I'll shoot you or Moses. Probably both, remember that," said the psychopath.

"Leave her be, Creep," said Moses. "Put the gun away and take me on. You've got fifteen, maybe twenty pounds on me. I remember those shitkicker boots of yours. My ribs still aren't 100%. You have every advantage. I know you'd like nothing better than to break the ribs on the other side."

Kressbach looked quizzical for a good ten seconds. A wry smile erupted into another crazy laugh as he said, "That's right. So that was you who I beat to shit the first night I hit town. Small world."

"Isn't it though," said Moses, "But it's understandable. It was pitch black that night, and you worked your magic boots at the darkest spot on the block, and I blended into the dark of night, invisible."

Moses' lip curled in anger as he spat, "Put the gun down. I'll let you have four chances to put me down before I tear into you. What do you say? Hard to resist putting me in my place, I'm betting."

"Later, maybe," said Owen. "I'll probably just shoot you. First, let me have the tape recording, and she gets a pass."

"Good enough. Eileen, take off," said Moses.

"Stay where you are, bitch," said Owen.

"I thought you agreed to her departure in exchange for the tape," Moses said.

"The order is the problem now," said Kressbach. "Produce the tape, and then she can leave."

"I was born in Lousiana, Kressbach," said Moses. "I wasn't born stupid."

Kressbach laughed again. His laugh was becoming higher pitched. Moses couldn't tell if he was getting under Owen's skin or vice versa.

"Enough, give me the tape."

"Find it yourself."

Kressbach stuck the gun against Eileen's head, just above her left ear. He was too far away for Moses to get to him before he pulled the trigger. The more Eileen leaned away, the more Kressbach pushed the point of his gun against her head. She closed her eyes and silently clamped her lips together, determined not to give the abuser the satisfaction of breaking down.

"Five seconds," said Owen. "Where is it?"

Moses counted to three in his head. "Alright, back off. I'll tell you where it is."

"Sensible, Nigger," said Owen. "Here in the Kitchen?"

"It's not even in the house," said Moses. "The tape is locked away in a hiding place in my apartment. A friend knows where it is and what to do with it if anything happens to me."

Owen smiled again and sang, "Heigh-Ho, Heigh-Ho, It's off to work we go." He motioned with his gun for Eileen and Moses to stand up. He backed up again so Moses could put on his leather jacket and grab his fedora, keeping the firearm against Eileen's side the whole time. Moses backed up against the wall while Eileen put on her coat.

Moses tried again. "You won't need Eileen. Leave her here, tie her up if you want. I can get you into the apartment, find the tape, and hand it over to you."

"No soap," said Owen. "This gun in her side will keep you acting like a choirboy. She is coming with us. We take my car. She drives. You sit in the back seat on the passenger side. I'll sit behind Eileen on the driver's side. Make a move, shithead, and one of you dies. I don't care which one. Now, let's go. I'm ready to blow town."

Moses tried to stay calm. There was no hiding place in his apartment unless the top drawer of his dresser that held his socks counted as such. He hadn't given instructions to Harry or Ross or anyone else in the event he went missing.

Stall for time. Think of something.

The short drive to **Southworth's Paints and Oils** store was uneventful. Moses had no safe opportunity to jump Owen to wrestle the gun away from him. For once, in January, the street was bone dry, and they met no other cars along the way, so Eileen had no option but to drive to their destination. Eileen found a parking spot in the block beyond the store. When the three of them got out of the car, Owen made Moses walk in front while he kept his gun discreetly sticking in Eileen's back.

A man and a woman, walking arm in arm, turned the corner at Burdick and started walking toward Moses. Owen might be hesitant to shoot here, in front of witnesses. Moses stepped in front of the man. "Got a light by any chance, sir?" he said.

The man was taken aback, especially when he looked up and Saw Moses and Eileen. He didn't say a word. He took his lady friend by the elbow, and Jaywalked across the street and turned down the first alley.

"Don't try that again, or your woman dies," said Owen.

"Sorry, but I could really use a smoke," said Moses.

"Forget it. Let's get inside," Owen said.

Moses unlocked the entry door to the foyer and stairwell up to the second floor. The wall on his left contained the mailboxes of the residents, of whom there were only three men besides Moses, who were currently occupying flats on the second floor.

Moses climbed the stairs first, followed by Eileen and Owen, holding her left arm with his left hand, his gun pressed against her side. As Moses fumbled with the key to his apartment, Jim Boyer, one of the three other residents, came out of the shower room, looked up, and said, "Moses, how's it going. How about coming down to my place for a game of cribbage on Sunday. Popcorn is included."

"I may not be available this Sunday, Bob," said Moses. Come to think of it, could you call Ross and…"

"Moses," said Owen, "I'm in a real hurry. I can still make the train if I can get that package."

Moses stopped addressing Bob and concentrated on unlocking his door. He briefly saluted Bob as he walked by and entered his apartment. Owen shoved Eileen ahead and shut the door, throwing the deadbolt.

"Webb, stay next to the table," said Kressbach. "Take that big pot hanging above the sink and set it on the table." Moses did as he was told.

"That's it, good," said Owen. "Now, where is this hiding place? If you don't tell me, I'll clock this pretty woman so hard the scar will be with her till she dies."

"You don't want to do that, Kressbach, or gun or no gun, I'll come after you."

"Well, what's it going to be," said Owen.

"I'll get the tape," said Moses, walking toward his dresser."

"Hold it," said Owen. "I want Eileen here to go fetch it."

"It's in the top drawer, Eileen," said Moses. Owen gave Eileen a shove toward the dresser while he swung his gun and pointed it at Moses, standing eight feet away in the kitchen. Eileen opened the top drawer and extracted the 7" reel. Her hand shook as she held it up for Owen to see.

"So much for the lock and hiding place," said Owen.

"I lied," said Moses.

"Put the tape in the pot, Eileen. Use the matches on the counter and set the tape on fire."

Eileen looked at Moses with despair. The evidence she hoped would reopen the investigation of her husband was her last hope.

"Go ahead, Eileen," said Moses. "We'll find another way."

She struck three matches one after another and tried to get the tape to burn, but her hand shook so severely that the matches all went out.

"Where's your lighter fluid, Webb," said Owen. "We have places to go."

From listening to the tape, Moses knew the celery bog was their next stop. He was getting desperate. If he were shot but could at least disable Kressbach, maybe Eileen would have a chance.

"There's a can of lighter fluid in the top drawer where the tape was kept."

"Good, said Owen. "Eileen, get it and set that fucking tape on fire."

Eileen crossed to the dresser, opened the drawer, and looked in until she spotted the small can of lighter fluid. Leaving the drawer open, she took the can over to the table, squirted the tape ten times, and lit a match. The tape whooshed up in flames, melting the tape. Eileen backed up to the dresser to avoid the heat. No one would be listening to that tape recording again.

Owen motioned Moses toward the apartment door, backing into the kitchen to keep a safe distance from the colored man. As Moses crossed in front of Owen, Eileen was out of sight for two seconds, long enough for Eileen to reach into the dresser drawer, pull out Moses' revolver, and point it at Owen. Her hand no longer shook as she said, "I've got a gun now, you bastard, and I won't miss hitting you at this distance. You're on your way to hell."

Moses knew the gun wasn't loaded. He never kept it loaded in the apartment. Owen, recovering from the shock of seeing Eileen holding a gun steady with both her hands, turned to Eileen and fired as Eileen pulled the trigger four times. Moses dove across the room, grabbing Owen's gun hand and gun. He saw Eileen slump to the floor from the corner of his eye.

Before a fight, Moses worked himself into a tensive state that carried him unafraid into the match and gave his fists the ferocity needed to win.

He needed no such workup to invent the wild fury he unleashed on Owen Kressbach as he wrestled him to the floor.

Eileen, Eileen.

Moses hit the table leg as he tumbled on top of Owen. The pain shot through his back and ribs. He dared not let go of Owen's gun hand. The gun went off again, a wild shot, hitting the Vargas calendar hanging on the wall beside his bed. He held the hand, gripping the weapon with his left hand while squeezing and twisting Owen's wrist with his right. Owen was beating Moses on his head and shoulders with his left fist and desperately trying to find something heavy to hit Moses. Moses didn't let go. Owen's hand began turning blue, and finally, he let the gun drop. Moses was able to get to one knee and kicked the gun under the bed, out of both their reach.

Owen curled into a ball and got both feet into Moses' chest. Kicking out, he broke free and stood up opposite Moses. Moses glanced at Eileen holding her arm, blood streaming onto the floor. She had turned ghastly white, something Moses didn't know was possible for a woman of color.

Owen was kneading his right hand with his left. He shook it to get the blood flowing and the color back to normal, readying himself for a brute-force fight with Moses.

Moses stepped in, jabbing with his right, hitting Owen rapidly in the solar plexus. Owen was throwing wild haymaker punches. Moses raised his left arm shoulder high (as high as he could lift it) to ward off Owen's blows.

With his right, he started jabbing at Owen's head, snapping it back each time.

Owen was already groggy, but the hate on his face kept him coming at Moses. The big man closed with Moses, bear hugging to catch his breath. Moses kneed the man in the groin and broke free of the clutch. Three jabs to Owen's head, an uppercut to his stomach, and a right cross to Owen's chin sent Owen to the floor.

Moses looked over at Eileen and decided he wasn't through with Kressbach. He bent over and hit him again and again. He picked the man up by the collar with his left hand and hit him some more, remembering every kick from the first time they met on that dark street and the second time when he was tied to the chair in the Cities Services station.

"That's enough, Moses," Eileen managed to whisper. "He's done."

It was true. Owen Kressbach was out cold, bloody, or swollen from eyes to nostrils to swollen lips.

Moses let go of Owen's collar, and the man conked his unconscious head on the floor. Moses rushed first to the kitchen for clean towels and then over to Eileen, swooning with a slight grin.

"I guess I just saw you in the ring. You must have been pretty exciting to watch, Moses," she said.

Eileen was holding her arm. Owen's shot had grazed her left arm. Moses examined the hole, determining that the bullet had passed through her upper arm, missing the humerus. Moses filled a pot of hot water. He helped Eileen to the table and used one of the towels to clean the wound with soapy water. Then he covered the arm in a gauze bandage and wrapped the whole affair in one of the dish towels, securing it with safety pins. Moses began to calm down. He didn't know how he got it, but he had a small cut above his left ear. He dabbed at it with another towel.

Owen was still out. Moses dialed the precinct.

"Police headquarters, how may I help you," said the duty sergeant.

"This is Moses Webb. Is Ross Kirkpatrick available?" said Moses. "I just made a citizen arrest of Owen Kressbach. Can you send someone over to take him to jail?"

"Ross came in with a reckless driving collar a half hour ago. He should be able to get to your place in another fifteen minutes or so. Hang tight. You're above the Paints and Oils store, right?"

"Make it as soon as you can,' said Moses. "My gal needs a hospital. She's been shot in the arm."

"I'll call for an ambulance," said the duty sergeant.

"Yes. Tell Ross to step on it."

34 | The Arrest

Owen stirred. Moses dug a clothesline out of his closet and tied Owen's hands behind him. Moses gagged Kressbach with one of his t-shirts and formed a slipknot with the end of the clothesline, cinching it around his prisoner's mouth.

Moses figured the wail of a police siren meant Ross was on his way. Ross burst through the apartment door in another minute, followed by Craig Sheid.

"Moses, are you OK?" said Ross, then he saw Owen Kressbach trussed up and curled on the floor near the bed. Eileen, looking about to faint, was lying on the bed.

"Yes, I'm fine, I guess," said Moses.

"The ambulance will be here shortly," Ross said.

"Craig, Get the handcuffs on this guy." While Ross held his gun pointing at the prisoner, Craig cut the clothesline, binding his hands. Owen looked like he'd been hit by a Mack truck. His eyes weren't tracking. Craig placed Owen's hands on his lap and handcuffed him.

The ambulance arrived, and two male nurses showed up with a stretcher. By that time, Eileen's color had returned. One of the nurses removed the makeshift bandage Moses had applied and looked at the wound. He recognized Eileen as a fellow nurse at the hospital. "Eileen, you must have been born under the right star. One inch over, and your arm would have been shattered," he said.

The nurse opened his bag, extracted a syringe and a tiny bottle, and administered the morphine solution into Eileen's shoulder. He waited three minutes and then took a bottle of diluted alcohol from his bag and splashed it in and around the wound. Eileen whimpered but didn't seem to mind the cleaning solution. The nurse bandaged Eileen's arm, slipped a sling over her head and arm, and said, "You should be fine, but I'm leaving three Kadian tablets for the pain. Take only one a day. Rewrap the bandage twice a day and watch for signs of infection. Here are a couple of aspirin. That shot will wear off in an hour or so."

Ross Kirpatrick's attention turned back to Owen Kressbach and Moses. "We'll need a statement from you and Eileen. If you want to bring Eileen into the station when she feels up to it, that will be fine. I prefer to get your statement right away, Moses."

Eileen heard the question and addressed the two officers, "I'll go to the station and make a statement now. I feel OK. The sooner I make my statement, the sooner Jeremy Fulton can get Marvin out of that cell.

"Please, Moses."

Ross looked at Moses and shrugged. "If she is up to it," he said. "The sooner we get a complete statement, the better, while things are fresh in your minds."

Owen Kressbach had revived. Craig handed him a large glass of water, which he gulped down. Owen acted unruly and defiant when Craig took him by the elbow to escort him to the patrol car.

"I'll drive Eileen's car and follow you, Ross. Be careful around that asshole," said Moses.

Moses helped Eileen bundle up, and they walked to Eileen's car. Moses swung the Ford Deluxe around and waited beside the patrol car, ready to follow Ross to police headquarters.

"So we no longer have the tape," said Eileen.

"True, Eileen, but that may work somewhat in our favor," said Moses. "Harry and I can testify as to what was on the tape. By innuendo, Jeremy Fulton may be able to get close enough to the truth to raise doubt in the jurors' minds about Marvin's guilt. Owen will be a hostile witness, but Jeremy may be able to trip him up or give him a reduced sentence in exchange for the other man's name on the tape.

"What will we tell Sarah," said Eileen.

"She may have to rewrite her article," said Moses. "But now she has the alleged attempted murder of Marvin's mother and friend to add more sensation to the article. People will read it, that's sure."

"I hope so, Moses," Eileen said.

"I'm hopeful, Eileen," said Moses. "For the first time in weeks, I'm confident we will beat this thing. Owen Kressbach will be locked up. That gives Jeremy leverage to press for a fast acquittal.

"It's Sunday morning now. The trial is scheduled to begin on Wednesday. Marvin may be eating dinner with us by Wednesday."

The patrol car pulled away from the curb, with Moses tailing close behind. Although the police headquarters was only two blocks away, Ross had pulled up to the Paints and Oils store in the patrol car pointing south on Burdick. Ross continued south on Burdick to South Street, turned east, drove one block, and then turned north. Moses followed. The streets were deserted (shortly after 1:00 a.m.)

Halfway to the station, Moses slowed as the patrol car stopped at the only stop sign. Moses was startled to see the rear passenger side door open. Owen jumped out, still handcuffed, and ran down the cross street. Moses leaped from Eileen's car as Ross exited the patrol car and leaned over the roof.

"Stop, Kressbach, or I'll shoot," Moses heard Ross say. Five seconds later, Moses heard two shots, presumably, according to police procedure, warning shots.

Craig then staggered from the car and turned to Ross for instructions. "Go after him, man," said Ross. "What are you waiting for."

Craig finally shook off his daze and began to chase the runner down the cross street. Moses leaned back into Eileen's car. "Honey, we can't lose him now. I'm going after him. Leave the car running and lock the doors. We should be able to find and subdue him quickly on a deserted morning like this. He still has the cuffs on."

Moses didn't wait for a reply from Eileen. He shut the driver's side door and yelled at Ross. "I'll help Craig out if Owen tries to overpower him."

"Great," said Ross. "I'll drive around the block and cut him off on the other end of this side street." Ross roared off to the north. Moses ran to catch up to Craig. He saw no one the length of the first block.

Moses heard a garbage can crashing on the street in the next block. Either Craig or Owen had tipped it over while running in the dark. Moses was on the right track. He continued running and found himself in more of a residential block east of downtown. About fifty feet away, Craig Sheid had scaled an eight-foot fence. Sitting atop the wall, Moses heard Craig yell at Owen. "Stop, I'm warning you."

Moses heard the patrol car roaring up the street towards his position, somewhere on the other side of the fence. Then, he listened to the muffled voice of Owen Kressbach. "Get the fuck away from me, Craig. You'll get your money. Back off."

Two more shots rang out. Moses saw the brief puff of smoke from Craig's gun. He hurried up to the fence and scaled it, dropping down on the opposite side. Owen Kressbach lay in a pool of blood. Moses checked, but Kressbach was dead. Nothing for it.

"What the hell was that all about, Sheid," said Moses.

Ross Kirkpatrick ran up, took one look at the dead man, and backhanded Craig Sheid, sending him kneeling to the ground, clutching his jaw.

"What the hell, Craig," said Ross. "I told you to take him alive. He was unarmed, for God's sake."

Craig stood up, looking defiant. "He was getting away," he said. "He wouldn't stop. I warned him. He was picking up that big rock. When I came off the fence, he would have clobbered me. It was self-defense."

"The body isn't near that rock, Craig," said Moses. "Those are exit wounds. It looks like he was moving toward you, giving up, maybe."

"The hell he was," said Craig. "You know how dangerous he was, Moses. Clearly, I shot him in self-defense."

Ross shook his head.

"Moses," said Ross. "Would you mind driving your car and reporting in at the station? We'll need forensics and a photographer. We'll stay put until they arrive. It may be an hour or two before we get to your statement. I suggest you take Eileen home. We'll have to take her statements tomorrow."

"Makes sense, Ross," said Moses. "We'll see you later today or tomorrow."

Moses couldn't figure out how to sugarcoat the events of the last twenty minutes. After scaling the fence, he strode back to Eileen's car. He climbed into the driver's seat and shifted to first gear.

"Did you find Owen?" Eileen asked. "Is he back in custody? How did it go?"

"It didn't go well," said Moses. "Craig Sheid shot him as he tried to escape."

"Oh, no," said Eileen. "Is he badly hurt? Did they take him to the hospital? I didn't hear any ambulance sirens."

"That's because he's dead. Owen Kressbach is dead. Shot twice in the chest by Craig Sheid."

Eileen stared out the side window for a few seconds and then wailed, "No! We needed him alive, didn't we, Moses? Whether he confessed or not, whether or not he implicated the other accomplice in the schemes involving the Shakespeare riot, the man was our last resort, and now he's dead."

Moses encircled Eileen with his arms, pulling her close to him in the front seat. When he thought she had settled enough, he said, "I need to go to the police station," said Moses. "Ross wants me to request a forensics team and photographer to investigate the crime scene. If you are up to it, we'll give our statements later after we get some sleep."

At headquarters, Mose left Eileen in the lobby and went to speak to the duty sergeant. He explained what had happened after the formal arrest of Owen Kressbach.

"That's a shame," said the sergeant. "Sheid will have to go through an internal review. He'll be on leave for at least a month, putting more pressure on the rest of the guys. We're short-handed as it is. Why don't you come back to the force, Moses? That collar last week of the Soebbing woman and now the capture of Owen Kressbach, who is wanted in three states. It's a match made in Kalamazoo heaven."

"Can't think about that until Marvin Simmons is back playing basketball as he should be," commented Moses.

Moses asked if Chief Hoyt was in by any chance.

"I have to call him about the shooting," said the sergeant. "You can bet he'll be here within fifteen minutes."

"I may wait," said Moses, "or take Mrs.Simmons home. She's been through the wringer today."

When Moses put the question of waiting for Chief Hoyt up to Eileen, she perked up. "Will you ask him if Marvin's case can be thrown out?"

"I'll ask. I think I'll wait and talk to the chief."

Moses returned to the duty sergeant's desk to check on the sergeant's progress in collecting the staff needed for the investigation of a police patrolman shooting an escaped prisoner. When he returned to Eileen, she lay on the bench, asleep. Moses walked over to the Chief's office to wait. The Chief of Police arrived within minutes and called Moses into his office, asking him to close the door.

"I've got to get out to the scene of the shooting. Give me the highlights; what am I looking at here."

"Boiled down," said Moses. "It goes like this. Owen Kressbach attacked me and Eileen Simmons at her house after dinner last night. When he found out the tape recording was at my apartment, we drove there. The tape was ignited with lighter fluid and is now a melted mess. Eileen saw my gun in the drawer and threatened Kressbach, not knowing the revolver was not loaded. During the distraction, I got a hold of Owen's gun hand, but he got off a couple of shots, one of which sliced through Eileen Simmon's arm.

"I subdued the man with prejudice and called Ross and Craig to make the formal arrest. Eileen and I followed Ross, intending to make our statements.

"Somehow, Owen opened the patrol car's rear door. Please don't ask me how or why it wasn't locked, and Owen, still handcuffed, ran away. After a warning shot from Ross, Craig followed Owen on foot, and I followed Craig in case he needed help. Ross drove to the other end of the street to block Owen's escape.

"I came upon Craig, sitting astride an eight-foot fence, and I could hear Owen Kressbach on the other side. I saw Craig fire twice, and when I got over the wall, I found that Owen Kresbach had been shot and killed.

"Ross sent me to round up a crime scene investigation crew, and I did that. There's your nutshell."

Chief Hoyt rocked back in his swivel chair with his eyes closed. "I can see I'm in a world of hurt over this," said the Chief. "The man hadn't been booked or tried, and yet he's dead. Rookie mistakes. First Madden, now Sheid."

"Don't include Ross in your frustration," said Moses. "Ross went by the book. I specifically heard him order Craig Sheid to capture and not shoot the suspect."

"Still," said Hoyt.

"Chief, let me ask you, of the three names you gave me to investigate in connection with the information leak from the department, did any of those three know about the tape recording?"

"There was no reason for anyone but Ross, you, and I knowing about that tape."

"Yet Owen Kressbach knew about it."

"You think Ross is working with Kressbach and the Shakespeare manager?"

"Not on your life; Ross is an honest cop… one of the most honest men I've known. No, it has to be Craig Sheid. He is around Ross enough that he could have easily heard Ross and me discussing the tape. I think you'll find more motive to this shooting by Craig than a mere rookie mistake."

"I'll speak to Ross," said the Chief. "I want his take on the rookie. I'll suspend Craig, of course, pending an investigation. That could go either way for Craig. The best he could hope for would be a justifiable shooting in the line of duty. I would fire his ass, and he'd never work in law enforcement again.

"Worst case, he goes to trial for manslaughter or homicide, and he gets a life sentence. Ross and I should be able to turn him against whomever he reports outside the department."

Returning to Eileen sleeping on the lobby bench, Moses gently nudged her awake. Moses acknowledged her perseverance and strength for all she was going through. She smiled, sat up, and arranged her tousled hair with her free hand. Moses decided right then that he loved the woman.

Eileen, I'll do whatever it takes.

Moses drove Eileen to her home and helped her to bed. She complained about the excruciating pain in her left arm, and Moses decided to let her take one of the Kadian pills. He stayed until the tablet took effect, and Eileen fell asleep. Figuring she'd be out for half a day, if not longer, Moses drove Eileen's car back downtown.

He spent the next two hours straightening and cleaning his apartment. He threw out the pot with the congealed melted tape. Then Moses stripped and remade the bed with fresh sheets and washed the blood off the furniture and floor.

He looked over the apartment and decided the remnants of Owen Kressbach had been vanquished like a dispersed ghost.

Then Moses called Harry Martensen. "How's your Sunday going, Harry," he said.

"The kids and Sarah are down for their afternoon nap, and I'm going crazy with boredom," said Harry.

"Harry," said Moses. "I could use you on a stakeout this afternoon that might stretch into the evening and night."

Harry answered quickly, "I can't believe I'm saying this, but a stakeout sounds better than total boredom."

"This one is a bit dicey, Harry. There has been a development. Owen Kressbach was shot late last night by Craig Sheid, Ross's partner. He's dead and out of the picture."

"I'm sorry for sounding callous, Moses, but that's a relief. I have been debating how much to tell Sarah about the danger that creep threatened."

"Well, that threat is off the table," said Moses. "What do you say to the stakeout."

"How dicey, Moses? Nothing illegal. The family comes first," said Harry.

Moses took a deep breath and explained, "I need you to keep watch while I break the law. If I get caught, I'll swear you had nothing to do with it."

"Well, at least you're being honest about it," said Harry. "Are there any dangerous 'Owen Kressbach' types involved?"

"I hope not, Harry. My problem if it comes to that."

The phone went silent while Harry thought it over. Then Moses heard, "This is important to you?"

"I'm out of options," said Moses. "The article Sarah wrote won't help because the tape has been destroyed by Owen Kressbach, and Owen has been killed by a policeman."

"Alright, I'll be at your place in an hour. Fill me in, then. It sounds like you had a hell of a night."

"Thanks, Harry. See you soon."

***

When Harry arrived at the apartment around four o'clock, Moses recounted the previous night's events.

"Do you think Sarah should come into town to look after Eileen?" said Harry. "We have a great babysitter who can look after the boys for a day or two."

"We'll ask Eileen when she wakes up," said Moses.

[305]

"So what's the job, and how am I not breaking the law," said Harry."

Moses had the Kalamazoo Avenue map spread out on the table. He pointed with a pencil to one of the spots he had marked. "This is Eileen's house on Parsons Street. Here is the north/south track of the Lake Shore & Michigan Southern railroad. You can see how close it is to Eileen's house.

"This other mark is the address of Beverly Simmons on Myrtle Street, literally two blocks from Eileen's house. Don't ask me how Beverly manages the rent. A side entrance on Pitcher Street faces the railroad track, and the front entrance on the porch faces Myrtle Street.

"Now, this third mark is a place on Porter Street to pull off next to the railroad track and diagonally across from Beverly's place. Parked in that spot, you can observe two sides of Beverly's house. If anyone comes or goes through the front or side doors, you'll see them. So far, so good?" asked Moses.

"No problem. You're hinting that you will be inside that house," said Harry.

"Yes, if a door or window is unlocked, I'll go in quietly. If everything is locked, I will make as little noise as possible, but I'm still going in."

"So you're looking at breaking and entering," said Harry. What are you looking to take out of there."

"Nothing," said Moses. "Not a thing, but I hope to discover something that will allow Ross to legally search the place and gather enough evidence to arrest Beverly Simmons."

"So, no burglary charge. Sounds too simple. Why can't you get Ross to search the place now?" said Harry.

"He has no justifiable reason at this point," said Moses. "My suspicions, without evidence, aren't good enough," said Moses.

"Just what are your suspicions," asked Harry.

"Just a minute," said Moses. "Want a coke?"

Harry nodded. Moses went to his refrigerator, took two bottles of Coca-Cola, and popped the caps. He brought the bottles to the table and handed one to Harry. Then Moses fetched the bowl of popcorn he had prepared while waiting for Harry to arrive and brought that to the table. After munching a couple of handfuls of popcorn and slurping on the coke, Moses moved the bowl of popcorn off the map.

"One thing has been gnawing at me since the beginning of this mess," said Moses. "No one has picked up on it, especially not the police or the district attorney. I could finally explain it after you took those pictures of Beverly at the funeral service and after I eliminated Melissa Soebbing as a suspect."

"What did the police miss?' said Harry. "They questioned Sheila, Curtis, Marvin, me, and Eileen. They wrote off Owen Kressbach's role as a myth. They haven't questioned our mystery man because they don't know who he is. What am I missing?"

"Alright, tell me this," said Moses. "How did Leroy Simmons come to be in Eileen's house. Curtis, Marvin, Sheila, or Owen never saw Leroy approach the house. Curtis would have seen him on Walbridge. Owen would have seen him at the other end of Parsons at Burdick, but they didn't."

Harry snapped his fingers. "Beverly's house." he said. The light bulb had flashed in Harry's head. "Leroy walked to Eileen's from Beverly's house."

"That's it. Once I found out how close Beverly's place was to Eileen's," said Moses. "Everything fell into place.

"Now, by the same token, that is how whoever murdered Leroy escaped detection after killing him.

"Marvin said that after he wiped the fingerprints off of Leroy's gun, he followed someone in a heavy coat out the front door, assuming it was Sheila. A snow squall came through, and Marvin lost sight of the person but hurried along to catch up to Sheila. Owen speeds off after Marvin fires a shot in Owen's direction. Then the police arrive and arrest Marvin."

"So you're thinking the snowstorm hid Beverly as she turned south on Pitcher Street and made it to the safety of her home."

"Certain of it," said Moses, "but we're out of time. With Marvin's trial starting tomorrow, I've got to find something today. I've got to try."

"Boy, my friend," said Harry, "You've got it bad for Eileen and that kid. I've sometimes known you to skirt the law, but this is new. Of course, I don't blame you. She's a beauty through and through."

"I just hope it works."

"Is there a plan," asked Harry.

"Barely. I need to get a feel for the inside of Beverly's place. I'll take Eileen's car and try a direct approach. You set up in the spot I marked on the map. If I don't get in, the windows should offer a clue. If I do get in, so much the better.

"Either way, when I'm done, I'll drive to Eileen's, park, walk roundabout to your car, and join you. Then we wait. Tomorrow's a work day. Beverly may go to bed early. I'll wait an hour after the place goes dark and go in. If she leaves, I'll go in. You brought your camera, didn't you?"

"Always, but it won't help us in a darkened house."

"Just in case, be ready with it. If the bedroom is upstairs, I can turn on a closet light or a lamp in the living room. Otherwise, I've got two brand new 'D' batteries in this flashlight that will have to do.

"Let's see. If Beverly goes out but returns while I'm in her house, blast the horn for a few seconds, and I'll skedaddle. If you hear police sirens getting close, give me two long blasts. If I hear three horn blasts, that means shotguns at the door, and I need to vamoose."

Moses crossed his arms and leaned against the car seat. "That should do it."

"Yeah, that sounds crazy enough," said Harry. "You're on your own on this one, Moses. Like I said, Sarah and the Kids come first."

"See that you stick to that rule," said Moses. "I've started over before. I can do it again. I'm not taking my gun, so I won't be shooting my way out of there. If it's the police, I'll come out peaceably, and you can return to the farm and family. Don't look back. Agreed?"

"There is no other way," said Harry.

"Eileen and Marvin have run out of time."

Harry shook his head. "Then let's get to it."

***

Moses parked in front of Beverly's house and walked up the driveway to avoid the snow that still covered the ground in the yard. Glancing over his shoulder, he gave Harry, who must have been ducking down in his car, a small salute. Moses knocked on the door, waited, and then knocked again. The third time was the charm.

Beverly opened the door a crack. "Whatever you're selling, go away. I ain't;, Oh, it's you," she said

"Beverly, Eileen, and I have been talking it over," said Moses. "Maybe we could help you out somehow."

Beverly shifted gears immediately and turned syrupy sweet. She opened the door and invited Moses in.

"Eileen is a good ole egg," said Beverly. "We had some laughs together back in the day."

By now, it was late afternoon. The long-sleeved housecoat Beverly was wearing didn't close over the top of the slip she wore underneath. For reasons that Moses could only guess at, she was trying to look alluring.

"Yes, we've become quite close," said Moses, stalling while he memorized the furniture placement in the living room and on the other side of the foyer in the dining room. There was a desk against the short wall beyond the dining table opposite the front windows. A beat-up credenza ran along one wall in the living room. The coffee table was littered with cigarette ashes. The décor of the living room reeked of 'early penitentiary,' void of pictures or knickknacks.

"I do a little basketball coaching," said Moses. "I helped Marvin put together a team for a tournament. His team won, by the way. He is an outstanding player."

Beverly didn't make eye contact. She was obviously bored but interested in Moses's proposal. She tapped out a cigarette from a pack on the coffee table, looked around for a light, and waved it in front of Moses, gesturing for a cigarette light. Moses feigned ignorance, so Beverly went to the credenza and flipped down a hinged horizontal cabinet door that revealed a mishmash of papers and junk in a cupboard. She found her lighter and lit her cigarette.

"Why don't we sit down, and you can tell me what Eileen has in mind," said Beverly, gesturing at the couch.

"Alright, Bev," said Moses. "Is it alright if I call you Bev?"

"My friends do," said Beverly.

Moses sat down on the couch while Beverly remained standing and smoking. She began to scratch her left arm through the housecoat.

"Do you mind if I get a glass of water, Bev," said Moses, standing up again.

Beverly put a hand to her cheek. "My heavens, where are my manners. How about a drink? I have some whiskey I snuck in from Windsor last month."

"Sure," said Moses, "You get the whiskey, and I'll get a couple of glasses from the kitchen and a drink of water."

Not waiting for permission, Moses marched toward the kitchen while Beverly returned to the credenza and located a bottle of Hiram Walker's Canadian Club. A quick glance around the kitchen and the bathroom he passed along the way was all he needed for orientation. A door, presumably leading to the basement, was closed, and Moses decided to leave that space for his return after dark, not to raise Beverly's suspicion. He drank a glass of water while he examined the kitchen, then brought his glass and one for Beverly back to the living room.

Beverly poured two shots of Hiram Walker into each glass and sat in the chair to the left of the sofa. Moses sat back down in the middle of the couch. He leaned toward Beverly. "We talked it over, and Eileen feels that in the interest of family harmony and so that Marvin doesn't lose contact with you, his aunt, she could give you $100.00 a month for the next ten months. That's a $1000.00 total, as long as you agree that the $1000.00 will fulfill your request for a settlement."

Moses could sense the wheels in Beverly's head turning. She remained quiet for more than a minute.

"The problem, Moses, is that I need $1000.00 now. I have expenses and a debt I must repay. So, she'll have to do better than a paltry $100.00 now and $100.00/month.

Moses was pretty sure Beverly would turn down the offer. He only had $20.00 in his wallet.

"I think Eileen's offering as much as she can. She has legal expenses for Marvin's defense."

Beverly instantly came up with a solution.

"You make good money, Moses; you could help her."

Moses made a show of his difficulty. He stood, walked over to the window, and looked to see if he could spot Harry in his car parked by the tracks. The vehicle looked empty, even though Moses knew Harry was there. Moses turned back to Beverly.

"You're right. Part of this is my doing as well," said Moses. "Alright, but I don't have that kind of cash on me. I can write you a check for $200.00."

Beverly smiled. A knowing grin. She had caught her fish. Now, to play him. Still smiling, Beverly sat in the chair. Her house robe fell open. She put one foot on the coffee table so that her slip slid back up her thigh. She had good legs and knew how to use them.

"Moses, you are starting to speak my language. How about a little more whiskey." Without waiting for a reply, Bev rose, bent over Moses, and put a hand on his thigh to steady herself while pouring more whisky into Moses' glass. Bending down allowed Moses a full view of Bev's cleavage. If it hadn't been for all the scraggly lines etched on her face and the fact that he had never been tempted to touch a white woman, he might have been influenced.

As it was, Beverly was not giving up. She tossed back her drink. Moses took another sip and set his glass on the end table. Beverly scratched her left arm vigorously and then rubbed the length of it, believing Moses wouldn't notice or perhaps didn't care.

"Maybe you can come up with a bigger check, Moses."

She took his hand and tugged on him until he rose from the sofa. "Bring your glass, and let me show you the upstairs." Beverly didn't let go of his hand as she led him up the stairs. There was a small table in the corner of the landing he would have surely bumped into if he hadn't scouted the house. The bedroom contained a double bed and dresser. There was also a makeup vanity with a set of drawers on the right and a mirror attached for Beverly to apply makeup.

"Before we get too far along, Bev, let me make out that check." Moses sat in the chair, ready to use the vanity to write the check. He took out his checkbook and opened the top right drawer of the vanity to look for a pen.

Beverly nearly closed the drawer on his fingers. "I have a pen on my nightstand." As she went to her nightstand on the other side of the bed, Moses stood and unlatched the window next to the vanity. His broad back hid the effort, and Beverly didn't notice.

Beverly retrieved a pen and handed it to Moses as he sat at the vanity. She put her left hand across the opened checkbook as Moses tried to write. "Make the check for $300.00, Moses. You're about to have a good time."

Moses looked up at Bev. She was using her right hand to massage her breast and make her nipple hard through the slip. Moses bent down and wrote the check for $300.00.

"There you are, Bev," said Moses. "Now, let's have no more discussion about money, OK?"

Beverly took the check, flapping it in the air. She took the check to her nightstand and set it under a perfume bottle. Then she came back to Moses and encircled his neck with her arms and rubbed up against him vigorously with her breasts and extended nipples.

Moses hugged her back, checked his watch, and pulled away, looking at the time. "Shit, Bev, I just noticed the time." He looked out the window. Daylight had turned to dusk.

Moses faked surprise. "I completely forgot about an appointment I made, Bev," he said. "I'm pulling the engine out of a 1920 Packard Roadster for a bigwig from Upjohn, off hours. This side job will help with the money I'm contributing. I gotta go. Now. How about I come back later. What do you say, for a little fun?"

"You are a devil, Moses Webb, but I won't tell. I'm going on a short trip, but I'll be back later."

"When will you be back," said Moses.

"I shouldn't be gone more than a half hour to an hour."

"That works for me; I'll work on that engine for at least forty-five minutes.

"Later," he said.

Moses scampered down the stairs and out the front door. He had managed not to kiss that scraggly pasty white face. A blessing.

***

Harry unlocked the passenger side door, and Moses slid in. "From what I could see through my lens," said Harry, you were successful. Maybe too successful. How far did you get up in the bedroom? It looked interesting."

"It wasn't. I kept thinking of prunes. It was hard to act interested."

"I get it," said Harry.

Moses closed his eyes. "Beverly said she was going out. Let me know when she leaves. I'm on my second day of no sleep."

***

Moses awoke to a jab on his arm. Sputtering awake, he began to sit up, but Harry had a hand on his shoulder and said, "Stay down; she's coming this way."

Moses hunched down in the car seat as a car passed.

"Some dude drove up in a coupe," said Harry. "He waited for a few minutes, then went to the door. Beverly came out, and they just drove by us. Hopefully, the house is empty."

Fully awake, Moses pondered his options. Michigan winters meant that complete darkness would arrive by seven o'clock. He already had to use his flashlight to tell it was 6:45 p.m.

Beverly had said she would be gone for half an hour to an hour. Moses' best chance was now. He put on his leather gloves and opened the car door, "I'm going in. Remember, don't get involved."

"Good luck, Moses."

In the waning dusk, Moses didn't need to turn on his flashlight to make his way to the front of the house. Looking around, he noticed the home next door had already turned on their living room lights. Moses walked up the porch steps and knocked on the front door. There seemed to be no interest from the neighbors, so he tried the door, but it was locked. He backed off the porch and walked around the house to the side entrance. That door wouldn't open either.

Moses could barely make out the bushes around the house in the darkness. No one would see him now unless he made too much noise. He systematically tried each first-floor window, but they were all latched tight.

Keeping his fingers crossed, Moses illuminated the garage's interior with his flashlight. There was a tall step ladder leaning against the back wall. The side door to the garage was unlocked. After retrieving the ladder, Moses leaned it against the house underneath the window he had unlatched in Beverly's bedroom.

Climbing up and standing precariously on the top of the ladder, the window was barely within Moses' reach. He pushed the window up three inches. Then, while doing a chin up on the windowsill and holding himself up with his left hand and arm, he opened the window with his right hand far enough to pull himself up across the sill and into the room.

Moses shut and latched the window, then played his flashlight about the room, pointing it toward the floor. Any observer passing by the house would only see a glow of light in the room. He carefully but rapidly rifled through the dresser drawers, checked the shelf in the closet, and opened all the drawers in the nightstand and vanity. The bottom drawer of the vanity held rubbers, assorted dildos, and lubricating gel.

Moses' heart stopped when he discovered his $300.00 check was no longer on the nightstand. Moses figured he could stop payment on it at the bank on Monday and went on searching the house.

He decided to get the basement out of the way and descended the stairs. The house must have been more than fifty years old. The spider webs in the basement were vast, and the dust on the stairs and the basement shelving units convinced Moses that he wouldn't find anything there.

On the first floor, Moses found the $300.00 check tacked to the corkboard on the wall next to the door leading to the garage. He smiled as he ripped it in two and pocketed the scraps. He checked all of the cupboards in the Kitchen and the broom closet. The next most logical place, the living room credenza, held only the bottle of contraband whiskey Beverly had smuggled in from Canada.

The last place Moses looked was the dining room. The desk held only an extensive pile of unpaid bills and a drawer full of pictures. Time was beginning to pressure Moses. He wanted to be out of the house within thirty minutes. Shining his flashlight on his watch, he determined twenty-five sweating minutes had passed since he left Harry's car.

The pictures included a family portrait of a gruff-looking man and Leroy, the father's arm around his shoulder. On the father's other side, standing a foot away was Beverly, and she was crying. The boy and the man weren't smiling either. There was a duplicate of all the pictures in the envelope, and Moses pocketed one of the copies of the family.

As far as Moses could tell, he had gently searched, leaving no telltale signs of his presence and no fingerprints. Yet he hadn't found anything of significance. Exhaustion and his lack of success made Moses clench his fists and cry out in frustration. He returned to the living room and beamed the flashlight around the room, ignoring the possibility of being discovered by a neighbor or passing car.

That's when he saw the wicker basket under the end table next to the sofa. He picked it up. Sitting on the couch with the basket on his lap, Moses opened the lid.

Jackpot.

All the paraphernalia for shooting up with heroin was contained in the basket. Moses saw the syringe, the length of rubber for a tourniquet, a small Bunsen burner, spoons, gauze, and more. A large mayonnaise jar was also in the basket. It had about a quarter inch of white powder inside. Moses had so far escaped the vice the basket represented, so he didn't know what all the pieces were for.

As he pawed through the basket, he found a belt. Moses pulled it out of the basket. He recognized the buckle and rough wear of the belt. This was Leroy's money belt. His initials were embossed on the tongue.

Double jackpot.

Moses unzipped the hidden compartment and thumbed three one hundred dollar bills. Then he heard the long blast of Harry's car horn. Moses put the moneybelt back into the basket, placed the basket back under the end table, and ran to the side door. He heard footsteps on the stairs to the porch as he unlocked the door, locked it again behind him, and hurried out. Moses ran quietly around the side of the house, retrieved the ladder, and put it back in its original position in the garage. Coming out the door, he hid behind the garage and waited.

Ten minutes later, Moses heard the front door open and close, and a few seconds later, a car started up and drove down Myrtle toward Walbridge Street. His breathing finally slowed, and Moses walked off across the neighborhood backyards in a wide circle and came up behind Harry's car, knocking on the window. Harry let him in.

"Jesus, Moses," said Harry. "I thought you'd never get out of there."

"For a minute," said Moses. "I thought I was cooked. Your warning gave me just enough time."

"Did you have any luck?" asked Harry.

"Yes," said Moses. "I suppose you didn't notice, but she's an addict. She shoots up heroin."

"Not familiar," said Harry. "How could you tell?"

"She scratches her arms and always keeps them covered. Pulling up her sleeve, you'd see the puncture marks of the needle. Heroin, or opioids in general, make your skin itch. She scratches without even knowing it."

Harry started the car and cruised along Pitcher Street.

"What's next, my friend," he said, pulling up to Eileen's house.

"Sleep," said Moses. "I'll check in with Eileen, see how she is doing, and get some shut-eye. With a clear head, hopefully, I'll figure out a way to end this. It has to be a legal way. Thanks, by the way. Give Janet a pat on the ass for me next time you milk her."

"Call me before the trial starts. Sarah and I will be there."

"Thanks again, Harry."

Moses left his shoes in the foyer of Eileen's house and quietly ascended the stairs. Eileen was asleep, her arm still in the sling. Moses went back downstairs and scrounged the leftovers in the refrigerator. He eyed the last piece of meatloaf covered with wax paper. Moses grabbed the ketchup and bread and made a sandwich with the meatloaf. He was famished. He washed his dinner down with a bottle of Coca-Cola. The bread drawer also contained a near-empty package of fudge-striped cookies. Moses ate them and threw the package away.

Back upstairs, Moses swished his teeth with toothpaste in the bathroom, stripped off his clothes, used the toilet, and crawled into bed with Eileen. She slept through the commotion, and Moses joined her in sleep minutes later.

Sunlight poured in the east window of the bedroom when Moses awoke. The alarm clock read 7:30 a.m. Eileen was not next to him in bed, and as he became more aware of his surroundings, he could hear rustling from downstairs in the kitchen and the smell of coffee.

Moses jumped into the shower, dried off, and dressed. His chin stubble would have to wait until he returned to his apartment and razor.

Eileen sat at the table. She was fully dressed in one of her Sunday outfits. The sling didn't seem to hamper her activity at all. She smiled and said, "I took two aspirins with my coffee. I decided not to take the Kadian tablet. With the trial starting today, I want to be alert in the courtroom. My arm feels better already."

"You look great, Eileen," said Moses. "In fact, the jury will probably take one look at you and dismiss the charges. How long have you been up?"

"At least an hour. I must have slept twelve hours after you left yesterday," said Eileen. "What were you doing while I was sleeping the day away."

Moses debated about how much he should tell Eileen. He had raised her hopes in the past, only to disappoint her when circumstances didn't achieve Marvin's release.

Instead, he said, "I have great confidence in Jeremy Fulton. I want to meet with him this morning, fill him in on Melissa Soebbing, and review his strategy."

"Alright, I could be ready by the time you are done with the breakfast dishes if you don't mind," said Eileen.

"Of course, I don't mind," said Moses, "but I need to do a few things downtown. Why don't we meet Jeremy later."

"Sure, I can drop you off downtown," said Eileen. "I want to shop for a new white shirt and tie for Marvin to wear in court."

"OK," said Moses. "Let's shoot for ten o'clock to meet Jeremy. That gives Jeremy an hour and a half before the trial starts with opening statements at 10:00 a.m.

***

Once Moses was alone, he walked to the Cities Service Station to let his boss know he needed the week off to attend Marvin's trial. Then, he made his way to police headquarters. Moses asked the duty sergeant to call Ross Kirkpatrick and ask him to meet with him at the station as soon as possible.

Chief Hoyt sat behind his desk as Moses knocked lightly on the door frame. The chief held the previous night's summary of arrests and scheduled interviews in his hands. He offered Moses a seat.

"How's your investigation of Craig Sheid progressing, Chief," asked Moses.

"Right now, the location of Craig Sheid has taken precedence," said Chief Hoyt. "He can't be located."

"Oh," said Moses.

"Not since I suspended him. No one's seen him. I sent a patrol car to his apartment address in Westwood, but he wasn't there. He may have skipped town. He was only renting and apparently had no relatives in the area."

"Or he's been silenced another way," said Moses. "He was the only link to the mystery man working at the Shakespeare Company that spearheaded the riot on December 1st.

"That man, whoever he is, is certainly not above using violence to further his ambition."

The duty sergeant leaned into the room. "Ross is on his way," said the sergeant. "I have reserved interrogation room 'B' for you to meet."

"Thanks, Sarge," said Moses.

The chief asked about Eileen Simmons' health. Moses explained she was healing and in as good spirits as possible with her son's trial about to begin. Moses thought it best not to mention Beverly's involvement in Leroy's murder. He still had no evidence in hand.

Moses had learned enough about the assistant prosecutor, Brian Verhage, to know he would be splashing a picture of himself standing next to Marvin outside the courtroom when the guilty plea was returned. Moses imagined the beginning of the article in the Gazette:

A rising star in the prosecutor's office secures a guilty plea in the murder of Leroy Simmons, a white man and resident of the Northside neighborhood. The neighborhood is safe once more, thanks to his efforts.

***

Ross opened the conference room door. Jeremy Fulton was at the head of the table, and Moses sat to his left. Ross sat opposite Moses after closing the door. "What's up, Moses? My shift doesn't start for three hours."

"Yeah, Moses, what gives," said Jeremy. "I'm not done prepping Marvin. Eileen will be here shortly with Marvin's shirt and tie, and I need to assure her and keep her calm as well."

"This is too important to wait," said Moses. "Thanks for letting me interrupt your agenda. I need your help, and the outcome of Marvin's trial depends on our next moves."

"Then get to it, Moses," said Jeremy, as irritated as Ross for the interference.

"I have discovered another suspect for the murder of Leroy Simmons," Moses stated. "Two suspects, in fact. I can't prove it yet, but we can together."

"Does the prosecutor know about these suspects?" said Jeremy.

"Hell no," said Moses. "Ross, remember the other greeter standing opposite Eileen in the church foyer."

"Vaguely," said Ross. "One glance and I made it a point to look the other way. Besides, Eileen was the other greeter. Now, there's someone I will always notice."

Moses ignored his friend. "That was Beverly Simmons, Leroy's sister. I believe she has a heroin addiction. Her arms are always covered, and she's constantly rubbing them.

"I can describe a logical scenario implicating either Beverly or her gentleman friend in the murder of Leroy Simmons.

"When I saw her in the church, I remembered her arguing with Leroy at the train station. She attempted to get money from him and was upset that his wallet was pretty empty. She overlooked his money belt at the time, but I watched him access that belt on several occasions.

"Beverly, or her friend Devon Drelles, or both, had a motive and an opportunity to be on the scene at Eileen's house on Christmas Eve."

"Who's this Devon person," said Jeremy.

"He's connected with the drug world on the Lake Michigan coast. He resides in St. Joseph, Michigan, and now in Kalamazoo," said Moses.

Jeremy and Ross both looked skeptical.

"You mentioned opportunity," said Ross, "Would you mind explaining?"

"Both of you have heard or read Marvin's statement of his activities on that night. Something to the effect that when he came out of the house with Leroy's gun in his pocket, he saw someone in a heavy coat up ahead and assumed it was Sheila. Then, the snow intensified, and the person seemed to vanish. Marvin kept moving down Parsons Street, hoping to catch up to Sheila. He eventually saw Owen up ahead and fired the gun. He never did find Sheila, and she made it home by her curfew deadline.

"Isn't that an accurate summary?"

"How does that put Beverly at the scene of the Leroy's murder," said Jeremy.

"Remember how terrible the storm was on Christmas Eve. Snow all day. Twelve to fourteen inches deep on many of the streets. Burdick Street, Kalamazoo Avenue, and several main streets were continually plowed. Curtis drove a truck with higher clearance and had trouble driving that night."

"Owen spoke of an unnamed accomplice on the tape recording at the Shakespeare building. That tape has been destroyed.

"My supposition is that Leroy and his accomplice made their way to Eileen's house on foot. Specifically, they came from Beverly's rental home on Myrtle Street, about two blocks away. After Leroy's murder, he or she walked in the snow along Parsons Street, turned south on Pitcher Street, and went back to Beverly's house.

"Sheila, Beverly, and Devon all wear long, heavy coats. I've checked. Marvin mistook Devon or Beverly for Sheila up ahead in the dark."

Jeremy interrupted. "Which one, do you think, shot Leroy, Beverly, or this Devon fellow."

"My money is on Beverly," said Moses. "That woman is a piece of work. She was still trying to extort money from Eileen at the funeral service. From how she scratches her arms, I'd say her habit is bad."

Ross played devil's advocate. "But you're saying she killed her own brother for the money he was carrying. We know Eileen had deposited her stash in the bank. There was nothing at Eileen's to be found."

"Listen," said Moses, "The prosecutor is willing to believe Leroy's son, Marvin, shot his father in the back in cold blood. Why not a sister. I've seen a picture of Leroy with a young Marvin and teenage Beverly, and there was a strange, angry look in Beverly's demeanor."

"Well," said Ross. This is all a supposition. A good one, I admit. What can we do about it? If Beverly shot Leroy, she is undoubtedly one cool customer. She's not running to the prosecutor and confessing to get Marvin off the hook."

"I say we go on the offensive," said Moses. "Jeremy, how long would it take to acquire a search warrant for Beverly's house for illegal substances. If drugs were discovered, couldn't we hold Beverly for questioning for forty-eight hours?"

"Twenty-four hours, at least," said Jeremy. "You're thinking she'll get desperate for a fix and try to bargain."

"That's my hope and dream," said Moses. "I'm convinced she did it. How realistic and fast could you petition the judge for a search warrant, Jeremy."

"My secretary can boilerplate the paperwork while I'm in court," said Jeremy. "I could take it to the judge during the afternoon break in the trial, but it's a long shot that we would find anything, right Ross?"

"Worth a try," said Ross, "There's nothing to lose. Where do I come in, Moses," said Ross.

"We keep this under wraps to ensure we surprise Beverly before she can destroy any evidence on the premises. Has Craig Sheid shown up yet? You have the worst luck with partners, Ross."

"Don't I know it, but just in case Craig wasn't the department leak, I'll advise the chief but keep the operation under cover until Beverly is in a holding cell. What about Devon Drelles."

"If he is at Beverly's house during the raid," said Moses. "Can't we hold him as a suspected accessory to murder?"

"And if he isn't with Beverly," said Ross.

"We find him quick before the two of them can coordinate their stories," said Moses.

Jeremy had been furiously taking notes and writing specific instructions for his secretary. When he looked up, he said, "I've got to get back to Marvin and meet with Eileen. The jury was selected last week. Four men and six women, all white. Opening statements come first at 10:00 a.m. Then, the prosecutor will put Sheila, Curtis, and a random student who witnessed Marvin threaten Leroy on the stand. Then he'll put the arresting officers on the stand and the forensics specialist who will testify to the gunpowder residue and Marvin's fingerprints on the gun.

"They think it's an open and shut case, all the way. I don't see it that way and will raise doubt on each point with the jury. Moses, you've given me plenty of alternative scenarios to work with. Thank you.

"There's no way we should lose this case, but this is America. It's 1949, and a person of color is on trial. That, in itself, gives the prosecution an advantage in the North and the South. I'll have that request for a search warrant in front of the judge by two o'clock."

"In the meantime," said Moses. "We should keep Eileen and Marvin in the dark regarding this new strategy. I've given her hope before that has turned to despair."

Ross decided to head first to Woolworth's soda fountain for a meal before coming to the courtroom. Moses accompanied Jeremy to the holding area to meet with Marvin and Eileen. Jeremy stopped at the desk and called his office to give his assistant directions for typing up the search warrant and subpoenas for Beverly Simmons and Devon Drelles.

When Moses entered the courthouse holding area, he waved to the officer on guard, an old acquaintance on the force. Eileen, one arm, hugged him. The sling made anything but a quick kiss awkward. Marvin stood up from the table and shook Moses' hand.

"Thanks for trying so hard to help my case," said Marvin. "Also, for taking care of my mom. I hope you'll be there for her whichever way this trial goes."

Moses admired Marvin's statements. Was Marvin wise for all of his sixteen years, or was he just a naïve sixteen year old that didn't really comprehend spending the rest of his life in a prison cell? Whichever the case, Moses was proud of the boy.

"As long as she wants me around," said Moses, "I'll stick. She's a strong, smart woman and really easy on the eyes. Her smile brightens my day."

Eileen punched Moses in the shoulder. "Let's get our thoughts back to the trial," she said.

Jeremy entered the room just as she said, "What will happen today?"

Jeremy took over, keeping the conversation professional but with a nice touch of empathy for the strange situation Marvin would endure.

"In fifteen minutes, Eileen, you'll sit in the first row behind the defense table. Moses and I will enter with the guard and Marvin and sit at the table. Marvin, you'll be next to me on my left. Moses, sit on my right. As my investigator, I want to rely on you to answer questions about the investigation if any arise. If you are called away, you can do so discreetly.

"Marvin, I can't stress enough how much I depend on you to sit up straight and pay attention to the judge. That shirt and tie look great, Eileen, by the way.

"Marvin, tell the truth, but do not under any circumstance offer embellishments or explanations other than what the prosecutor or judge asks. Understand?"

"I think I understand," said Marvin.

"That's not good enough," said Jeremy. "Can you follow my instructions, or must we review them again?"

"I understand, Mr. Fulton," said Marvin.

The officer standing at the door said, "It's time."

***

The morning passed quickly. Brian Verhage, the assistant prosecutor, outlined the charges against Marvin, describing him as a premeditated murderer who was disgusted with his father for accosting Marvin's girlfriend on the grounds of Central High School.

Later, Marvin decided to eliminate the man from his life. He helped Leroy Simmons rob his own mother's home for traveling money. When no money could be found,

Marvin, in a fury, shot Leroy Simmons in the back, killing him.

Jeremy Fulton, in his statement, painted a completely opposing picture. Marvin, a 3.2-point sixteen-year-old, is dedicated to basketball, his mother, and his girlfriend, Sheila Rohan. He found his father shot dead on his own kitchen floor. He picked up Leroy Simmons's gun and pursued the murderer out the front door and along Parsons Street, eventually catching up to whom he thought was the murderer and firing the weapon as a warning. The police arrived on the scene, ignored Marvin's pleas to pursue the car with the possible suspects, and instead arrested an innocent teenager.

At the noon recess, Marvin was returned to the holding area for lunch. Moses and Eileen tried the sandwiches at the small cafeteria in the courthouse. Jeremy went to check with his office.

***

When Moses and Eileen returned to the courtroom, Marvin sat beside Jeremy. Moses accompanied Eileen to her seat and then sat next to Jeremy. Jeremy whispered, "The judge didn't argue the search warrant. Here is your warrant, signed and sealed. This afternoon, the prosecution will present their case. With my objections at every turn, I imagine that will take the rest of the day. Brian will have to get used to it. His grandstanding is going to sound ridiculous. He'll paint Marvin as a dressed-up gang member, a man of color and therefore suspicious, and Brian will ride that image into the ground. Moses looked around the courtroom but didn't spot Ross Kirkpatrick. He patted

Marvin on the back, stopped at Eileen's chair, and whispered, "Jeremy wants me to track down some evidence that may help our case. I'll be back. Stay positive."

"OK, Moses," said Eileen.

Moses headed over to the police station. He located Ross and showed him the warrant. Ross took the warrant. "I've lined up two other officers for the search, and Chief Hoyt supports the effort. Let's surprise Miss Simmons."

Since Ross had not been assigned a new partner, Moses rode up front with him. The other two officers followed in a second patrol car. Ross pulled up in front of a house two doors from Beverly's address. The other patrol car parked behind Ross.

"Moses," said Ross. "We don't want to risk any evidence of corruption by involving a citizen. You stay in the car. I've gone on searches with these two guys in the past. They're pros at it. If anything is there, we'll find it."

"Do your best, Ross," said Moses. "This may be the boy's last chance. Isolate Beverly and Devon if he's there, so they can't flush the evidence."

"I've been to this rodeo before, Moses; hang tight."

***

Twenty minutes later, one of the officers returned, opened the trunk of the second squad car, and grabbed a forensic tackle box used for dusting for fingerprints. Moses rolled down his window and spoke to the officer, "Any luck?"

"No, we haven't found a thing, Mr. Webb," said the officer. "Between the three of us, all we've found is the stub of a possible marijuana cigarette. That's why I need the kit."

When the officer climbed the stairs to the porch, Moses hammered the dash with his fists.

God Damn it. Are they really going to overlook that sewing basket in the living room?

Five minutes passed. Suddenly, the front door opened, and Ross jumped off the porch in two hops down the stairs. Rushing to Moses' side of the patrol car. Moses rolled down the window. Ross said, "We found her stash. For God's sake, she kept everything in a basket under the end table in the living room. The rest of the house was clean.

"There's also a money belt in the basket. We're dusting it for prints. 'LS' is embossed on one end. Leroy Simmons. It's his money belt.

"Moses, did you know he used a money belt."

"I did," said Moses. "I saw him put money in and take money out several times behind the trash barrels at the train station."

"We have to get the basket to Jeremy," said Ross. We have another hour of cleanup; a forensic team will finish. I can probably leave in twenty minutes to a half hour."

Moses closed his eyes and snoozed while he waited. A noise from the rear of the house awakened Moses. He caught sight of Devon Drelles before the garage hid him from view.

No one came out of the house after Devon. Moses rushed to the rear and opened the mud room door far enough to see one of the police officers lying dazed on the floor. That made Devon's exit an attempted escape. Moses turned around and ran behind the garage. He saw Devon, still running, a quarter mile ahead in the field. Moses started after him on the run. The snow hampered the progress of both men, but Moses was in better shape and continually gained on Drelles.

Devon made it to the next area, where houses were clustered and disappeared after turning down an alley. Moses was only thirty feet behind. When he turned the corner, Devon was bent over, holding his knees, gasping for breath.

"You're done, Devon," said Moses. "Let's go back. Don't give me any trouble."

Drelles couldn't speak and still gulped air. When Moses approached him, Devon came alive. He threw a wild haymaker with his right fist at Moses. Moses saw it coming and feinted to his right as the swing sailed by his left ear. Then he came back with an uppercut to Devon's gut. That further took the breath out of Devon, who began to retch from lack of oxygen.

Moses twisted Devon's left hand behind him, pressing on the man's palm pressure point, Devon screaming in pain. Moses led the man to the road. A minute later, Ross, in the squad car, pulled over to the curb. He put handcuffs on their captive and helped Moses deposit Drelles in the back seat.

On the short drive to police headquarters, Ross began to explain. "Jim and I found a sewing basket in the living room full of paraphernalia for shooting up and a small glass pickle jar full of heroin. Enough that Beverly qualifies as a dealer as well as a user.

"Her arms are a mess, by the way. I made her roll up her sleeves. I believe she needed another fix when we interrupted the two of them. In another hour, she'll be coming down hard.

"The belt is the real evidence of her involvement in Leroy's murder, of course. Beverly is in the other squad car.

We'll book each of them into separate cells far enough apart that they won't be able to work up an alibi together. One or both of them will crack."

***

Moses slipped into the courtroom and sat next to Jeremy. Marvin looked a little ill, probably the result of the prosecuting attorney continuously referring to him as 'a juvenile delinquent with the adult capability to kill Leroy.' Then Marvin apparently invented a story about chasing his so-called father's killer down Parsons Street until the police officers arrested him. As Brian Verhage released one of his witnesses, Moses leaned over to whisper to Jeremy, "We found Beverly's drugs. Even better, Ross found Leroy's money belt. I believe that will tie Beverly to Leroy's murder, although she is denying it."

The judge spoke to the assistant prosecutor. "Call your next witness, Mr. Verhage."

"That was the last prosecution witness," said Brian. "I believe we have proven our case beyond a shadow of a doubt."

"Leave the editorial for your summation, Mr. Verhage. Mr.Fulton, are you ready to present witnesses for the defense?"

"Yes, we are, your Honor," said Jeremy.

"Then we'll start with the defense witnesses first thing in the morning. If there are no objections, we'll begin at 9:00 a.m.

The bailiff took his cue from the judge, "All rise."

When the judge had left the courtroom, the bailiff announced, "Court is in recess until 9:00 a.m. tomorrow."

***

Eileen, Moses, Ross, and Jeremy met in Jeremy's office. Ross had checked the basket and contents into the evidence room after making a detailed list of its contents.

"From what you describe, Mr. Kirkpatrick," said Jeremy, "that is Leroy's money belt. You say you found it while searching the property identified in the warrant?"

"Yes," said Ross. "The search was successful. My fellow officers found the basket containing the belt today at Beverly's house."

Jeremy looked at Eileen. "We'll go to the evidence room in a minute. That should clear Marvin if you recognize the belt and can testify in court.

"Ross, I assume you photographed the basket's location in the house and the contents before removing it from the premises."

"You bet. All above board and by the book," said Ross.

Moses remained in the corner, smiling. Eileen beamed at him and kissed him, ignoring the rest of the inhabitants in the room.

Everyone walked over to the police station and waited outside the evidence cage for the officer to retrieve the basket and set it on the counter.

"The belt has Leroy's and Beverly's prints all over it," said Ross.

"That's Leroy's money belt," said Eileen. "I'm positive."

Despite the exhaustion that hung over the group due to the day's activities, Jeremy suggested that Ross, Moses, and he secure the interviews of Beverly Simmons and Devon Drelles that evening."

"Eileen," said Moses. "I'll drive you home and return for the interviews."

Eileen gently removed the sling from her arm. After flexing her arm a few times, she declared, "The arm is well enough to drive, Moses. I can make my own way home. The jury's sympathy over my skirmish with Owen Krssbach is not as important now."

"You are a sly one, Mrs. Simmons," said Jeremy. "I think it is safe for you to discard the sling."

***

A guard brought Beverly into Interview 'B.' Moses, Jeremy, and Ross sat on one side of the table, and a court stenographer sat at the end of the table. Beverly was urged to sit across from Jeremy.

Beverly was in the throes of heroin withdrawal. She had been given a blue short-sleeved smock to wear. The heroin puncture tracks were evident from the opposite side of the table. Between the puncture dots, long white scratches four, five, and six inches ran up both arms.

"We can make this short and sweet, Beverly. You stole Leroy's money belt on Christmas Eve after you shot him in the back. By the look of you tonight, grabbing money from Leroy to support your habit was your motive. You walked to Eileen's home with Leroy. Easy, even in a snowstorm. You shot him, dropped the gun, took his money belt, and returned to your house undetected. It almost worked."

"I didn't shoot Leroy," said Beverly.

"You're kidding," said Moses. "You're as guilty as Judas."

Beverly exploded. "Get that nigger away from me. This is a frame-up. That man wrote me a check for $300.00 in exchange for the best blow job he would ever have."

"I don't know where you're coming from with this nonsense," said Moses. "Thank God I never had to touch you.

"Sure, I visited you at your home as part of my research of possible suspects. Jerry Fulton, Marvin's lawyer, hired me to do just that. Where is this check you refer to? Maybe you have a deposit slip for a bank account for $300.00.

"I lost that check," said Beverly, "but I had it. I'm done talking until the nigger gets out of here."

Jeremy stood up and looked at Ross. "Ross, can you keep taking Miss Simmons's statement. I need to speak to Moses for a few minutes."

"My pleasure," said Ross. As Moses left the room following Jeremy, he heard Ross say, "Use that language just once more, and I'll smack you into the next county. Understand?

"Now tell me what you think happened on Christmas Eve."

Once the door was closed to Interview room 'B.' Jeremy turned to Moses.

"I thought we should try interviewing Devon Drelles," said Jeremy.

"Great idea, let's see how far we get."

They went over to interrogation room 'D.' Devon sat at the end of the table. Jeremy entered and sat on Jeremy's right. Moses took the seat to Devon's left. A second court stenographer sat at the end of the table, and the guard stood in the corner.

Jeremy looked at his notebook. "You have been arrested for assaulting a police officer. Moses, what kind of sentence can Mr. Drelles expect for that lapse in judgment."

"Two to seven years, Jeremy," said Moses. "I suppose if he had escaped, he might have not done any time. Idiots think like that."

"It might have been worth the risk. The murder rap will get Mr. Drelles life in prison," said Jeremy.

"What are you talking about. I haven't murdered nobody," said Drelles.

I'm sorry, Devon," said Jeremy, "but Beverly says she didn't fire Leroy's gun. That leaves you."

Devon Drelles was becoming more agitated by the minute. "Did she say I did it? That I used that gun? I wasn't even there!"

"She's implying it," said Moses. Another hour without a fix, and she'll be telling us what clothes you were wearing, where you were standing when you shot Leroy, and how she begged you not to do it."

Devon smiled and relaxed. He was busy figuring out how to drop his association with Beverly Simmons, the drug addict.

"What about the assault charge? How about that."

"The officer's pride is bruised more than his jaw," said Jeremy. "Tell us the truth, and we'll see about dropping the assault charge."

Devon stayed silent for a minute. He was ready for a whiskey drink from the bottle at Beverly's house.

"Alright, like I said, I wasn't there. I don't need to steal money. I've got plenty of cash coming my way.

Leroy came by the house at 8:30 p.m. The two of them argued for a half hour about where the money might be hidden at the wife's home. Leroy flashed the gun several times, saying he needed it in case someone surprised them. Then, they left for the wife's house on foot in the snowstorm.

"An hour and a half later, Beverly came in, and I watched her put that money belt in that basket. I can't tell you what happened at the wife's house because I didn't go over there."

Moses looked at Jeremy, who nodded and stood up. Moses stood up and opened the door.

"We'll need to see if Beverly will corroborate your story, Mr. Drelles. We'll be back."

***

When Moses and Jeremy were seated in interrogation room 'D,' Ross summarized his conversation with Beverly while they were absent.

"Miss Simmons has now asked for a doctor several times. She says she is sick and needs her kit to help her out. In the last five minutes, she told me that Devon Drelles did accompany Leroy and herself to Eileen's house, and at some point, Devon shot Leroy in the back. Then Devon and Beverly left the house and walked back to Beverly's house. For giving up Devon Drelles as the murderer, Beverly expects to have a doctor's prescription of Kadian or something similar to help her get well."

Jeremy and Moses were amused, but neither bought it.

"Unfortunately, Beverly," said Jeremy. "Your version of the events on Christmas Eve does not mesh with the testimony of other witnesses or the facts of the case.

"Marvin Simmons followed you after you left Eileen's house. He has been unequivocal. He only saw one person leaving his mother's house. Not you and Devon. Just one person.

"Furthermore, we're typing up a statement by Devon Drelles that states that you and Leroy walked to Eileen's house without him. He will testify that only you returned carrying Leroy's money belt. The belt has your fingerprints and Leroy's, but not Devon's."

"I need a doctor," said Beverly. "I'm sick."

"Tell us the truth, and we'll have a doctor here within minutes. Are you ready to make a complete and honest statement?"

Beverly shrugged, suddenly looking ten years older. Her shoulders slumped, and she rubbed her arms.

"Leroy was worse than scum. Since he was eight, he could get money from Papa at a moment's notice. Papa would laugh at him when Leroy asked, but Papa gave in every time. He never gave me nothing. Papa beat me for asking. He said I was old enough to work for it. He didn't care how or what work I did. Papa liked to set me up with men. Yeah, I hated the man. Mama was wise to leave.

"Papa left us when I was sixteen and Leroy was twelve. I guess I was supposed to take care of us, but Leroy was much better at taking care of us than me. He started hawking shit the minute Papa left. Leroy was stingy with the money, claiming he was building up. For years, I believed him, but eventually, I caught on.

Yeah, I hated Leroy as much as Papa. They were two of a kind and wanted to control Mama and me."

Leroy got me hooked on cocaine. I moved to heroin on my own.

I saw my chance when he put the gun down to search a drawer in the dining room.

"Yeah, I was high. It felt so fucking good pulling that trigger and watching that shit for a brother pitch forward dead. I never have to look at him again.

"I'm ready. Get me a pen and some paper, and call that doctor."

***

An hour later, after Beverly and Devon had been returned to their respective cells, Jeremy's assistant entered interrogation room 'D.' and handed Jeremy the confession she had typed based on the court stenographer's shorthand. Jeremy looked it over and gave it to Moses, who read it.

"Mission accomplished," said Jeremy. I'll send for a doctor for Beverly, and early tomorrow morning, I'll apply for subpoenas for Beverly and Devon, just in case we need them to testify in court.

I suggest we get a good night's sleep. I want to be optimistic, but you never know what the judge might do. We have done everything we could."

Eileen sat at the kitchen table holding Moses' leather jacket and fedora, urging him to finish his coffee and toast so they could leave for the courtroom. She wore her excitement with a smile that hadn't stopped since Moses had come to her house last night with the news of her sister-in-law's confession. There was no love lost between Beverly and Eileen. Beverly had objected to her brother marrying Eileen from the first, over sixteen years ago.

Eileen had always suspected a shady side to her husband's sister. As Moses told Eileen about Beverly's attempt to extort money in the form of a $300.00 check, he thought she might vomit; she became so pale. He described Beverly's antics while offering sex. No, there was no love lost for her former sister-in-law by Eileen and no sympathy for yet another member of the Simmons clan that proved to be scum.

Eileen and Moses were the first to arrive in the courtroom. Eileen could hardly sit still. Her excitement kept bubbling forth to anyone who filtered into the audience section. Moses sat in his assigned seat at the defense table. Eileen continuously leaned forward to pat him on the back or rub his shoulders. When Jeremy arrived, he assured Eileen that he would present Beverly's confession to the court.

Jeremy went over the articles he had collected for his presentation. The bailiff would bring in Beverly's sewing basket containing the drug paraphernalia and money belt upon a signal from Jeremy. The pictures Ross had taken during the search were lined up at the top of the table. Jeremy had requested an easel be set up near the witness stand that would hold an 18" x 24" poster board with an enlarged map of the city streets pertinent to the case. The illustrated area included the Kalamazoo River, Parsons Street, and Bosker Street to the east. Sheila's house was marked on Bosker Street. Eileen's house on Parsons Street and Beverly's house on Myrtle Street were highlighted. The railroad tracks next to Beverly's home and running north near Eileen's property were also called out. The map accurately represented the distances and proximity of the sites on Christmas Eve.

Moses congratulated Jeremy on the thoroughness of his presentation materials.

"I have a photograph that may or may not be pertinent, but it might generate some interest to the court," said Moses.

"Let's see it," said Jeremy.

Moses laid the Simmons family picture on the table to examine. "I think it is interesting," said Moses. "Leroy looks to be the favored son with his father's arm around his shoulders, and Beverly almost seems like she might belong to a different family. The father is ignoring the girl, almost disowning her."

"You're right, Moses. The picture might portend Beverly's long-term jealousy of Leroy. I could play it that way, regardless. I don't think we'll need it, but thanks; where did you get it?"

"I swiped it from Beverly's house," said Moses. "It's a duplicate. You could suggest it may have been among Leroy's effects."

"Definitely not admissible as evidence," said Jeremy, "but useful for background context."

Marvin entered the courtroom from a side entrance accompanied by his police guard. Before he sat down, he turned toward his mother. She gave him a thumbs-up and smiled.

Jeremy leaned Marvin's way and said, "We're going to enter a motion to dismiss the charge. Stay calm." Upon hearing that news, Marvin looked back at Eileen, smiled, and nodded.

The judge entered the courtroom, and the bailiff called, "All rise, the honorable Judge Archibald Mcdonald presiding." Everyone in the courtroom stood; the judge sat behind his desk and gestured for everyone to sit.

"Is the defense ready to present?" said the judge.

"We are your honor. At this time, I am filing a motion to dismiss the case against my client, Marvin Simmons, on the grounds of a signed confession in my possession by the actual person who fired the fatal shot that killed Leroy Simmons."

The buzz in the courtroom was immediate.

The judge quieted the crowd with his gavel.

"Let me see that confession, Mr. Fulton," said the judge.

"Your honor, this is absurd," said Brian Verhage. "No foundation has been laid for this surprise announcement. I certainly had no knowledge of any confession."

"I have a copy of the transcript for you as well, Mr. Verhage," said Jeremy, walking over to the prosecution table with a copy of the confession. "Your honor, this confession was obtained last evening after the court adjourned. That is why the defense is now making the court aware of it."

"Let's all be quiet," said the judge. "Give me a chance to read it through."

"Judge, you haven't responded to my objection," said Verhage.

"And I won't until I'm ready to," said Judge McDonald.

Brian sat back down and proceeded to read and then reread the confession. After which, he still couldn't contain himself.

"Your honor," he said. "Let me point out that the person named here admits to having drugs in her possession. She repeatedly requested a doctor and was not provided medical assistance until she signed this confession. This is a clear case of confession via intimidation and isn't worth the paper it is printed on."

"So now you've elevated yourself to judge in this case, Mr. Verhage," said the judge. "I'll thank you for leaving that responsibility to me." I see the name of Ross Kirkpatrick of the police department and also Moses Webb. Mr. Fulton, what is Mr. Webb's connection to this case."

"Your honor," said Jeremy. "Mr. Webb has been investigating the circumstances of this case from the beginning under contract with the public defenders' office. He was instrumental in acquiring the evidence that points to Beverly Simmons as the culprit in the crime."

"Is this Beverly Simmons in custody?" said the judge.

"Yes, your honor," said Jeremy. "She is in a holding cell at police headquarters, pending a charge of murder in the first degree, by the prosecuting attorney."

'Alright," said Judge McDonald. "I want to see Mr. Verhage and Mr. Fulton in my chambers. I also want to see Mr. Webb and Ross Kirkpatrick regarding questions about this confession. Bailiff, arrange for Beverly Simmons to be transferred to the holding area in the courthouse in case I need to speak to her as well. The court is adjourned for an hour and a half while I straighten this out."

"All rise," said the bailiff.

Eileen tugged on Moses as he headed out of the courtroom with Jeremy.

"I thought it would be over, Moses," said Eileen. "What's going to happen?"

"Eileen," said Moses. "Jeremy is doing the best he can. Don't forget whose court this is. It will always be twice as hard for us to get justice. Don't start worrying. The evidence, confession, circumstances, and motive are overwhelming. We have to grind the gears a little longer."

***

Judge McDonald worked in a large office on the uppermost floor of the Courthouse. All the players were present. Ross was the last to appear. The bailiff had arranged chairs for everyone around the judge's desk.

"Now that we're all settled," said the judge, "Brian, what's your argument."

"Reading through this confession and the description of how it was obtained, anyone can see that it was coerced. The suspect asks for the doctor on at least five occasions. Sober, I doubt Beverly would have confessed to being a pick-pocket, let alone a murderer. We have the guilty party in custody, Marvin Simmons."

"Mr. Fulton," said Judge McDonald, "Can you and Mr. Webb give us a brief preview of what we could expect in court if I should rule for you to proceed with a defense."

Indeed, your honor," said Jeremy. "Moses, can you use the poster to show the judge how Beverly Simmons escaped detection and arrest on Christmas Eve."

The easel had been set up in the corner of the office, and Moses crossed to it, holding a pencil, and described the sequence of events on the night in question. He spoke of Marvin and Sheila walking from Curtis' truck to Eileen's garage. Moses traced Beverly and Leroy's steps to Eileen's house from Beverly's house on Myrtle Street. He told the judge how Marvin had returned to the garage for a flashlight and how Sheila had panicked and hurried home.

Jeremy broke in with an explanation for Marvin picking up the gun and that he had sworn statements from Marvin on at least two occasions that there was only one person he followed out of his mother's house before the person vanished in the storm. It was Beverly that disappeared. She had turned left from Parsons Street onto Pitcher Street and then walked to her house on Myrtle Street. Marvin had assumed the person who vanished was his girlfriend, heading home, and he continued to follow her on Parsons Street. Moses stayed at the poster and pointed out the route as Jeremy described the sequence.

"Your honor, we have photographs taken on the premises of Beverly Simmons of the sewing basket we will produce in court containing needles, spoons, a Bunson burner, and more. All items used by a serious heroin addict. The woman's arms show the effects of using that needle. She becomes desperate for a fix in a very short time. Without a fix, a doctor can only prescribe morphine to ease her withdrawal."

"The basket also contained the moneybelt worn by Leroy Simmons and identified by Eileen Simmons, the deceased's wife, as his everyday attire.

"We will gladly hand over all of our documentation and evidence concerning Beverly Simmons to the prosecuting attorney's office."

"Judge," said Verhage. "I have a strong case against Marvin Simmons for the murder of Leroy Simmons. We have his fingerprints on the weapon, he was arrested with the gun in his possession, and a record of a violent and physical incident regarding the defendant's girlfriend and Leroy Simmons.

"Do you really think, your honor, that a sister would shoot her own brother in the back for the small amount of money in a money belt? Whereas Marvin is of African descent, a race still evolving in terms of controlling their violent, animalistic nature."

Moses gathered his right hand into a fist. Jeremy put a hand on Moses' shoulder, holding him down as he addressed the judge. "Your honor, we believe we can show that the relationships in the Simmons family have been strained for years. There was certainly no sisterly love for Leroy. Their cooperation in the burglary of Eileen Simmons's home mutually benefited them. With a money split, Leroy could have left town without paying off his debts. Beverly could afford her habit, at least for a while longer."

"Your honor," said Brian Verhage. "Shouldn't the jury decide this matter on the evidence presented by the prosecution? Isn't that the way of the legal system in this country?"

"Mr. Verhage," said the judge. "It is up to me to decide what is presented to the jury, not you. Could you stop trying to tell me how to do my job? You're out of order."

"Yes, your honor," said Brian. "I apologize."

"Now," said the judge," the court will be back in session in half an hour. I will announce my decision at that time. Thank you all for your patience."

When the courtroom came to order after all the parties had returned and the judge and audience had been seated, Judge McDonald arranged his notes and looked out at the crowd. Eileen, Marvin, Jeremy, and Moses tried to keep their excitement in check. Brian Verhage and his assistants at the prosecution table looked somber.

Sheila clenched her fists, and her mother put a hand on hers. Council Hawes and more than twenty patrons of the Pacific Club took up three rows. Harry and Sarah Martensen sat behind Eileen.

News of the confession had somehow flashed through the Northside Neighborhood and Kalamazoo Central High School. Nearly thirty residents were sitting in the last few rows. Curtis and most of the junior varsity and varsity basketball teams were in attendance, as was Coach Quiring.

A reporter and photographer from the Gazette and reporters from the Detroit Free Press and The Grand Rapids Press were also on hand.

The judge gaveled the room to quiet.

"I will now rule on the defense's request to admit the confession obtained from Beverly Simmons into the court record. After reading through the confession and listening to arguments from the prosecution and the defense, I find the confession valid and pertinent to this case. The motion by the counsel for the defense is sustained.

"I will say that even if the confession were ruled invalid, the investigation into Beverly Simmons's activities would certainly throw more than a shadow of doubt on the guilt of Marvin Simmons.

"I, therefore, dismiss the charge of murder in the first degree against Marvin Simmons.

"Mr. Simmons, will you please stand."

Jeremy stood and helped a shaking Marvin to stand tall as well.

"The charges against you, young man, have been rescinded," said the judge, "and will not appear on your record. Marvin and Mrs. Simmons, I sincerely apologize for what you may have suffered these last months. You are free, Marvin.

The judge looked at the audience and said, "The case is dismissed with prejudice."

***

Many people gathered in the hallway outside the courtroom. Most wanted to congratulate Marvin and ask when he hoped to return to basketball. Moses was surrounded by neighborhood folk. A few wanted to talk to Moses about a problem they wanted him to investigate. Moses asked them to contact him at the Cities Service Company.

Moses found his way over to Eileen and asked if she would mind if he listened to the court session next door for a while. He broke away from the neighborhood entourage and tried to get close to the courtroom next door. The overflow crowd spilled into the hallway.

The judge in that courtroom was hearing accusations about the December 1st riot at the Shakespeare factory from another prosecutor out of Brian Verhage's office. Moses spotted Walter Deering of the Shakespeare Strike Committee looking over the crowd on tip-toes outside the courtroom. "What's happening, Walter," said Moses.

"I think they have finished reading indictments against eleven union management people. Some out of Detroit and some from our local union."

"What are the charges," said Moses.

Walter referred to the pocket notebook he was carrying. "Eight are charged with conspiracy, four are charged with destruction of property."

"What about the rank and file," asked Moses.

"No charges," said Walter. "Union folks really stuck together. The detectives couldn't get anyone to testify against other union members. My union members are safe since Leroy Simmons and Owen Kressbach are out of the picture. Fingers crossed.

"There will probably be a hefty fine against the union for the damages to the factory. That will definitely involve litigation. Just a second, I think I heard the gavel."

"Yes, that's it," said Walter, "The court's adjourned."

"Any indictments against senior management of the Shakespeare Company?" said Moses.

"No, damn it. What do you think, Moses? Sound fair to you? If we had Owen or his confession. We don't."

"Walter, I learned a lot these months about sparring with the bigs in this world. I'll stick to providing neighborhood help. Sometimes, my people don't have anywhere else to turn."

"Well, I'm glad it worked out for Marvin. He is a good kid. Gonna be a great basketball player."

March 19, 1949

Moses nervously sucked on his Camel cigarette among a group of ten men and women smoking between the third and fourth quarter. Crisp fresh air whistled through the cracked open door in the hallway leading to the locker rooms. The March wind offered a slight clearing of the cigarette smoke. The Class A Championship basketball game pitted Kalamazoo Central against Saginaw Arthur Hill. The game was being played at Jenison Fieldhouse in East Lansing. The Maroon Giants of Kalamazoo had a six-point lead.

Moses squashed his cigarette butt with his toe and hurried back into the gymnasium. The crowd was immense compared to the regular season games in Kalamazoo. At least five thousand high school fans anxiously awaited the scoring table buzzer to signal the start of the last quarter.

The teams broke their huddles as Moses found his seat next to Eileen and Sheila, and Saginaw tried to inbound the ball. The Saginaw guard threw the ball to his forward, who was immediately swarmed by Marvin and Curtis. The Lumberjack player's pass was picked off by the other KCH forward.

Marvin brought the ball across center-court at point guard, working a give-and-go play with a Giants forward at the corner of the key. Marvin flashed by the screen, received the pass, evaded the Saginaw double team, and dumped the ball into Curtis' outstretched arms, who turned and tapped the ball against the backstop and into the hoop.

Throughout the quarter, the Kalamazoo Maroon Giants displayed consistent, measured teamwork. Marvin was on fire. His speed and height at the guard position gave the opposing team fits. Marvin was making up for all the time he sat in his cell, practicing his moves in his head and doing pushups until he could fall onto his cot and sleep.

Marvin made his share of the points in the last quarter, as did the rest of the starting five, as Kalamazoo pulled away from the Saginaw team. Marvin made four of his five shots at the line in the last three minutes as the other team desperately fouled him to get a chance to run a play.

The final score was 53-37 in favor of the Kalamazoo Central High School Maroon Giants.[41]

The crowd rushed onto the court to congratulate the players and Coach Quiring. Even though Marvin was the only player of color on the team, he was hugged and backslapped as much as the rest of the team members.

Moses was as proud as a father. Marvin, exhausted, suffered through hugs and kisses from Sheila and Eileen. Kalamazoo Central High School had won the championship for the first time in over ten years.

***

The 'Mystery Man' behind the Shakespeare riot was never discovered. Craig Sheid's body floated to the surface in the celery bog along the Grand River two miles north of Eileen's house in May.

The final verdict against eleven CIO Union managers was read on October 6th, 1949. Each defendant was freed with one-year probation and a $1,000.00 fine.[42]

End Notes: Kalamazoo Historical References

[1] Paints and Oils Store – Business on Burdick street before the mall

[2] Cities Service Station – Currently: Bell's Eccentric Cafe

[3] Shakespeare Company - The Shakespeare Company has been a leading manufacturer and supplier of fishing equipment and other sporting goods since it was founded in Kalamazoo in 1897 by William Shakespeare Jr. This followed his original patent in 1896 of the level winding reel, which enabled fishing enthusiasts to rewind their line evenly on a spool, rather than having to guide it with their thumb. While the reel was the first product to be manufactured by the company, rods, lines, and bait were added. One of the most popular baits was the rubber frog.

[4] Dr. C. Allen Alexander's - Known primarily as Kalamazoo's first black surgeon, Alexander's intellectual pursuits, married to a love of people, drove his calling to better understand and improve the human condition.

[5] Van Avery Drugstore - By 1963, most of the residents living in the neighborhood were African American, and since most of the store's customers were black, activists argued that it was reasonable and fair to expect that local businesses hire staff that reflected the community in which the store operated. Up until then, there existed a whites-only hiring policy, one which increasingly became the source of friction between black customers and store management.

[6] Model 27 Hoover - From 1941 to 1945, Hoover ceased all vacuum cleaner production and converted the North Canton, Ohio factory to support the war effort. When World War II ended in 1945, Hoover started producing cleaners again and unveiled the Model 27 for post-war America to enjoy.

[7] Kadian Tablets - KADIAN® (morphine sulfate) Extended-Release Capsules, for oral use, CII - Initial U.S. Approval: 1941

[8] Local architect Ernest Batterson, drafted an Art Moderne styled structure featuring a multicolored brick exterior, large gymnasium, snack bar, library, and several social rooms spread out over three levels. The building was completed in 1941 and formally dedicated with great fanfare on February 16th. The new Douglass Community Center was hailed as one of the finest facilities of its type and remained the association's home for over forty years.

[9] Fetzer purchased the station for $2,500. He essentially ran the station as a one-man job, serving as technician, engineer, disc jockey, and sales staff. The station began operations as WKZO in September 1931, and soon became a success.

In the 1930s, '40s and '50s, WKZO carried the CBS schedule of programs, during the Golden Age of Radio. Listeners heard dramas, comedies, news, sports, soap operas, game shows and big band broadcasts.

[10] The New Burdick Hotel - For much of the 1930s and 1940s the Burdick Hotel was the home of Kalamazoo's first radio station, WKZO. In 1931 Fetzer moved the station to the seventh floor of the Burdick, in a suite of elegantly appointed office and studio space.

[11] Hanselman Building - One of the tallest and most visible landmarks in the city. It was finally eclipsed in height in 1929 by the fifteen-story American National Bank, today's Fifth Third Building. Tenants came and went, but the building always maintained a healthy occupancy rate.

[12] F. W. Woolworth Company - A pioneer of the five and dime. Frank Winfield Woolworth opened The Great 5 Cents Store, in 1879. The first thing he sold was a five-cent fire shovel.

[13] Fountain of the Pioneers - Opponents of the sculpture have deemed it racist, "horrendous," "a monument to mistreatment," even "evil." The figure of the Indian was sometimes described as "kneeling," although even a casual examination makes it clear that it was not, but simply stood at a lower level than the pioneer. Supporters maintained that erasing the past does not change it. The controversy persisted, however, and the city commission voted on 6 March 2018 to remove the fountain.

[14] Kalamazoo Central High School – (The Fourth Building) Local architect Rockwell A. LeRoy designed a classroom building that would connect the north wing to the gymnasium and also to the new auditorium. The two classroom buildings, completed in 1923, would add sixty new rooms. It was estimated that the entire complex would hold 1500 to 1800 students. The Kalamazoo Gazette reported on 17 August 1922, "…the Central high school plant will in the not far distant future be one of the finest and most complete in Michigan." The new auditorium, completed in 1924, seated close to 3,000 people and became more than just a location for school productions; it became a community auditorium.

---

[15] Lincoln School - Built and dedicated in 1922, the Lincoln School replaced the aged and overcrowded Frank Street School, which was torn down in 1924. Henry L. Vanderhorst's firm won the bid to build the school. At the time of its construction, the three-story school was both the largest facility in the school district, and one of the largest in the country.

[16] Kalamazoo College Angell Field - The field, to the southwest of the main College campus was dedicated in October, 1946. The football stadium and pressbox, lights for night contests, and a quarter-mile track were provided by Mr. and Mrs. William R. Angell, in memory of their son, Chester M. Angell. Lt. Angell was killed in action over Sardinia in 1944.

[17]Downtown YMCA - The YMCA returned to Kalamazoo in 1885. The Y's 270 members moved into the organization's first building in 1892, where it stayed until a fire destroyed the building in 1911.

Undaunted, the YMCA staff and members set about constructing a newer, better building, and they succeeded in spectacular fashion. Over 50,000 people were on hand as President William Howard Taft laid the cornerstone of the new building at the corner of West Michigan and Park Street.

[18] Mt Zion Baptist Church - The congregation, in 1945, moved into a vacated church building on the corner of North Edwards and Parsons streets.

[19] The State Theater - When the State Theatre opened on the corner of S. Burdick St. and Lovell Streets in July 1927, it brought the "atmospheric" movie palace experience to Kalamazoo. Built for the W. S. Butterfield Theater chain, it was constructed in 9 months for $350,000. Originally it featured vaudeville shows and silent movies.

[20] The Pacific Club - What makes The Pacific Club's story so unique for mid-century Kalamazoo life, was that its manager drafted an eligibility pledge that mandated members "to promote integrity and good faith, the application of just and equitable principles between Americans of different racial stock and creeds, and thereby prevent controversies in the community."

[21] Council Hawes Jr. - Hawes hailed from the St. Petersburg area of Florida, and like many blacks dreaming of access to better opportunities that were off limits in the Jim Crow south, Hawes Jr. joined the millions of blacks who migrated north, hoping to find work and less racial prejudice. While in New York, Hawes' brother found a job in Kalamazoo. So, in 1939, Hawes landed in southwest Michigan,.

As the second world war raged, the government draft board came calling, and the 33 year-old found himself a "jughead" in the segregated Marine Corps. It was during his time in the service as a sergeant assigned to galleys and mess halls that Hawes developed an awareness of his leadership potential and capacity to function as a liaison between black and white soldiers, often resolving conflicts.

Back in Kalamazoo after the war ended, Hawes sought to be his own boss, and considered opening a private, racially integrated night club that would serve liquor. Because Kalamazoo was a "dry" city at the time, liquor could only be sold in private clubs. Hawes used the bridge club that he and his wife belonged to as the foundation for The Pacific Club's legal classification. Nonprofit organizations were also expected to have a charitable purpose, and so he included a rider that provided for club profits to be used to help children attend summer camps. According to Hawes, he spent $40,000 in legal fees before the license was granted in 1951 after a prolonged battle with the Michigan Liquor Commission. Because he had been the first proprietor to apply for a liquor license and the last to receive one, his suit alleged discrimination.

[22] Kalamazoo Armory Building - Demolished in August of 1978, the Kalamazoo Armory Building (aka Michigan Armory Building) stood at 162 E. Water Street for more than six decades, serving as the headquarters for Company C battalion of the Michigan National Guard.

[23] Bob Quiring - The Kalamazoo Central High School basketball team was coached by Bob Quiring. Bob Quiring was inducted into the Kalamazoo Central High School Athletic Hall of Fame in 2003.

[24] Michigan Central Railroad Station - Kalamazoo celebrated one Sunday morning in 1846, when the Michigan Central ran its first train into town. Eventually four rail lines converged at the edge of downtown, but the Michigan Central played the major role. The Kalamazoo Telegraph announced in a special edition for 1887 that Kalamazoo had a fine new station as well. Built of red brick and stone on the site of the old village park, it offered Kalamazoo the fashionable "Romanesque" architecture that Henry Hobson Richardson had made popular in the East. Heavy arches and turrets gave it something of the massiveness of a medieval castle – a fit new structure to bring Kalamazoo into what Willis F. Dunbar called in All Aboard, the "Golden Age of Rail Travel."

[25] Baton Rouge Refinery - Baton Rouge Refinery in Baton Rouge, Louisiana is the fifth-largest oil refinery in the United States and thirteenth-largest in the world.

---

[26] Checker Motors Company – Som sources suggest that Markin decided to move his business to Kalamazoo for expansion because the chief engineer he wanted, Leland F. Goodspell, refused to move to Chicago. Other theories propose that Markin sought to put distance between himself and the violent taxi wars being waged between rival cab companies on Chicago's streets. Markin's own house in Chicago was destroyed by a bomb in 1923. Whatever the reason, Markin and Checker would find Kalamazoo an ideal location in which to prosper.

[27] Oak Lawn Hospital - When opened in 1925, Oaklawn only had 12 beds. It was housed in a private residential home, not even 5,000 square feet, with the third floor accommodating operating, emergency and maternity rooms, a baby's bath and a nursery. The building was furnished with draperies, sheets and pillowcases made by area churches.

[28] Percy Jones Hospital - In August 1942, the United States Army purchased the near-vacant main Battle Creek Sanitarium building and converted it into a 1,500-bed military hospital, with crews working around the clock for six months to complete it. Dedicated on February 22, 1943, the hospital was named after Col. Percy L. Jones, a pioneering army surgeon who had developed modern battlefield ambulance evacuation during World War I.

Percy Jones Hospital was one of the army's 65 stateside General Hospitals, providing more complex medical or surgical care—those more difficult and specialized procedures requiring special training and equipment. Percy Jones Hospital specialized in neurosurgery, amputations and the fitting of artificial limbs, plastic surgery, physical rehabilitation, and artificial eyes.

[29] Borgess Hospital - Throughout the 1930s, with the country in the midst of the Great Depression, Borgess faced serious financial struggles. Nonetheless, Borgess saw many advances in healthcare during this time. These advances included Dr. Roscoe Hildreth's radium and radon therapy and the many inventions of Dr. Homer Stryker, including his famous CircoLectric bed. Dr. Richard Upjohn Light also began the first out-state neurosurgical and neurological outpatient services at Borgess at this time.

[30] Federal Housing Administration (FHA) loan - The Federal Housing Administration's justification of discrimination was that if African-Americans bought homes in white suburbs, or even if they bought homes near these suburbs, the property values of the homes they were insuring, the white homes they were insuring, would decline. And therefore their loans would be at risk.

The term "redlining" ... comes from the development by the New Deal, by the federal government of maps of every metropolitan area in the country. And those maps were color-coded by first the Home Owners Loan Corp. and then the Federal Housing Administration and then adopted by the Veterans Administration, and these color codes were designed to indicate where it was safe to insure mortgages. And anywhere where African-Americans lived, anywhere where African-Americans lived nearby were colored red to indicate to appraisers that these neighborhoods were too risky to insure mortgages.

[31] Congress of Industrial Organizations (CIO) - was a federation of unions that organized workers in industrial unions in the United States and Canada from 1935 to 1955. Originally created in 1935 as a committee within the American Federation of Labor (AFL) by John L. Lewis, a leader of the United Mine Workers (UMW), and called the Committee for Industrial Organization. Its name was changed in 1938 when it broke away from the AFL.

[32] Kalamazoo Gazette - added a photoengraving department in 1937, and wirephoto service in 1945. The paper moved to its present location on South Burdick Street in 1925 and has expanded its building several times. In the early days, of course, type was set by hand. The linotype machine, introduced in 1900, made the process less time-consuming. In the 1960s punch-tape typesetting began the process of automation. In May 1980 computerized typesetting and editorial video display terminals were installed. They began operation on the 13th, a day no Gazette employee will ever forget because it was also the day a killer tornado hit the city. The staff persevered and produced the tornado "Extra" on the new system.

[33] Water Street Police Station – 1913-The police department moved to a new headquarters at 122 E. Water St. on August 4.

[34] Oakland Gymnasium - The Oakland Gymnasium of The Western Michigan College of Education was built in 1925 in the historic East Campus and historic Heritage Hall."

Built between 1904 and 1909, East Hall gained its historical significance through its example of the Georgian Revival style of architecture.

[35] Funicular - A type of cable railway system that connects points along a railway track laid on a steep slope. Most of the oldest and original Western Michigan University buildings are collectively known as East Campus. Because of the steep grade elevating the campus above the city, the Western State Normal Railroad was established in 1907 to

carry students and staff up and down the hill with a funicular. It operated until 1949.

[36] Chief Howard W. Hoyt was appointed chief of KPD in 1945. Chief Hoyt served as president of the Michigan Association of Chiefs of Police in 1948-49.

[37] The Gibson Mandolin-Guitar Manufacturing Company. – The company first moved to a larger facility at 523 E. Harrison Court. In 1917, the company moved to its permanent location, 225 Parsons Street, where it remained for nearly seven decades. Over the years, the Parsons Street plant expanded five times into a 120,000 square foot building spread out over an entire city block.

As America's musical tastes evolved during the 1920s and 1930s, so did Gibson's. Banjos, ukuleles, and guitars became increasingly popular. In the early '20s, the company introduced a truss rod neck construction which streamlined a guitar's neck. Now standard on most guitars, this innovation allowed easier fingering and faster playing. During the 1920s, Gibson was also one of the first manufacturers to experiment with the electric guitar, twenty years before it found popular success. In 1934, Gibson introduced the "Super 400" guitar, which revolutionized standards for tone and volume. Unfortunately, the consumer's buying power had been drastically reduced during the Depression. To remedy this, Gibson produced a lower-cost "Kalamazoo" line of guitars that helped keep the company afloat during the lean years.

During World War II, Gibson contributed to the war effort by manufacturing electrical and mechanical radar assemblies, glider skids, and precision machine-gun rods. The company was even awarded three Army/Navy "E" awards for production excellence.

Gibson experienced remarkable growth in the 1950s, aided in part by the introduction of the famous Les Paul guitar in 1952. Named after the famous guitarist, it was designed to his specifications. The company's success continued during the 1960s, when it manufactured over 1,000 guitars a day and employed nearly 1,000 workers, but a sharp nationwide decline in guitar sales contributed to Gibson's difficulties during the 1970s and 1980s. The company moved its headquarters to Nashville, Tennessee, in 1981, and three years later it closed the Kalamazoo plant.

[38] The Shakespeare Factory and Administration building - In 1939, operations moved to the old multi-story Kalamazoo Paper Box factory at 241 E. Kalamazoo Avenue. A one-story Art Deco style building was

added just to the west of the factory and used as an office building. Currently Shakespeare's Pub, a popular bar and restaurant.

[39] Unites States Representative Clare Hoffman - Hoffman was born in Vicksburg, Union County, Pennsylvania, where he attended the public schools. He graduated from the law department of Northwestern University in Evanston, Illinois, in 1895.

Hoffman was admitted to the Michigan Bar in 1896 and commenced practice in Allegan, Michigan, where he also became prosecuting attorney for the county from 1904–1910.

In 1934, Hoffman ran as the Republican candidate for Michigan's 4th congressional district, defeating incumbent Democrat George Ernest Foulkes. Hoffman was elected to the Seventy-fourth United States Congress and was re-elected to the thirteen succeeding Congresses, serving from January 3, 1935, until January 3, 1963. He was seen as "a bitter lone wolf" during much of his time in office, unable to work with either the Democrats or the Republicans. Hoffman voted against the Civil Rights Acts of 1957 and 1960, as well as the 24th Amendment to the U.S. Constitution.

Hoffman was a vocal opponent of the National Polio Immunization Program, claiming that the U.S. Public Health Service had been heavily infiltrated by Russian-born doctors. In addition, he was known as an anti-Semite with fascist sympathies, even speaking at rallies held for the far-right America First Party (1944).

[40] John Walsh - The longest serving editor of the Gazette, and certainly one of its most influential personalities was John K. Walsh, who served in that capacity from 1912 to 1959. A native of Melbourne, Australia, Walsh came to this country to further his education and made Kalamazoo his adopted home. At his retirement, Walsh described his life's objective as "molding the character of the Gazette, in its evolution from a provincial, partisan small-town journal to its present independent, cosmopolitan status." His active campaign helped to give Kalamazoo the first licensed airport in Michigan. He is also remembered for his advocacy of the city's arts and education.

[41] Bob Quiring coached Kalamazoo Central to a Class A State championship in 1949 in one of the greatest tournament upsets in Michigan high school athletics history. The team, 9-7 in the regular season, won 53-37 over the previously undefeated Saginaw Arthur Hill. It went on to win championships in 1950 and 1951.

[42] 1948-49 Shakespeare Company Strike and Riot - In September of 1948, contract negotiations had come to a standstill, and Local 3619

of the United Steelworkers went on strike, affecting approximately 700 Shakespeare employees. A riot ensued in December, resulting in a conspiracy trial that broke all previous records for length of criminal cases tried in Kalamazoo County. Finally, in August 1949, a mistrial was declared, in September the strike was declared illegal, and in October, more than a year after the strike began, the picketing ended.

Workers at Kalamazoo's Shakespeare Company walked off the job in September 1948, but a couple of months later, the sporting-goods maker had made no concessions. That's when a "flying squadron" of strike supporters arrived from Detroit.

"They ransacked the company offices," says historian Tom Dietz. They also overturned cars downtown and got into scuffles.

One lawmaker saw the disturbance as much more than one day of unrest. He saw it as proof that communism had come to the Paper City, and he demanded that Congress investigate.

Dietz told the story of "Red Terror in Kalamazoo," at the Kalamazoo Public Library downtown. He previewed the talk in an interview with West Southwest.

Kalamazoo was not a particularly strong union town, Dietz said.

"Part of it had to do with its size, part of it had to do with kind of a longstanding - this is my opinion - a longstanding tradition of kind of a benevolent paternalism, 'we take care of our workers here,'" he said.

The steelworkers who came in a "flying squadron" from Detroit to support the strike would have had a three-to-four hour journey on the roads at the time, according to Dietz. They assembled in Galesburg, then launched their action in Kalamazoo early in the morning.

"Of course that action alone is terrifying to a lot of people, because by the time this is happening of course, the Red Scare is starting to pick up, the fear that communism is everywhere, the Cold War has kicked in."

U.S. Representative Clare Hoffman of Allegan saw the incident in Kalamazoo as proof of a communist, "Red Terror" presence in Kalamazoo. Politically, Dietz said Hoffman was "at the very least, on the far fringe" of the Republican Party.

"He's the one who saw the 'communist conspiracy' and promised that he was going to hold hearings," Dietz said.

www.ingramcontent.com/pod-product-compliance
Lightning Source LLC
Chambersburg PA
CBHW021238190726
48289CB00005B/1375